The Make-Believe Man
A Friend of Mary Rose

Two Novels by
Elizabeth Fenwick

Introduction by Curtis Evans

STARK
HOUSE

Stark House Press • Eureka California

THE MAKE-BELIEVE MAN / A FRIEND OF MARY ROSE

Published by Stark House Press
1315 H Street
Eureka, CA 95501, USA
griffinskye3@sbcglobal.net
www.starkhousepress.com

THE MAKE-BELIEVE MAN
Originally published by Harper & Row, Publishers, New York, and
copyright © 1963 by Elizabeth Fenwick. Copyright renewed December 24,
1991 by Elizabeth Fenwick Way.

A FRIEND OF MARY ROSE
Originally published by Harper & Row, Publishers, New York, and
copyright © 1961 by Elizabeth Fenwick Way. Copyright renewed
February 13, 1989 by Elizabeth Fenwick Way.

Reprinted by permission of the Elizabeth Fenwick estate. All rights
reserved under International and Pan-American Copyright Conventions.

"Hello, Miss Fenwick: Getting Reacquainted with a Crime Fiction Great"
© 2022 by Curtis Evans

ISBN: 978-1-951473-67-9

Book design by Mark Shepard, shepgraphics.com
Cover design by Jeff Vorzimmer, ¡caliente!design, Austin, Texas
Cover art by Tom Lovell
Proofreading by Bill Kelly

First Stark House Press Edition: April 2022

Hello, Miss Fenwick:
Getting Reacquainted with a Crime Fiction Great
By Curtis Evans

When the psychological crime thriller *The Make-Believe Man* was published in 1963, one of the novel's many laudatory reviewers, a young North Carolina newspaper columnist named James Alexander Dunn, in the *Chapel Hill News* perceptively placed his finger on the signal quality of the author's crime fiction. "Elizabeth Fenwick has successfully combined a believable situation with people who matter—not that they are important people," he observed. "On the contrary, there is not an entity in the lot. But they are familiar people whom you would not like to be in the situation Miss Fenwick places them in." In reviewing the same novel that year, Robert R. Kirsch, longtime literary editor of the *Los Angeles Times*, echoed Dunn's sentiment, trenchantly declaring: "The great gift of Miss Fenwick is to take the ordinary situation and translate it into nightmare." Elizabeth Fenwick's own colleagues concurred in these judgments. The next year *The Make-Believe Man* placed second for the Mystery Writers of America's Edgar Award for best novel to Eric Ambler's *The Light of Day* (perhaps better known under its film adaptation title, *Topkapi*), along with Dorothy B. Hughes' *The Expendable Man,* Stanton Forbes' *Grieve for the Past* and Ellery Queen's *The Player on the Other Side*—an estimable lot of crime fiction.

Arguably this was the high point in the career as a crime writer of a woman who in her lifetime never received, despite the praise afforded her, sufficient due, both critical and monetary, as such; and who herself well knew from personal experience about the desperate struggles of people sunk in the depths of situations they do not want to be in, yet which they have somehow to navigate in order to reach the shelter of a safe harbor. That shelter was something which Elizabeth Fenwick herself never quite achieved until later in life, despite her many remarkable accomplishments. Yet she persevered, leaving readers all the richer for her work.

The crime writer known as Elizabeth Fenwick went through several authorial appellations in life, but she started off as plain Elizabeth Jane Phillips. Born on April 6, 1916 in St. Louis, Missouri, Elizabeth was the second daughter of Jerome Jay Phillips and Elizabeth Jane Nicholson, who called each other Jay and Beth. Elizabeth grew up as an only child, her slightly elder sister Eleanor having passed away in 1920 during the dying days of the deadly flu pandemic; and as a solitary child she lived a precarious, peripatetic existence with colorfully quirky parents.

Beth Nicholson was a pretty, spirited young woman of pious, patriarchal Canadian Scots-Irish descent who rebelling against a repressive father left her home in Canada at the age of seventeen in 1903 to settle with relatives in Boston. Over a decade later she met Jay Phillips while dining alone at a rathskeller at a St. Louis hotel during a tour with the Ziegfeld Follies. Small and bowlegged, Beth to her chagrin had been hired by Florenz Ziegfeld, the Great Man himself, after he got a good look at her gams, strictly to play boys. No mere boy himself, Jay—six feet tall, blond and blue-eyed, good-humored, well-mannered and single, of prominent family and in control of his own considerable fortune—seemed an enviable catch indeed for the Follies performer. Beth soon hauled him into her matrimonial net, wedding him at Greenwich, Connecticut on February 3, 1914 and bearing him a daughter, Eleanor, later that year. However, the couple's promising fortunes were undone by the improvidence of Jay, an amiable drinker and gambler who remained, even after his marriage, under the thumb of his formidable widowed mother, Nellie Usher Curlee Phillips, and refused to leave St. Louis for Boston.

Nellie Phillips, known among the family she dominated as "Mommy," came from a prominent Mississippi family that had transplanted itself to St. Louis in the twentieth century and done very well there indeed. The Curlee House in Corinth, Mississippi, which served as headquarters to both Union and Confederate generals during the Civil War and today is a National Historic Landmark, had been the childhood home to several of Nellie's cousins, one of whom, Shelby Hammond Curlee, founded the nationally prominent Curlee Clothing Company in St. Louis and at his death in 1944 left an estate valued at over a million dollars, or about sixteen million dollars today.

Reflective of the effort at the time to recover and apotheosize a rigorously scrubbed, pristine version of the country's complicated past through architectural restoration (the most famous example of which is found at Colonial Williamsburg, proudly dubbed the world's largest living history museum), both Shelby Hammond Curlee, Sr. and his brother Francis Marion Curlee, Sr., an attorney and Great War veteran known in the press as "Colonel Curlee," were heavily involved with historical restoration, the former buying back and restoring the old Curlee home in Corinth and the latter purchasing and restoring the homestead of Nathan Boone, where Boone's father, famed pioneer Daniel Boone, had died. "This place will never become a 'hootch' joint or a roadhouse," Curlee passionately vowed in 1926, two years after the exclusionary Immigration Act of 1924 was passed. "Italians were trying to get the property when I bought it," he added darkly, "and if they had succeeded, it is probable that they would have made a roadhouse of it …" Both the Curlee House and the Daniel Boone Home, as it is known, are publicly owned house museums today, with nary a bottle of hootch in sight, one surmises.[1]

Jay Phillips, who himself was known to enjoy a tipple or two, lacked the drive of either his mother's dynamic cousins Shel and Frank Curlee or his own late father Joseph Phillips, a former trader of Atoka, Indian Territory (later Oklahoma) who became a prominent bank director in St. Louis, and he frittered away his once comfortable estate in a series of failed agencies. (Successively he fitfully sold automobiles, cut glass and Corona typewriters.) "[Jay's] entire personality was so mysterious and admirable to her that [Beth] was unable, even years later, to make sense of his disaster," Elizabeth Fenwick in her unpublished memoir *Beth: My Mother's Story, 1886-1965* recalled of her lovable, wayward parents, whom she likened unto birds of paradise. "She went over and over his virtues, and still found them sound. There was the glorious sense of humor, the kindness and generosity, the handsomeness and lovely manners, and a fine intelligence—'very deep'. She could only conclude that it was his mother who ruined him. The two women never got along well."

Leading an uncertain existence as an adolescent, Elizabeth over the years moved around the eastern half of the country—sometimes with both Beth and Jay, sometimes just with Beth—to Boston, Detroit,

---

[1] In a strange twist which could have come out of a mystery novel, both Shelby Hammond Curlee's nephew Francis Marion Curlee, Jr. and his son and principal legatee, Shelby Hammond Curlee, Jr., died untimely accidental deaths shortly after his own unexpected demise in January 1944. Francis expired in an automobile accident in February, while Shelby in September was found dead in the swimming pool of a St. Louis racquet club. In the latter case the county coroner speculated from a bump found on the top of Curlee's head and other marks about his head and face that the dead man "may have struck the bottom of the pool in diving" and then "lost consciousness and drowned." Colonel Curlee was the lone survivor of this mayhem, passing away in 1958.

Cleveland, San Antonio and Dallas. The Boston move came only after her parents had divorced in the early Twenties and her mother had returned with her to the city she had adopted as her home. There Elizabeth saw much of her beloved Uncle Fen, aka John Fenwick Nicholson, a commercial traveler from whom she would derive her prominent authorial surname. After Beth married another, older man, she and Elizabeth lived briefly with him in Detroit. The marriage soon failed, however, and Beth, not liking life as a single working mother, in 1927 remarried Jay, who had been living with Mommy while desultorily laboring at "some sort of job with Uncle Shel" and falling thousands of dollars behind in child support.

With the onset of the Depression and the realization, as Elizabeth bluntly put it, that "[n]either of them was much good at making a living," Beth agreed to reside in an apartment in St. Louis with Jay and Elizabeth, supported by a stipend from Mommy, whom Beth and her daughter, offended by her disdainful and imperious behavior, refused ever to see again. Jay sank into semi-invalidism after Mommy, when Beth was away visiting relatives, had him receive an experimental injection for a growth on his neck, and Beth herself, likely motivated by the disasters that had befallen her husband and her elder daughter, became a zealous advocate of Christian Science, leading Elizabeth for a time to question her mother's sanity. For several years the family moved around Texas on account of Jay's health, before finally settling down for good back in St. Louis, supported by Mommy's grudging benevolence.

Despite her aptitude in English, Elizabeth, who had blossomed into an extremely comely blonde with a pretty pert nose and delectable Cupid's bow mouth, never attended college after graduating from high school in San Antonio, instead learning shorthand to take up secretarial work and earn money of her own when the family moved back to St. Louis. However, in 1936, when she was twenty years old, Elizabeth joined a remarkable writers' circle centered on a trio of male Washington University literature students: future U. S. Poet Laureate William Jay Smith; poet Clark Mills McBurney; and future landmark playwright Thomas Lanier "Tennessee" Williams. There were also several young women besides Elizabeth, including Louise Antoinette Krause, who was writing a thesis on John Donne and composing her own metaphysical poetry.

William Jay Smith later recalled that the little group, which grandly dubbed itself the "St. Louis Poets Workshop" on the letterhead of their own stationery, "met usually at Tom's house at Arundel Place, a few blocks from the university, first in the living room where Mrs. Williams received us, and afterward on the sun porch, where we sat for hours criticizing one another's poems." He added wryly that Mrs. Williams, familiarly known as "Miss Edwina," presided over the Williams' two-story modern brick craftsman house "as if it were an antebellum mansion."

In his memoirs Tennessee Williams recalled that the "little poetry club … contained only three male members," characteristically adding snobbishly and chauvinistically (and not entirely accurately, at least concerning Elizabeth's economic standing) that "[t]he rest were girls, pretty, with families who owned elegant homes in the county … and who at meetings] provided lovely refreshments and décor." At the time Williams could vaguely recall of this pulchritudinous, refreshments-bearing feminine contingent only a girl named Betty Chapin and "the wealthiest, Louise, who took us all out in the family limousine to a ballet performance one night." On the other hand, the rather-less-full-of-himself Bill Smith—"the handsomest of us three boys," allowed Williams—to his credit remembered "Elizabeth Fenwick Phillips," who "as Elizabeth Fenwick wrote several fine mystery novels."

For Elizabeth's part her association with such adepts of Literature as Tom, Clark and Bill in what she lightly termed "our Poetry and Chowder Society" inspired her first published literary effusions, which appeared in the magazine *Poetry* in 1936, under the modest name Betty Phillips. "[W]hat wonders the others lived with, and passed on to me!" she later exclaimed in recollected awe, revealing how the Poetry and Chowder Society altered the course of her life. "Proust, Kafka, Rilke; Brahms, Debussy, Vivaldi; French books, movies and records; endless free or cut-rate tickets to the symphony, the ballet, the opera, the plays that came to town—and best of all, talk. We never stopped. Our talking became to me like air to breath." (I am reminded of lyrics in the B-52s' 1989 song "Deadbeat Club," about another garrulous group of arty types in another college town: "I was good, I could talk / A mile a minute / On this caffeine buzz I was on / We were really humming." People are the same all over the world.)

Evincing the same cosmopolitan wanderlust which had taken hold of her mother nearly four decades earlier around the turn of the century, Elizabeth, as the advent of the Second World War loomed closer, resolved, like her friends, to move to New York: "The lively minds were all there, waiting for us. My gang assured me that I was probably better equipped to make a living there than any of them. I meant to go."

Yet in spite of this brave resolve, in 1940 Elizabeth still resided, at the age of twenty-four, with her parents at their place at Donaldson Court Apartments, located at 613 Westgate Avenue, University City (an inner ring suburb of St. Louis), where, like Dolly Parton in the 1980 hit film, she worked as a stenographer from "nine to five," Mondays through Fridays, making $1080 that year (or about $21,500 today). This was the family's only actual earned income (distinguished from Mommy's stipend), and it covered the rent at the attractive art deco apartment complex, which according to the National Register is generally regarded as the most attractive one that was built in the eastern part of University City during the Twenties.

The next year Elizabeth finally made her big move to the Big Apple. After a bout of emotional recriminations from Beth (she "disowned me, assured me I should never see or hear from her again," her daughter recalled, although this rage fortunately soon passed), Elizabeth found her parents a cheaper apartment in St. Louis and settled far away into her own place on West Eleventh Street in Greenwich Village (an extremely posh address today). Within a few months, however, the single working girl abruptly moved in with one of her old poetry circle compatriots, Clark Mills McBurney.

After he left St. Louis in 1937, Clark spent a heady year at the Sorbonne and then resignedly obtained a position teaching French at Cornell University, which is located to the west of New York City at the town of Ithaca in the Finger Lakes region. In her memoir of her mother, Elizabeth states unambiguously that she and Clark wed, although I have been unable to discover any marriage record for the couple. For his part Clark in his 1943 U. S. Army enlistment record gave his marital status as "single." However, there is a later record of a marriage between Elizabeth and Clark having been annulled, so evidently Clark, for reasons of his own, simply lied about his matrimonial status, or the two wed after he enlisted.

Three years older than Elizabeth, Clark Mills McBurney was an imposing figure at six feet tall and 180 pounds, with brown hair and hazel eyes, over which he wore the spherical glasses of the intellectual. Tennessee Williams, who idolized his friend at the time, referred to the poet in his memoirs as not only "brilliantly talented" but "handsome" too. In 1940, the year before Elizabeth burst into his life in a bold new way, Clark, who published his critically praised and cutting edge but decidedly unremunerative poetry simply as "Clark Mills," had confided to Tennessee Williams that he planned to commit suicide. "[Clark Mills] came over and told me quite seriously that he decided to kill himself within the next year," Williams recorded. "He is tied to an academic job at Cornell which smothers his creative life and he sees no possible escape, as his poetry, very fine but completely noncommercial could never support him." Williams talked his friend out of self-destruction, but it was an ill omen for the potential stability of Clark and Elizabeth's coupling.

The pair remained together in Ithaca until Clark was inducted into the Army at Syracuse in June 1943. Over the rest of that year Elizabeth lived with him at camps in South Carolina, Wisconsin and Maryland, additionally spending six months with her mother in Cleveland, where Beth had gone to live with a sister after Mommy had placed Jay in a nursing home and turned her daughter-in-law, in the latter woman's querulous words, "out into the world with 'a few hundred dollars' and 'a train ticket.'" Jay passed away not long afterward in 1942. Clark was sent overseas to Europe in 1944, leaving Elizabeth alone but hardly idle.

In December of 1943, Elizabeth as "E. P. Fenwick" published her first detective novel, *The Inconvenient Corpse*, which she probably wrote in Ithaca during the first half of the year. (The novel is set in the Catskills region of New York.) Thus was launched her career as a novelist, albeit of mysteries. Two more detective novels, *Murder in Haste* and *Two Names for Death*, rapidly followed in 1944 and 1945, prompting the impressed crime writer and reviewer Anthony Boucher rapturously to dub her the first "student" of pioneering suspense novelist Elisabeth Sanxay Holding and "a possible major contender" in the mystery field. However, Elizabeth soon changed tracks as a writer, Boucher's praise notwithstanding.

In the meantime, there was a grave personal matter with which Elizabeth had to deal: she had been callously deserted by her husband. Her marriage to Clark had been a great relief to her mother and aunt, Elizabeth later recalled: "Now I no longer would be 'unprotected.'" They never lost the feeling—in fact, it increased as they grew older—that single women were in some great danger, and to be regarded with pity, anxiety and a bit of scorn. No woman could possibly choose to stand open to the wind, so, if she could help it." With Clark absconded, however, Elizabeth had again become one of those unprotected, pitiable and pathetic women.

During the war years of 1944-45, Clark served as a master sergeant in the Counter Intelligence Corps, where men with foreign language skills were in particularly high demand. Afterward he stayed on in the newly created Central Intelligence Agency, a product of the National Security Act of 1947, at posts in Berlin, Bonn and Frankfurt, not returning to the United States and the teaching profession until 1951. After months of not hearing from him, his letters to her having unaccountably ceased, Elizabeth was granted an annulment in November 1946. Apparently she never saw Clark again, although two decades later, her daughter from her second marriage reports, she referred witheringly to his having married again. This was "a terrible time" for Elizabeth, her daughter has written: "Much later she wrote in a journal about the loss of hope for the home and family she thought she had found."

During this difficult time Elizabeth determinedly had started work on a mainstream (i.e., non-criminous) novel entitled *The Long Wing*, which she proudly published with Rinehart under the name Elizabeth Fenwick in February 1947. Concerning a young woman and her mother-dominated father and his family, the novel, which is set in St. Louis, obviously is heavily biographical, having clearly been inspired by the author's need to work though her ambivalent feelings toward Jay and the Phillips/Curlee clans, which after all those years, she finally realized, had accepted neither Beth nor herself. She sadly reflected that, after receiving a brief telegram at Ithaca from one of her father's brothers notifying her of Jay's death, "I never could bring myself to write. For the first time, I began to understand the depth and breadth of the gulf that had separated us for years from my father's people; it was too sad to try to bridge it now." Still, she transmuted the situation into art with *The Long Wing*, an impressive novel which likely none of the St. Louis Curlees and Phillips ever read. Nor, it would certainly appear, did Tennessee Williams, even though the put-upon "Edwina" of the novel seems to reflect aspects of both Tennessee's mother Edwina and his sister Rose.

The Long Wing received extremely good reviews, critics generally lauding it as a most promising first novel by an up-and-coming young author. In the *Saturday Review*, Nathan L. Rothman, in a notice tellingly titled "Mama's Boy", pithily summarized the plot of the author's "brilliant little novel" as follows: "A man returns to his mother's house for a two-week visit and doesn't get away again." Elizabeth, however, was not going to make this same mistake. She returned to New York City, altered her birth year to 1920 rather than 1916 and found employment as a secretary to a professor at Columbia University, devoting her evenings to writing in a bid to make it as a "serious" novelist.

In June 1947, Elizabeth encouragingly was featured in a *Life* magazine article, "Young U. S. Writers: A Refreshing Group of Newcomers on the Literary Scene is Ready to Tackle Almost Anything," along with ten other hopeful neophytes, including Gore Vidal and Truman Capote. To be sure, the star attraction of the piece was the elfin "Tru," who appeared on the first page of the article in a three-quarter photograph of him "on a couch in a checkered waistcoat, a cigarette in his hand," soulfully gazing out "with big eyes and a wistful look on his face"; but at least Elizabeth's photo was bigger than Gore Vidal's, who was quite vocally disgusted with receiving second billing, along with all the others, to the likes of Truman Capote.

The next year Elizabeth was invited to spend the summer as a guest at the famed Yaddo artists' colony at Saratoga Springs, New York, along with such future famous names as Flannery O'Connor, Chester Himes and Patricia Highsmith. Flannery O'Connor, then just twenty-three years old, became a lifelong friend of Elizabeth, who in 1949 found Flannery a place near her own to live while in New York. After Flannery retired to reside with her mother on a farm in Georgia upon her terminal lupus diagnosis in 1951, she and Elizabeth corresponded up until her death in 1964, although her last in-person meeting with Elizabeth was in 1958.

The late writer Fredrick Morton, who was also at Yaddo during the summer of '48, recalled Elizabeth as "a kind of sexy creature, very attractive physically," and with this estimate Flannery—who in old-fashioned southern lady fashion always referred formally to Elizabeth as "Miss Fenwick"—clearly concurred, although not in quite those words. "She … is a big soft blonde girl and real nice to be around except that she bats her eyelashes," Flannery wrote a friend about Elizabeth in 1960, "we get on famously." This is far more than one can say about Flannery and Patricia Highsmith, who obviously loathed one another at Yaddo as only temperamental polar opposites can. (Elizabeth, on the other hand, should have appealed tremendously to Highsmith; it may be, however, that their time at Yaddo just missed overlapping, Highsmith having been there for only two months in the early summer.)

At Yaddo Elizabeth worked on her second novel, *Afterwards*, which she published in 1950. Twentieth-Century Fox purchased the film rights to the new novel, assigning the projected flick, which was to star Joseph Cotten, to producer Julian Blaustein, who in 1951 would produce both the sci-fi classic *The Day the Earth Stood Still* and the psychological thriller *Don't Bother to Knock*, based on the Charlotte Armstrong novel *Mischief*; but sadly the project fell through and the novel was never filmed. (This would not be the last time that film adaptation would narrowly elude Elizabeth.) Despite piquing the interest of a Hollywood film studio, *Afterwards*, about a divorced couple with a child who get back together in Boston after several years apart (the author again was clearly drawing heavily on her own life), was not as well-received by critics and Elizabeth would not publish another novel for six years.

Yaddo and *Life* notwithstanding, the writing career of "Elizabeth Fenwick" was wobbling. While her books, especially *The Long Wing*, had won her flattering plaudits from reviewers, to be sure, very little actual money had gone along with that praise. "I wrote a novel a few years ago," Fenwick with evident bitterness recalled in a *San Francisco Examiner* article on women mystery writers in 1971, after she had long shifted over to publishing crime fiction. (The novel to which she referred was surely *The Long Wing*.) "I got my picture in all the magazines, a few bucks and a lot of letters from nuts."

She was desperately lonely as well, as she had been so often as an adolescent. "I returned to being the child and girl who belonged nowhere, was obsessed with other peoples' homes, and wanted only to *have someplace where I belonged*," she later reflected of this time in her life. "I thought I had found it in Ithaca, with Clark, and when I lost it after Clark went back to Germany, I went back to being 'homeless and no family' me in New York." In 1950, the year *Afterwards* appeared, Elizabeth wed her second husband, David Jacques Way, a twice-divorced partner in the small New York publishing and printing firm Clark & Way who was a couple of years younger than she, and in October she gave birth to her only child, Deborah. Yet domestic bliss again cruelly eluded her, as did that sense of belonging as a wife. To be sure, she had a dearly loved daughter to care for, but her spouse proved an altogether thornier presence in her life.

At 6'4" Elizabeth's second husband was even taller than her first one, although in 1940 his recorded weight was just under 150 pounds. Gangling, brash and brightly red-haired, with glasses and a mustache and one blue and one brown eye, David Way was a distinctly memorable individual. Initially Elizabeth deemed him a "charming and funny and brilliant" man who seemingly knew "everyone and everything." Unfortunately her estimation of David proved as errant as the one her mother had made of Jay, though in an even worse way, as it were.

To obtain a better environment for the baby (Deborah's carriage was covered over in a film of soot every morning), the couple at Elizabeth's insistence departed from the village, settling in the coastal town of Stonington in eastern Connecticut, which would serve as the fictionalized setting for her 1971 crime novel *Impeccable People*. David commuted to work in the city, staying at an apartment during weekdays and returning to spend weekends in Stonington. Elizabeth raised Deborah and ran the little book and game shop that was semi-attached to their house at 110 Water Street.

After two years, however, the family returned to New York City, for Elizabeth felt isolated and unhappy in Stonington. David having proven a rageful and violent husband, she lived apart from him with Deborah in the same apartment building, with David visiting them at dinnertime. He began seeing a psychiatrist, but according to Elizabeth these visits failed to help him, since even his psychiatrist was mortally frightened of him. Elizabeth and David would attend cocktail parties and never get invited back again because of his aggressive, angry behavior. David and Elizabeth's own daughter described her father as "terrifying" in his "rages."

After several years Elizabeth consented to live with David again and the pair moved with Deborah to Mamaroneck, a city in wealthy suburban Westchester County, where, Deborah recalls, Elizabeth and David occupied separate bedrooms in a "very pleasant Cape Cod style house" located at 911 Stuart Avenue, just a three minutes' drive, as it turns out, from the house where famed detective novelist John Dickson Carr lived with his wife in the early Sixties. There David joined the Episcopal Church, made a great hit with both the rector and the deacon, and sang, along with Deborah, in the choir. Meanwhile Elizabeth after four years had managed to complete her third mainstream novel, *Days of Plenty* (1956), but with the book decidedly failing to ignite the literary world, she resolved in Mamaroneck to try her hand at crime fiction.

Crime writing might at least prove lucrative and finally make Elizabeth financially independent of her frighteningly moody and mercurial husband. With two small rooms at the top of the house at her disposal, her bedroom and a tiny writing-room/study, Elizabeth, working during the winters when her daughter was at school, between 1957 and 1963 published a half-dozen crime novels—*Poor Harriet* (1957), *A Long Way Down* (1959), *A Night Run* (1961), *A Friend of Mary Rose* (1961), *The Silent Cousin* (1962) and *The Make-Believe Man* (1963)—that established her as one of the preeminent authors of domestic suspense from those years.

During the summers Elizabeth would drive with Deborah to Cleveland to visit her mother Beth and her aunt, trips which were something of an idyll for the author and her daughter, as Deborah has recalled:

We went on these trips as soon as school was out, and each time we drove away from Mamaroneck in great high spirits, very early in the cool of the June mornings. She seemed to leave all of her troubles and worries behind as we headed off to Cleveland. We would stop at a "homey" motel in the mid-afternoon when the heat became unbearable, and no matter how cheap and homey the motel was, it had to have a pool, for us both to jump in and cool off. We were always welcomed to the house in Cleveland with great joy, and we would spend our week there in great comfort, my mother sitting peacefully with my grandmother and (great) aunt, with their endless conversations, myself playing contentedly around the house, or with the neighborhood children.

Unfortunately Elizabeth's crime novels, well-received as the majority of them were, failed to earn their author enough money to free her for good and all from David. Despite being published in the United Kingdom as well as in the United States, each book, Deborah recalls, typically only netted her mother royalties of about a couple of thousand dollars, or around $20,000 today. This was about as much as Elizabeth annually had made, in other words, from the nine-to-five stenographic work which she had performed in her early twenties—a dispiriting reminder to us today of the pecuniary limitations of even a lot of critically-acclaimed mystery writing. While all of Elizabeth's crime novels were loyally published in the U. K. by Gollancz, her publication record was spottier in the United States, where, despite the high praise afforded her first two crime novels, *A Night Run* never found a publisher and *The Silent Cousin* was not picked up for four years. Nor was Elizabeth fortunate, on the whole, with paperback publication.

Whenever Elizabeth did receive a check from her publishers, David, his own publishing business having been "constantly on the rocks" for years according to Deborah, responded by halting his own checks to the family until Elizabeth's money ran out, meaning she was damned if she wrote and damned if she didn't write. This continually stressful situation to which her husband subjected her inevitably began to exact its physical toll on Elizabeth, who started to suffer physically (aside from David's outburst of violence toward her), developing migraines, facial rashes and numbness in her extremities. Her friend Flannery O'Connor, nearing death herself, was convinced that Elizabeth like she was suffering from lupus, but it turned out "merely" to be Raynaud's Syndrome. 1964 saw the demise both of Flannery and Elizabeth's mother Beth, who, afflicted with dementia, had been placed in a nursing home. Deborah, then barely in her teens, remembers "how frightening that tiny, sharp, disheveled, toothless person" had become, asking "the same questions over and over and over."

Back in Mamaroneck after her mother's funeral, Elizabeth again was faced with that same question which faced so many of the female protagonists of domestic suspense fiction from the period: How to extricate herself from the terrible, soul-destroying marriage which she had made with a man who was entirely unworthy of her. According to Deborah:

She racked her brains to think of a way to support herself so she could leave him—the writing just did not bring in enough for financial independence. She thought of going back to secretarial work, but she was so much older, had no recent experience and it would mean my coming home to an empty apartment after school. She thought of divorce and alimony, but could she support us on that? My father did not want a divorce, and seemed to be clinging tightly to this life he had made. She wondered how long she could stick it out.

With cruel and classic irony it was David himself who settled the matter for good in 1966 when he, like Clark had before him, abandoned Elizabeth, leaving her for a graphic designer in his firm, who, at twenty-three, was proverbially young enough to be his daughter. Upon sixteen-year-old Deborah's graduation from high school in June, Elizabeth sold the house in Mamaroneck and with her daughter set out for the West Coast, as if to put as much distance between herself and her old life (and her faithless husband) as she could. However, there was more purpose to this western venture: Deborah was going to college in Portland, Oregon while Elizabeth, ironically, was going to stay with David's family in California. "They had always loved her dearly and preferred her company to his," Deborah bluntly recalls, "and invited her to come to them when the marriage broke up."

Over the next six years Elizabeth in California completed five more crime novels, her final published works: *The Passenger* (1967), *Disturbance on Berry Hill* (1968), *Goodbye, Aunt Elva* (1968), *Impeccable People* (1971) and *The Last of Lysandra* (1973), the last two of which were published only in the U. K. Over the summer of 1966, before Deborah went away to college, Elizabeth, while renting a small apartment in Pasadena, started writing *The Passenger*, a "road" novel which reflects some of her traveling experience with her daughter. She completed the novel later that year, but during the bleakly lonely winter, she later admitted to Deborah, she had, like Clark back in 1940, seriously contemplated suicide.

Fortunately the next year Deborah transferred to the University of California at Berkeley and Elizabeth was able to purchase a small house with a rose garden in Walnut Creek, closer to her daughter and to David's kindly son from one of his prior marriages, with whom she and Deborah had long been close. There Elizabeth was able to live off her royalties, along with the alimony she had exacted from David as a condition of consenting to a divorce. Presumably she was divorced by November 1971, when an article on women mystery writers in the *San Francisco Examiner* referred to her as "a tweedy, English-looking

Walnut Creek wife and mother who writes books of what she calls 'domestic menace.'" Perhaps in spite of herself Elizabeth, like her mother, still saw something pitiable in the state of a single woman, second wave feminism notwithstanding.

Disappointingly, an attempt by producer-director Robert Aldrich to film Elizabeth's "domestic menace" novel *Goodbye, Aunt Elva* as *What Ever Happened to Dear Elva?* or *What Ever Happened to Dear Daisy?*— the third in a trilogy of his so-called "psycho-biddy" films, following *What Ever Happened to Baby Jane?* and *What Ever Happened to Aunt Alice?*—fell through in 1971, film success thus eluding Elizabeth again, as it had two decades earlier. Then ideas for stories finally just stopped coming to her a couple of years later, after the publication in the U. K. of *The Last of Lysandra*. She ceased writing for publication, instead quietly keeping her diaries, caring for her roses and her dog and cats and receiving visits from her family. Her writing reputation began to wane, even as her personal contentment waxed.

About a decade later Elizabeth moved to Colorado, where Deborah had taken a residency in radiology. She again found a little house with a lovely garden to tend, but in 1987, when she was seventy-one years old, she was diagnosed, sadly recalling the experience of her mother Beth, with dementia and Alzheimer's disease. From these afflictions she suffered for nine more years, until she passed away in her sleep at the age of eighty on November 20, 1996.

□ □ □

As public tastes in crime fiction changed, many works by women writers of mid-century domestic suspense fell into unmerited neglect after their deaths, but Elizabeth Fenwick's books fell, quite unaccountably, into even greater neglect than most. With the exception of *Goodbye, Aunt Elva*, which the publisher Academy Chicago reissued in 1987, it appears that until this year not a single Fenwick crime novel had been reprinted in paperback for half a century. Yet several of the author's crime novels were embraced in their day as true classics of suspense.

Perhaps the most lauded of these novels were *Poor Harriet* (1957), surely one of the most raved debuts in the history of crime fiction, *A Long Way Down* (1959), *A Friend of Mary Rose* (1961) and Edgar-nominated *The Make-Believe Man* (1963), which were published successively in the United States by Harper & Brothers' prestigious "Harper Novel of Suspense" imprint, edited by the hugely influential crime fiction editor Joan Kahn. Throughout the Fifties and Sixties (and beyond), Kahn through this imprint published an impressive array of talented crime writers, including Patricia Highsmith, Michael Gilbert, Julian Symons, Andrew Garve, Dick Francis, Maurice Proctor, Lionel Davidson, Gavin Black, J. J. Marric, John Ball, Elizabeth Linington, Nicholas Freeling, Peter Dickinson, Nicholas Blake, Shelley Smith, Sara Woods, and John Dickson Carr. What is remarkable about this list, aside from the notably few exclusive practitioners of classic detection like Carr and Sara Woods and the heavy preponderance of British writers, is how phallocentric it is. There are a wildly disproportionate number of men, especially when one considers that the editor of the imprint was a woman. Not only are traditional detective novelists of the British Crime Queen school absent, but so, largely, are women authors of "domestic menace," like Celia Fremlin, Margaret Millar, Charlotte Armstrong, Ursula Curtiss and Jean Potts. It appears that it was left largely to Elizabeth Fenwick (along with British suspense writer Shelley Smith) to hold this flag high. And hold it high she did, despite her adversities, although between 1966 and 1968 she was affiliated in the United States not with Harper but with Atheneum, publishers of British crime writer P. M. Hubbard and the spy novelists Eric Ambler and Len Deighton, among others.

Obviously Mr. John Nicholas, the protagonist of *A Friend of Mary Rose*, is male, but a most atypical "sleuth" he is: No tough dick or posh amateur sleuth, but rather an eighty-three old blind man—intelligent and decent, to be sure, but hardly a Mr. Marple in the making. Yet it is his very normality which makes him so memorable. Certainly visually impaired detectives were not unknown in crime fiction at the time. There was, for example, Clinton H. Stagg's Problemist, Thornley Colton, deemed the mystery genre's first blind detective; Ernest Bramah's brilliant blind Britisher Max Carrados; and Baynard Kendrick's canny Duncan Maclain. Yet all these men are, to some degree or another, essentially super-sleuths, in no wise different, really, from Sherlock Holmes, John Thorndyke, Hercule Poirot and Ellery Queen, despite their physical impairment—if such it really is in their cases.

Mr. Nicholas, on the other hand, is an everyday elderly man who suffers the everyday indignities of the aged, like the well-meant but patronizing treatment afforded him by his fretful daughter-in-law, whom he with exasperated humor dubs the Martyr. When fate places him late at night in a dim attic with an eleven-year-old girl (the titular Mary Rose) stalked by a man with the darkest of intentions in his heart, readers are kept on edge, because they have no assurance that this frail old man will survive the experience, let alone successfully bring a fiendish miscreant to justice. Realism—both of intimate domestic detail and horrific criminal malevolence—is the keynote to this crime novel and gives it its understated power.

Mary Rose received raves across the Anglo-American world. "This is a wonderfully original and entertaining yarn," wrote Ruth Hard Bonner of *Mary Rose* in her "Books in Town" column in Vermont's *Brattleboro Reformer*, "a fine blend of chill and warmth." In Australia's *Melbourne Age*, features writer Alan Nicholls echoed Bonner's sentiments, perceptively adding: "The suspense, which is acute from cover to cover, depends upon fear for this old man." Perhaps most surprisingly, in the United Kingdom the curmudgeonly Grand Old Man of mystery Francis Iles (aka Anthony Berkeley Cox) chimed in with his own hymn of praise for *Mary Rose* in the *Guardian*, for once keeping both his national and sexual chauvinism mostly in check: "Here the smallest touch of sentimentality would have ruined the whole thing, and in ninety-nine transatlantic cases out of a hundred it would have been ruined; but Miss Fenwick, although an American, most nobly holds herself in until, perhaps, at the very end, when it no longer matters." British Paperback publisher Penguin reprinted *Mary Rose* in 1966 in an eye-catching edition.

Altogether expectedly, Anthony Boucher, the dean of American crime fiction critics and perhaps the most avid admirer of Fenwick crime fiction, emphatically agreed with all the encomia in his review of *Mary Rose* in the *New York Times Book Review*, declaring: "It's a beautiful specimen of the modern manner in suspense, quiet but powerful, recognizably set in everyday life with a strong interplay of interesting people." Strikingly he also took the opportunity to review the author's distinguished criminal career, as it were, going back to the now remote "E. P. Fenwick" days, when as a young woman she "published three mysteries in fifteen months ... and good books they were—somewhat influenced by Elisabeth Sanxay Holding, and therefore well ahead of their time in 'psychological suspense.'" He added that while her earlier mysteries had been, unjustly, little noticed, "Elizabeth Fenwick" was now justly "recognized as one of the few American women writers to compare, in subtlety and insight, with such English writers as Celia Fremlin and Shelley Smith."

These same sterling qualities are found in *The Make-Believe Man*, probably the most popular of Elizabeth Fenwick's novels. American paperback publisher Avon reprinted the novel in 1963 as "Elizabeth Fenwick's masterpiece of terror." Here a close mother-daughter relationship is central to the tale, which is set primarily in Detroit. Norma Hovic is left alone at her mother Mrs. Moore's house with her eleven-year-old son, Jimmy, where they have been residing since the death of her husband, when Mrs. Moore goes to stay in another town with Norma's pregnant sister and her family, until the new baby is born. While her mother is gone, Norma receives an unexpected gentleman caller: Mrs. Moore's previous tenant, a nice young man named Cliff, whom Norma displaced when she came home again to live. Strangely Cliff turns out not at all like Norma expected ... This is another unassuming nail biter of a tale, where suspense slowly but surely builds and does not let relent until its smash finish. Anthony Boucher rightly deemed *The Make-Believe Man* "a quiet, even a gentle novel, with warm understanding of its characters ... and a firm chilling insistence on the menace of the unpredictable mind at large."

That unpredictability in domestic life—the way the cozily familiar can, in the blink of a disoriented eye, turn into the crazily off-kilter—is something Elizabeth Fenwick, drawing on her sometimes painfully lived experiences of forty and fifty years, powerfully depicted in the eleven crime novels which she published between 1957 and 1973. Her body of mid-century crime fiction is an important and compelling one, making Stark House's reprinting of *The Make-Believe Man* and *A Friend of Mary Rose* and after the author's long era of neglect a welcome event indeed. Welcome back, Miss Fenwick! The suspense is finally over—and it has only just begun.

—February 2022
Germantown, TN

Curtis Evans received a PhD in American history in 1998. He is the author of *Masters of the "Humdrum" Mystery: Cecil John Charles Street, Freeman Wills Crofts, Alfred Walter Stewart and British Detective Fiction, 1920-1961* (2012) and most recently the editor of the Edgar nominated *Murder in the Closet: Essays on Queer Clues in Crime Fiction Before Stonewall* (2017) and, with Douglas G. Greene, the Richard Webb and Hugh Wheeler short crime fiction collection, *The Cases of Lieutenant Timothy Trant* (2019). He blogs on vintage crime fiction at The Passing Tramp.

The Make-Believe Man
Elizabeth Fenwick

CHAPTER 1

At four o'clock in the morning, in November dark, Norma Hovic came down the stairs in her mother's house. Shut into his own small room upstairs, her son still slept. In the big front bedroom her mother was struggling by lamplight with her best corset; her struggles were audible. But she said she didn't want any help.

Not entirely awake, Norma turned on the hall lamp, and in its faint light went on out to the kitchen. She could easily have made the journey in darkness, and had done so many a time—the little house was as familiar to her as her own life, and had contained a great deal of it. But the hall lamp meant that they were officially awake and the night over.

In the kitchen she put water on to boil, lit and opened the oven for quick warmth, and then went down cellar to open the furnace damper. When she returned to the kitchen (with smudged hands: the furnace was old and difficult), her mother was there.

She said at once, "Now don't try to fix me anything to eat, Normie. There are things I want to take with me. I want to think what they are."

Mrs. Moore was tubular in the splendid corset and wore, rather than pack it, the purple wool dress in which she would visit the hospital when Tom's baby should be born. She had powdered her face and neck dead white.

"Leave the cellar light on," she added. "It'll remind me. There's some things down there I want to take—some of the preserves and pickles for Tommy, poor darling, driving round this time of night in weather like this! I wish just once," she said, controlled, "Edna could have a normal time."

"Nighttime's normal, mama."

Pouring boiling water in the aluminum coffee maker, Norma heard it begin its rapid drip against the room's stillness. She added, "Don't you want a piece of toast?"

"No. Well, one. And just drop an egg in that water you've got left, dearie. I don't mean night, I mean November," her mother said. "I had all my plans made for next month. And if it had only been Christmas vacation, the way it should have been, I could have taken Jimmy with me. I don't know how you're going to manage, Normie. I just don't."

"Don't worry about us. We'll make out fine. It'll be sort of fun."

Mrs. Moore gave her a sharp glance.

"You won't think it's so much fun when you have to come home and cook and clean after a day's work, my girl. And what's Jimmy going to do until you get here? I don't think he's old enough to have that key. You'd better have him go next door and wait for you," she said firmly. "The Hausens owe us, anyway, from when they both had their grippe. And besides, it gives them something to do. You send Jimmy over there after school, Normie."

She shouldn't have said that: about it being fun. To have the house to themselves a little while, as if it were their own. As if they had a house of their own again.

In obscure apology (and changing the subject), Norma said, "Don't you want to take your own comforter? You said you wished you had, last time."

"Yes, I do," her mother agreed, instantly distracted. "Lordie, I'm glad you thought of that! I nearly froze at night, last time. A year January, that was, when Cassie came. Edna's never had a summer baby, has she—come to think of it."

Norma left her thinking of it, over the poached egg, and went upstairs after the comforter. Her mother's room, tidied, the bed already made, added its own reproach. Of course they would miss her. What had made her say that, about it being fun?

She came back to find Mrs. Moore clearing away plates and cups.

"Leave those, mama. There's all the time in the world before I have to leave. And don't you want some more coffee?"

"Well," said her mother, undecided, "I ought to go down cellar and get those things ..."

"I'll get them. I know what Tom likes. And there's plenty of time. It's going to take him a good hour to get in town: those streets are slick. Just in patches," she added hastily, to her mother's look.

Apparently incapable of saying anything right this morning, Norma escaped to the cellar. If she could only wake up! But the tidy rows of preserves, of jellies and pickles, were soporific in themselves: it was like choosing in a dream to choose among their colors, their memories, their unchanged richness....

Her mother's voice called faintly from above. Norma rapidly transferred jars to basket and ran back up the steps. Mrs. Moore, standing over the table, was tugging to close a small bag.

"The zipper's caught," she said, breathless. "Nasty things!"

"You've got too much in it. Here, put some of those little things in the basket, there's room."

She began to make napkin nests, transferring bottles and small boxes. Wonder at last invaded her drowsy mind.

"What on earth are you taking? Edna must have a medicine cabinet too!"

"I'm not going to count on what Edna may or may not have, with three little girls falling down all day long. Put everything in, Normie."

"Poor mama," she said, suddenly touched by her mother's need to transfer all the comfort and safety of her own home to her daughter-in-law's house. "I ought to be going out to Tom's, and you staying here with Jimmy—why didn't we think of that? I could get a vacation week now, I know I could!"

But her mother said only, "Don't talk nonsense, Normie," and finally zipped the zipper. Calmed by this triumph, she sighed and sat down. "Well, that's all I can think of. Pour me another cup of coffee, will you, dearie?"

The cups were already washed and put away. Norma took them down again.

"I don't think it's nonsense," she said.

"Well, it is. You've got your son to support and look after, and that's plenty without taking on more. Besides, it's harder to be a young widow than an old one. I remember how it was for me after your father went. And I was a lot older than you."

Norma was unprepared for this—an extremely personal statement, by her mother's standards. She could not think of an answer, and a brief silence occurred between them, reinforced by the deep silence of the hour.

Then her mother added, "Not that you aren't doing very well, Normie. You are, and I'm proud of you. I always mean to say so, but somehow I don't. That first year is a very hard one, dearie, and you've come through it just fine."

"Well ... I had you."

"That's not always a good thing," said her mother firmly. "It's not easy to come back and be a daughter again when you're used to being a wife and mother, with a house of your own. Especially when your mother's an old lady as set in her ways as I am."

"You're not any of that," said Norma, beginning to smile.

"Oh, yes. Sixty-three next April. And I guess I've been keeping this house pretty much the same way for thirty-five of those years. If that's not set, I don't know what would be."

"Well, whatever it is, we love it," said Norma.

It was past five, now. The darkness outside still seemed absolute, but there were beginning to be small sounds of an awakening world around them. An occasional swift car went by. A man, coughing, walked with sharp steps past the house; a nearby window went shut with a hard sound.

Tom didn't come.

Mrs. Moore said suddenly, "Maybe it will be fun for you two to be on your own for a while. I hope it will. Just don't worry about a thing, dearie—let the house slide and enjoy yourselves."

"Oh, mama—"

"No, I mean it. Don't be like Cliff. My goodness, he must have just killed himself while I was gone, washed all the windows, and polished floors, and I don't know what all. He said it was because he was lonesome, but I don't know. I think he was afraid I'd come back and the house wouldn't look right and I'd think it was his fault. He was a little bit that way, poor boy."

"Cliff? You left him here alone?"

Cliff was her mother's one roomer—an experiment doubtfully tried, but apparently a great triumph. Norma and her son, coming home, had ended it; the house was too small for all of them, and so Cliff had to go. But triumph or not, it was hard to imagine Mrs. Moore leaving her house to a stranger for so long.

A little defensively, she said, "Well, certainly he stayed here. Where else would he go? Besides, he was a very quiet man, I never worried about him for a minute. Of course I never dreamed he'd work himself to death like that while I was gone!"

She was smiling—a curious, remembering smile that lightened her poor face, already marked by fatigue.

"That was when Cassie came—a year ago January," she went on. "And we were sitting here just the same way, waiting for Tom. Except it was ten o'clock at night, that time. And all of a sudden, Cliff says no, he thinks he'd better go to a hotel after all. He doesn't think he'd better take the responsibility! After I'd just finished making him all sorts of lists about the milk, and the furnace, and telephone numbers, and what-all. I guess I took him up pretty sharp," she said, her smile growing. "But it was the right thing, it straightened him up. He lacked confidence, you know, that was his trouble. I knew he'd be perfectly all right if he just set to and did it, and he was. And quite proud of himself, too."

Through her faint astonishment at this story—so unexpectedly familiar—Norma caught her brother's step on the front porch. She pushed back her chair.

"Here he is!"

But for a moment, her mother seemed not to know whom she meant. Her smile wavered, confusion crossed her look. Then Tom rapped on the door, and her expression cleared.

"All right, dearie—all right, we're all ready!"

She called out the last of this to the opening door, her voice following

Norma out into the hall.

Tom came in, as large and harassed as if it were the first time. Norma put her arms around him, in a rare close embrace.

"You come have coffee. It's all ready."

But he couldn't; he'd left the kids ... and was this all that went out to the car? The comforter, the preserve basket, the zipper case ... No; the big suitcase was still upstairs. Just by the bedroom door. Mrs. Moore, coat-bundled, went up after him—the hat she wanted to wear was up there too. They met and struggled round each other on the stairs with hardly a word, intent on their separate preoccupations. Then Norma remembered her mother's purse in the dining room sideboard and ran for that. And the porch light wasn't on....

In its sudden glow, Tom reappeared for a second load. Mrs. Moore, holding her hat as if to a high wind, appeared breathless on the stairs.

"Normie, my purse ..."

"Here; I've got it."

"Don't forget the milk ..."

"I won't. Call me ..."

She kissed her mother hastily, clutched at her brother's arm.

"Tom—I'm so glad for you, dear—"

He looked at her as if she had hit him over the head. Then he suddenly grinned.

"Then wish me a boy," he said, "so she'll quit this jazz!"

Her mother murmured an automatic, "Oh, Tommy," and then they were two solid backs, going down the steps, down the walk, out of the porch light's radiance and into the dimmer one of the street lamp. Norma went in.

Pressed to the front window, she watched the double huddle by Tom's car; saw it break into two, her mother entering, Tom shutting the door and striding round. Then he waved! His arm went up, and hers shot up in answer.

Still arm in air, fingers faintly moving, she watched the car start and drive away, out of sight. Then there was nothing but the deserted, early-morning street.

And the deserted house around her.

Perversely, she was wide-awake now.

After a lost moment, she returned to the kitchen. Two cups on the table were the only evidence of her mother's recent presence. Of Tom's, there was none. It was hard to believe they had both been with her so recently. What a lonely thing it was, to be the one who stayed behind!

With over an hour to spend before she could, fairly, make her son get up, she began to make a stew for that night's dinner. It was a weird occupation, at such an hour, but it took off the shock of aloneness. I'm like Cliff, she thought. With his window washing and floor polishing.

Somehow it wasn't a comfortable idea. Besides, he must have kept at it the whole time she was gone, to do so much. How funny. He'd worked, had a job. Surely he ate out, saw friends, went to the movies. Where had all those empty hours come from that he had needed to fill as she was filling this one?

Uneasily, she began to wish that her mother had told her either more or less about the displaced roomer. The glimpse she had left behind was hard to flesh out and as hard to get rid of. Rather creepy company, in fact. She began to imagine a larger Oliver Twist, dragging home each night from some arduous job to swallow his crust and then feverishly, doggedly set to work polishing up her mother's house. Her implacable, tyrannical mother, of course. Mrs. Bumble, in fact.

This was cheerful enough, but by the time Jimmy came down, to a disconcerting fragrance of stew and oatmeal mixed, she found she had coaxed herself out of believing in Cliff at all. And serve him right, for leaving behind such a highly moral legend!

CHAPTER 2

The Hausens, next door, had captured Jimmy before Norma came home from work that evening.

She had barely time to notice her house was dark, and wonder about it, when their neighbors' aluminum storm door opened just enough to show a beckoning arm under the porch light. A hollow voice called, "Normie ... Normie ... over here!" Then arm vanished, door shut; she came up the walk to a closed fastness, and had to ring.

Mr. Hausen let her in, with suitable care to avoid drafts. He was retired; and so far as Norma could tell their sole winter occupation was fighting off (or having) a plague known to them as *la grippe*. Secondarily, they tried to keep a watchful eye on the neighborhood, but under such handicaps of enclosure that this occupation really belonged to summer.

Why did they have Jimmy?

Her son's face, showing controlled despair, made her ask, "What's wrong?" Jimmy said at once, "Nothing."

Mr. Hausen then begged her to open her coat and take her boots off so she wouldn't sweat on going outside again.

"I can't stay, thanks," she said. "If you'll get your things on, Jimmy? And where's your key?"

"Mr. Hausen has it," said Jimmy, with the same control, and took down his coat.

"Oh, you knew he had the key?" said Mr. Hausen, disappointed. "We thought maybe he kind of—you know, snuck that one your mother keeps under the clock. Didn't seem to us like she'd want him to be carrying a key to the house round all day, at his age."

His expression said, clearly, that he was sure she wouldn't. Mrs. Hausen's voice added from the dining room, where she had gone to avoid drafts, "Besides, it would worry us, Normie, to think of a little boy alone there all that time. You'd much better have him come here, you know. It's no trouble to us, we don't mind."

Jimmy pulled on his knit cap, with clenched knuckles. She didn't look at him again, but said, brightly smiling, "Oh, Jimmy's eleven—he's very responsible. And it's only a little over an hour. I wouldn't want him coming here from school every day, with all the germs he must pick up there. He'll be fine at home. Thank you, though."

There was a small pause, after which Mr. Hausen said warily, "He hasn't got anything, has he?"

"No, but I'm sweating," Jimmy muttered.

Norma immediately made a small aperture in the doors and pushed him through, Mr. Hausen recoiling from the suck of air.

"No, no, Normie—that's not the way, let me do it!" he exclaimed. But she was already outside herself, nodding and smiling.

Then she had to ring the bell again to get back the key. And wait for that.

Going down one walk and up the other, they exchanged looks.

"Well, I'm sorry," Norma said. "But did you behave?"

"Yes. They're awfully nosey, though."

"About what?"

But he, shrugging, didn't want to go over it, and she didn't particularly want to hear. They came into the warm and silent gloom of their own hallway, and Jimmy closed the door with his back, with a sigh. Norma turned on the lamp.

"I'd better leave this on in the morning, when we go. Then you won't come home to a dark house."

"It's not dark when I come home. Besides, I wouldn't care. You don't think I'd be scared, do you?"

"No, not scared. But a light is like someone here."

"The house is like someone here," he said, scornful. "I've been here when there wasn't anybody. I like it."

"When were you alone?" she asked; and as they went back toward the kitchen, turning on lamps along the way, he reminded her. Sure enough, he had been; and it was clear that he not only liked it, he loved it. Some real delight of proprietorship had been taken from his grasp by the Hausens, but he would have it again. She would see that he did.

The wrapped sandwich she had left for him caught his eye, but her hand was quicker than his.

"No, too late. I'm starting supper now. Didn't they give you anything to eat?"

"Yes. I think it was celery juice. They make it in a blender. You know? And little brown crackers," he said thoughtfully. "They can't eat salt—salt isn't good for them. That was why they tasted like that. The crackers."

"Well, you'll be good and hungry for dinner, then," she said, in a no-comment voice.

A few minutes later the telephone rang. It was Mr. Hausen, to tell Norma that their cellar light had been on all day. He thought maybe she didn't realize it.

It seemed to Norma, saying thank you, hanging up, that she simply passed this intelligence on to her son with a simple request that he turn the light off. There was no way of explaining the wild fit of giggles that hit them both and then led to some unfortunate demonstrations by Jimmy of Mr. Hausen fitting his spyglass between the venetian blind slats while trying to keep his chest covered. Norma felt obliged to discourage this; but it was funny. Their good humor remained throughout dinner and settled afterward to a luxury of content.

Yet they did miss her mother. This exhilaration of being alone together was quite different, hard to explain. When Mrs. Moore called, around nine o'clock, Norma's heart turned over for the tired, familiar voice coming out of the receiver.

She just wanted to let them know everything was all right, Mrs. Moore said, and find out how they were. No news from Edna yet, but everything was all right. How were they?

Norma said they were fine, but missed her.

"I forgot my elastic bandage," said Mrs. Moore sadly. "And that little bottle of Lapactic pills, in my dresser drawer. Could you make a little package and mail them out, dearie? It seems so wasteful to buy more, out here."

Norma said she would mail it from the office, next day. Then she motioned Jimmy to come and talk, which he did, very nicely. Then Mrs. Moore asked for Norma again, apparently to say that she thought it was a toll call from suburb to city, so she had better not run it up any more. Good night to her darlings, she missed them so much.

Sobriety entered the room, after they hung up. Ought they to be so content, when poor Grandma was not? Norma remembered the supper dishes, still undone, and Jimmy—at the merest suggestion—went upstairs for the night. She heard him bumping around up there for a while; then he was silent. The little stretch of light which his window made on the frozen ground of the back yard disappeared before she had finished in the kitchen. He had turned himself out without even being told.

Should she go upstairs too? It had been a long day, with that early beginning. Only coffee had got her through the morning and her luncheon might as well have been solid Mickey Finn. Yet now that she was free to collapse, she had lost the need.

She stood at the front window, looking out on the quiet, rather shabby street where she had grown up. It wasn't so different outwardly, but all the houses had changed hands, some of them many times. Families moved out into the suburbs now; these city blocks had become backwaters, a little stagnant. Business crept closer all the time, too, and parking had become a problem. Wasn't allowed at all, in fact, on Mrs. Moore's side of the street. Yet one lone car sat in front of their house, in spite of this prohibition.

A long hardtop, without lights, it had—she realized—been sitting there as long as she had been standing at the window. Well, unless it had M.D. plates, someone was inviting a fifteen-dollar fine.

A man got out of the far side and shut the door.

Instinctively, Norma moved back. That there should have been someone in the car all this time gave her a slight sense of shock. She had been standing there looking out, as she supposed, on an empty street, and here all the while there had been an observer of her observations.

Not that it mattered. Recovering, she glanced out again, curious to see where he was going. He wasn't going anywhere; he was coming up their front walk.

She moved without haste to the hall and switched on the porch light. After a moment, quietly, she slipped the night chain in place. With equal quietness, he was coming up the steps.

She forestalled the bell-ringing that might rouse Jimmy and opened the door slightly, saying from that ambush, "Yes? Who is it?"

"Is that Norma?"

The voice was light, pleasant. Not familiar. She looked out through her guarded aperture and saw only an illumined hat, shading the face beneath.

He removed this, and the porch light shone down on butter-blond hair, waving back from a high forehead. The rather fleshy face below, still shadowed, offered a tentative smile.

"It's Cliff, Norma. Cliffy Wilson."

Cliffy?

His low voice, offering this unfamiliar diminutive, trembled slightly. Could he be drunk?

She said cautiously, "Oh, yes ... Cliff."

The chain ought certainly to come down now. Instead, after a moment, she said impulsively, "I thought that car was empty."

"No," he said. "No ..."

The chain seemed to disconcert him. As well it might. She took it off and stood back, inviting him to come in. But he hesitated.

"I didn't see your mother ...?"

"No, she isn't here just now. Won't you come in?"

Cold air was coming in, plentifully, while he continued to hesitate there.

"She—is she coming back soon?"

"She's out at Tom's. But won't you come in? I'm afraid we're letting the whole night in."

"Oh. Oh—yes."

Startled, obedient, he slipped inside and stood just by the door (by her) while she shut it. She moved somewhat away and saw, with shock, that there was something very wrong with his face.

He put up his hand against her look, but it shaded only the enormous bruise round his eye. Below that, meaty-red abrasions covered one jaw and the side of his neck.

"Why, you're hurt, Cliff!" she said. "What is it—have you had an accident?"

He shook his head, keeping the hand in place.

"No—please, it's all right, Norma. But—you see why I didn't like to come in. I mean, if she wasn't here."

But what if she had been? Norma looked at him in increasing discomfort, less because of his face than because of his strange maneuvers to hide it.

"Well, she isn't. I'm sorry. Is there anything I can do?"

"No—no, thank you, Norma. Except, I wonder if you'd mind if I wait for her? She won't be too late, will she?"

Now he took his hand down, in some return of confidence, and he really did look awful. What in the world had happened to him?

The polite smile he kept essaying only made things worse.

She said slowly, "She's staying there. They're having another baby."

"Oh."

She had given up asking him in, and was not prepared for the sudden advance he made—past her, as if she had not been there, to the middle of the living room. He stood there, looking round.

Then, in his pleasant light voice, he said, "I was here, the last time. I stayed here alone while your mother was gone."

"Yes, I know."

But not Oliver Twist, not Oliver Twist at all, with those pouched and weary eyes, those softening jowls.

"She told you about that?"

The smile he managed then was more natural and showed small, good teeth. With his profile toward her, she could see the straight nose, the high forehead, which together made an attractive line. And he carried himself well, very erect. It was possible to reconcile this view of Cliff with her mother's "nice young man"—only not a very young man. He was older than she, older than Tom. Forty, surely. The boyishness was there, but it was not a matter of years.

She became aware that she was still in the hall, as if waiting for him to come back. To leave. He seemed unaware; but she moved forward at once.

"Won't you sit down, Cliff? Take your coat off?"

"Why, thank you, Norma."

He smiled again and went back to the hall, removing and hanging up his coat, hat on top. It was a gesture of custom; he performed it carefully. When he came back and sat opposite her, he seemed entirely to have forgotten his ruined face.

"This is where I always sat," he said. "I must say, it's nice to be back. And I hope," he added, carefully, "you'll forgive my saying 'Norma' all the time. It's the way I learned to think of you, you know—and to tell you the truth, I wouldn't know what else to call you!"

"Well, my name is Hovic now. But 'Norma' is fine."

"You probably think of me as Cliff. I hope you do."

She said after a moment, "Of course."

"Maybe you wondered why I never came around to meet you, Norma. It must have seemed rather strange, almost hard feelings! But I'm sure you don't believe that."

"Believe what?"

She was listening toward the stairs, uneasy lest Jimmy should come down while this queer visitor was here. Yet he was not likely to do this; nor was there any real reason why he shouldn't.

"Why, that I had any hard feelings toward you," Cliff was explaining. "Because of having to leave. I certainly didn't. You certainly had first place here, and I know your mother was very pleased to have you back. It wasn't anything like that."

On the other hand, it wasn't like him to sleep through a visitor's arrival. Not this early. Then she saw, glancing at her watch, that it was past ten.

She forced her attention back. Cliff seemed unaware that it had been divided.

"Actually I wasn't in town. I'd been offered another connection, you see, and when your mother told me that she would have to ask me to leave—quite rightly, of course—I decided to make a clean break of it, to relocate completely. And so—that's what I did."

"I see.... Well, I'll tell mother, Cliff. I know she'll be glad to hear about you. Where did you go?"

His failure to answer lay between them, like a strange answer. She met his eyes—large and blue—and found them fixed steadily on her face.

"Why, St. Louis, Norma."

It wasn't true. Why he should lie to her about this, she had no idea; and yet he was lying.

She received the lie in silence. And then got up.

"Would you excuse me a minute?"

She left him standing too, saying something polite, and went out of the room and up the stairs.

CHAPTER 3

Jimmy's door was closed. She had needed to know that. But more, she needed privately to consider a most peculiar notion.

Was this Cliff?

More than real doubt, perhaps, she was juggling surprise. In no way did the man downstairs fit in with the idea she had come to accept, casually, of her mother's roomer. It was true they had not discussed him much. The overwhelming fact of her new widowhood had absorbed and quieted them both; beyond that, her mother was not given to much discussion of other people (or even of themselves). Still, from a few phrases, she had somewhere formed a most definite picture of Cliff: a nice young man, with such lovely manners, who was no trouble at all.

The man downstairs seemed to her, simply, a middle-aged shifty customer. If he had been selling something at the door, she wouldn't have taken the chain down for a minute.

How to reconcile them? *And what about Oliver Twist?*

It was no use. She could not make it fit. Either Cliff had changed drastically, or he was a completely different person with her mother.

As soon as she thought this, it seemed to her the answer. Of course he was different with her. He was the kind of man—lonely, pseudo-boyish—so appealing to older ladies, so unappealing to his contemporaries. And naturally, ill at ease with her, he showed at his worst. That was all.

Yet why the lie? And what had happened to his face?

She had wandered into her mother's room, was standing by the windows looking down at the illegally parked hardtop, when it occurred to Norma that she was almost hiding. Her reaction to Cliff edged on fear! She was dreading going back to him.

At once, she left the room and ran briskly downstairs again. Cliff was instantly on his feet to greet her.

Before she could speak, he said eagerly, "I see you've moved into your mother's room, Norma."

She stared at him, taken aback. But he went on quickly, "I only mention it because it gave me an idea—well, a hope, really—that you wouldn't mind my using the second bedroom for a few days? That was what I wanted to ask your mother, actually," he confessed, "but I felt a little shy with you at first, until we got to know each other. Really what I had in mind was the day bed, in the dining room, and if you'd prefer my taking that, I certainly wouldn't mind. It's only for a few days." He added, "I know, of course, your little boy has the small room. Tom's room."

Why did he say that? There was no reason why he shouldn't know about Jimmy, who was hardly a secret. Yet she might have been trying to conceal her son's presence in the house, his remark startled her so.

To his waiting smile, she said finally, "I'm sorry, Cliff, but I'm afraid I couldn't do that."

He became serious too.

"Well, I know how you feel, Norma—about being responsible for the house. I felt that way too, when I was here alone. But after all, it's only me. I do feel so sure your mother wouldn't mind. In the circumstances."

What circumstances? She didn't want to know. It was a time to be firm.

"Well, she probably wouldn't mind, if she were here. But she isn't, Cliff. And I know she wouldn't think it was right for you to stay here when she's away and—we're alone."

She couldn't bring herself to say, "I'm alone," but he understood the point at once, and was silenced by it. His silence closed on him, like a defeat.

She found herself adding, "Would you like me to call Mrs. Walters, down the street? They often have an empty room."

"No. No, Norma—thank you."

She had remained standing, by the portieres, but as if this no longer mattered, he sank down in his chair again.

"To tell you the truth, Norma, I simply don't feel up to going to strangers yet. You know how reluctant I was, even to come in to you. Well ... I've had a really ... disgusting experience, and it's left me pretty well shaken up. It's the sort of thing you don't believe can happen to anyone, certainly not to you, and I just—I suppose you might say it's broken my spirit, for the moment."

He turned his marred face up to her, like a kind of evidence. Between pity and repulsion, she could only murmur, "I'm sorry, Cliff."

"I wouldn't dream of distressing you with the—very sordid details. I'll just put it this way, that I'm through with that Chicago deal and on my way back east. And I would like, very much, a few days of respite here before I go on my way."

Chicago, then. Why hadn't he wanted her to know?

The disastrous face waited, still upturned. She said unhappily to it, "I wish it were possible, Cliff. But it just isn't."

He surprised her by saying then, "I'm sorry I told you I'd been in St. Louis, Norma—I suppose my mind is just trying to deny the whole experience, or something like that. Because of course you knew it was Chicago I'd gone to, didn't you? I think I told your mother?"

"I don't know. It doesn't matter, Cliff."

"Perhaps not, though," he said, growing thoughtful. "I guess I didn't see her before I left, did I? Everything happened pretty fast, and it was a rather unhappy time for me—I probably felt that she had too much on her mind just then to be bothered with me anymore. And as I say, it was a very quick decision—I'd had the offer a couple of months before and turned it down. I hadn't any intention of taking it, actually. But then, when I knew I had to leave here, I just decided to relocate completely."

She felt as if, in her confusion, she must have missed something.

"You don't mean you changed your job just because you had to move?"

"Yes, it's exactly what I mean, Norma," he said, faintly smiling. "Is that so hard to understand? You see, to me, this house and your mother were Detroit. I came here my first week in town, and very frankly, your mother and this house were far more important to me than a mere job. After all, my work is more or less the same wherever I do it. It's the personal element in life that gives it whatever real worth it has. And I'm sure you know that I was very happy here with your mother, Norma. This place meant a great deal to me, it always will."

Too astonished for caution, Norma sat down on the arm of the nearest chair.

"But what sort of work do you do, Cliff?"

He gave her, before answering, the same steady sort of look that had preceded his saying "St. Louis," earlier. But apparently for a different reason.

"Norma, you're almost persuading me that your mother has just never gotten around to mentioning me at all! But of course I know there were many other concerns between you when you came," he said, making her explanations for her. "And perhaps, if she did mention me, you had other things on your mind. Something like that?"

"Yes, I suppose so."

She was regretting her impulsive question. But it was too late; he was going on to answer it.

"As for my work—why, I'm a display artist, Norma. I create those—I hope—very tempting displays of merchandise that bring you ladies into the shops. And I also have considerable merchandising experience, of course. You force me to tell you this, but I'm really quite favorably known in my field, which is why relocating is never a problem with me. I certainly wasn't bowled over by receiving that Chicago offer, although it was very good…. It just came at a time when … it was urged on me," he said suddenly, "with *very great personal warmth*."

His pleasant voice sharpened. He began to speak more quickly.

"I think I'm just as well qualified to distinguish real friendliness from business friendliness as the next man—maybe a little better! But unfortunately there are men for whom business relationships are their real relationships—they simply have no other life that counts. Do you know what I mean, Norma?"

"Cliff, you don't need to—"

"Now this man—nameless, of course—has quite a successful chain of specialty shops. I happen to know he had quite a long struggle to get even the first ones established, but then—about ten or twelve years ago—they simply began to go like wildfire. Well, by then, that business had become his sole interest, you see. He's a married man—I happen to know he has rather an elaborate home, out in Highland Park—but *he never asks anyone there!* I doubt if he goes there himself, very much. His real emotional life, you see, is centered in those shops! Now that would be harmless enough, I suppose, if this man had a *normal* emotional life. But he does not. He does not!"

"You don't have to tell me all this, Cliff," she broke in.

He seemed to hear her, but the rapid voice went on, without acknowledgment.

"He regards his entire staff as a possible stock of cronies, if you can understand me, and he requires them—requires them, mind you!—to become his companions in his amusements. And I have no intention of telling you what *they* are," he said tightly.

"No, don't. Cliff—I'm sorry you've had this trouble, but—"

"Oh, don't look on me as a helpless victim, Norma," he said, suddenly cold. "I assure you, I made myself perfectly clear from the first! As soon as I realized what his ideas of *fun* were, I made it quite clear they weren't mine. He could take it or leave it. And he took it, of course. He wanted me there. I was doing an excellent job for him. And in return," said Cliff, in a reasonable tone, "I had no objection to a certain amount of good-natured teasing on his part. What I *took* to be good-natured teasing. But there was deep resentment underneath, Norma. Deep resentment. I suppose he felt that I had rejected him as a person. And so I had! That part of him, anyway."

"Cliff—"

"He's not a stupid man. Not by any means. Whether or not he's sane is another matter, and I have my own opinion about that! But he did manage to establish a kind of relationship between us that I would accept. That I did accept."

The voice stopped. Norma got up. He gave her a startled glance and said quickly, "Occasional dinners, I mean. Or even a late evening now and then, talking things over. At his club or sometimes at his apartment. He was a bawdy talker, he didn't seem to be able to say anything in a clean way, but a certain amount of allowance has to be made for the way people *are*—I know that—and *on my terms* I had learned to make allowances for him. *Which was what he had planned.*"

To her horror, she saw that tears had begun to run down his maimed cheeks. She could think of only one thing: to stop him; and she said in a sudden, clear voice, "I don't want to hear the rest of this, Cliff!"

He stared at her. She turned and went out into the hall—stood there, knowing she must go on somehow, or he would.

In as normal a voice as she could manage, she said, "Your car's been there a long time, Cliff. You know they're very strict about the no-parking rule on our side of the street. Don't you think you'd better move it?"

After what seemed a long time, she heard him get up. But when she moved to see him, he was just standing there, by the mantel.

Then, slowly, he started toward her. She took down his coat and hat and held them, like a barrier between them; but although he came up to her he did not take them.

He said in a low voice, "You only know the safety of this house—a life like this house. You have no idea of the evil there can be in the world outside. The malice, and cruelty, and evil."

She could make neither sound nor movement.

"He had a woman there in his apartment," he said then. "She was there all the time. And when she came in the room with us, she had nothing on. They had planned it that way, it was a joke. They both acted as if nothing were wrong, but they were smiling. Watching me. She—"

"Cliff. Please go."

"I got up to go. He put out his leg and tripped me, and when I fell down he sat on me. He sat on me as if I was a horse. He was laughing, he told her to come over there. He said, Now you can—"

Norma opened the front door, wide. The cold night air swept in; his monotonous voice rose above the current of it."

"... She kicked me. She had shoes on. Just shoes. And when she kicked me, he laughed. And then he—"

"Shut up," she said. "Shut up, Cliff! Stop it, stop it!"

In a blind thrust, she put his coat out at him, half dropping it. He caught absently at that—then stooped for his hat, which had fallen.

She said, fierce, "Did you come here to tell my mother this? Did you?"

He gave her an empty look and put his hat on. His coat held in a careless bundle, he walked out the door. And down the steps.

Shaking, she put the chain on the door.

Then upstairs—far enough to see Jimmy's closed door. Back in the hall, she came to a dead stop.

I told him where mother is. He knows where she is.

But Tom was there too.

She had an instant certainty that he would not go where there was a man, a young and able-bodied man capable of protecting her mother from such behavior, and in the relief of this thought, she sat limply down on the stairs.

But her mind was blank with shock. No trace was left of anger, of pity, of fear. Just nothing.

Presently she got up and went to the window. The car was gone. She began numbly to wonder, Where had he gone?

Where would he go, with his hurt face, his compulsion to talk, his deep resentment? For he had been full of resentment, she realized. It was what she had felt most strongly in him, from the first: beneath his need to placate, to reassure, it had glowed out at her and filled her with unease. Resentment that they had put him out in the first place. And this was what had happened to him, because they put him out.

A forty-year-old man.

She shivered and moved away—going back through the house, turning out lamps. The hall was last. With her fingers on that switch, she looked round and saw the small mantel clock slightly askew. She withdrew her fingers and stood quietly a moment. The brief journey she made then was hardly necessary. She knew before she looked that the spare key her mother kept there would be gone.

CHAPTER 4

By morning, Norma felt she knew what to do about the situation.

She was up early, with the false alertness that follows a broken night, full of canceled decisions. Now, in daylight, her course seemed clear.

First she tackled Jimmy about the key. It was the one he was to use, and the strict rule was that it must be replaced under the clock every night so they would not spend precious morning minutes trying to find it. Since she had watched him replace it yesterday her questioning was perfunctory, but it had to be done.

"You're sure you didn't take it down again?"

"Why would I?" he said, reasonable.

"I don't know why you would, but *did* you?"

"No, I didn't. Maybe that man took it," he said hopefully—and then evaded her stare. "I just heard him come in. I didn't listen."

She was inclined to believe him, partly because of that closed door.

"Who was he?" he asked then; and she was sure his innocence was real.

"The man who used to live here. Grandma's roomer."

"Oh," he said. "Well, then, he prob'ly took it."

"Well, I don't know why he should do that. It's no use to him with the chain up," she added incautiously.

He corrected her at once.

"Yes, it is. They know how to reach in and get those things off easy. What you have to have is a police lock, that's like a long stick only it's steel, and they sink one end in the floor with this plate. And then you fasten it up like a brace on the door lock. We could get one."

"No," she said; but shaken. "Good heavens, Jimmy."

"But maybe he just wants to get in while we're gone," he said, comforting her. "Sometimes they do that when they want a hideout— you know, fix up a place like in the attic and stay real quiet when we're here. And then he could come out every day while we're gone. You can tell if the food keeps getting used up, or things like that."

She gave him his breakfast and a helpless look.

"Who tells you these things?"

"I read about it. Aren't you going to eat?"

"I did. I want to call Grandma now and see how Aunt Edna is. Will you finish your breakfast and then do your teeth?"

"Sure," he said, miles away.

She went out and shut the door.

Her call was legitimate, even though her mother would have called her by now if the baby had been born during the night. Still, concern was natural. She listened sympathetically to a full account of Edna's condition: pains had stopped, then begun again, then stopped. Pros and cons of Edna coming home again; they would know today. So hard on Tommy. But the children were angels. And maybe Norma had better not mail that little package till they were sure what was going to happen.

Norma made a mental note to get the bandage and pills as soon as she hung up. Then she said, "By the way, mama—your old roomer came by to see you last night. He said he was just passing through town."

"*Cliff?*"

"Yes. I told him where you are, but I don't think I'd get too much involved with him if he does come out. He's been in some sort of trouble in Chicago and left his job, and he seemed pretty upset. I think you've got enough on your hands without taking him on again, don't you?"

"Well, for pity's sake," said her mother. "Poor Cliff—I'm sorry to hear it."

"Yes, I knew you would be. But don't get involved, mama. Don't even ask him in. He's sort of hard to get rid of, and he might upset the girls."

There was a pause, then Mrs. Moore said, "Did he bother you, Normie? Did you have any trouble?"

"Oh, no. No. But then I wasn't doing anything special, and you are. Just don't ask him in. It's hard to stop him once he gets started."

"Oh, my," said her mother's faraway voice. Then, "I'm so sorry, dearie. If I'd just been there.... But he mustn't come and bother you. I'll tell him so, if he comes out. And if he should come back, you be firm, now. It doesn't help him a bit to feel sorry for himself. And he's a little that way."

Jimmy had come into the hall and stood waiting for her to finish. She said, aside, "Get your things on!"

"Aren't you coming?"

"Yes, go along," said her mother's voice in her ear. "And mind what I say, now, Normie. He's not to bother you. Just be firm."

Norma said she would and hung up. She and her son usually walked part way together in the mornings, as far as Norma's bus stop. But she wasn't going with him today.

He said with interest, "Are you going to get a police lock?"

"No, I'm not."

But she was going to have the present lock changed.

It was a momentous decision—to take out that lock her father's key had turned. She had considered and rejected the idea during the night as being rather hysterical. But now, Jimmy's information quite aside, she realized that she couldn't leave the house unprotected all day long with no one there. Perhaps coming home to find Cliff waiting! Or if he simply kept the key, for some indefinite future use, that would be a prolonged uneasiness. Better to end it. She thought her mother would agree, when it came time to tell her; she had always been extremely careful of keys, herself. There were only four: her own, Tom's, Norma's, and the one under the clock. Cliff's.

Promptly at nine she called the nearest locksmith, asking him how soon he could come over and change the lock on their front door. To her dismay, he eventually gave her, not an hour, but a day when he could get there.

"Oh, it must be done today," she said at once. "It's really an emergency. I'm—I'm alone here, with my little boy."

He said, Well, in that case. He considered, and thought he could get by later in the day. He couldn't give her an exact time, but he would, he said, get there. That day.

So there was nothing for it but to call the office and explain that she would not be in all day. No, she wasn't ill, and she'd be back tomorrow. It was an emergency.

But now that she had yielded to alarm and disarranged everybody, she began to doubt. Was Cliff really an emergency? And what was she going to do with herself while she waited? Wash the windows and polish the floors … but it wasn't funny. There was no Oliver Twist.

But there was always ironing. She put up the board and began to sort.

The telephone rang a little later, and her heart jumped. It was Cliff who came first to mind; Edna far behind. But it was neither. Mr. Hausen next door had noticed she didn't go to work this morning. They hoped she wasn't feeling poorly? She said she wasn't, just had some things to do.

He said, probing further, "Anything I can help you with, Normie?"

"Not unless you're a good ironer, Mr. Hausen," she said cheerfully. But that was a mistake: he was a good ironer, had been doing the ironing for years, on account of Mrs. Hausen's bursitis.

She went back to the kitchen amused and resumed her time killing. It began to feel rather peaceful to be at home in this way in the morning, with mild November sunlight in the windows, a quiet house, and more time than she needed. The night's alarm seemed gone out of her entirely.

Yet it was not. The moment the key turned in the front door lock—the moment she realized what that small clicking sound meant—alarm sprang up inside her undiminished. It was in her throat, filling her throat; she couldn't speak past it.

Nor could she remember if she had put the chain on after Jimmy left.

She managed a sound, then a random movement. That rocked the board, and the iron began to topple. Catching it, she called out clearly, "Who is it? Who's there?"

There was no answer of any kind.

She unplugged the iron, stood holding it without purpose for some time. Then, still holding it, she went to the front of the house.

No one was there. The door was shut, the chain up.

She moved carefully to one side of the door and peered out. No car stood at the curb, Cliff was not in view. Not in her view. She went into the living room presently and looked up and down the street, but no Cliff.

All external evidence said to her, Mistake. Nerves. But it wasn't so. She hadn't a moment's doubt of what she had heard. The sound of the lock was too familiar, too clearly heard, to have been anything else. No; Cliff had come back and used his key, found the chain up, and gone swiftly and quietly away.

She accepted this, and the acceptance sobered her. She thought, as if to someone else: So you see, it's right to change the lock. It's necessary....

The locksmith came soon after midday in what, he explained, would have been his lunchtime. This martyrdom established (he didn't want anything, thanks), he set to work desecrating her mother's door while Norma, wrapped in her coat, sat on the steps to keep him company. He seemed to expect this, in return for his own favor, and furthermore he wanted to know what her trouble was. He made this clear by some bald guesses—about all the trouble there seemed to be nowadays with parents getting divorces, fighting over the kids.... Well, if she was a widow, she was a mighty pretty one, and he just hoped she'd be careful after this who she picked up with.

The truth seemed so harmless by now that Norma simply told it to him. It gave her an odd relief to tell someone.

"It's just that a man who used to room here, a year or so ago, came back last night and—well, stole the spare key while he was here. I can't imagine why he did it, but I didn't like the idea."

He was most cordially in agreement with her. She was, he said, so right; and he only wished other people showed a little more good sense about the locks on their houses. The way they moved in and out, family after family, lordie knew how many keys were lost and scattered around, but the same old locks, why, it was just a wonder there wasn't more trouble than there was. And there was plenty at that. He had a nice series of grisly examples, of careless householders, faulty locks not replaced, forgotten keys larcenously used, and he leisurely entertained her with these as he worked. She watched him take out the lock they had all depended on for so many years and replace it with one so aggressively new, so golden, that her mother would see it the minute she got out of Tom's car. Norma would have to tell her before she came home.

When the locksmith had finished and cleaned up, he said he had better look at the rest of her locks while he was here. She followed him round obediently. The back and side doors both had simple open keyholes that almost any key, he explained, would open; but they also had firm bolts, and he kindly allowed that she was safe enough if she remembered to keep the bolts shot. Then he paused over the small, waist-high milk chute, by the side entrance. This had double doors, about two feet square, with a bolt on the inner one. The outer one was left unlocked so that the milkman might set the milk inside.

To Norma's dismay, there was not only forgotten milk in the chute, but the inner door was unbolted.

"Now there's your real danger," he explained, still kind. "To my mind, they ought to do away with these things. Nobody remembers to keep 'em bolted, you usually got your hands full of bottles anyway, and what's the result? Why, your house is wide open. Wide open." He went out the side entrance and showed her—sticking his hand and arm in, reaching round to work the bolt on the side door as he pleased.

He was perfectly correct. The house had been wide open.

By two o'clock the locksmith was gone, leaving her much poorer and rather depressed. She didn't know why, except that the new lock was so glaring a reminder. It seemed to be visible from almost anywhere and to admonish her (like Cliff) that life within this house and life without were two very different affairs. She hadn't yet found this to be so; but perhaps that had only been her luck. Or maybe there was a peculiar kind of unluckiness, which Cliff had, by which the world really became a constant enemy.

When the time came, she left the lonely house with relief and walked up to meet Jimmy—checking all bolts first and using the new lock for the first time. The air was mild, after a day of sun, and the sky through dry branches a gentle blue. She began to feel less sad, coming past the empty playground, seeing the bicycle racks full, glimpsing through big, bare windows the end-of-day bustle of which Jimmy was somewhere a part. It was like old times, coming to meet him. She stood content and waited for the bell.

He was astounded to see her, almost dismayed.

"Hey! What happened?"

"Nothing. I just never got to work. Besides, you haven't any key."

"I know, I remembered."

"And what were you going to do?"

He hesitated, then grinned at her.

"Come downtown. I know how." He thrust a hand in his pocket, showed her a nickel and a dime. "I saved it from lunch. Pretty neat?"

"Yes," she admitted. "If you're sure you remember where to get off?"

"Of course I do! And it would be after four by the time I got there, and I could do homework, and then we'd come home."

She was impressed by such foresight, and showed it. After this good beginning, she found it easier to tell him about the new lock. He was interested, but mainly, she thought, in seeing the lock itself. She couldn't even tell him what kind it was. Of Cliff she said nothing—only that she thought Grandma would want the lock changed, with a key missing.

Mr. Hausen was much more excited. He came out on the walk, well bundled up, to meet them. Perhaps to have another stare at that golden shine on the old brown door. He just didn't know what Mrs. Moore was going to think about that, and he certainly hoped Jimmy would take a lesson from it and learn how important a lost key could be! She listened patiently, and Jimmy, with a glance at her, did not protest.

Afterward they grinned at each other, on their porch, and she let him be the first to use the new key.

CHAPTER 5

Their golden weather ended in the night. Norma woke next morning to cold rain and the news that Tom's fourth daughter had arrived.

Tom was back home, and took turns with their mother on the telephone. Both of them sounded lightheaded with relief and happiness, everybody was fine, the little girls were squealing in the background or calling into the telephone—it was like a party, and Norma could picture all of it.

She hung up smiling, the rain-darkened morning transformed for her as it was for them. For the moment, anyway. Yet there was nothing she could do—except make up the small package her mother wanted.

She did this, and then woke her son—who received the news politely and reminded her about his extra fifteen cents. He was making his trip downtown that afternoon, to meet her.

Her secondhand glow survived even the damp journey to work. She came into the newspaper advertising office where she worked so cheerful that sly jokes greeted her. About yesterday's emergency.

"Must have gone too far to get back in one day," mused Mr. Hopkins, from the salesmen's Bull Pen. "Just where were you calling from, Mrs. H.?"

"Maybe the car broke down," someone suggested. "That's an emergency."

"I have a new niece, that's all," Norma protested. But Al Hines called out, "A new *what?*"—crossing some other suggestion, which was hushed. It was amiable hazing, but they were reluctant to leave it, perhaps because it was the first time in her months among them that she had given them any opening. She shook her head, smiling, and escaped into her own office next to Mr. Bennig, who was always impersonal.

Even he looked at her, for once. But he said only, "Everything all right now?"

"Yes, thank you. And I have a new niece."

She hoped this would cover it; and with his minimal interest, it seemed to. He said that was fine and stood waiting for her to get her wet things off.

The day went back to normal.

When she came back from lunch, there was a number on her desk for her to call. It wasn't Tom's, or the school's, yet it seemed vaguely familiar. No wonder: Mr. Hausen's cautious voice answered hers. He sounded very doubtful.

"I don't know if I did right about something, Normie," he began. "Just thought I better check with you, in case."

"About what, Mr. Hausen?"

"Well, we always keep pretty much out of our neighbors' affairs, I guess you know that. Ordinarily I would have just shut this fellow off, you know—figured it wasn't his business nor mine where you worked. But this was the fellow used to live with your mother, before you came back—I recognized him right away. Nice-spoken fellow, too. So I didn't like to just shut him off."

"He wanted to know where I work," said Norma. "Yes, Mr. Hausen?"

Something in her voice destroyed his confidence. He became even slower.

"Well, now, I knew for a fact he'd tried to reach you a couple days running—he'd come there, you know, and wasn't anybody there. So I knew that was true, and of course he'd lived there quite a spell, and I know your mother never had any complaints about him—"

"You told him?"

"Well, yes, I did, Normie. And if I did wrong about that, I'm mighty sorry. But it didn't seem to me like—"

"No, it's perfectly all right. Please don't worry about it. When was this?" she asked.

"Well, now, I hope it is all right, Normie. I can't see why it wouldn't be, him living right—"

"Was it very long ago, Mr. Hausen?"

"Well, not so long. Around ten, maybe. I wasn't even going to bother you about it, but Mrs. Hausen, she says I shouldn't have done it, and so I thought I better tell you about it. See if I did so wrong, like Mrs. Hausen says I did."

He was both aggrieved and upset; her repeated assurance that it was perfectly all right didn't comfort him. He began to argue a little: it wasn't like he didn't know the fellow and know for a fact Mrs. Moore'd left him all alone in her house last time Tom's wife had a baby, so it looked like if she trusted him all that much, why, Mr. Hausen could at least....

She forced more strength into her reassurances and got rid of him. And then sat there.

Why?

Why did Cliff want to know where she was during the day?

What could he hope for, by coming here? It happened that she was alone in her office; but doors opened on either side to the sales manager and the assistant sales manager. Outside sat the whole Bull Pen of salesmen, ready to inspect anybody coming from the elevators to her door. (Or from the stairs, for that matter.)

She couldn't believe he would come here. If he did, there would be no reason to fear him.

Later it occurred to her that he might mean to meet her as she came out that evening. At once Jimmy came into her mind—who would be showing up alone downstairs, around four, when the rainy dusk was like evening. She glanced at her watch: quarter past two. If she called school before three and told him to stay there—right there, inside the school—then she could pick him up....

Mr. Bennig, who had been dictating, stopped. "What is it?" he asked.

"I'm sorry, I just remembered something. It's all right."

She didn't know how long the school remained open or if there would be some group staying after hours. Some group that he could join, among whom he could wait. Perhaps if she spoke to the principal....

Mr. Bennig had stopped again; so, she saw, had her pencil. Fortunately, the telephone buzzed.

To her embarrassment, he handed over the receiver. With visions of Mr. Hausen, Norma said repressively, "This is Mrs. Hovic."

Not at once, and speaking slowly, a man's voice remarked, "You shouldn't have done that, Norma."

"What?"

"You must hate me a lot, to do a thing like that."

The slow, dull voice was Cliff. He sounded like a man talking to himself, neither expecting nor desiring an answer. At home alone, Norma might not have found one. But the office, Mr. Bennig's presence, gave her the presence of mind to reply.

"No, of course I don't. But you shouldn't have taken that key."

His voice quickened.

"Then you shouldn't have taken mine!"

Before she could speak, he went on rapidly, "That's really why you changed the lock, isn't it? You wanted to get rid of my key—it wasn't very nice to know you had my key all the time. Was it? You had to make it worthless, didn't you? So you could throw it away ..."

She was too paralyzed by this to make a sound.

"That was always my key, waiting for me. You knew that. You didn't like knowing it, did you? I imagine you feel very glad now it's no good anymore. You're very happy, aren't you?"

He was talking to himself again. More and more slowly.

Norma met Mr. Bennig's sharp gaze.

"What's the matter?" he said, brisk.

She shook her head. Nothing more was coming from the receiver. Mr. Bennig leaned and took it from her wavering hand, listened. Replaced it.

"Nobody there now," he said.

"That wasn't sane," Norma said suddenly. "A sane man wouldn't say those things."

"What things?"

She went on staring at him, earnest and mute.

He got up, leaving her fixed view, and presently reappeared to put a glass in her hand.

"You look like you need blood," he said, "but maybe this will help. Drink it."

It was whiskey and water, not much water. She drank what she could and put the glass down.

"No, all of it. Come on."

"Excuse me," she said. "I have to call my son's school. I'll be right back."

But she didn't move. He pushed his phone toward her.

"Use this one," he said.

She could not manage the dial. Some impediment lay between her fingers and her brain, with its clear and urgent message. Mr. Bennig stood observing this clumsiness.

"Wait a minute," he said finally. "You don't want to call him yet."

But mortification was coming to her rescue. She shook her head and tried again—dialed outside and then the school's number. Got the receiver under control.

"This is Mrs. Hovic, Jimmy's mother," she said steadily. "In 6-A. Can you give him a message for me? It's important."

When she had finished—arranging for Jimmy to stay with the

detention group until quarter past four, when she would pick him up—she was all right again. Mr. Bennig had sat down on his desk top near her, to wait.

"Fine," he said, when she hung up. "Now who is this nut? And why is he pestering you?"

She felt she really owed him some explanation. Besides, the need to talk about Cliff was becoming urgent in her—to the point where she was afraid of breaking down and telling Tom and her mother.

She looked at Mr. Bennig's businesslike face a moment, and then said frankly, "It's a man who used to room with my mother. Over a year ago, before Jimmy and I came home. I'd never even seen him, until he came by the house. Night before last ..."

He listened head down, letting her sort out and relate the story at her own pace. What slowed her was not embarrassment, she was past that, but the need to keep to facts. To define what had happened to herself, as well as to him.

"He wanted to stay there a few days. He'd been in some kind of trouble in Chicago—only he said it was St. Louis, at first.... His face was badly hurt," she said, beginning to lose her way.

"You didn't let him stay?" said Mr. Bennig, bringing her back to the point.

"No. Mother isn't there; she's out at Tom's. Perhaps he might have been different if she'd been home; I don't know. But I didn't like him. He frightened me."

"How? What did he do?"

"Well," she said, "the way he acted. And that funny lie, about St. Louis. And then he wouldn't go—he just kept talking, I couldn't stop him. Finally he began to tell me about what had happened to him in Chicago, an awful story about his boss and some girl who'd played a horrible joke on him. That was how he'd gotten beaten up, I guess. And I couldn't *stop* him. I don't think he could stop himself."

But that wasn't a fact.

"Anyway, I got rid of him, finally. I'm still not sure how. But after he was gone I found out he'd taken the spare key off the mantel."

She looked into Mr. Bennig's thoughtful face and began to speak to him directly, with less care.

"That did scare me. I didn't know what to do, I thought about it all night. Then in the morning I decided to have the lock changed—that was why I stayed home. And I called mother and told her as much as I could without scaring her—just that Cliff was back, and in some kind of trouble, and not to let him in if he came there. Then he came back and tried to use the key."

"When?"

"That morning. While I was waiting for the locksmith. The chain was up, and he went away again—he was very quiet and quick, I didn't even catch sight of him."

"And now what does he say?"

But she needed not to leave anything out. There had been Mr. Hausen's call and the fact that Cliff had come back again today and found the lock changed. And then, hours later, the telephone call crystallizing into certainty all she had sensed about Cliff from the first and had tried not to admit.

"It's very hard to decide that someone isn't normal," she said slowly. "I don't know why it should be, but it is. You excuse all sorts of peculiarities as long as you can. At least, I have."

He smiled down at her—an ordinary, friendly smile that surprised her only because she hadn't known he could do it.

"We all do. We have to. You know the old Quaker saying?"

"About thee and me? Yes."

"Well. All right," he said, and went back to his chair. "And you know what the next step is, don't you? Right now."

She did. But it troubled her.

"I think I'd better call Tom first. So he can go home and be with mother. Only I hate to do this to them, just now!"

"What are you doing?" he asked, reasonable. "It wasn't even your roomer. I'd say your mother's safe enough," he went on. "Sounds like she's Friend, you're Enemy. But that's just my opinion."

Put like this, it seemed to her better to call the police first and Mr. Bennig offered to do it for her. He said he knew a man at Headquarters who could at least connect them up right, and Norma gratefully accepted.

She was taken aback to hear her confusions still further compressed, though. It seemed that Bill Bennig's secretary had a psycho after her— fellow that used to room there, kept trying to get in, and now had started calling her at the office. Who should she talk to?

"Sure, I could bring her over," he said. "Except she wants to get out to school pretty soon and pick up her son, in case this guy has any ideas. Any way you could see her out at her place?"

He said across the desk, "Where do you live?" She told him, and he relayed the information, with her name. Then he hung up and nodded to her.

"That's a better deal," he said. "Go on by and pick up the boy and go home, and somebody will come talk to you there. How old's your son?"

"Eleven."

"Good. He's big enough to know. All right," he said and got up. "Leave this stuff—your mind's not on it anyway. And take a taxi—you got enough money?"

"Yes, thank you," she replied. And then, scarlet, remembered the locksmith.

Between the daylong rain and the time of year, the afternoon she came out into was no lighter than a late evening. The downtown streets were cheerful enough, with multicolored lights doubled in shining reflections. But as the taxi went beyond West Grand Boulevard, up Second Avenue, the darkening damp closed in. Worse, that brief period of having someone to talk to—someone decisive (and normal)—had torn holes in her new self-dependence.

She was now at the point of recovery from her husband's sudden illness and death, where only the unexpected threw her back into the helpless despair of those first weeks without him. Even the throwbacks she could bring under control; it was months since she had fallen back on her mother's standby, the Twenty-third Psalm. At least, in the daytime.

But this wasn't daytime, no matter what the clocks said. And she was in no condition to explain to Jimmy what she could barely understand herself. So very quietly, looking out on drizzle, she began to remind herself: "The Lord is my Shepherd ..."

CHAPTER 6

No matter what it did to Mr. Bennig's ten dollars, she kept the taxi standing outside school while she went in and found Jimmy. Rescued, he couldn't understand about the detention class.

"It doesn't even count ahead," he explained out in the hall. "Why couldn't I have watched orchestra, or something?"

She said of course he could; she was sorry; she just hadn't known. More than apologies, however, the taxi cheered him up. He sat on the jump seat and stared over the driver's shoulder, helping to drive.

This was the time in which she had meant to prepare him for the police interview; but it was too short. She could only hope they got there first.

However, a car was standing before their house when the taxi turned the corner. A plain car, but on the no-parking side.

"This may be the police, Jimmy," she said hastily. "I reported that key.... Will you go on out in the kitchen and get something to eat while I talk to them?"

"Is that why you're home early?"

"Yes, it is."

He said nothing more, nor did she. As their taxi drew up, a door opened in the car ahead and a man in an ordinary raincoat and hat got out and walked back to meet them. He said her name and mentioned his—a blur to Norma. Mr. Hausen was probably taking all this in, suspecting her of a wild social life in her mother's absence. Well, she didn't care anymore.

"Are you headquarters or precinct?" Jimmy inquired politely.

She gave a nervous twitch at his arm, although the man answered good-naturedly and smiled at them both. Inside, she sent Jimmy out to the kitchen at once, rubbers and all.

To her dismay, she found that she was extremely nervous—more so than with Cliff himself. Why? The detective was perfectly pleasant (although he wouldn't take his coat off), but she found it hard to repeat the story she had told Mr. Bennig. For one thing, he kept interrupting. He wanted Cliff's full name and description; he wanted information about him she could not give, such as where he had come from, where he had worked in Chicago or even in Detroit. She didn't know any of this.

"My mother could probably tell you these things," she said at last, reluctantly. "I haven't wanted to upset her about it, but I suppose she'll have to know if you really need all this information."

He said he thought they had better have it, and she parted with Tom's address, her mother's name. He put his notebook away and stood up.

"Let us know at once if he comes round again, Mrs. Hovic," he said. "Don't let him in, of course. We'll have the patrol cars keep an eye on your house, and you call this number if you want any help."

He gave her a card, which she tightly held.

"You'll call me as soon as you catch him, won't you?" she asked.

He looked at her gravely and said they'd be in touch with her. It wasn't the same thing.

As soon as he had gone she went out to the kitchen (totally and ominously quiet all this while) and found her son still fully dressed, peeling an apple with microscopic care. She made him look up; his eyes were shining.

Without a word, she went out again and shut the door. To call Tom, at the office. As soon as he answered, she said rapidly, "Tom, there's been a little trouble here, and the police are coming out to your house to ask mama some questions. About that fellow that used to room with her. Can you go home right now and be with her when they come?"

He said, not at once, "What are you talking about, sis? What trouble?"

He must be exhausted, after last night. And his mind already divided. But she couldn't waste a minute, if he was to get home in time.

"He's been trying to get in here and calling me at the office. I've reported him to the police, but they want to know things about him that I don't know. The main thing is, mama's going to be awfully upset about the police. About my calling them."

He said then, "Normie, you and Jim pack your things. I can call mother, and then I'll—"

"No, wait, Tom—listen. We're all right. I've got a new front-door lock and all the bolts up, and you know the storm windows are on. And the police are watching the house. Just go home and be with mama. Please, Tom."

"Well," he said, giving up, "I'll talk to you from there. You stay there, Normie. Don't go out, and don't let anybody in. You sure it's the same guy?"

He lived about ten minutes from the plant, he ought to be home in time to prepare their mother, besides being with her.

Now there was nothing more to do but wait.

She was getting dinner, in a tattered show of normalcy, when the front doorbell rang. She cried first, "Don't answer, Jimmy!" Then, realizing it must be the police, she ran out and took the chain off.

With shortened breath, a second later, got it back in place. Turned on the porch light and peered out. Mr. Bennig stood there, his black hair brilliant with rain drops.

He gave her his new, friendly smile and came indoors, looking round.

"Just stopped by on my way home to see how you made out," he explained. "Who did they send?"

"A precinct detective," said Jimmy, from the kitchen door. "His name is Joris."

"Well, good enough. This your boy?"

Norma introduced him then, but so repressively that he followed them at a distance and in silence. Unlike the detective, Mr. Bennig took his coat off when asked and came in to sit down.

"I'd keep that porch light on all the time if I were you," he remarked. "Makes you easier to find, for one thing. Well, how'd you make out?"

"All right, I guess. He wanted to know a lot of things about Cliff I didn't know, so I had to send him out to mother's. He must be there by now."

"Are they going to put out a prior, Mr. Bennig?" said her son's small voice.

"Jimmy, will you please—"

"No, it's all right," said Mr. Bennig. He looked at Jimmy a moment and then answered, "Probably. It helps if they can get something to hold him on," he added to Norma.

"Something to hold him on! But what more do they need? Surely he isn't *allowed* to do these things?"

"Well," he said, mild, "what things? You say he's stolen a key, but you can't prove it. And in any case that doesn't exactly count as larceny. You say he's tried to enter your house with that key, but you can't prove that either. Your neighbor thinks he just tried to call on you, which is no doubt what he'd say himself. He didn't behave very well while he was here, but you did ask him in, and he didn't commit any offense while he was here. Not legally. And that telephone call isn't any kind of evidence. Even if he'd actually threatened you—which he didn't—it still would be your word against his."

Her first indignation had died down as she listened. But she didn't understand what point he wanted to make.

"Then why call the police at all?" she asked.

"Because you'll get all the protection you're entitled to, on a complaint. And meanwhile they'll be checking to try and find out if the man has any prior arrests or detentions. Or maybe he's been a mental patient. And he can certainly be picked up if he comes here and bothers you again."

She remembered the evasive answer the precinct detective had given her, "Let me know when you catch him"; and colored faintly.

"I see. But 'picking up' isn't arresting, then."

"No, it certainly is not. You wouldn't want it to be. Suppose somebody had complained about you—said you were calling them up and threatening them, coming to their house, so on. Would you want to be arrested on that kind of evidence? The law works for everybody, Norma. It has to."

"Are you a lawyer, Mr. Bennig?" said Jimmy shyly.

"No."

Just no.

Norma said once more, "Jimmy, please ..." and he backed reluctantly round the corner.

"Why don't you let him in on this, Norma?" Mr. Bennig asked quietly. "He's old enough. And it's better for both of you."

"Well, maybe. But I just—I don't want it to come near him. Any part of it."

"Well," he said. And left it. "Oh, there's another thing. I know of a rather unusual sitter, used to be a policewoman. She's also a grandma and a darned good cook—My sister-in-law uses her when she has to be away overnight. Why don't you have her come over here for a few days? My treat," he added. "I need you downtown, in good shape."

She was impressed by this offer, and touched by it, but it implied a beleaguered state she didn't feel they had reached.

"Oh, I think we're all right—if I can leave a little early and pick Jimmy up at school. He can stay a little late, for a few days. I can't believe this will go on very long," she said suddenly.

He didn't reply. In the silence Jimmy's low voice said from the hall, "Can we eat?"

To her surprise, Mr. Bennig accepted her invitation to stay. "If you're sure you've got enough."

"Yes, plenty. It's very nice of you to stay with us, it does help. But I don't want to upset your arrangements."

"I'm not arranged. I'm a bachelor," he said, grinning. "You didn't know?"

Since he was flagrantly eligible, and famous for it throughout the entire building, this was teasing.

She said with dignity. "Even unmarried people have their arrangements, Mr. Bennig," which seemed to amuse him even more.

But he did have to call someone named Ginny and tell her not to expect him.

"My sister-in-law," he explained, coming to the kitchen door. "I eat over there quite a lot—my brother's in Milan Correctional. Five years served, two more to go, we hope."

He handed her this, like a kind of test.

"Oh," she said. And then, "Are there children?"

He gave her a look, friendly enough.

"Three. The eldest's just started junior high school. That's Sheila, then Rob's about your boy's age, and there's a nine year-old fiend name of Bill. After me."

They were alone; she had sent Jimmy in, hastily, to lay the dining-room table. And she wanted to go on talking about his brother, easily, as he seemed to be able to do. But her wonder wouldn't take acceptable forms. What on earth had he done? And did Mr. Bennig have to support his family all this time?

"That's a Federal jail, isn't it, Mr. Bennig?" her son's voice inquired, round the corner.

"*Jimmy!*"

"Penitentiary, yes," Mr. Bennig replied, as if she hadn't spoken. "Why?"

"Well, I just meant, the Federal ones are more big-time, aren't they?"

There was an awful silence, in which Norma's heart sank.

Mr. Bennig said to her, "Who does that boy play with?"

"Sometimes I wonder," she said, attempting lightness.

"Sometime maybe you better find out. Like soon." He said to the dining-room door, "Who told you a stupid thing like that, Jimmy?"

Too late, her son was silent. She said suddenly, "*Men With Guns.*"

"What? Oh, that. That's not much of a program for kids to watch, is it?"

Norma was stung to reply, "Do you ride herd on your brother's children too, Mr. Bennig?"

"Darn right I do," he said, but absently. His attention was still on the dining-room door, and to it, he said presently, "I'll tell you one thing that *is* true, Jimmy. Nothing's big-time when you live in a cell. Nothing and nobody."

How they were to get through dinner after this, Norma didn't know. She was more than slightly on her son's side—after all, he hadn't brought the subject up. And he'd only been trying to be tactful. Which was hard enough for grownups, in the circumstances. But Mr. Bennig was the guest.

She made him say Grace, however. He got through it. Then, to show Jimmy he wasn't an outcast, she said, "Jimmy's going to be one of our paperboys next year, when he's twelve. You have to be twelve to qualify."

"Is that right?" Mr. Bennig was trying too. "Well, I was about nine, I guess, but that was up in Hamtramck—I guess we didn't go much by the rules up there."

Shut up, thought Norma, smiling kindly at her son. He didn't make a sound.

"Were you a paperboy long?" she asked.

"Oh, sure. Years. Then I graduated—my brother had an old jalopy—"

"A what?" said Jimmy.

"A junk heap. An old car. He let me take it, and I got to be the guy that delivered the kids and papers to each other. A very big deal. Then somebody noticed I wasn't old enough to have a driver's license, so they put me on downtown, helping to load the trucks."

"Didn't you go to school?" said Jimmy.

"Sure I did. This was a morning paper, we had the trucks rolling long before breakfast. I didn't go back to the afternoons till I got my license, and by then I'd found out about the guys who just went around selling ads. I did that all through college. Sort of edging my way into the Bull Pen."

They were both almost free of constraint as Mr. Bennig went on to explain to Jimmy about the Bull Pen. Norma, excusing herself to answer the telephone, felt it was safe to leave them. She thought it would be her mother, or Tom, calling about the police visit. Cliff had fallen so far to the back of her mind that the strange male voice saying "Mrs. Hovic?" gave her an ugly shock.

But it was a Lieutenant Radick, wanting to come out and talk to her. She said, Yes, she would be there. He didn't say why he was coming, and she didn't ask, but she went directly back and told Mr. Bennig.

"Do you want me to go or stay?" he asked, dropping his social efforts. It was as if he had been wanting to ask this for some time.

She said, "Stay," without thinking, then added, "If you can. I'd be very glad. Is this your friend?"

"Yes. He's a very nice guy. You don't need me, you know."

"I'd be very glad if you could stay," she repeated firmly. To Jimmy she added, "Finish up, now, and go upstairs and do your homework."

"I already did it, in the deten—"

"Then do tomorrow's," she said, so outrageously that he gave up and obeyed.

CHAPTER 7

"Try the one with the porch light," said Radick, hunched down beside his driver.

It was the only lighted porch on the block; a quiet, rather shabby block just off Woodward Avenue, whose other citizens were apparently in for the night or economical. The lighted-up place was a dark brick bungalow, early-twenties style, with the porch almost obscured by tall rhododendrons.

Radick, coming up the walk, noted the lush planting with a professional eye: an army could hide in that. A new lock gleamed on the elderly front door. He shook his head and rang.

She looked out at him through the chain, but took this off to see the credentials he held out to her. He shook his head again.

"Look first, unchain after," he said gravely. "That's an old trick, honey. You Mrs. Hovic?"

She was a pretty little brunette, big eyes, young enough to be wearing one of those bridey aprons. Inside he saw why: Billy Bennig standing there in the living room. He looked a bit chip-on-the-shoulder, Radick was interested to note.

"Well, Bill," he said. "You still in on this?"

Bennig said, Just passing through. There was a coffee service on the table, three clean cups. The little brunette was about ready to fly. His movements became slower, as he removed and hung up his coat.

"Ginny and the kids all right?" he inquired, coming back. He glanced to see if he were giving anything away, but the girl knew. From that moment his interest in her doubled.

He was a man who liked to know things. Almost anything. He had been known to leave home on a fast call, passing the janitor in violent altercation with the trash-man, and come home twelve hours later, sunken-eyed, to stop in and find out why. The once that this kind of nosiness paid off, he argued, balanced out the hundred times it didn't. But he did it for love and knew it: no principle could have sunk so deep.

Tonight, once more, his curiosity had paid off. That relayed complaint to precinct needed no follow-up; in fact, a follow-up at that point was sheer nosiness. But he had established his brash need years ago, it was more or less accepted, and precinct passed on what it had without comment.

"Chicago, huh?"

"Or St. Louis. The girl says—"

"No, Chicago. Now hang on, hang on."

He was back on the line, complacent, in two minutes.

"Clifford Wilson, right? Thirty-eight, five-ten, one-eighty. Blond, blue eyes, no dis—*may* be marked or bruised ..." He read on, skipping, to precinct's patient ear. "Well. No problem here. We just wrap him up and hand him over."

"What's it for?"

Radick told him. Then, scorning the brief information on his desk, he got onto Chicago for the rest of the story.

It was a queer one. Drinking his coffee, sizing up the comfortable brown room in which he sat, Radick wondered if the girl was good for once more around, about her visitor. He could have done without Bennig sitting there, well aware that the lieutenant's visit was not routine.

He attacked these problems obliquely.

"Well, now, I thought you'd like to know this is going to be simpler than an ordinary complaint," he said kindly. "I expect what you want is to get rid of this fellow—right? And it just happens we can do that. There's a prior complaint in Chicago. So it's just a matter of picking him up and shipping him out."

"What's it for?" asked Bill, in the words of precinct.

"Questioning," Radick replied, bland. "Now I think he told you about some kind of fracas he'd been in up there, Mrs. Hovic. Just what did he say?"

It wasn't going to be that easy. Her regard was intelligent and searching.

"You can send him back to Chicago, just on a complaint? Isn't that like an arrest?"

Bennig was poker-faced. Radick, after a glance, replied cordially, "Yes, that's right. They've got a right to question him, you know, and they can't very well do that if he's someplace else. Now, about this visit—"

Really big eyes. She looked from one to the other of them and then gave it up, poor girl.

He got his story. And in a detail that clearly took Bennig by surprise: the night-owl boss and Cliff's long hold-off; the doll with shoes and no clothes and Cliff on the floor, staked down for her attentions. The girl got it all out, under Radick's expert guidance, and didn't falter. She seemed too fatigued for any more emotion, even embarrassment. Maybe even fear.

When Radick had, finally, to bring up the matter of the policewoman he meant to install on them, she only looked at Bennig.

"Is that the one you told me about?"

"No, this one's free," said Bennig, playing up nicely. He explained to Radick, "I was trying to sell her Ma Owens."

"Couldn't do better. Except, like Bill says, this one's free."

She was also, he then revealed, sitting out in the car—waiting the way no wife would, he said, humorous. He went to the door and signaled her in: a slender, youngish woman in a suit and topcoat and carrying an overnight case. Norma, with a glance at the dark house next door, received her calmly and got another cup.

Not even the news that the police would prefer her and her son to stay home for a couple of days shook her into protest.

Radick explained, "That should give us time to check out the hotels, and find him—it doesn't sound like he knows anyplace else to go in town, except here. Couple days ought to do it, Mrs. Hovic. Either he's moved on, or we'll pick him up."

"All right," she agreed, listless. And then looked up at him. "He's done something ... awful. Hasn't he?"

"Well. Let's say he may have taken more part in that fracas than he told you. But that's for Chicago to decide, we just deliver him," he reminded her.

She made a helpless gesture and asked nothing more.

Bennig left the house with the lieutenant, not unexpectedly. On the walk, he asked, "Which is it, the man or the woman? Or both?"

"Oh, the lady. Little Miss Shoes."

"How?"

Radick paused at the curb, glum under the cold seep of rain which still came down. He opened the door of his car.

"Get in—your head's getting wet. Why don't you wear a hat?"

"I haven't got one."

He waited until the lieutenant had groaned his way under the steering wheel, then followed him into the car. Radick handed him a handkerchief.

"Wipe your hair. You're not all that young anymore." He said, watching, "That your girl?"

"I don't know. Probably not."

"Why? She's a nice girl. Nice looker, too. Widow or divorced?"

"Widow." He balled the wet handkerchief and threw it back. "Come on, Uncle Dorothy. What about it? What happened to this girl in Chicago?"

"Oh, she's dead," said Radick. "It's a funny situation. They had the boy friend in for it—man called Max Gordon, runs a chain of specialty shops in Chicago. Calls 'em Jolly Dame; that's French. So he told them the tale about this fellow that works for him—how Gordon and his girl friend played a little joke on the guy, and he turned very sour. Kept calling the girl up at home the next day and saying funny things. Gordon tried to get hold of him, but couldn't—fellow never showed up, didn't answer at home. Gordon says he wasn't really worried, mostly exasperated at the girl for getting hysterical about it. He said the guy was a milksop, forget it, so on. Then the next day they pulled him in—Gordon, that is. The girl was dead."

"How?"

"A knife. All over. Twenty-three wounds," he said, precise.

"My God."

"Well, they weren't too sold on this joke idea at first, naturally. But then it turned out Gordon had been in a Turkish bath when his girl friend got it—between midnight and two A.M., that was. About twenty-four hours after this alleged joke took place. So they checked the other fellow out, and sure enough he was gone. Packed up and gone."

"And it's this roomer?"

"Same name, same description. And you heard your girl friend's story. A real brooder," said Radick, with satisfaction. "'Course, that may be all he is, that's up to Chicago. But they want him, and they'll get him. If he's still around."

"You're all-out looking, are you?"

"All-out."

His hand on the door handle, Bennig turned back.

"Your policewoman knows what she's up against?"

"Oh, she knows. Don't worry, your girl's all right."

Bennig got out, shut the door, watched the car drive away. He crossed the street and walked to his own car, legally parked. From this distance Norma's porch light seemed negligible—a candle in a forest of shadows. He started the windshield wipers, lit a cigarette, and watched a while. But the quiet street had nothing to show, and presently he drove away too.

CHAPTER 8

A very nice policeman came out to see Mrs. Moore that evening, at her son's house. The girls were in bed, and she and Tom were having a serious talk in the kitchen over some Ovaltine, when the door chimes made them both jump. They were aware that Tom's house was under surveillance—that was part of what they were discussing—and the man out on the step clearly wasn't Cliff, so Tom let him in.

This was an older policeman (although a lieutenant, which seemed a young man's title) and much more leisurely than the first one, who had given Mrs. Moore an edge-of-the-chair feeling. The first thing he told her was that he had just come from seeing her daughter, and everything was all right there; he'd left a woman to stay with her, from the Department, so they needn't worry about her being alone.

"A policewoman?"

He said, Yes, and a fine girl too. Mrs. Moore looked at Tom, who said he was relieved to hear it.

He added, "I don't suppose you have any news of this fellow yet?"

"Well, it takes a little time to check out the hotels and motels," the lieutenant replied. "I imagine that's where he'd go, don't you? I don't suppose you've thought of anybody he might go see."

"There isn't anybody to think of," Mrs. Moore said sadly. "Cliff was a stranger here, you know. He just worked very hard and then came home. And I know he made a point of keeping his working relations very impersonal—he said he always did, because it avoided quarrels."

"Did he have any quarrels? Or would you have known?"

"Oh, yes, I think so. I could always tell when he was upset—he'd just go right up to his room. But it was never anything much. Somebody'd hurt his feelings, or a display hadn't worked out right. I'm sure if he'd had any real trouble he'd have told me. To tell the truth," she confessed, "I got so I had to stop him telling me things. I'd just say, Now, I don't want to hear about it, Cliff, and you don't want to think about it, do you? I'd make him get out the cribbage board, and we'd play a while. To break his train of thought. It always worked."

Tom said, "Lord, mother—if I'd had any idea ..."

"Of what, Tommy? I didn't mind. I like cribbage. And it was time somebody had a little patience with him," she added. "I didn't encourage Cliff to talk about his troubles, but he'd certainly had them. Why, he told me once his father was eighty-five years old!"

"When he was born?" said the lieutenant.

"Well, at some point—when he was a boy, or something like that. And his mother was afflicted, I don't quite recall how ... "

"Where was all this, Mrs. Moore?"

She thought it was somewhere in the East. Cliff hadn't said just exactly where he came from, and of course she had never asked him questions, but he usually talked about himself as an Easterner. She thought that was part of his trouble—being in a strange part of the country.

"Well, he sounds like a handful to me," said Tom. "I don't know why you put up with it so long."

"I didn't put up with anything, Tommy. Cliff behaved himself perfectly while he lived in my house. I guess I was a little bit proud that he did," she admitted to the lieutenant. "He was a difficult boy, anybody could see that. A bit too touchy and inclined to feel sorry for himself—and he didn't forget about things the way most of us do. Unpleasant things, I mean. For instance, when he first lived with me, he used his coffee spoon for his egg one morning and it turned black. I always put out a stainless steel spoon with eggs, and I showed him about that. Well, he was terribly upset. He wanted to clean the spoon himself, he couldn't get over it—and as long as he lived there, that man claimed he could tell the spoon he spoiled! Every once in a while he'd come up with it again. Now somebody made that boy feel terrible about *something* for him to grow up like that! You understand I'm not excusing him for one minute," she added firmly, "for the way he's acted to Normie. I must say that does surprise me."

"Mother's still convinced he wouldn't hurt anybody," said Tom. "She wants to go back home and wait for him so she can talk to him herself."

"Oh, I wouldn't advise that, Mrs. Moore. I think you'd be very foolish to try and deal with this man yourself, the way he is now. He hasn't called you yet, has he?"

"No," she admitted. "But he wouldn't, out here. He knows I have my hands full, and Cliff never liked to intrude. I just have this feeling that he's waiting for me to come home."

Both men looked at her. She added, "I may be entirely mistaken, of course."

"You might be right, too," said the lieutenant. He looked at her a moment longer. "You would report to us, if you heard from him, wouldn't you?"

"Oh, yes," she said at once. "Don't you have any doubts about that, Mr.—Lieutenant. My first concern's for my daughter, and I think Cliff's behaved very, very badly to her. Besides, I never coddled him. And I certainly wouldn't start now."

Tom said, "I don't give a damn what this guy wants, but I would like to know where you think mother ought to be. For my sister's sake and her own. There's no problem about us, I can get someone in—"

"Oh, I think I'd let things ride the way they are, Mr. Moore," the lieutenant said. "For a day or so, anyway. If we don't pick him up by then, we can always try your mother's idea."

"You mean, use her for a decoy?" Tom said bluntly.

"If she wants to try being one," the lieutenant agreed. "It would probably just be a matter of her answering the telephone herself, or something like that. Naturally they'd have plenty of protection. But there's no use crossing that bridge yet," he said, heaving himself up. "He may not even be in town by now. Your daughter hasn't heard a peep out of him tonight."

"No, we just talked to her," Mrs. Moore agreed. "Poor Normie—what a thing to happen! She must think I'm out of my mind, telling her about my nice roomer!"

"Well, you saw one side of him," said the lieutenant. "She saw another."

Mrs. Moore then said, formally, that they were very grateful for all the help and attention their police department was giving them, and she thought it was very nice of them indeed. Tom said nothing. But he followed the lieutenant out on the front step and pulled the door to behind him.

"What is it, Lieutenant?" he asked then. "Has he got some kind of record?"

"Well, if he has, we haven't turned it up yet, Mr. Moore. He may have been in some trouble in Chicago, though. Between us, that's what we want him for—to send him back there."

"Oh, God. I knew it. What kind of trouble?"

"Something like this. It got a bit rougher. But your family's all right now, don't worry about it. Just make sure your mother understands that this isn't anything to fool around with privately. Will you do that?"

"She won't. I guarantee it."

Tom went in, thoughtful, to find the living room empty. The kitchen was empty as well. He stood there, saying "Mother!" more loudly than he would ordinarily have done. There was an answering "Hush!" from the hall, and she came out of the bedroom she shared with Cassie. Her eyes were reddened, still damp.

"Hey," he said. "Hey!" And put his arm around her. "What's that for?"

"Oh, I don't know, Tommy. It's just so sad, and awful."

He couldn't deny that, but he could remind her that, after all, it might have been much worse.

"What scares me is all the time he lived there alone with you. He could have gone over the edge then, just as well."

"No, I don't think so."

He moved back to see her face.

"Mother. Now, listen."

"Oh, you don't have to say it. I know Cliff's way past any little help I could give him, Tommy. There's something else wrong, I know that. They wouldn't be making all this fuss just because he bothered Normie."

"Well," he said; and then, "Yes, there is something else. I don't know what, myself. But I do know you mustn't have anything to do with him, Mother, no matter what. Can I trust you about that?"

"Tommy, I'm pretty foolish sometimes, but I'm not an idiot," she replied soberly. "I'm really not."

He knew she wasn't, and looking at her expression, he was satisfied.

CHAPTER 9

Central Display, the firm for which Cliff had worked in Detroit, was large enough to have three addresses. One was suburban, a branch; one a warehouse, from the address; and the main office, a good-sized suite, was in a downtown building.

This was where Radick turned up next morning. He was alone. The Chicago detectives, two of them, had arrived with their warrant. Cliff had now been placed in the vestibule of the girl's apartment around midnight, and fingerprints in his abandoned apartment had been matched with those in the girl's. A little blood and skin from this boy, Chicago said, and it looked like they had a good, tight case. Radick left them to their happy thoughts and went his own way.

The check of hotels and motels he also left to itself. So far no Clifford Wilson, nor anyone of his fairly blatant description, had turned up. Radick hadn't expected it. He had by now an instinct for when to start digging, and his excavations, calm and separate, were already running parallel to the city-wide search.

What Radick hoped for here, at Central Display, was some background: the names and dates that employment files ought to give. But he was, as usual, open to any other impressions. For instance, when he got in past the girls and men, Central Display turned out to be a Miss Lally, and Radick was interested in her reaction.

"Our Cliffy, is it?" she said, sizing him up. "What's he done, stuck a knife in somebody?"

He regarded her gravely. She was a skinny, lively, attractive woman with jangly bracelets and a nice grin. Not much of a mother image. Her tone, however, was indulgent.

"You'd expect that?"

"Oh, Lord—don't quote me! What do you want, his file? I've got it." She told a box on her desk to bring Cliffy's file, dear, and then sat back. "Last I knew he was in Chicago. But I didn't think he'd stick Max Gordon very long. *Sheer* madness. Is he back?"

"We think he might be, ma'am."

"Oh-oh. Doesn't sound so good. Just tell me one thing—is it something about Max?"

"Is what about Max, ma'am?"

"You. Or let me put it this way: how is Max Gordon, Lieutenant?"

Radick said he didn't have any information about that. She ignored his tone.

"Well, you would, if he was lying in the lily pond, wouldn't you?" She took the proffered file and held it, scratching her chin with its edge. "Now what on earth would it be? Don't even consider embezzlement. I don't care what Max says. Our Cliffy is terribly upright, and I'm sure it's real. The knife—I'm kidding. Blood would make him faint. So what could it be?"

She was honestly puzzled. And as curious as a monkey. (Or as Radick himself.)

He said, with some sympathy, "We're just answering a request from Chicago, ma'am. If he's not here, they'd like to know where else he might be."

"Yes, but *why?* Oh, all right—here." She spun the file over the desk to him, and he caught it. There was a short silence, jangly on her part, while he looked at it.

"Previously employed in Buffalo, New York?" he murmured, still reading.

She burst into instant response.

"Oh, Buffalo—that's nothing. He was just pouting around up there. Manhattan's what counts—didn't he put that? That's where I saw his stuff, several years ago, and I liked it very much. But he didn't want to come out here then. So later, when I heard he'd left town, I hunted him down and asked him again. That's the Buffalo part. It was brief, love, brief."

"Then New York City would have been his real home?"

"Never," she said quickly. "What are you thinking of—Sodom and Gomorrah! Anyway I don't think he'd go back there," she added, thoughtful. "I don't think he *could*. He'd pretty well worked his way through that lot."

"How do you mean?" asked Radick.

"Well, our Cliffy was quite a sorehead. A walker-outer. You know? I knew it. But I thought, what the hell—I'm pretty good with the oddballs, and he does work like fury while he's around. Calculated risk," she said and grinned. "And he did do some lovely things for me. I've got pictures—but you don't care about that, do you? Well, I'll just say this," she said, and her grin widened, "you send him back here, when he gets out of jail, and I'll take him. I never had any real trouble with Cliffy. Max just gave him the old razzle-dazzle and he couldn't resist. Actually, I expected him back before now."

Their equally curious glances met and held. Radick disengaged himself.

He asked, "Would he consider you a friend?"

"Why?"

"What I mean is, would he be likely to look on you as a person to come to, if he wanted help?"

"Oh, I'm going to die of this," she exclaimed. "What help?"

"Personal help, of any kind. Perhaps a place to stay."

"Well, he could hardly stay with *me*. After all, he looks male. And I *think* I look fairly—"

She was abruptly silent. He glanced up and caught her swallowing delight. His heart sank.

"What is it, Miss Lally?"

"What is what, Lieutenant?" she replied sweetly.

"Something occurred to you?"

"But you're forcing me to think like mad," she complained. "And it's so *early*. How can I imagine poor Cliffy doing anything serious enough to have policemen out looking for him? It just clogs my mind, and I'm no help to you at all. Am I?"

Amused, he asked, "If your mind got unclogged, what might you think about?"

"A place he might go," she said softly. "Oh, let's have some coffee—wouldn't that be nice? How do you like yours?"

He told her, and she told the box on her desk.

"And it won't be drugstore coffee, either," she assured him. "We make our own, we're very fussy. Just like Cliffy."

With this slight push, she settled back, expectant.

He said, "Would you like to know why Wilson left you, Miss Lally?"

Her eyebrows went up.

"Not Max?"

"No. He lost his room. Where he was living."

She examined the idea.

"Do you mean they put him out? What for?"

He told her about it.

She had never heard of Mrs. Moore or the little bungalow and was deeply interested to hear of Cliff's private life. Over their coffee, to this kindred soul, Radick told of the cribbage games, and the egg spoon, and threw in the eighty-five-year-old father. She listened absorbed and not—he thought—entirely pleased.

"But that's fantastic! And not a word about it to me. What a queer child," she said, cross. "And here I was flattering myself I'd made him such a happy little nest, with his dear old Lally-pally, and his ..." She checked herself, but absently.

Radick went on.

"Well, I think they were surprised, too. That's how we knew he was back in town—he went out there. And turned pretty nasty about it, when they wouldn't take him in. Tried to use a key he'd stolen, and so on. I've had to put a policewoman in the house," he added. "Just till we pick him up."

She made a small face.

"Well, that's not very pleasant, is it?"

There was a small pause, then she said abruptly, "He has one of my keys, too. Oh, I knew it. I wasn't worried. That's one reason I thought he'd be back. Not to my apartment, of course." She was looking at him directly now, across the desk, her face older in thought, undisguisedly intelligent. A little fearful. "We keep a glorified storeroom over on Sandusky Street. A big place, everything you can imagine. Cliff adored it, I let him practically take it over. He used to spend whole days there when something went wrong, and I let him. He's terribly careful, I never had any fear he'd set the place on fire, or damage anything. *Au contraire.* I even put in a phone for him." She rummaged in a desk drawer and brought out two keys on a labeled ring. "Here. It's two keys, actually, and he has both. I think what I most want to know at the moment," she added, with her grin diminished, "is that he *isn't* there."

"Thank you," he said. "But wish that he is. That would settle it."

She gave a little shiver.

"No, settle it somewhere else, please. And don't tell me any more—I've changed my mind."

He got out, before she changed it again.

The storeroom was in a loft building, occupying the entire second floor. Even in midmorning of a working day the narrow street was quiet. One truck, loading enormous paper rolls; a two-by-four luncheonette; an occasional passer-by comprised its visible life. Behind dirty windows light burned here and there, but many of the windows seemed closed on vacancy or some habitual disuse.

Radick left the police car at the end of the street and with its driver walked to the loft. The building door was unlocked, giving access to the ground floor premises of a bottle-cap company. No sign directed them, but at the head of narrow stairs one opaque-glass door had a lettered cardboard notice: "CENTRAL DISPLAY. NO ADMITTANCE."

Three other doors were blank, with painted-over glass.

Radick used his key and pushed the door back on what seemed only a wide path in cluttered gloom. A switch on the wall just inside produced, strangely, two pools of shaded light: one from a kind of spotlight arrangement, pointing down; the other, farther in, a muted glow from Tiffany glass on a heavy standard lamp.

Radick said, "Police officers. Anybody here?" But the enclosed silence awaited them listlessly, with no echo or fall of recent sound.

They came in, careful but curious. The fragments of a whole world of clever contriving lay about them, its meanings jumbled and lost, contexts forgotten. Strange structures of wire, of heavy cardboard, or papier-mâché; of tile, marble board, pasted cloth, shaped thin metal. Odd chairs and benches, stands; recherché tables, wickerwork; screens, vases, bowls. Boxes.

By the Tiffany glass lamp, a long and sturdy worktable offered a surface entirely bare. Nor was it dusty. Radick peered beneath the table and drew forward a good-sized box. Within, neatly folded, lay an assortment of heavy draperies and hangings.

He decided this could make up into a bed. Closed the box again, pushed it back.

The other man had gone ahead, checking two smaller adjoining rooms with closed doors which formed a sort of corridor to another large room at the front of the building. These smaller rooms were little morgues of women's figures. Half figures, portions of figures. Arms, heads, hands.

"Jeez," said Radick's companion. "What a racket."

There were ceiling lights in each of these rooms. No one had gone to the trouble of wiring up shaded lamps. Fluorescence, unexpected and unkind, lit up the large front room.

This seemed to be a kind of workroom, with cluttered shelves and unpainted plywood cabinets whose drawers and cupboards were jammed with odd utensils: scissors, knives, brushes, pots of paint and glue, trimmings, sequins, glitter. There was a long sink on one side, dry except for a thin ring of water caught round the drain. An enclosed toilet completed the corner.

Radick was interested by a stretch of bareness along the window wall. He examined the floor, scuffed and darkened by years of careless use:

a doubtful record of anything. Nevertheless, he thought the worktable in the other room had stood here.

"He must have moved it in there for sleeping. He didn't drag it, either. How in hell did he get it through those doors?"

He went back to find out and discovered it was dismountable. The long top, which looked like a flush door, merely lay across three trestlelike supports. A hell of a job, just the same. He shook his head, looking round the triumphant disorder.

"Not just a one-night stand, then. But where's his stuff?"

"In his car," the other man suggested. "He probably wants to keep portable. Besides, don't they use this place, daytimes?"

Radick wasn't satisfied. He said, "By the way, I want every garage around here checked for that car. Private or public. Anyplace he could make a deal to stash it. And we'd better keep somebody here for a while. Twenty-four hours."

He was moving round the room as he spoke—as much as it was possible to move through that exasperation of obstacles. And in an overcoat. The room was chilly despite an old radiator whose occasional sad clank alone broke the dusty silence.

"You go on back," Radick said presently. "Take the car. Get onto those garages right away, will you?"

He had made his way into a thicket of clutter. From the outside it looked as if he might never get out again.

But there was, if you used care, a kind of path. Alone and curious, Radick followed it. His gloved hand went into tall vases, back into drawers, into every interstice. He examined what he found with impartial wonder. A white-painted hall rack and seat, wildly ornate, proved to be his destination. The seat lid came up, disclosing tissue-enfolded packages.

Five shirts. Underpants and vests. Socks. A plastic case containing shaving things, toothbrush, and paste. Brushes for hair, clothing. To one side, in more tissue, a dry folded towel. And pajamas!

Unpacked, yet.

Radick went back to the workroom and the telephone. He wanted that stake-out man right away, didn't intend to leave until he came. In case Cliffy came home. Because that's what it was, he thought, returning to the glow of the Tiffany lampshade: home sweet home. Lord, how complicated could a man get?

He went on exploring in his solitude and came up with the dirty laundry—logically in a basket. A gilded basket. But only two days' discarded clothing—why? There should be three, unless Cliffy was getting careless. Or had found someplace else to stay. But in that case, why hadn't he taken his wardrobe with him?

Radick went back and called Miss Lally. He wanted to ask her not to put the storeroom to use, even for casual visits, until she heard from him again. She said, "Oh, Lord!" and then, "You mean he's using it, don't you?"

Radick said it looked that way.

"All right. Don't tell me. We won't come near it. Oh, dear—you don't think he'll come out to my place, do you?"

"He looks pretty well settled here," Radick assured her.

But he looked up Miss Lally's apartment later and notified her precinct to keep an eye on it and have a quiet word with the superintendent. He couldn't figure out that missing day's laundry. It must mean something, but he didn't see what.

CHAPTER 10

Norma's day at home was like no other day in her experience, and by evening the idea of repeating it—indefinitely—began to make her feel desperate.

The long sense of strain was in no way due to their policewoman. She was their one bright spot: cheerful, a willing magnet for Jimmy, and a good sharp Monopoly player. Her name was Mrs. Cunningham, but she was firm about being called Ann.

She was also firm about all of them staying indoors.

"You'd better market by telephone today," she said, when Norma proposed walking down to the corner. "I know it comes higher, but it won't be for long. We've been asked to stay indoors, period. Sorry."

"What if it snowed?" said Jimmy. "Couldn't we even go out and shovel?"

She said they would worry about that when it snowed, which didn't seem likely.

The weather, in fact, had cleared again, and they were having one of those mild and light-drenched autumn days which make imprisonment harder to bear. If it had only been like yesterday, rain all day, Norma thought their long enclosure might have seemed more natural.

Or perhaps it wouldn't have made any difference.

For the real sense of strain came from her constant idea of Cliff. To be shut in this way because he was somewhere outside made it seem as if he were everywhere outside. In every car that passed, in every sound of footsteps (the mailman mounting the porch steps, the milkman coming round the house); in any shrubbery that moved, in any loiterer who didn't.

Yet this was only her mother's roomer. The same Cliff with whom she had been alone here, and not really frightened, however strange and repugnant she had found him. Even that telephone call, she argued silently, had not frightened her of Cliff as a person. If he had been with her, if she had had to respond and force him to respond again, his peculiar reasoning would have lost its power to shock.

Driven to this kind of interior argument, Norma went round her mother's house in outward obedience. She ordered the groceries over the telephone. She allowed Ann to take in the mail and the paper. She answered the telephone herself, since she was told to, but it only rang once, and that was her mother.

In spite of this she had an experience which sobered her. The cellar steps paused halfway, to form a side entrance to the house. She went down these to take in the milk, unbolting the small milk door and taking the bottles from the shelf. But the outer door was open too. She was reaching out to draw this shut when—real as flesh upon her flesh—she felt the seizing hand that might catch and imprison hers and hold her there.

The next thing she knew, the inner door was shut and she was feverishly bolting it again. What she had done about the outer door she had no idea, probably nothing. It was a moment before she could even pick up the milk bottles and return to the kitchen.

Ann chose that moment to appear.

"What is it?" she said instantly.

Norma shook her head.

"Nothing."

"Please answer me, Mrs. Hovic!"

This was a new Ann.

"All right," said Norma. "I will. I just went down to take the milk in. You've seen the milk chute, you know it has two doors. Well, the outer door was open for some reason, and I had to put my hand and arm out into the air to pull it shut. And it scared me silly. That's what happened, Mrs. Cunningham. And that's all that happened."

Ann didn't smile.

"Why was the outer door open?" she asked.

"I've no idea. Probably the milkman didn't shut it properly."

"Has he ever done that before?"

"I don't know. You'll have to ask mother, she's the one who takes the milk in."

Without reply, Ann went down the steps, and there was a sound of opening and shutting. When she came back up she said seriously, "Let me take in the milk after this, will you?"

"With pleasure," said Norma.

This ridiculous episode—which Jimmy fortunately did not witness—had one good effect. Norma's internal arguments ended. Reasonably or not, she was now afraid of Cliff. And recognized that she was.

The strain increased with that recognition. Perhaps her silent arguments had been an attempt to keep it down. By afternoon, she was trying other methods. The next time she caught Ann by herself, she said bluntly, "I think if I knew more about Cliff's trouble in Chicago, I'd imagine less. Do you know what he's being arrested for? It is an arrest, isn't it?"

"Oh, it would have to be, for Interstate," said Ann readily. "But it can be 'On Suspicion,' of course."

"Of what?"

Not quite so readily, but still with her frank air, Ann replied, "I don't know too much about it, but I believe it concerns a woman's death. In Chicago."

Norma felt no surprise. Some part of her had known.

"What sort of woman, Ann?" She added, to the other's hesitance, "I mean, was it someone like—my mother?"

"Oh, goodness no! A night-club hostess, or something. I really don't know too much about it, Norma," she repeated firmly.

Clearly, this was all she meant to say. It was enough. Norma's first reaction was of disbelief. A night-club hostess! Then there was surely some mistake. Cliff in a night club—or dating one of the hostesses—was beyond her power to imagine. It must be some sort of mix-up with the man he had worked for: the horrible *bon vivant*.

Except that the girl who had helped to play that joke might have been a night-club hostess. And Cliff hadn't said how he got free.... But the man, the boss, had been there too. From the sound of him, he would have been able to protect the girl.

Or had Cliff somehow fought both of them off and injured the girl fatally in doing so? But this was more impossible than Oliver Twist. A sort of Western-style hero. Not Cliff at all.

By evening a queer mixture of relief and exhaustion claimed her. She had reached some middle ground in which her vague terror of Cliff was replaced by a conviction that he was undoubtedly off balance, at least right now, and that reasonable care was certainly called for in avoiding him. But this business of not being able to walk down to the grocery store, in broad daylight! That was too farfetched. It simply led, she decided, to being afraid of the milk chute.

Bennig came by that evening after dinner. Ann went tactfully upstairs to take one of her naps.

Bennig asked, "Where does she stay at night?"

"Down here on the day bed. With her clothes on. She says she can go on for days like this, catnapping."

"She probably can. But let's hope she won't have to. How are you and Jimmy making out?"

"Jimmy's fine," she said. "I'm not, though. I don't think I could get through another day like this if Cliff were twins. And I know about that woman in Chicago," she added abruptly. "Do you?"

He did, of course. But he was taken aback that she should.

"Who told you?" he asked, frowning.

"I deviled it out of Ann. Please don't tell on her. She didn't say much, just that they thought Cliff might be mixed up in it. A night-club hostess! I couldn't understand that, at first—but it must be the woman who helped play that joke on him, and then he hurt her somehow, trying to get away. He never did tell me how it ended, I didn't let him. But it must have been a fight, don't you think?"

He said, "Probably"—a minimal sound.

"Perhaps he doesn't even know how seriously he hurt her. If it was he."

This time he said nothing.

"Well," she said, a little embarrassed. "What happened in Chicago isn't really my business, I know that. All I meant was that it doesn't seem necessary for us to stay cooped up like this all day, even in—in the circumstances. I don't see why I couldn't take Jimmy to school, and go on to work—Ann could pick him up. We could all use taxis, it wouldn't break us for a few days. Doesn't that seem reasonable to you?"

He got up and put his hands in his pockets.

"Well, I know this is a strain on you," he said. "Waiting and not knowing much about it. It's a bad combination. Maybe you would be better off moving around. Why don't we talk to Radick about it?"

"Would I have to do that? Get permission?"

"I think you should. He's doing his best to protect you, and you asked him to. You ought to check with him before you make any changes. Why don't you give him a ring in the morning? I'll leave you the number."

"I'd like to call him now, if you think that would be all right," she persisted.

He hesitated. He was a poor dissembler, she knew that by now—he hadn't the patience for it. There was something he didn't want to tell her.

She said wearily. "Or is there some other reason for waiting?"

He smiled then and sat down again. Nearer.

"Norma, you know how I feel about cards on the table. It seems to me the average human being is a lot better off knowing what he's up against than sitting around wondering. On the other hand, this isn't my party. I would wait till morning."

He must mean, they expected to have found Cliff by then. She was suddenly convinced of it.

"All right," she said and smiled back at him in the pleasure of her relief. His own smile vanished.

"Now don't go getting your hopes up, Norma. These things are very chancy."

"I understand that. But it will be nice to have a *little* hope to get through the night on. Then if it doesn't happen—well, I can still call."

"Good girl," he said, relieved by her quiet manner. "And you're right, that's the way to wait something out. Make short objectives. Go from one to the next. Plan from day to day, or week to week, if it's a longer wait. Nobody can sit around with his clock stopped. People don't work that way."

Was he talking to her, or to his sister-in-law? She looked at him doubtfully and saw that he was very much with her—watching her as he spoke, half-smiling, attractive and attracted.

Somehow the discovery didn't comfort her. She had spent months beside him, in far deeper, more difficult trouble than this, and been ignored. Why? Was it only disaster he recognized and not ordinary troubles and sorrows?

Her wonder must have showed; his own expression was changing.

"What is it?" he asked.

"Nothing. You're right."

"But what? I'm butting in too much?"

"No, not a bit. I'm really very grateful to you, Mr. Bennig. You must know that."

"Bill," he said, patient. "Out of the office, anyway, for Pete's sake." She smiled, but didn't correct herself; he didn't like it. "Or is this against your policy?"

She saw she would have to make some attempt to explain herself, without hurting his feelings. It wouldn't be easy. But he said he preferred cards on the table, and she believed him.

"I don't have a policy," she said. "But this trouble with Cliff isn't going to last—it might even be over tomorrow. And it isn't really my trouble, no matter how close it comes. Even if he had really hurt one of us, it would have been like an accident that could happen to anybody."

He listened impatiently, not pleased, certainly not enlightened.

"Well, what difference does that make?" he said.

"Just that I don't really belong to the people you're close to, down at the office," she said frankly. "Miss Munn, in Accounting, for instance. And old Mr. Pollack. And Al Hines, in the Bull Pen, that nobody else can stand. I used to wonder about them, but I think I know what it is, now. They're all in some sort of real trouble, aren't they?"

"Good Lord," he said. "What is this? You think I'm running some kind of blues club?"

Well, wasn't he? She didn't reply.

He was beginning to get angry.

"The hard-luck kids—is that it? And you're not that hard up—you don't have to belong. Is that the way it looks to you?"

"I don't think I qualify," she said, her own temper stirring. "Not on your terms."

It was an offer to quarrel; she was immediately ashamed, but did not know how to withdraw.

He had better command of himself.

"Norma, I don't have any terms," he said, quietening. "Or a hard-luck club either. I think you know that. It's true I know a little more about— those three people you mentioned than the rest of you, but there's a reason for that. Once in a while, somebody gets hit by something that's more than he can cope with, and if it's happened to you, you know the signs. You know what it's like, and you know how to help, a little. That's all there is to it."

"Yes, of course," she said at once.

"It's not that people don't exist for me unless they get clobbered," he said doggedly. "I think that's what you meant, isn't it? And I admit maybe it looks that way, a little, around the office. Partly because I'm not much on social life at work, anyway. I wouldn't say you are either, are you?" She shook her head. "No, I know you're not. It's one of the things I like about you."

She could think of no answer to this, and made none.

After a minute, he added, "I can see how it would stick out, though— any kind of other association, I guess you might call it, around there. I hadn't meant for it to, I'm glad you pointed it out."

"It doesn't stick out," she said. "Please."

"Well, you noticed. It's noticeable. I'm sorry about that."

She was by now heartily sorry, herself, for having mentioned it.

"I'm with you more, that's all. Please don't think any more about it, Mr.—Bill."

He acknowledged this effort with his smile. But he was still thoughtful.

"Would you like some coffee?" she asked. To escape.

"Yes, sure. Thanks."

But he followed her out to the kitchen.

"There's something in what you say, though," he said from the door frame, leaning there. "I'm damned if I know what it is, but it's something."

"Maybe so. I don't know either, really."

He was quiet, then. But as she passed him he stopped her, his hand on her shoulder, then on the back of her neck. She stood still to his intention and to the brief, warm shock of his kiss. He let her go immediately.

"Don't be sore. It's just something I had at the back of my mind a long time. You're awfully pretty, Norma."

That was the end of it—a form of communication, or reassurance, she supposed, that canceled out his other dissatisfaction. But he continued thoughtful and went away soon after he had drunk his coffee and made some desultory talk about her morning plans.

He kept a little of her lipstick on his mouth, and she didn't tell him—let him go away with it, for some later discovery, and that was a small private satisfaction to her.

CHAPTER 11

Radick lived in an old, comfortable apartment on Chicago Boulevard, alone with his wife and innumerable framed pictures of their grown children and grandchildren. He claimed this was the ideal family set-up, which he had worked for thirty years to achieve.

"They're all out of town, too. Brazil, Toronto, and Akron, Ohio. Eight grandchildren, and no noise, no baby-sitting. How's that? You have to start young, though, or you're too tired to care."

He offered this tip to Bennig with increasing emphasis as the years went by. He had been, when the Bennig boys were little, the cop on their beat, and it was to him that Roy Bennig had come for advice and eventual submission to arrest. Since then Roy's wife had found him something of a nuisance and said so.

"Damn it, he's got kids of his own! Why does he have to hang around here so much?"

"Because his kids are in Brazil, Toronto, and Akron, Ohio," said her brother-in-law, grinning.

"I wish he was too," said Ginny.

But on her dark days she called him, and Bill knew that she did.

He himself saw less of the old cop, these days, but on the morning following his visit to Norma he made an early stop by the Radicks' apartment. Mrs. Radick was always up early, with coffee and a luxury of newspapers. Radick himself was still asleep.

"I thought he might be," said Bill. "What happened about that kook, do you know?"

He was rubbing his cheek absently as he spoke; she looked up at him, entertained.

"You bachelors. I haven't got lipstick on, Billy."

He stopped rubbing and grinned.

"That's right. You're the one I can trust."

"You'll get the right mark on you one of these days. Then you'll be proud." He accepted his coffee and said nothing. More tactful than her husband, she went on, "I don't know about that fellow, Billy. Nothing's in the papers, but I guess it wouldn't be. I don't even know what time dad got in, except it was late. Why don't you call Headquarters?"

"Well, I will," he said. "You know my secretary's in hock till they get him. I miss her."

"Sure, you would," she said, with continuing tact. "It's not so nice for her either. I hear she's a nice girl."

"She's a very nice girl. But she thinks I only like people if they're in trouble. How about that?"

"No. Is that what she said?"

She gazed at him, interested, but he didn't want to go on with it after all.

"Can I call from here? I'd like to get moving on this."

She said he could, but in the living room he met Radick emerging in his bathrobe, yawning and grumbling.

"What's all this yak, yak? This is supposed to be a quiet house now. You have to come around here and holler?"

Sometimes it was disconcerting to discover how thoroughly they knew each other—two who met only a few times a year, now, and were not even recognizable as the people they had been: the cop, the younger Bennig kid. Yet Bill's trip to the telephone ended right there. Nor did he repeat his question about the capture. It hadn't happened. Something had gone sour.

He stuck his hands in his pockets, with a shrug, and turned to the living-room window. Stood whistling under his breath and looking down into the wintry street. It was in his mind that he could stop by and pick her up, maybe drop the boy off at school. Yesterday he would simply have done it, but today he was looking twice at every move he made. Maybe looking through her eyes.

"Billy, come eat," said Mrs. Radick from the breakfast room. He turned and went back, hands in pockets still.

"I ate, thanks. Get dressed, I'll give you a ride down," he said to

Radick, who notoriously rode buses.

"He's running a jitney now," said Radick to his wife, who was taking curlers out of her hair.

She paused, under his stare, and then said with dignity to Bill, "Excuse me, I'll go dress. One sloppy is enough."

"Hah," said Radick. When she had gone he inquired, "That's why you're here, naturally? To give rides?"

"Sure. But the one I really want to pick up is my secretary. She says she can't come out if you don't tell her."

"That's right," said Radick, chewing. He said presently, "See her at night. You'll get further."

"No, but how about it? I'll take her down, she'll take a cab back, or I'll bring her. Your lady cop can get the boy. Why not?"

"What's the hurry?" Radick countered, smearing toast. "It's Friday, that's only one day, then the week's over anyway."

"One day can be a long time, pop."

Bennig sat down, looking seriously across the table at Radick, who considered him in return.

"She's jumpy, huh?"

"Why not? It's a very jumpy deal. Besides, I miss her."

This was bait Radick never refused. His consideration deepened.

"I think you like this one. Right?"

"I'm crazy for her. I can't work if she's not there."

Radick went back to his toast.

"Well, it could be a while yet," he admitted gloomily. "I thought so, I didn't think he would show last night. This is a very screwy guy, Bill."

"You don't think he'll come back there?"

"Who knows? He didn't. He might yet."

"Maybe he's left town," Bill suggested, but Radick shook his head.

"He's around. We got his car yesterday, everything in it. Even money. He hasn't been near it since he put it in. What he needs, he took. Then he doesn't come near that either. So tell me what he's doing."

"He's got a friend his size."

"He's got no friends, any size. I can't figure it."

"Hospitals?" Bill asked. Radick gave him a glance of approval, but shook his head.

"If something happened to him, it's strictly private." He pushed back his chair and got up. "All I can hope is something scared him off. When he calms down he'll come back. Because he's got to wait," said Radick, to the tabletop. "He's got to wait for that old lady to come home."

"Call your girl," he said, leaving the room. "Tell her half an hour, we'll pick her up. I want to talk to her anyway."

Alone in the Radicks' living room, Bill looked up Norma's number. It was the same as yesterday. He dialed it, frowning, and after two rings a high, faraway voice said in his ear, "Hello? Who is it?"

It took him a minute to realize this was Norma. Then he said quickly, "It's all right, this is Bill Bennig. What's the matter—he called you?"

"Oh," she said, and was silent. He had caught her being scared; she didn't like that. "Oh, good morning," she started again, and made the effort, "—Bill."

He said patiently, "What happened, Norma?"

"Well, nothing, really," she said in her own voice and added something that sounded like, "Another milk chute, I guess."

"What?"

"A call that wasn't anything, that's all. It rang and I answered, and then there was a funny noise and nothing. Somebody realized they'd misdialed and hung up."

"Oh, come on, Norma. Of course it's something. You answered, didn't you?"

"But I didn't say anything. I didn't have a chance. Before I could even get the receiver up I heard this noise and then nothing."

"But the line could still have been open. You did speak then, didn't you?"

She said after a small pause, "No. I just listened a minute and then I hung up too."

Too scared to make a sound. He could see her carefully putting the receiver back in place. Standing there looking at it.

"Well," he said. Then, "How long ago?"

"About ten minutes. It sounded more like dropping the phone than hanging up," she added. "I mean, it wasn't just one noise. More like a lot of bumping."

She let him think about it. He gave it a puzzled moment and then said, "If you went to work, what about the phone? He'd know it wasn't your voice."

"Oh, Ann wouldn't answer. She'd just let it ring, as if the house were empty."

"You still want to go?"

"I'm dressed," she said simply. "I'm just waiting till nine to call the lieutenant."

"He says you can go. We'll be by in about half an hour to pick you up. If this guy wants to call you back meanwhile, I guess that gives him time. So I'll get off the line. Half an hour."

"Bill! Wait." She said carefully, "If the phone should ring again, do you think I ought to say 'hello' or just wait?"

It was an idea. He examined it.

"Just listen. Why not? He's got to know—make him ask. Unless this will give your mother fits, if it's her."

"Oh, I've already talked to mother. She knows we're all right. She won't call again till evening."

So she really meant to get out of there.

He hung up, smiling, and then wiped it off as Radick came into the room. Going down in the elevator he told Radick about the call, and he listened, nodding.

"Like he dropped it, sort of. Well, maybe he did. Maybe there's something the matter with him, that's why he doesn't show. He doesn't drink at all, the old lady said so," he added thoughtfully. "Too bad."

As soon as the car drove up in front of Norma's house, the front door opened, and she and her son came out. She shut the door firmly, on an apparently empty house, while holding Jimmy in check with the other hand. All the way down the walk she kept a hand on his arm. He looked as if he needed it, to keep him from breaking into a run. He grinned at them all the way.

Radick grunted.

"There's a happy boy. Look at him! How to keep the kids amused. Hah!"

But he got out as they came up to the car and took his own grip on Jimmy.

"You're late for school."

"I know," said Jimmy, startled. "I've got a note."

"Late's late. Get in here with me."

Radick had shut Norma into the front, and now pushed Jimmy in back and climbed in after him. This was partly so he could watch the backs of their heads all the way downtown, Bennig knew, but partly too from a real physical hunger for any available child.

In front of the school the lieutenant kept them all waiting while he got out of the car again and looked things over.

"You play out in that playground, do you?"

"Yes, sir," said Jimmy, radiant with pride.

"Don't leave it. I know all about sneaking over to the candy store."

"No, sir, I won't."

"And don't talk to anybody you don't know."

"I wouldn't! I know all about that. We had movies."

"Did you," said Radick, who had distributed them. "Well, go on—hurry!"

"Where's your note?" he demanded, making Jimmy turn and fumble for it. "All right—get!"

"Nice boy," he remarked, back in the car. Norma, still looking at the closing door of the school, said only, "Yes."

"Do you want to leave early and pick him up yourself?" Bennig suggested.

He hadn't, until he said it, any idea of saying such a thing. Nor did he expect, because of it, a look of gratitude from Norma—so welcoming that his mind stalled briefly.

And the old man in the back, not missing a thing.

On the way downtown Radick asked Norma if anybody had called again, and she said no one had. Then he wanted to know if she thought her mother could take the conditions at home, if she came back early.

"Say tomorrow," he suggested. "Your brother says it's all right with him, and she's willing. But I wouldn't want to put a nice lady like that under a strain she couldn't take."

She understood what he meant: that her mother's presence was to draw Cliff out of hiding, so that he might be captured. Her mother, naturally, would understand this too. Norma thought about it.

"Mother can do it, if she says she will," she said finally. "She won't like it. But I don't think she'd be afraid, waiting for Cliff, the way ... others might be."

"Good," said Radick, satisfied. "Then your brother can bring her home, just like normal. We'll leave Mrs. Cunningham right where she is. You won't mind that."

They dropped Norma off at the newspaper building so Bill could take the lieutenant over to police headquarters before garaging his car. She was hardly out of sight before Radick asked, "How old is she? Thirty-two, -three? The boy's about eleven."

"I don't know," said Bennig, with shut teeth.

"Well, that's young. And she's had the first one early."

Bennig blew up.

"By God. I don't know why any of your kids ever got married, Radick!" he snarled. "They ought to be vomiting by the time they're twelve, even to hear about it! *Now shut up!*"

The old man was too surprised to answer at first. Then, with gathering outrage, he stammered, "My kids—my kids, what are you talking about? My kids know what to do, they've got some sense—not like *some smart schnooks!*"

In finally achieved fury, he got out and slammed the door—in the middle of traffic. And Bennig drove off and left him there without a backward look.

CHAPTER 12

It was a slight shock to Norma to find how completely their return to the office changed Mr. Bennig. Not only did he become Mr. Bennig again—as if no Bill had ever existed—but he was Mr. Bennig in a bad mood, sharp and hard-driving. By midmorning she had asked for a girl from the stenographic pool and sent this victim in to cope with the whirlwind, shutting the door on them, too.

She thought, He didn't like what I said last night. I suppose I shouldn't have said it.

But the alternative was to become another Miss Munn. Or Mr. Pollack. Or Al Hines.

The day began to seem interminable. And the week end ahead would be no better, with her mother shipped home sad and nervous for such a grim purpose. They probably wouldn't even be allowed to go out to the hospital to see Edna and the baby.

And Ann there all the time, a constant reminder, nice as she was. A stranger in her readiness to function.

And always, always, the background wonder and fear of Cliff.

By lunchtime she had no appetite nor desire to go anywhere. She sent out for coffee and a sandwich, and could manage only the coffee. Mr. Bennig came out, in a fast tangle with his overcoat, as she was bundling away these remains. He gave the discarded sandwich a sharp glance.

"Surely that's not necessary?" he said.

"I didn't want to go out."

"Did anybody tell you to stay in? The police?"

"No."

He hesitated, still at odds with his own overcoat and clearly wondering, Is she afraid?

"Do you want to come with me? Just across the street."

"No," she said. To her horror, her voice shook. She didn't dare add so much as "Thank you."

He stood looking down at her, a man suddenly defeated by an overcoat, which looked by now as if it would neither go on nor come off. Then his mood changed; she could feel it. A couple of shrugs and the coat came into place.

He said quietly, "Come on. We'll go over to Charlie's and have one drink and some minestrone. This is no good."

He took down her coat, and she got up and put it on. They went down in the elevator and out on the cold street, equally silent, but no longer at odds.

She felt very tired. The warm gloom of Charlie's, and one glass of wine, almost put her to sleep. Her head against the back of the banquette, her eyes closed, she heard him say, "This is a let-down, Norma. Because you hoped it might be over, and it isn't. You'll get your second wind pretty soon."

She nodded, too tired to speak.

He said abruptly, "Are you sore?" and that opened her eyes.

"What about?"

"I don't know."

"I'm tired," she said, explaining, and he nodded.

"Well, that's natural. Try to get a lot of sleep this week end. Ginny's got some good knockout pills, I'll bring you a couple if you want them."

"No, I don't need them," she said. The soup came, and she sat forward, hoping this would rouse her. And heard herself ask, "Do you live there, Bill?"

"Where? Ginny's? Lord, no." Halfway through the minestrone he asked, "Why?"

She didn't know.

"The fact is, the kids are wonderful, but I can't take an awful lot of Ginny," he said presently. "She's a good kid—she really works over those kids, and she's one hundred per cent for Roy, she always has been. But she's still just like when they got married—seventeen years old. I swear those kids have got more sense than she has. You don't notice it so much, when Ray's around, but it makes it tough for all of them when he's away. The kids can face it," he said abruptly, "but she can't."

He shut up then, leaving her both puzzled and curious. She tried again. "Is your brother like you?"

"Well, we're brothers. Anybody can tell that." He smiled suddenly— not for her, for some memory. "You know Radick, the lieutenant, was the cop on our block when we were kids. It wasn't a very good neighborhood. And I was the one he had the trouble with—the hell-raiser. You know? I'd be maybe eight, nine, and Roy's not much older, but he's home. Hitting the math. And here comes Radick, dragging me home to Roy. My dad worked nights," he explained. "He'd get the supper, leave us in— we were supposed to stay in. Roy did. But not me. Maybe it got so I was out there hunting for Radick, making him hunt for me. I don't know. But he always did. Finally he got so he'd take me over to their place for the night. He got transferred when I was twelve, but I still went over a lot. They're nice people."

She was lost—fascinated and lost in this fragment of his past which he obviously enjoyed recalling. She didn't want to break into his enjoyment with questions. But what did it mean? Where was their mother? And what had happened to good Roy, who stayed home?

More cheerful now, he was ordering more food—urging her to have some more wine. She did what she could to respond, but it wasn't enough; he felt it.

Sobering, he said suddenly, "I don't have a very good family situation. I know that."

"Well ... all families have their troubles," she murmured. "Besides, this isn't really your family now, is it?"

"Sure it is—who else? There's only Roy and me. My dad died when I was in college, and I couldn't have swung that anyway without Roy. He's a very smart guy, you know—kind of a mathematical genius. I'm not kidding, there's nothing he can't do with figures. When he was fourteen, he was keeping the books for three stores on our block. He used to make out everybody's income-tax forms. He was earning as much as my dad by the time he was seventeen!" He said, checking himself, "But it wasn't really such a great deal for him, you know. He ought to have had scholarships, gone on and done something in physics. He could have. But when a boy starts living like a man too soon—he doesn't go back. He doesn't want to. Maybe it would have been different if my mother had lived, maybe not."

"What did he do, Bill?" Norma asked then.

"He kept books for the wrong people," he said grimly. "And handled their tax returns."

"You mean, criminals?"

"Yes."

Since he wouldn't soften this, she found herself needing to.

"Perhaps he didn't realize ..."

As if she hadn't spoken, he said abruptly, "It's a kind of garbage-type big business. Known as the rackets. The money comes from everywhere—some of it borderline legitimate, most of it not. Every bit of it needs to be accounted for at least two ways—sometimes more. I think even Roy must have had all he could do to keep the books straight. I know he was fooling around with the idea of IBM machines, before ...

"Sure he knew," he said, coming this way round to her question. "If he didn't, there wasn't anybody who did. He knew, and he didn't care. For him it was all figures." It was a chilling answer; he couldn't take it himself, and needed to add, "But the funny thing is, he's the nicest guy in the world to know. Everybody likes Roy—he gets along with people a hell of a lot better than I do. Nothing bothers him, so long as Ginny and the kids are all right, and the figures come out even. He'll get his parole, all right, and I know at least two places that'll be glad to get him, when he does. But I still don't think he knows what hit him. Even after five years to think about it. And Ginny sure isn't the gal to help him find out. They're both scared careful by now," he said, wry. "But that's about all."

"Well, it's something to begin on," she said, for comfort.

"Not much. It's not that I'm scared Roy will get into trouble again," he said slowly. "He won't. But it does something to a man, to get slapped down hard like that for being the way he's always been. Either he starts to think, or he starts to fold. With Roy I can't tell yet which it's going to be. I can't tell."

"If he's really so much like you, I don't think he'll fold," she said.

He looked at her sideways, not sure what to say.

She added, "Besides, with three children, he can't fold, can he?"

"Well, it's been known to happen. But they're really what I'm betting on," he admitted. "People can really learn from their kids—you know? Kids like that. And someone like Roy. When he gets home and sees how it is with them," he said earnestly, "I'm betting he'll start to breathe again. And think. They're really marvelous kids, Norma. It's the truth, they are."

She believed him and said so.

By the time they came out into the street again her fatigue was gone and the depression which perhaps had led to it. He looked better too and took her arm—a comfortable arrangement. She smiled at him.

"Thank you, Bill. I'm glad you made me come out."

"Sure, there's nothing like moving around. Change pace and move around. It keeps things from closing in on you."

He was hopeless. But it no longer irritated her. She thought she understood why, now. What had happened to his brother had been the shock of his life; he still couldn't absorb that pain or bear to see an echo of it in others.

But she thought she would have liked to know the cheerful "hell-raiser" he had been—slugging his way up through the newspaper— before his private life fell in on him.

They went back to work, amiably, until three o'clock, when he reminded her that she had better leave. She didn't need reminding. The air was still light outdoors and would be for another couple of hours. She would take a taxi, as she had promised, but fear was very far from her then. More a memory than a present possibility.

He asked her when her mother was coming home and she said she wasn't sure. That night or perhaps in the morning.

"Well, you'll be all right, then. I guess you won't want to have me come by this week end."

"Yes, come by if you can," she said gravely. "It would be a good deed."

He wasn't sure whether to smile or not, until she did. This time she waited outside the school in her taxi. Jimmy seemed disappointed to find her alone.

"How come we don't have anybody?" he asked, climbing in beside her.

"We've got the taxi. And Ann, at home. What more do you want?"

In fact, their street lay so harmless and quiet-seeming in the autumn afternoon that even the idea of Ann, lurking indoors, was incongruous. Yet Norma had no doubt she was there. And necessary.

She got out her new key and picked up a package lying on the steps. Apparently Ann wasn't answering the doorbell.

"It's for the Hausens," she said absently. "Take it over, will you?"

He held out his hand, but with a grimace, and she drew the package back.

"Oh, all right. Here. Tell Ann I'll be right back."

She gave him the key and ran down the steps again. Halfway across their frozen lawn she felt a sudden check of caution and stopped to look back. But it was all right, he had just shut the door behind him.

Standing on the Hausens' porch she could see her mother's milk chute door gaping outward once more. So the catch must be gone. Ann would have shut it when she took in the milk.

But wouldn't she also have noticed a faulty catch? A spasm of irritation drowned her slight anxiety. Not the milk chute again. And no, Ann wouldn't necessarily have noticed. Obviously, she hadn't.

In her preoccupation, she found she was ringing too insistently. The poor Hausens would think it was some disaster. She began instead to clear out their mailbox.

There was still no answer, so she opened the storm door to tuck package and mail inside, but as she leaned down, the inner door yielded at last.

Well trained, she straightened and slipped inside as quickly as possible.

"I'm sorry, I thought you ..."

How dark the room was, with all the venetian blinds closed and no lamps lighted! Were they ill again? She peered doubtfully at the man against the door, who was a stranger, not Mr. Hausen at all.

"What—"

Her voice died. This was no stranger. It was Cliff.

CHAPTER 13

And he was terrified.

Still pressed to the door he had so quickly shut behind her, his stretched fingers clutching the knob, he stared at Norma as if she were some invading Fury—an apparition of doom—that had come through the walls at him.

As if to an apparition, he whispered, "Go away. Go away."

She did not move. There was no way in which she could dislodge him from the door, to obey. Nor was he even speaking to her, as she stood there, but to a Norma still outside. Ringing and ringing the bell. Starting at last to come in.

Did he think she had a key?

He was staring at her hands now, as if to discover what magical properties they held, to let her invade his privacy in this way. Very slightly—her arms nearly numb with shock—she extended the parcel and letters.

"I was bringing these ..."

She could not tell if he understood her or not.

In the dull light filtering into the shuttered room, she saw that he had deteriorated badly since their last meeting. He was tidy still: his fair hair combed, his battered face shaved. Even his shirt seemed fresh, although it was much too small. But he had become another person. Private, staring. Impossible to reach. Impossible to address.

She stood very still.

At last he drew a long shaking breath and spoke again. Very low, but no longer whispering.

"What is it?"

"Some mail. A package."

He still gave no sign of understanding, but his large eyes came slowly back to her face, examining it. She looked down from their empty gaze.

"Why are you here, Norma?" he asked then.

A kind of despairing courage rose in her at this more normal voice. She said in the same way:

"Why are you here, Cliff?"

"I'm staying here," he said quickly. Then nothing more.

"With the Hausens?"

"What?"

His attention was gone again, gone inward. She did not repeat her question. A long time went by—she could not guess how long, but she found she was trembling: a faint, constant tremor that made the papers she held susurrate together. She moved to quiet them, a slight movement, but it recalled his notice to her.

"Norma."

"What is it?"

"Who is that woman in mother's house? A young woman. She never comes out."

The shock that went through her took a moment to define. It had nothing to do with Ann. He had said "mother's house" as naturally as she or Tom would say it. Finally and simply announcing his claim.

She couldn't speak. In the silence, the poor light, his expression changed: his head turning slightly, his glance becoming upward and oblique.

He said slyly, "I know she's there."

She made herself answer.

"Yes, of course. That's Ann."

He accepted this, but thoughtfully, like one searching his memory. She let him. The world in which she might have said, That is a policewoman, who knows I am here, was a world outside these doors. In here one moved and spoke as if in a strange dream—Cliff's dream—with care not to break it. For it broke in only one way: into violence. She had never understood anything more clearly, more immediately, in her life— perhaps because on that understanding her life could depend.

"What Ann?" he said finally, with a frown. But going on at once, he added, "A man brought her. There are two men. Who are they?"

She risked a show of dignity, as her mother might have done, and answered simply, "My friends. My guests."

But in some interior function her mind registered his awareness of Ann's arrival. Two days ago. He had been there that long.

He did not like her implied rebuke and quickly offered one in return.

"But it isn't your house. It's not your house, Norma."

Then where were the Hausens? Two days ... two days! And the total, utter quiet of the rooms around them ...

Without warning, tears came into her eyes—more from shock than from any rational idea—and once begun they kept flowing and spilling down her cheeks. She made no attempt to deal with them.

He observed this weeping and seemed to find it natural.

"You tend to forget that, I think," he said.

She no longer had any idea what they were talking about.

At some point he had let go of the door and pushed himself upright again, standing in a relaxed and thoughtful way beside her. His terror was over. Now he seemed to accept her presence—even to find it natural.

His tone was natural, though slightly petulant, as he remarked, "We'd better sit down. I haven't been very well."

When she did not follow him into the room he turned and looked at her—simply a look, from his large blank eyes, but a shock of terror went through her that produced its own convulsive movement. To cover this, and in part obedience, she turned and slowly put down on the console table beside her the letters and the package she still held. In the mirror above, his waiting figure was reflected.

Then behind it, far behind, another figure appeared and stood still. It was so improbable an emergence—the light so poor, and her vision so blurred—that it evoked no belief.

Then she turned. And saw Mrs. Hausen standing in the archway.

"No, no—go back!" Cliff suddenly cried.

His voice rose, grew thin—his hands came up and battered on air, a gesture of abhorrence that belonged to an apparition rather than the small old woman who stood there.

"Go back, please! I—go back! *Go back!*"

To this final scream, Mrs. Hausen turned and stumbled away. Down the hallway which led, in this one-story house, to the bedrooms and bath. There was no further sound from that part.

Nor had Norma been able to produce a sound.

Cliff was badly shaken. The minute they were alone he fell into random walking, desperate gestures with stretched hands. A babble of words.

"Horrible—horrible, impossible creature—and this ghastly, ugly, horrible house! How can people live this way, with such mean, horrible ugliness? *How can there be such people?*"

He stopped, staring at her out of a face gone white. Gone shining, with a burst of sweat from every pore. And cried out again, "You don't think I *want* to be here, do you? Do you think I *choose* to be in this hell—shut up in this mean, ugly hell ... day and night, *shut up?*"

He came back to where she stood, herself now pressed back to the door—as far, as close as she could come to freedom. A hand behind her on the knob she could not turn.

He cared for none of this, but went on raging at her. "You chose this for me, Norma! This is where you force me to wait—is that what you came to see? Is this what you wanted to know? *How I could bear it?* Is that it? Is it?"

Now her head was pressed back as far as it could go—face upturned and helpless, to his closer, shining, dead-white face, contorted with furious grief. Forcing her to see him.

She shut her eyes. Instantly his hands were at her, fingers pushing up the lids.

"No! You wanted—*you came here to*—"

"All right," she said, sudden and loud. The voice sound made him pause. She went on rapidly, "All right—you win. You win. Come back."

He stood over her, checked: a hard, sobbing breath, no other sound. She made herself go on staring up at him, as if there were some meaning in her words, which he must receive.

Then his breathing stopped. He turned away from her, a little away, standing head down by the console table. Staring at the scatter of papers there. Breath burst from him—in a laugh, a sob, she could not tell what—and he began with shaking fingers aimlessly to touch the letters.

She tried to go on. "Your key ..." Something about his key, but she could not. Nothing more was possible.

Perhaps it was better so. Her silence seemed, gradually, to reassure him. He gave her at length one of those oblique, upward looks and said uncertainly, "You admit that?"

"Yes," she said at once.

He did laugh, then: a brief and shaky sound, but a laugh. And said with tired bitterness, "Well. So you see how simple it was, after all. How simple."

He was in motion again, with resumed thought. Restless motion, hovering near the table. Near her.

But when he should move to the center of the room she would turn the knob at her back and slip sideways. And be out.

The telephone in the room with them began to ring—a tiny, tuned-down ring. He paid no attention beyond a glance, and that was toward the mirror.

The reflected room in the mirror seemed to hold him. He said into it, presently, "I try and try to think about your strangeness to me, Norma. The very strange, complicated way you've behaved to me since the first moment I came. Why? What reason could you have had? *Did you have any reason?*"

He looked to the mirror, which did not reflect the slow shake of her head, and went on more rapidly, "The coldness, the rudeness—the absolute lack of courtesy, even a stranger ... Why should you have behaved that way to me, without any reason? The very moment I came. Do you know? Do you?"

The tiny ringing went on. He would never move away.

She repeated numbly, "I admit it...." He gave her a blank stare and turned away.

"You admit it. You admit it rather late, don't you think?"

He stopped three steps away, with his back to her. Head down.

"Why should I come there now? It's spoiled, it's impossible. You've made it impossible, and you don't even know why. You say you admit— but you're afraid now. You're afraid of what she'll say, aren't you? When she comes back and finds out. She will know. She will know, Norma."

The ringing stopped.

He added without turning, "Besides, that woman is there."

It took her a moment to grasp what he meant, to form a minimal reply.

"She can leave ..."

"You mean you would ask her to leave?"

"Yes."

"In my presence?"

He turned enough to give her that upward look—a sly watching.

"If you like. *If you like.*"

A sudden exhausted fury burst from her, frightening Norma. Disconcerting him.

He turned all the way round. Said uncertainly, "Well, if you find that humiliating ... it's you who've, you are the one who ..."

She stared back at him, capable of no more of this insane improvisation. It was all useless, anyway. It could go on forever, until she said—was forced to say—the words (whatever they were) that would enrage him again. And end it.

Quietly, almost at random, she said one honest thing to him.

"My mother's coming home tonight, Cliff."

He gave no sign of hearing her. Nor of hearing the telephone, which had resumed its thin ringing. When he did begin to speak, it was as though he had finished some private deliberation of his own.

He said, "I refuse your invitation, Norma. And I deny your right to give it or to withhold it. It's too late for you now. It's too late."

His color returned while he was speaking. He had raised his head, and stood looking down at her proudly with his large, empty eyes.

No reply was possible.

He did not want one. As if she had ceased to exist, he turned to walk away. From her, from the room. Her numbed fingers slid more tightly round the metal knob at her back, trying to make ready for the fast wrench that would free her. As soon as he should reach the dining-room archway....

He did not reach it.

With a sudden choked cry, he stopped dead, his proud posture shattered, his hands rising. His voice rising, too.

"Why are you there? I told you to go back!"

He was staring where Norma's vision could not reach, beyond the archway to that part of the dining room where the bedroom hall began.

She made no attempt to see, but in a sudden ducking movement wrenched the door open and crowded through, seizing the storm door's aluminum handle. She had it, was pressing it down, pushing against the door itself, when he pulled her back into the room.

Violently. And violently slammed the door behind them. Swung her, in violent rejection, half across the room. She fell across the large television set and hung leaning there, without word or breath.

It was total defeat. He was back in that frenzy of panic, or rage, or both, in which he had held her pressed to the door and tried to pry her eyelids open. Almost incoherent, his thin voice screamed, over and over, "What's the matter with you? What's the matter with you? *Are you both mad? What's the matter with you?*"

She made no attempt to answer, but raising her head a little, saw what he had seen: the little ghost woman, standing mute at the opening to the bedroom hall. Just standing there.

Without hope—perhaps in warning, Norma gasped, "Mrs. Hausen ..." But the ghost woman did not move.

Instead she cried out too, a thin wail, *"Oh, Normie!"*

Cliff's hands went over his ears.

"I won't have this," he said rapidly. "I won't endure it. I've told you, I've asked you ... *You are not to come out here.*"

Without moving, Norma said, "I'll take her back." He made neither reply nor any movement. She saw that his eyes were shut, his hands still covered his ears. Mrs. Hausen had begun a faint whimpering.

It took all Norma's courage to leave her corner and come out into the room—passing him, crossing in front of him, making steadily for the little old woman whom he could not bear, for some reason, to see. He was aware of Norma's passing. His hands came slowly down, his eyes were open. But he let her go by.

She passed through the dining room and reached the small waiting figure, which instantly and heavily attached itself to her. The low whimpering broke into a keener wail that she tried to hush, while turning and urging her mother's neighbor back to whatever refuge there might be.

He let them go. He wanted them to go. Nor did he follow. The spare room was closest, and Norma bundled them both in there, pushing the door shut with the weight of their united bodies, falling back against it. She leaned there in utter exhaustion, holding Mrs. Hausen in her arms, and Mrs. Hausen put her head down on Norma's shoulder and began to cry.

CHAPTER 14

Norma couldn't let that go on. For one thing, it was too audible.

As soon as she could gather the strength, she guided Mrs. Hausen over to the diminutive chintz chair which no normal person could have sat in at all. But tiny Mrs. Hausen went into it with room to spare, and thus detached, looked up at Norma in dazed obedience and grew quieter.

But she didn't want to be left, to let go of Norma even for an instant. Her whimpered protest followed Norma back to the door and made almost useless any attempt to listen there. But if Cliff had followed them, he was being quiet about it.

She saw that the door had an interior bolt, like that of a bathroom door, and she turned this. So that had been Cliff's problem: he could not, from outside, lock the old lady in.

A frantic whispering burst out behind her. She turned, putting a finger to her lips, but it was no use.

"... mustn't do that, Normie! He doesn't like it, you mustn't lock the door ..."

Norma came back and knelt down by the chintz chair, taking Mrs. Hausen's hands in hers. They were like trapped small birds.

"... and you mustn't make a noise, and don't ever try to use the telephone, Normie—*he hits you!*"

"I know, I know, dear. It's all right, don't be afraid."

In here, the venetian blinds were closed too. The windows were on the far side of the house, looking on neighbors she no longer knew. But the drop to the ground could not be more than five or six feet. She started to rise and found her hands still held.

"Just for a minute," Norma whispered. "I just want to see something."

No use. Mrs. Hausen hung on, looking pitifully up. Norma bent to her. "What is it, dear?"

Nothing. Then, in the smallest of whispers, Mrs. Hausen made her confidence.

"Mr. Hausen is in the closet, Normie ..."

Involuntarily, Norma straightened. Her glance shot behind her.

Mrs. Hausen was tugging again.

"No, no—in our room, that's why I have to stay here! Oh, Normie— it's a big closet, do you think he'll be all right?"

Helplessly, Norma nodded. She sank down again, to hear the rest of it.

"I heard him sliding the doors," Mrs. Hausen whispered. "When he took Mr. Hausen in there, I heard him sliding them. And Mr. Hausen isn't anywhere you can see him—I looked, when that young man was asleep. But those doors make so much noise, Normie, I was afraid to try.... He hears you, he always hears you. You mustn't think just because he's asleep he won't hear you, Normie!"

Feverishly, she whispered on.

"I tried to call your mother this morning. Because he used to live with her. You know? But he heard me ..."

Then that was the call without any voice. From right here; from next door. Norma rose to her feet, unable to bear any more of this knowledge until they should be out of here. This time Mrs. Hausen let her go. Without protest or hope, she followed Norma with her eyes.

The venetian blinds would not move. Cliff had nailed their wooden slats to the window frame on either side. Not all of them, but enough. There were two windows, one at the side, one at the back. They were fastened with equal thoroughness.

Norma stood regarding this strange piece of work. She had turned on the bedside lamp, in a gesture of protest, even of anger, at their gloomy imprisonment, and the warm light steadied her.

Mrs. Hausen, blinking, said dully, "He nailed them all up, Normie."

"It doesn't matter."

Norma came back by the chintz chair. She said in a low, firm voice, "The police know I'm here, Mrs. Hausen. Don't be afraid anymore. When they can't reach me, they'll get in. He can't keep them out long. And meanwhile, he can't get in here."

She noticed, as she spoke, that the door seemed a solid one, and the hinges were on their side. Nevertheless, in a kind of restless need, she went over and stood by it. It seemed to her that she would know if Cliff were out there, no matter how quiet he remained. She felt that she would sense him there, listening. Trying to listen, to hear what they said of him.

She could sense nothing. And yet, she could not move away. Was he there or not? Here was a nightmare increase of the waiting she had done next door for Cliff to appear. Now, he was in the same house. She knew where he was, but not what he was doing. Or planning to do.

Where was Ann? What could she possibly be thinking, to wait so long? It was past four; Norma had picked Jimmy up only a little after three-thirty, surely—and surely they had not taken more than five or ten minutes to get here, to part at the steps. Still ... it was less than half an hour that she had been here. She had thought it to be much longer, and her heart sank as she realized that such a visit, to elderly neighbors, might not concern Ann at all. Especially with Jimmy explaining that you couldn't get away from the Hausens, that they really hung on to you. She could almost hear his voice, and Ann's amused rejoinders, as the two of them moved round the kitchen, fixing an after-school snack, talking. Perhaps it had not been Ann at all, then, on the telephone. Almost certainly it had not....

If she went on thinking this way, despair was going to engulf her absolutely. Nor could she continue to stand and listen. Because if you listened long enough, you began to hear. Whether there was anything to hear or not.

She forced herself away, back to Mrs. Hausen. This time Norma drew up a straight chair for herself, and they sat side by side, like ladies visiting. Mrs. Hausen accepted all of this, in her new numbed way, and made no more attempts to cling or whisper. After her first outburst, she had fallen into a passivity of exhaustion, or renewed hopelessness. Sitting there as she must have done for the better part of two days, now. Simply enduring.

Norma took her hands, stroking them. Then she saw a bruise on the fragile and colorless cheek and gently touched it. Mrs. Hausen's dry lips trembled.

"I tried to call your mother this morning, Normie," she said faintly. "Because that's the young man that used to live with her. But he didn't use to act this way."

"I know. The police know too, Mrs. Hausen. Don't worry, they'll find us soon."

"He hit Mr. Hausen, too, you know. He knocked Mr. Hausen right down, right in our own living room. And then he put him in our closet. Mr. Hausen only wanted to use the telephone. You mustn't ever try to use the telephone, Normie," she whispered earnestly. "He always hears you."

Silence closed on them again. The silence which Cliff required. Demanded.

Norma couldn't bear any more of it.

She whispered, "When did he come here, Mrs. Hausen? How did he get in?"

Mrs. Hausen's mouth trembled again. She said, in old grievance, "Mr. Hausen let him in. He let him right in, Normie. Just to spite me, because I told him he shouldn't have told that young man about where you worked. That wasn't any of his business, was it? But Mr. Hausen got mad and called you up, and he didn't like what you said, either, Normie. And when that young man came back, he invited him right in the house."

"But when did he come back? That same day?"

"Yes, he did," said Mrs. Hausen, remembering injustice. "And Mr. Hausen asked him in. He said if you had something against him that was your business, but he knew your mother didn't, and that was good enough for him. He just wanted to show me I was wrong."

"But what did Cliff want? Why did he come back?"

"He said he wanted to stay here. A few days, he said. But we don't ever have people to stay, we're not well enough. It's too much for us. Mr. Hausen told him so. He told him we never have people to stay with us anymore. But he wouldn't go away," said Mrs. Hausen, with a tiny whimper. "He just kept sitting there and talking. And he wasn't nice, Normie. He wasn't talking nice at all, and Mr. Hausen didn't like it. We didn't want to hear all those things, and Mr. Hausen told him so. But he wouldn't stop."

"I know. It's all right."

"He wouldn't pay any attention at all, Mr. Hausen got terribly upset, and he said he'd have to call the police if that young man didn't go away. And then he pushed Mr. Hausen, just because Mr. Hausen tried to use the telephone. He slapped him, and he pushed him so hard he fell down. Right there in our own living room."

Dry-eyed, solemn, Mrs. Hausen paused. Waiting to be told how this was possible, what it all meant.

Norma said, "Was Mr. Hausen ... hurt?"

"I don't know," said Mrs. Hausen, with her small whimper. "He was just lying there, and his eyes looked so funny, and that young man wouldn't even let me go to him. That's why he made me come in here, Normie, because he said I was making a noise. And he shut the door, too. But I could hear him sliding our closet doors, you can always hear that. I know he must have put Mr. Hausen in the closet ... but I don't know why, he wasn't making any noise.... It's a big closet," she said, with recurrent anxiety. "It's almost the whole wall. Do you think he'll be all right, Normie?"

Two days ago. Did she realize how long it had been, in this room without night or day? Norma, murmuring some reassurance, could not meet her eyes.

Nor could she go on sitting there, so intimately, with this new horror in her mind.

Mrs. Hausen watched her rise, watched her wander back to test, hopelessly, at the fastened blinds. And murmured again, "He nailed them shut, Normie."

Norma did not reply. Anger was beginning to rise in her, a moving anger, enemy of patience and of stillness.

She crossed suddenly to the dresser and turned on that lamp. The dresser top was spread with an embroidered cloth, on which lay (for the benefit of that guest they would never have) a celluloid or plastic dresser set: brush, comb, mirror. Nail file. This last she took up, holding it tautly as if it were a weapon, and went back to the blinds. Worked the coarse file in between slat and window frame and began to pry. At the first use of force, the plastic handle snapped.

Mrs. Hausen gave a tiny cry. Norma caught at the remaining file, working it so fiercely that it cut her finger. But there was no result. There was no leverage here sufficient to part solid nail from solid wood.

She stood in anger, thinking without coherence, But why didn't someone hear him, hammering in all those nails? If it had only been on our side, we ...

They would have thought nothing of it. Mr. Hausen was always hammering something.

She dropped the file and returned to the dresser. Nothing else on top, except an enormous bottle of cologne, with a ribbon on it. She began to pull out drawers, careless of sound: empty, empty, empty. A folded blanket, hideously rose.

Behind her, an agitated whispering went on.

"Oh, Normie, don't make so much noise—he'll come, Normie! And he'll find out the door's locked, and he doesn't like you to lock the door ..."

More quietly (but only for Mrs. Hausen's sake) Norma shut the last drawer. And stood still. Because there was nothing else, her fingers closed around the bottle of cologne. Gardenia (illustrated). Glass, alcohol, a weight of ... what? A pound?

She turned and found Mrs. Hausen staring at her as if she were a stranger. A frightening stranger. Norma came back and sat down beside her.

"Don't be afraid. I'm only looking for something to get those nails out."

Complete bewilderment. No impression at all.

Norma took her hands. That was better. Then she tried a quiet question.

"Does he let you use the bathroom, Mrs. Hausen?" The old lady's face cleared.

"Oh, yes. But you mustn't go anywhere else, Normie. And you mustn't stay too long. He—"

"Then I'm going to the bathroom. I'll be right back. Will you wait here? Just a little while."

But Mrs. Hausen did not want to part with her. Her face clouded again, her skeletal small fingers tightened. And she began, with a child's random purpose of engaging, "You know, he uses the ... closet in the cellar. I can hear the pipes. Do you think he makes Mr. Hausen go down there too? Because he never comes to the bathroom, Normie. I listen for him, but he never comes."

Norma looked down. She said after a pause, "Perhaps. ... You will wait here, won't you? I'll be right back. Please don't come out?"

The fingers didn't slacken.

"You know, if you lock the door, he won't bring you any tray," Mrs. Hausen confided. "You'd better not lock it anymore, Normie."

"I'll unlock it."

She was allowed free, then. But with reluctance, and the little whisper following, as if to keep her within listening distance.

"He's using all the things out of the freezer, Normie. Everything.... I don't know what Mr. Hausen is going to say ..."

The lock turned with a click. The door opened with another. Mrs. Hausen fell silent, and answering silence came into the room with them.

Norma made no attempt to gauge it. He was not there, immediately in view: that was all she waited to know.

Shutting Mrs. Hausen in, she went down the short space of carpeted hall to the bathroom which lay between the two bedrooms. Its door stood open. She went in and shut it behind her.

In that gloom she stood briefly without moving, finding that she was trembling, not knowing when this had begun. Then she turned on the light. Her first discovery was that she was still wearing her coat, and for some reason this distracted her. She had a brief confusion of wondering what had happened to her handbag and when. There was a little pair of folding scissors in it, a present from Jimmy, faithfully and uselessly carried round....

But this was getting her nowhere.

She began to search the bathroom cabinet. A large bottle of Lysol caught her eye, and she had seized this, taken it down, before she understood the impulse that moved her.

What she was really looking for was a weapon. Not against the nailed blinds—against Cliff. Accepting this, in some wonder, she considered the Lysol. What was it, thrown? Like lye? Blinding, disfiguring?

Slowly, she put the bottle back. A little shudder went through her and she drew a long breath. It was contagious, then. To be with madness, helpless before it, had its own contagion.

Like poor Mr. Hausen, noisily struggling for the telephone. Perhaps it was he who, to an overwrought Cliff, had suddenly seemed mad, to be stopped at any cost. And she could still hear Cliff crying out, when he had thrown her back from the door, *Are you both mad?*

She thought, I'm too tired now. I can't figure this out.

And yet, within her, some conclusion had been reached. She shut the cabinet and stood examining the room itself. A tub occupied the outer wall, with a narrow window over it which was completely blinded. The slats of the blind hung loose. She stepped quickly into the tub, and supporting the bottom slats with one hand she pulled the cord which ran the blind up. Then she saw why Cliff hadn't bothered. The sashes were, many times over, painted to the frame. This window was kept modestly and permanently shut.

She put the blind down again, as quietly, and left the tub. The room. In the hall she went as far as the threshold to the dining room and (like Mrs. Hausen) paused there.

Into unbroken silence, she said, "Cliff."

Her voice fell into deadness, itself died away. After a time she moved a few steps forward, until she could see into the living room. A lamp had been turned on, showing her vacancy, an unguarded front door. She considered it and then turned to consider the closed swing door to the kitchen, which was much nearer.

No running.

She began to walk slowly toward the swing door. Reaching it, not touching it, she said Cliff's name again. When the dull air had totally absorbed this second sound, she pushed the door. Then pushed it wide.

The kitchen was lighted, empty.

Her first reaction was a rise of panic, almost a loss of control. Her inner balance was too tightly guarded to allow of any surprise. Frozen at first, she then found herself halfway back to the bedroom before reason brought her to a stand.

Wherever he was, she could get out.

But Mrs. Hausen.

No. Not time now.

Soundless, fast, she reached the front door and pulled it open. On a shock of darkness. The daylight was gone, and like a beacon their street lamp was burning, steady and safe.

Out on the porch she glimpsed the car at the curb, with its red roof light. It meant nothing to her. Single-minded, incapable of new decision, Norma ran over the frozen lawns toward home.

CHAPTER 15

The little house was like a fortress. Solid doors, solid locks, every window sealed shut with aluminum sash. Even the inner blinds were tightly drawn, revealing only the smallest leak of light from rooms within. This was the only sign of life which the guarded, encircled house gave back to them. There might have been no one at all within.

By now there were three patrol cars out in front, their men dispersed and wary. Still-approaching sirens wailed toward them from various directions. The precinct detectives' car arrived, spilling out its two occupants almost before it had come to a stop. These, striding up Mrs. Moore's walk, were met by two converging patrolmen.

"Any sign of him?"

"No, sir, no sign of anybody. Lady in here, she says he's down in the basement next door. There's a milk door we could—"

"Whose place is it?"

"Some old lady. She's in there, supposed to be, but nobody—"

"All right. What's the milk door?" interrupted the detective, who was young.

The patrolman, who was not, gave him a glance and led the way. All kids, nowadays. Not one of them, he would bet, had ever shaken down a coal furnace in his life.

At the side of the house, he pulled open the cupboard-like aperture by the side door. A further small barrier resisted the detective's pressing hand.

"This is it? It's locked."

"Yes, sir. But that's the weakest bolt in the house. A tire iron—"

"Okay, get one, will you?" he said to his confrere. "Better check round the house, see it's posted. This guy supposed to be armed?"

"Well, he's a killer. Knife, though, I think."

Another patrol car slewed to a stop out in front. The street was beginning to look like a block party, with emerging neighbors, adventure-hunting private cars.

The detective said to an approaching patrolman, "Put those new guys on traffic, will you? Keep it clear. How many men around the house?"

"Six, I think."

"Okay. Everybody on traffic that shows up now—except I need two. But get those damn spooks out of the street before somebody gets shot."

The first patrolman came back with a tire iron.

"Your party," said the detective and stood aside.

They waited restlessly through the brief ensuing crackle of splintering wood. Then they looked in on a square of shadowed wall, reflecting light from above. The patrolman put an arm in, withdrew the side-door bolt, and turned the key in the lock. The opening door showed darkness below, a lighted kitchen above. They were on a half landing.

"The cellar switch'll be up in the kitchen, head of the stairs," said the first patrolman, with melancholy pride.

"Okay, go up and turn it on, will you? Then stay up there—one of you go with him," he said to the two men rapidly approaching. "Take the rest of the house. And watch out for an old lady."

When the cellar lights came on, the two detectives started warily down. Upstairs, with equal caution, the two men moved through an empty kitchen. Looked into a back entryway which had been enclosed and now contained an enormous freezer. Nothing seemed out of place except a man's shirt, worn, thrown over the back of a chair. They looked at this without touching it and moved on.

The swing door pushed open, spilled light into a gloomy dining room. At the farthest edge, in a shadowy aperture, a small and motionless figure stood. A woman. She looked toward them without a word.

They exchanged a glance, and one of them spoke. "You all right, ma'am?"

No answer. One of the men moved toward her, the other branched off to cover the living room.

"Anybody else here with you, lady?"

Couldn't she talk? Her eyes were wide open, watching him come. Then she gave a little whimper, sharp in the quiet.

"Where's Normie?"

"Who?"

"Dame next door, maybe," the first patrolman muttered. He raised his voice. "It's all right, ma'am. She went home. You alone here?"

No answer again. But one bony little hand began to rise, like an urge to communicate. As soon as it touched a sleeve, closed on cloth, she began to whisper.

"Mr. Hausen is in the closet," she told them carefully. "In our bedroom—down there. It's a big closet ... do you think he's all right?"

They exchanged glances again. A wanted man was supposed to be hiding here; what the rest of the deal was, who these people were, no one yet knew. The first step was clearly reinforcements. One of the patrolmen went to open the front door. The other, with surprising difficulty, uprooted the old lady from her post and led her, tottering and protesting, out into the living room. She seemed terrified by the journey.

Then, the way clear, they went with drawn guns down the narrow hall, kicked open the indicated door, and advanced with all caution toward the closed closet and whoever might be hiding there.

Radick came in while they were looking down at him: a small, elderly man, full length on the closet floor. He had been there a long time. There was no immediate way to tell why he had died, but it wasn't their job to say, only to be sure he was dead.

He was very dead.

Radick said nothing. He went back through the house, out of it. The darkness was complete now, it was close to six o'clock. But the entire neighborhood would have to be searched: every house checked, every garage. The space under porches, behind shrubbery, within cars. Either he was very close, Radick thought, or very far. It depended on how much time had gone by.

Sandusky Street, with the warehouse. Or the son's place, out in Dearborn.

Radick sat on in his car, still holding the transmitter, after he had covered everything he could think of. The ambulance arrived, sliding bulkily in ahead of him. He handed the transmitter to the man beside him and pointed.

"I'll be in there."

On the walk, he stopped the intern.

"There's an old lady in there that'd better go to Emergency. Shock, maybe malnutrition, I don't know. She's had a bad time for a couple of days. Her husband's dead in there, she doesn't know it yet. Let her sleep, I'll see her in the morning."

He went up Norma's walk, frowning. Jimmy opened the door before he reached it; his mother and the young policewoman stood just behind him, in equal and silent anxiety.

Radick said in general reassurance, "All right." And as if this were a permission Jimmy burst out, "Did you get him, Lieutenant?"

Radick put his hand on the boy's head, sliding his fingers along the slender nape, as he said to Norma, "Now tell me what happened. When did you go there, how did you get in? In here," he added, herding them out of the hall. "We'll sit down. And take off your coat, Norma. Mine I'll keep," he said to Jimmy's eager help. "Thank you. Go make your mother some coffee, you can do that."

"You haven't found him," said Norma, ignoring her son's backward withdrawal.

"Not yet."

"I knew it. As soon as I could think, I knew he must have left. All that time we were in the bedroom, afraid to move, he must have been gone."

"Then tell me," said Radick. "Also, the times, if you can."

This was something she and Ann had been trying to straighten out between them. She knew now that it was 3:40 when she and Jimmy had arrived home, and then she had taken the Hausens' package next door....

Radick listened, asking an occasional question. How did Cliff look, what was he wearing, how long had he been there? How had he got in?

Radick made a long mouth for the answer to this one, and Norma broke off to ask, "Did you—are the Hausens all right?"

"I sent the old lady to the hospital. Just to rest. Her husband you know about, she told you."

But Norma hadn't quite believed. Couldn't, still. "You mean—really in the closet? But what—she said Cliff just pushed him—"

"Well, we'll know later what happened," he said. "Right now, when did you see this fellow last? Was it light, getting dark?"

She tried to remember, but those gloomily shuttered rooms had been lightless and timeless. There had been no living-room light when she arrived; he must have turned it on when he made ready to leave. The kitchen she didn't know about. The only time she had looked at her watch was when they had first been locked in the bedroom: that had been ten past four. Otherwise she had lost all track of time.

Ann remembered better, she had been more conscious of time. Especially after the unanswered telephone call. She had let Jimmy ring up, she explained, only to give his mother an excuse to leave; up till then it had been a joke. That was at four. Afterward, she had had to decide whether to take the responsibility of calling a patrol car, just because ... She had checked with the telephone company, tried to determine from Jimmy just how peculiar these neighbors were....

"All right," said Radick. "I see your problem. So when did you decide to stick your neck out?"

She had called in at 4:15, Ann said, and the car had arrived at 4:21. Say two or three minutes to make the situation clear, and then the officer had tried for normal entry at the front door. Gone round back, tried again, checked what he could, and come back to Mrs. Moore's door to confer with Ann—all of it taking perhaps ten minutes. And the front of the house under surveillance all that time, of course.

"Then we heard Norma—heard someone coming out, next door, and the minute she told us, we called right in," Ann finished, slightly nervous.

Radick nodded.

"So between 4:10 and 4:20, probably. By the back door and down the alley. Your mother was coming home tonight—you told him?"

"Yes. He didn't—she's on her way now," said Norma, and Radick's look sharpened.

"She called you? When?"

"Just before you came. Not mother, a neighbor—she's staying with the girls, so Tom can drive mother in. They asked her to call and tell me...."

But the girls are out there alone with that neighbor," she said suddenly. "He could be—Cliff could have taken Mr. Hausen's car—!"

"No," said Ann, at once. "It's there."

"Then he could have taken a taxi! There's a stand just—"

She was alive with sudden fear, not knowing its source, nor how to defend against it—finding only new reasons to fear, with every shift of thought.

Radick rose, saying firmly, "The children are all right, Norma. There are men all around that house by now, they should always be so safe. Don't be afraid for them. And your mother will be safe here. Say, fifteen minutes ago the neighbor called. They just left?"

"I—don't know. She just said they were on their way ..."

"All right, in less than an hour your mother will be home, right? And we'll give your brother an escort back. In fact," he added, to her rising distress, "describe your brother's car to me. We can pick them up on the way in."

She said instantly, "It's a Ford. Blue, a two-door sedan. About four—five years old." There was a desolate small pause before she confessed, "I don't know what Tom's license is."

Radick said kindly, "All right. Don't worry. Go help the boy with that coffee now. And drink some."

Norma obeyed, not caring that he wanted to speak privately to Ann before he left. What difference did it make? All she could think of was Tom's little house, Tom's car innocently journeying home with her mother in it. Surely the police would warn the neighbor? Or should Norma herself call and say ... what? Without throwing the woman into a panic?

She came into the kitchen, and Jimmy's flustered voice said at once, "It's all right—I don't need help." But she scarcely heard him, saw without interest that he was down on the floor wiping something up.

Six-thirty. Then they should arrive by seven-thirty. Before that. But not after, unless they stopped. Only why would they stop? Surely there was no way in which Cliff, even if he had somehow acquired a car, could make her brother's car stop. Could make Tom get out....

She said suddenly, "What's Uncle Tom's license number, Jimmy?" He, looking up in surprise, told her a series of numbers and letters which she took back at once to Radick, who was just going out the door. He sent Jimmy his congratulations.

Somehow this cleared her mind. She could even smile for her son, standing over a muddy sink with the ruined tea towel in his grip.

"It's cooking now," he said quickly. "But it'll be a little while."

"That's fine," she said. "You're wonderful. And starving, aren't you?"

She glanced at the clock again, but only from habit, and opened the refrigerator door.

CHAPTER 16

It wasn't the most convenient time in the world to leave the girls, Mrs. Moore thought, and she would have liked to get one more good meal inside Tommy, too, before she went. But if this was when the neighbor could come, well, there wasn't much choice. After the girls' bedtime would have been so much better, though. In case they made a fuss.

They weren't making any fuss at the moment. Alone in Cassie's room, rearranging her zip bag so it would close all the way, Mrs. Moore could hear tranquil dinner-table sounds from the nearby kitchen. Remarkably tranquil, in fact. Except that Cassie was singing instead of eating.

The zip bag just wasn't going to. Mrs. Moore wedged a facecloth in the opening, to keep little things from falling out, and straightened her hat. This was all. Tommy had already taken out her big suitcase and the comforter, and she was temporarily leaving her empty preserve basket for her eldest granddaughter, who had made a doll bed out of it. Her own bed was made up freshly, for the woman coming in tomorrow. At ruinous expense. And what the poor babies would make of that...

A teary sting at her eyes took Mrs. Moore by surprise. What nonsense—cry when you leave home, cry when you go back, she thought severely. I suppose at my age you just cry if you have to move at all.

She glanced at her watch, seeing that it was only five-thirty, although so dark! But that was late enough, considering how far they had to go, and Tommy must be getting impatient. She went briskly out into the kitchen, where three little faces turned toward her, as did the neighbor's.

"Well, this is awfully nice of you, Jean," Mrs. Moore said, keeping her eyes firmly on the neighbor's face, which was pleasant and young and perfectly calm. "We'll be as quick as we can, but I expect it'll be a couple of hours."

"That's all right, Mrs. Moore. We aren't going out till eight-thirty, and I'm a fast dresser."

"I think I left everything where you can find it."

"Don't give it a thought, we pinch-hit all the time around here."

"Well, we appreciate it," said Mrs. Moore. Cassie was beginning to make questioning sounds; the other two were ominously silent. Their grandmother went quickly round the table, with a firm kiss for each, and then opened the back door. Cassie let out a tentative wail.

"Be good girls, now," said Mrs. Moore blindly and kept going. Along that rickety little covered way, whatever they called it, breezeway, and into the garage door.

The lights were turned on, and shone in her eyes, and the motor was running, so she couldn't hear a thing from the house. Just as well, probably. The only way was to leave very quickly, never go back. When they heard the car drive out they would know it was no use. She backed in the open car door as hastily as she could, the only way to get in these modern cars, and even then your hat always....

"Go on, Tommy, go on," she said, leaving the hat tipsy till she got her coat inside the door so that it would shut properly. And then that nasty little zip bag slid off, somewhere around her feet, but there was only the one "plop"—the washcloth must be holding. If she could only pick it up carefully....

"Go on, dearie," she panted, groping with one hand, holding her hat back with the other, but he just sat there. She had no more breath, but cast an impatient glance at his legs.

Her groping hand stopped.

Still in that crouch, from behind her own raised arm, Mrs. Moore peered timidly upward. Because it was not Tommy. For that one moment, not anybody real. Just, impossibly, not Tommy.

Then each of them made a sound. The man said one shaken word: "*Please ...*" and her immediate answer, quite involuntary, was a sound such as Cassie might have made. In the night, dreaming.

Both of them moved, then—she in a galvanic attempt to straighten, still clutching the hat, while he suddenly turned from her to the car's controls. They began to shoot backward out of the garage.

The fast motion threw her forward again. Both her hands flew out, the hat fell over her face at last. But in one moment of perfect vision, with the headlights flooding the empty garage, Mrs. Moore saw her son's wide eyes staring back at her. He was crouching or sitting in the corner by the other door, where the car had hidden him from her, and the bottom of his face was all tightly covered!

She screamed then: "*Tommy!*" and the backing car made a wild swerve that seemed the preliminary swing to a total capsize. Somehow it wasn't. They slewed into the street instead, jolted to a dead stop, and then began to rush forward through the suburban darkness.

Mrs. Moore found both her hands clapped over her own mouth. Her eyes felt the way Tommy's had looked: as if they would never close again. Another car was shooting toward them, another glare of headlights with a winking red light above it. By the time she sorted this out and turned her head sharply, the car was past: a dark blur, there might as well have been bears driving it.

What she did see, in the dashboard lights, was Cliff's face. Tears were pouring down it—really pouring. His whole face looked drenched and shiny. He turned and met her stare briefly, but without caring that he was seen—perhaps even to make sure that she saw? In any case, she went on staring—unable to stop, unable to speak; and the car flew on through winding suburban streets.

She suddenly managed his name: "*Cliff!*" and an answering sound burst from him. Not a word nor anything she could define. The car swerved again, jolted and swerved. She regained her balance in a dizzying vacuum: the car had stopped.

He had fallen forward, she thought he was vomiting. Then she saw his arms round his head, his hands clutched in his own hair, and knew these were sobs. He was crying, crying too hard to drive, crying as she had not known a man could cry.

A whole lifetime of impulse died in her, with this knowledge: the instinctive impulse to comfort and draw close. No closeness was possible to such wild isolation. They were as separate as if each had been enclosed in glass. Or as if one of them were real and the other a violent vision on a screen.

She stared now at her own hands, clutching her hat in her lap, and still all she saw there—anywhere—was Tommy's eyes staring after her, in the bouncing shine of the moving headlights. Staring. She made her own eyes close; and in this relief—as if the relief were Tommy's, too—she spoke again.

"Cliff, no. *No.*"

He heard her. His body began to rock and then flung backward, his head against the seat back with his guardian elbows now sticking up into air. The sounds were worse, unmuffled, and beat hoarse and monotonous on her mind like an exhausted child's screaming.

She could not touch him. Nor speak to those sounds.

Instead, putting out a timid hand, she pushed down on the curving bar in the steering wheel. That was the horn, on Tommy's car. It worked at once, sending out a long, one-note blare of sound into the night. She kept it sounding; and as if her vision were widened by the burst quiet she could see that they were still in some suburb. Perhaps Tommy's. The houses were more infrequent, but they were there. There was one not more than a hundred yards away, with little lights shining in it.

With her hand on the horn, her eyes on these lights, she sat and thought: Tommy. Her whole purpose was in his name; the noisy agonies beside her were only something that would have to stop before her purpose could begin.

They were stopping. Cliff was straightening, bringing his arms down. He removed her hand, a fumbling impersonal touch as if to correct some mechanical fault, and she did not resist. In the renewed silence he took out a handkerchief and wiped his face, blew his nose, attended to himself in an automatic way like a man alone. He still made diminishing sounds of grief, but these seemed automatic too, of no interest to him.

When he leaned to start the car again she said, "Cliff, you must take me back there. I must see to Tommy. Now, Cliff. Take me back now."

He did not answer, but still sighing, still brushing at his face, put the car into a slower forward motion. She might not have been there at all.

She began to insist, talking urgently to the hat in her lap. Not touching him.

"Cliff, I cannot go anywhere until I know Tommy is all right. I mean it. Now take me back there, right now."

He said dully, "We can't go back. You know that."

Her control broke. She cried, "You did something to Tommy—"

"I didn't. I didn't. There's nothing the matter with him. *There's nothing the matter with him.*"

Warned, she lowered her voice as his voice rose. But hers had begun to tremble.

"You did. He couldn't get up. And he couldn't say anything—"

"It's only clothesline," he said sullenly. "And a scarf. It's his own fault, I tried to talk to him, and he behaved like a madman. It's entirely his own fault." He frowned then, and said, "Your comforter got soiled on the garage floor. We'll have to have it cleaned."

She was silenced by the picture this evoked: of Tommy, laden with comforter and suitcase, backing into the garage, pulling the door to behind him. And Cliff suddenly at his elbow, saying one of those mad, polite things into poor Tommy's ear....

"I want to know if you hit him, Cliff," she said with sudden anger. "You must have hit him. Didn't you?"

He drove, ignoring her.

"I want the truth," she said sternly. "Did you hit him?"

He said suddenly, in a high voice, "The truth is that *I don't hit people.* I'm not a savage, and you know it! If I have to defend myself I will, I have the right to defend myself, anyone has that right! What are you talking to me this way for, as if you didn't know I—*as if you believed them—*"

His voice broke. In the silence that fell between them, she looked away at last, out the car window.

They were going faster now, on some small road she did not know. The groupings of houses were gone; she could not tell where they were going or even in what direction.

All the same, he must have hit Tommy. But it could not have been too hard a blow, or Tommy's eyes would not have been open. And his eyes had been open. She clung to that last vision now, as she had once tried to escape from it: Tommy's wide eyes, seeing, knowing what he saw....

"Cliff, stop this," she said abruptly. "I can't talk to you this way. I can't even think. Take me back. You can come with me. There's no sense in this."

"I didn't choose it," he answered at once. "Do you think I would behave this way if there were any other way—if they'd left me any other way—*if there were anything left?* You know how we used to live," he cried out, with sudden passion. "How quiet it was, the way we wanted it—the way that we are. And *whatever they've told* you, I only tried—I only wanted to wait for you, the same way, just to wait.... Do you know that I had to come in by the *garage*, to see you tonight? That I had to leave the taxi in another *street*, like some—like a stupid *burglar*, and come through backyards and creep into a garage—and even then, they— Do you know where I've had to wait for you, all this time?"

He wanted an answer, turned to receive it. Her hands moved on the hat; it was all she could manage.

"Do you know where I've been, what I've had to do?" he demanded.

"No," she said, very low.

"Shut up with an old, old woman—caring for her, keeping her alive. Cooking her food, carrying it in and out on trays—a horrible, helpless, half-witted old creature, I—I don't want to think about her, I don't even want to think of it. But I waited," he said. "I waited.... And then tonight she came, because she knew you were coming back, she came and she said ... *invited* me," he said, with such bitterness, such loathing, that she looked back at him. "As if you wouldn't know, then, how she— But I don't bear tales, I never have. You know that I don't. But I have the right to defend myself *in my own way*, against ..."

He fell silent, his lips working. She went on looking at him, in growing astonishment.

"Cliff, I don't understand who you're talking about," she said finally. "What old woman?"

"It doesn't matter. I don't want to talk about it. But that was when I knew," he said, with quieter emphasis. "There was no use waiting anymore. I couldn't go back there. I couldn't let you go back. There's nothing there anymore, for us. It's all destroyed. We'll never go back again," he said quietly.

She went on looking at him.

Presently, and as quietly, she asked, "Then where are we going?"

"I thought of Vermont."

She made no sound. He glanced toward her.

"Do you know Vermont?"

"No."

"I've been thinking of it all the time, recently. Sometimes I think it's all that's kept me sane. Those old villages, so quiet, and orderly, and clean. The old houses, with their gardens—you'll love them. They're your kind of house. You'll see. We'll be very happy there."

He said after a while, in a lower voice, "There's one thing I ought to tell you"—and she felt a stab of such fear that it was like pain. Physically like pain. No—don't, she thought ... but no sound came out.

He went on, "I'm not—I'm finished with my profession. I've known for years that it wasn't—it isn't my world, a world I can live in anymore. Because the people are ... But it doesn't matter," he said. "It makes no difference. I can do so many things, there's so much that needs to be done. We'll be all right, I promise you."

He was a different man, now, from the hysterical, sobbing creature who had first greeted her. Even his breathing had grown slow and even, with no more of the catches and deep sighs of recent weeping. He was quite calm, relaxed, even drowsy-seeming. He had begun to yawn, at intervals.

Yet neither of these was the Cliff whom Mrs. Moore had thought she knew. With a growing and timid wonder, she found herself watching him as he drove. What clue she looked for, what hope she could take from such a clue, she did not know; but she could not stop. And he did not seem to mind her attention. After a particularly deep yawn he would glance her way with a little smile, in apology.

"This doesn't really mean I'm sleepy, don't worry," he said. "I seem to have given up sleeping. I just have spells of feeling rather groggy, and then they pass."

She murmured, "Perhaps you should ... stop and have some coffee."

"Perhaps," he agreed.

An increase in her heart's beat made Mrs. Moore look away, in a confusion of duplicity. Would he stop? Would they really go into an ordinary lunchroom, like the two ordinary travelers he seemed to think they were? She tried not to show any more interest, but she could not help looking fixedly ahead now, down the dark road they were traveling.

It was not one of those wide highways Tommy always took, if they were going any distance. She did not know what road it was nor what to expect from it—only that it did not seem to be much traveled or populated. The infrequent lights ahead always turned out to be houses.

Then she saw red neon lighting and watched it come nearer in desperate and silent attention. Gasoline pumps. But the neon was on the house behind these, so surely ... Yes. A little restaurant, or bar.

Something.

She said, low, "I think that's a place," and Cliff turned his head sharply.

"What?"

"A place for coffee."

He slowed a little and glanced out, but not as if he meant to stop.

She added with an urgency that she could not help, "And gas, too. Don't you want some gas?"

He swung off the road then, not answering, beginning to frown again.

They were on the opposite side of the road. Mrs. Moore didn't say a word or look at him. Nor did she look across the road for fear he should see her expression.

The car moved again. More slowly. Turned, to cross the road, and bumped over the rough surface by the lighted tanks. Kept going, to a darker area where other cars were parked outside the restaurant.

Here they drew up, and Cliff turned off the motor.

CHAPTER 17

She could not open her door enough to get out. They were too close to the car beside them. She looked helplessly back at Cliff and saw that he was rapidly combing his hair, straightening his tie and coat.

He said in a curious, breathless voice, without turning his head, "Please stay here, I'll see what it's like. Just wait here a minute, please."

"But I want to go in, Cliff. I want—"

"Please. I'll be right back."

He was out of the car then, in a fast, lithe movement that surprised her. Shutting the car door firmly he ran over the ground and up the wooden steps—was inside the place, whatever it was, before her surprise subsided. She had not known he could move like that!

But it didn't matter. She knew (because of the children) that it was not possible to lock anyone inside the car from the outside. She had only to get across the seat and push the handle in order to get out.

This was easier in thought than in deed. Her body, so sturdy and serviceable that she scarcely thought of it these many years, now revealed itself as utterly unsuitable for the kind of fast action she had in mind. How could it be this difficult, and slow, only to crawl across a car seat and under the wheel? Gasping a little, tangled and bruised by the wheel's contact, she leaned at last to push the door handle—only to see, as it yielded, the restaurant door partially open and Cliff appear.

He did not come out. Nor did he glance her way. He just stood there, like a man taking stock of the weather. So that she could see him?

Astonished, chilled by this performance, Mrs. Moore let her hand slide from the door handle. As if aware of this, Cliff disappeared again.

She leaned there a moment, breathing unevenly, then brought her body as nearly as possible upright under the wheel. And opened the door. She had one foot on the ground and was struggling with the rest of herself when he came out again.

This time he came clear out and over to her. She watched him with despair. How could anyone move that way, without even trying?

She said at once, with what breath she had, "I'm coming in to the ladies' room," but he paid no attention.

"We'll have to leave. I'm sorry. Please get back in."

She didn't move.

"I'll just go in to the—"

"No. Please get back!"

Even if she had wanted to obey, Mrs. Moore felt that she had exhausted her capacity to move for the moment. And she did not want to obey.

He leaned down, lifted her foot, and replaced it in the car. Not gently.

She said in startled protest, "*Cliff—!*" but he was saying again, in that rapid, high voice, "I'm sorry, but we'll have to leave. Please get back. *Get back!*"

It was as if he were speaking to someone else. As if she were no longer there at all.

The restaurant door opened again, and a man in a checked flannel shirt came out. Cliff shut the car door and turned with his back to it. The man saw him and started forward, saying, "I'll have to charge you for the can. Deposit. When you bring it back—" He stopped and then said in some surprise, "Is that your car? Why, we can roll that back to the pumps, you don't—"

Then Cliff hit him. He stooped, picked something up, and hit the man—all in one movement, all at once.

The man's face looked the way Mrs. Moore felt—totally unbelieving. Then, grimacing, the man made a stumbling lurch forward. Cliff hit him again. This time the man fell forward on the ground. Cliff turned at once and came back to the car.

Mrs. Moore's hand came up at the same time his did, on the other side of the glass. She pushed down the little button that locked the door. That was supposed to lock the door, from the inside.

She saw now that it did.

Cliff stood holding the handle that would not yield and stared in at her. He didn't make a sound, nor did she. A pop bottle still dangled from his other hand—that was what he had hit the man with, a pop bottle. From the rack of empties. In a moment, Mrs. Moore thought numbly, he will break the window with it too.

But he had no need to do that. After a moment he straightened and let the pop bottle drop and thrust his hand into his coat pocket. For the keys. He would have a key that would force the button up.

Even if she continued to push it down?

Her hand had not moved away; it didn't now. She felt the little button beneath her finger trying to rise and pushed back hard, concentrating all her attention on it. Someone's breathing was audible, but nothing else—until a queer stifled sound just outside the car warned her, and she saw Cliff's distorted face sinking downward beyond the glass, with another, equally distorted face rising behind it. Then a plaid-covered arm swung forward, and both men fell.

She could only hear them. Dreadfully, horribly, she could hear them, on the ground beside the car. She could not bring herself to look; but abandoning the door button, she got her hand onto the bar that sounded Tommy's horn and kept it there, until the restaurant door opened.

It was the most embarrassing time of Mrs. Moore's entire life.

To feel such a trivial emotion at such a time, with Cliff held down huddled and sobbing there on the ground and the other man wild with pain and rage, added to her shame; but she could not help it.

Because of course they knew nothing about her. And for quite a few moments after they got her to open the car door (it was only confusion and fright that kept her from opening it right away) they must have thought she was talking about Cliff. When she kept saying, over and over, "Please call my son's house—please let me call my son's house, he's hurt. He's been hurt!" All those suspicious, staring faces. She had not known other people could stand in a circle and look at you like that. Perhaps they thought she was like that mother with the gangster sons, Ma Whatever-it-was. And with her hat off and all mussed and crumpled....

At the time she hadn't even considered what they might think, if she could just get to a telephone. But they wouldn't let her go anywhere, they would hardly listen to her, except as a dreadful kind of curiosity. The man in the plaid shirt kept saying. "Nobody moves—nobody goes anywhere, we wait right here till they come!" She knew he must be half-savage with shock and pain, she didn't blame him, but his loud angry voice went on, telling his grievance over and over. "Why, the bastard, I just come out to give him the can of gas, and he—just got me outside and was standing there waiting with that empty—just swung on me the minute I—"

And Cliff on the ground, abandoned to weeping. Beginning to moan, "Help me ... help me ..." to the pebbled rough ground they held him against. When she noticed how they were holding him, she couldn't help protesting—there wasn't any need at all to hold him down like that, anybody could see that. But they were incapable of looking, at least with normal vision. Incapable of hearing or understanding anything; just a ring of staring, alien eyes and greedy ears.

Her embarrassment had sunk into a dull horror by the time the police car arrived. Even then, for a while, nothing changed. She sat there, in her limbo, and the loud talk and the moaning went on eddying round her.

And then everything changed. One of the policemen came up to the car and, bending down, said to her, "You're Mrs. Moore?"

His voice was different. She was restored to her innocent identity, to the rest of humankind again. But the shock had been too great.

Her eyes filled with tears. She murmured, "Tommy ... please, Tommy ..." and felt her head sink against his shoulder, and then nothing more.

She never saw Cliff again.

He was gone when she was finally helped from the car; gone long before that, probably. Even before she became aware of the glass they were urging her to drink from, of the voice kindly repeating, "Your son is all right, Mrs. Moore. He's been worried about you too, but now he knows you're all right. We've just been in touch with him, it's all right."

It was spirits, in the glass. Her eyes stung with it, her throat burned. But she managed to gasp "Thank you" and to see past the helping policeman the same circle of staring eyes. No longer hostile, she understood that. Perhaps even sympathetic. But she couldn't bear to meet any of them, just then. And that was when, looking down, she saw the place on the ground where Cliff had been.

An unreasonable fright made her ask at once, "Where's Cliff?"

Well, he was in police custody, of course. Her wits told her that, even before they did. And there was nothing more to fear. And she wouldn't have to see him again.

But some memory of that rough holding made her pause and murmur to the policeman, "You know, he isn't—he isn't right. You know that."

He said they did.

Oddly, Cliff fell right out of her mind after that. What she wanted, almost to the point of obsession, was to get back to Tommy and see him with her own eyes. Feel him with her own hands, hear him speak. When this finally came about, she couldn't get enough of it—just seeing him, the way he ought to be, instead of tied up (or tied down) and staring in that awful way.

Tommy began to protest, after a while.

He said, "But the poor guy hasn't got any punch at all, mother. I never was completely out—if I hadn't had all that stuff, and the damn comforter unwinding all around me ... He sure was quick with the rope, though," Tommy added thoughtfully. "Should have been a sailor. I never saw anything like it."

They didn't know then about Mr. Hausen. Or the woman in Chicago.

Mrs. Moore was at home, the next day, before she learned the real measure of Cliff's desperate activities. And she made Norma go over the whole thing with her. Not so they could sit there, in her bedroom, and talk about it: neither of them wanted that. Any more than they wanted to talk to newspaper people, or solicitous friends, or even the rest of their own family. But they had to work out, between them, as much as they could of the truth—the tragic and terrible truth. That was something they needed to be clear about, together, so that each of them would understand as well as possible and would know the other understood. Then that was enough.

Yet, like the image of Tommy in the garage, that of Cliff as she had last seen him kept recurring in Mrs. Moore's quiet hours. For a long time. There wasn't the helpless urgency of the Tommy vision, that dream feeling of needing to move and not being able to. No; in recollection as in fact, Mrs. Moore did not try to reach Cliff. But she continued to hear him, crying "Help me ... help me ..." into the ground; and closing her eyes, sitting very still, would add her soundless voice to his: "Lord, help him. Help him."

Radick was downtown when they brought Cliff in, and he got a considerable surprise. For Cliff in exhaustion, in the stillness of dead end, had got back the looks he must have started with.

At least, Radick supposed that was it. No description so far had prepared him for the aloof young man he saw now, with his large, steady eyes, his small full mouth firmly held. Cliff looked about twenty-five. Ill-used, of course, and aware of it, but with his own reserves.

He had nothing to say about the Moores; nothing could goad him to acknowledge even their name. But the Chicago charge, on which he was being removed almost immediately, brought a flush of anger to his face.

He said at once, and coldly, "I have a great deal to say about that, in the proper time and place, and I'm perfectly willing to do so. There's been no need for all this—humiliating disorder. I had every intention of reporting the whole disgusting episode myself, as soon as I am in a ... as I am capable, and well ... and I am capable of defending myself, and

I have every right to defend myself."

"With twenty-three stab wounds?" inquired the man from Chicago. Cliff stared at him.

He said, remotely, "I don't accept your language, or your concepts. Or your manner, or your sources of information. I have nothing more to say to you."

And he had not.

But when Radick talked to him about Hausen—an old man with a broken neck, lying for two days in that closet—Cliff was terribly shaken. Confusion destroyed his proud looks; it was as though his mind had not had time to absorb and transmute such an idea. Had neglected even to try. Radick believed that he quite honestly could not remember who the man was.

And yet feared he might.

"But it was an old *female* person I stayed with," he protested, tight with panic. "My dear man, I *fed* the creature— I had to do the simplest things for it, it was simply and totally incapable of ... I kept it *alive*, I tell you! *An old woman.*"

Radick was almost sorry to see him go off to Chicago, on their prior (and graver) charge. He would have been interested to hear what Cliff had made of Hausen by next morning.

CHAPTER 18

Bill Bennig offered to take Jimmy over to his sister-in-law's the next day, Saturday, which seemed to Norma an extraordinarily thoughtful idea for a bachelor to have. The minute he suggested it, her tired mind seized on the idea with relief. Ann was gone; she and her mother could just shut up the house and pull themselves together in adult peace.

Nevertheless she hesitated, not quite knowing why. "But would he want to go, Bill? He might feel strange."

"Well, ask him," he said, reasonable.

Jimmy wanted to go. Whether it was to see this fascinating family whose father was in a penitentiary, or to have unchecked access to Bennig for a while, or just to get some action, Bennig didn't know; but Jimmy accepted instantly. This of course put an end to Norma's hesitation, but not, he thought, to the doubts that underlaid it.

He had his own doubts. He understood hers very well, even if she did not. Taking Norma's boy for the day, and into the heart of his own guarded private life, was an offer of intimacy more than he had yet made or she accepted. He had made it deliberately, and by now he knew

Norma well enough to be sure that her acceptance would have meaning too, however tired and uncertain she might be.

But it was not an easy step, for either of them. Past thirty, weighed down with old loyalties, it just wasn't easy.

And now he had Ginny to watch. Because his sister-in-law was "thrilled"—that was what she had said when he had talked to her about bringing Jimmy over, and he didn't doubt that she meant it. In her own way she was just as bad as Radick about any girl he showed interest in. A little worse, maybe, out of some crazy guilt feeling. He would have to watch it.

He caught himself in a short, hard sigh and saw Jimmy, beside him in the car, watching him sideways. He grinned, and Jimmy said at once, a little anxiously, "I forgot their names, Mr. Bennig."

Bill told him their names. And their ages and something about each. Then Jimmy asked, diffident, "Is it—do they say anything about their father?"

"Yes, of course." Bill added, "I'd let them bring it up, though. One of them probably will. They don't go to visit him, but they all write letters a lot, back and forth."

"Yes, sure," Jimmy said quickly. He continued to watch Bill, but more directly. Then he said, "Mother and I talk about my father a lot. Grandma doesn't, though. Maybe it's because she didn't know him too well, we always lived in Wisconsin."

"What did he die of, Jim?"

"Meningitis," said Jimmy, as directly. But nothing more.

"That's a bad one."

"Yes." He asked, not quite so directly, "You didn't know my father, did you?"

"No, Jim. I didn't even know your mother until last year. We're all new to each other."

"That was what I thought," said Jimmy. "I wasn't sure, though."

"You were right."

On this sober understanding, they tackled the rest of the Bennigs together. It wasn't too bad. Bill had overlooked his sister-in-law's main virtues, from an eleven-year-old boy's view: she was a meltingly pretty blonde, and she dispensed food tirelessly. Good food. So no trouble there. Sheila was annoying for a while, in and out with a couple of other giggly thirteens, and young Bill had to have some quiet disciplining in the kitchen a couple of times. But Rob, solidly obsessed like his father, took Jimmy firmly into his room where his elaborate train set lived and kept him there. Apparently it was all right. The couple of times Jim wandered out, it was just to make sheep's eyes at Ginny and collect more nourishment. Then he went back. Around two, when he heard Jim saying "Beat it" to young Bill through a crack in the door, Bill decided it was all right to take a nap. He came down at four to find the house completely empty and a note on the refrigerator: GONE SKATING. BACK SOON.

No time or signature, of course. The writing could have been anyone's except Rob's, who wrote very well. Bill made himself coffee and a snack. Around five he called Norma and explained the delay. They were supposed to be back around five.

She sounded much better, but a little anxious still.

"Has it been all right?" she asked.

"Well," he said, spreading it a little, "it's all right unless you want him back. I think they're planning to keep him."

She laughed then—a real, audible laugh of pleasure.

It was nearly six when Ginny's car came into the drive, and an incredible number of people got out. Some of them scattered into the dark, and the ones that belonged there trooped in, very noisy and pink. Bill saw that he hadn't been spreading it much; young Jim was definitely one of the ones that belonged.

"You should see him skate, Uncle Bill," said Sheila. "He's absolutely boss. Isn't he, Rob?"

"He's better than us," said Rob matter-of-factly, opening the refrigerator. "What's for dinner?"

"Steaks," said Ginny. "Bill, honey, just stick them in? I'll be right back."

He took the steaks out obediently, still smiling, making some remark; and then all at once the kitchen was quiet, and there was nobody in it except himself and Jimmy, looking at him.

"Are we going to stay, Mr. Bennig?" he asked politely. Suddenly polite.

Bill turned on the broiler.

"Well, whatever you like, Jim. I talked to your mother, she knows why we're late. But it's up to you."

Jimmy wanted to leave. All of a sudden, full of triumph, he was full of doubt too. He wanted to touch home base again. But he didn't like to say so. He said nothing.

"Why don't we eat and run?" Bill suggested. "These steaks look pretty good."

"Could we do that?"

"Sure, why not?"

"Okay, fine," said Jimmy, and was all right again. It was that quick. That strange.

They were on the road by seven, due more to Bill's firmness than the boy's. There had been a strong drift back to the train room after dinner, but Bill remembered that look and got them going.

In the car he said, "So you're a pretty good skater, are you?"

"Just medium. Everybody skates in Wisconsin." He added presently, "My father was good."

"Did he teach you?"

"Yes."

He was getting up nerve to say something else. It took quite a while, but he got it out.

"Is that your house, Mr. Bennig? Where we were?"

"No," said Bill. "It's my brother's. I live in an apartment."

"Oh. I thought you sort of lived there, like their father. It sort of sounded like that."

"No, I just visit there, Jim. Like their uncle."

"It's a nice place to visit," said Jimmy politely.

After a day of perfect accord, and considerable success, they were back at polite distance. Accepting his disappointment, Bill acknowledged the reason for it: he had hoped to bring back a glowing boy, testimonial to his fine relatives and his own sure touch with the young. Instead, the kid looked like he'd been chained in a cellar all day. Well, it wasn't easy. Any of it.

He said mildly, "Okay, Jim. Nearly there," and getting no answer, discovered that Jimmy had gone to sleep. Or seemed so.

At least he didn't fling himself on his mother, when they got there. Or even his grandmother. The one he seemed most interested in was Radick, who happened to be there. And who had brought his wife.

Their cordial approval finished Bill. He suddenly felt the way Jimmy looked, standing there being lovingly handled, encouraged to speak up when he had nothing left to say. The boy was the lucky one: he got sent upstairs. Bill got a chair between Mrs. Moore, still trying to make head or tail of him, and Radick.

He looked at Radick. Just a look; but Radick began to explain their presence.

"Well, we just dropped by on our way downtown, Bill. Make sure everybody's all right."

"It's very nice of you both," said Mrs. Moore. "You've all been so kind. And thank you for telling me about Mrs. Hausen, Mr. Radick. You're sure it's all right for me to go and see her tomorrow?"

"Sure, do her good. She's all right, you know. Except she's still sort of looking around for her husband. Maybe you can get her to understand about that. I wouldn't mention the broken neck, right away. Let her think it's heart, maybe."

"Yes," said Mrs. Moore, a breathless sound. "Yes, I—I will."

"Maybe you can get her to let you make the funeral arrangements. They don't have any people, right? No use leaving the poor fellow down in the morgue any longer than we have to."

Mrs. Moore seemed incapable of reply. Unfortunately no one else said anything either.

Then, in the silence, Mrs. Moore raised her head. She said firmly, "I wish you would tell me one thing, Mr. Radick."

"What's that, ma'am?"

"What could I have done—what should I have done, to stop—these terrible things from happening?"

"Nothing," said Norma quickly. "There wasn't anything anyone could have done, was there?"

Her mother paid no attention. She sat with her eyes fixed on Radick's face.

He considered, then said gravely, "Well, I can think of one thing. You could have raised him from a pup. That's about all."

Tears came into Mrs. Moore's eyes. She got up, murmuring, "Excuse me, I'll get us some coffee ..." and left the room.

Mrs. Radick, smiling at Norma, began to button her coat. Radick considered this signal without moving. Then he called out toward the kitchen.

"Don't bother about us, Mrs. Moore. We can't stay." To Norma he added, "Guess you people have had enough of this, right? Well, it's over. Forget it. Get out and take a ride, maybe—you got a new baby to go see, isn't that right? Boy or girl?"

Norma told him a niece, and he nodded. Pushed himself up.

"Well, that's the best thing you could do. Go see the baby. Maybe Bill here could drive you out."

Bill said nothing. A little embarrassed for him, Norma took the Radicks to the door and shook hands with them both.

"You're a lovely girl, dear," Mrs. Radick murmured. "Your mother must be proud."

She squeezed Norma's hand and passed it to Radick, who kept it. And leaned to murmur, in his turn, "Don't mind him—he never took anybody over there before, it's hard for him. You know?" The jerk of his head said Bill—still presumably standing in a corner of the living room.

Norma could find no immediate reply. Radick smiled at her.

"All right. I know what you're thinking. A handsome boy, right? Very smart, good job, big heart ... but all this stuff with Roy and Ginny and the kids! And on top of that he's got to take care of the whole world! So what's left over for you? Right?"

"Believe me, Norma," he whispered, before she could draw breath, "this is nothing. Nothing! You know what ends it? The first kid. I know this, believe me. I was the same way."

"So what ended with you?" his wife murmured.

"Please, Sophie. I'm talking."

But he was through talking. Bill was in the hall with them.

He said simply, "You're leaving or me?" and Radick's smile became a snarl.

"Good-bye *schnook*," he said, and bundled his calm wife out the door.

When Norma turned round, Bill was still standing there. He looked as if she had just shut him in.

She said gently, "Don't fuss, Bill. I didn't mind. I like them."

"I love them," he said gloomily. "And I guess they go with me. Like Roy and the rest of it. If we ever got as far as a wedding, they'd take it over. You realize that."

She considered this, as if it were rational speech, and then said, "Jimmy wore you out, didn't he?"

"No. And he did have a good time. All day."

"Well, I'm glad. It was a big thing for him. We hardly see anybody, any more. He misses that."

He said in a low voice, "Shouldn't we ... won't your mother be wondering where we are? Or maybe I'd better go, she seemed pretty upset."

Norma murmured back, "No, she's making coffee, we'd better have some." Then she said, in her own voice, "You're making me nervous, Bill. It's just mother!"

"Your mother," he replied.

They looked at each other seriously, there in the small hallway, with its quiet lamp hardly disturbing the shadows. She was still pale, with darkness round her eyes, and he reached out and drew his finger down the outline of her cheek.

She said, "It's hard, isn't it, Bill? You can almost understand about people like Cliff that stop trying. To meet somebody else halfway, I mean. Because even mother wasn't real for him. Not the way he thought of her. He just made my mother up," she said steadily. "And that was all he had ..."

"I know. But don't cry."

After a minute, he leaned and kissed her. She came toward him, close within his arms. Then a sound from the kitchen brought his head up.

He said, beginning to smile, "Come on. Let's go meet your mother halfway and drink the coffee. Then I'll beat it. Only don't cry?"

"No ..."

He kept his arm round her till they reached the swing door, then pushed that open, and followed her into the kitchen.

THE END

A Friend of Mary Rose
Elizabeth Fenwick

Chapter 1

On the day they were to move, Mr. Nicholas rose in darkness at his
usual hour. An unacceptably early hour, he knew, to the adolescents and
middle-aged adults with whom he lived; but rather late for his cat.

This cat, an illegal companion at night, started Mr. Nicholas off every
day with the same problem: to get it downstairs undiscovered. It was
a wretched cat, as a co-conspirator, and moreover very lively and
hungry at this hour. It would not let itself be caught and carried down.
So the moment he opened his door he had to be ready to follow, and
follow fast—the slightest pause meant yowls, and yowls meant the end
of his game. For Mr. Nicholas had his scruples. He would not have taken
the cat up at night with him, if she had actually told him not to. And
as soon as she knew, she would of course tell him not to.

Fortunately, they were all heavy sleepers. But this morning, as soon
as he opened his door, he heard his daughter-in-law's voice. Awake
already! Behind the closed bedroom door her quick voice was already
talking, talking—talking his poor son out of sleep, no doubt. Mr.
Nicholas, who had been waking to silence and solitude for years now
(until he thought of the cat), listened sardonically a moment. That
moment was too long; the cat cried out to hurry him.

In the deep quiet of the upstairs hall, the cry sounded incredibly loud.
Providentially, the cat pressed against his leg just then, and he gave a
half-shove, half-kick, that knocked it down some of the steps. He
followed as rapidly as he could. It kept going, luckily. The next cry came
from the kitchen door, and that was all right. They were both downstairs
now, both in the kitchen. Nothing could be proved, they had won again.

His satisfaction, as he groped for its can of food (the cat loudly, legally
crying at him now), was as solid as ever. His day had begun once more
with purpose, with achievement, and he was not ashamed of its nature.
At eighty-three, you made your life out of whatever you could, or had
none.

She came in on them while he was hunting his own breakfast. At
once—nervous and patient—her voice began to pour over him.

"Now, Father—what are you looking for in there? You know there's
nothing—look out for those bottles! I don't know what they're doing in
there, Alan was supposed to take them all back yesterday.... What *is* it,
dear?"

"I can't find my bananas," he said. When she gave him the chance.

"Well, they wouldn't be in there!"

He said nothing, while he rummaged.

"Well, there were two left. I put them aside specially. You *sure* you didn't eat them, Father?"

He never answered nonsense of this sort. He began in silence to leave the kitchen. There were no bananas.

"I suppose the children got them, then ... though they know perfectly well they're not to eat the last ones, ever. I'll have to make you something," she said, resigned. "What would you like, dear?"

A martyr already, and not even six o'clock.

"Never mind," he said.

"Or if you want to wait I'll send one of the children down to the store. Would you rather do that?"

"All right. Don't fuss."

A last word like that she wouldn't let him have. Her anxious voice followed him away: "It's true I've been letting things run out, but they know they're never to touch the last of the bananas, I just can't believe they ..."

Sounds echoed, with curtains down and rugs up. He was aware of his own quiet footfalls, the regular descent of his rubber-tipped stick, and overhead he could hear—heavy and slow—the tread of his son getting dressed. Plunk plunk. Plunk plunk plunk plunk plunk. Plunk. No other sounds than these—certainly none of children. There were no more children here, not what Mr. Nicholas called children—that woke with the light and came welcome into his room. No more of those; they were gone. And the big strangers in their beds would sleep till they were shaken out of sleep, meeting morning as late as possible, like an outrage. He would wait a long time for his bananas, if he waited for children to bring them.

He had no such idiot intention. Unbolting the front door, he went out onto the porch. The morning was freshly cool, light air from the southwest moved upon his skin. She was not going to have a rainy moving day after all, poor Martyr, she would have to make do with other, smaller grievances. Well, he would help her along, he would start her out right, if she would just give him time to get going.

Sometimes she had an intuition that dismayed him, and when at last—beyond the gate, the gate quietly shut behind him—he found himself on his way, he was surprised at his luck. Or at her failure in vigilance. He set a safe boundary for himself, beyond which he could pretend not to hear her, and reached that, too: the swollen part of the sidewalk where the great tree root had wrenched it up, in front of Thompsons'.

He was now out of her territory, in public domain. And he was going to fetch his bananas for himself.

From the curtainless hall window, Dorothea Nicholas watched him go. He was past the worst spot; the rest of the way was clear—or should be clear, at this hour. Unless some child had left a tricycle or a wagon out overnight, for him to fall over and fracture his poor old bones, and be bedridden from then on.... Her tic jumped; she put an absent, gentle finger on it, and then stepped out onto the porch. From here she could see the sidewalk all the way to the corner, where the little grocery store was, and it was clear. Besides, he was using his stick very carefully, ahead of himself.

She let him go. This was his last morning in his old home; she would let him have his adventure, and go up to the store for himself. It couldn't set any precedent.

Standing there a moment longer, consciously indulgent, she continued to examine the street that she was leaving. It was years since she had seen it so empty, so clear of people. So *clean* of people. It seemed almost itself again, the way she had first known it twenty years ago when she had come here as Johnny's bride, to visit his parents. Even then it had been going down, and the big clapboard and shingle houses had been a bit shabby; but most of the yards were kept up, most of the old owners still lived there. Now this early look of emptiness restored much of its old dignity. Because *people* were what had ruined DeKuyper Street—too many people, more and more of them crowding in as the old houses changed hands, the houses that were too big for single families nowadays. Or too big for the kind of families that came to live on DeKuyper Street. Apartments and rooms, makeshift apartments and furnished rooms, had multiplied all round; and the people who rented them had multiplied, too. They were transient people, not many stayed long enough to seem familiar, but they seemed to replace each other by some inexorable law of progression—two for one, four for two—until sometimes Dorothea was haunted by wonder at where and how they all must sleep. Children in cellars? In closets without windows, in beds with too many other children or adults? There was no way to know, they were all strangers. Except for old Mrs. Thompson next door (desolate at their leaving), and the Rudds with their corner store—and the Haydens going to wrack and ruin at the other end of the block—she no longer knew anyone at all. Well, it was time—past time—to be moving away. She was moved by this last, familiar view of the street where she had lived for nearly ten years, but it did not change her mind in the least. She was glad, relieved, to be going from it at last. If only the moving were over....

She gave a last, resigned look at her father-in-law's progress—he was almost there—and then went inside.

Immediately, as if safety had abandoned him with her leaving, she thought of the store being shut. It never seemed to be—early, late, Sundays, holidays, one or both of the Rudds always seemed to be there. To be open was their main commodity, in fact, and allowed them to survive along with the big chain stores that offered more, and cheaper, but not always. Six o'clock, though ... she had never tried them this early.

The telephone was still connected (because of Father, in the night), and she rang the corner store and got Mrs. Rudd on the second ring.

Cordial with relief, she said: "It's Mrs. Nicholas, Mrs. Rudd. I just wanted to be sure you're open this early...."

"Oh, yes, we're open, Mrs. Nicholas. My, *you're* getting an early start today, aren't you?"

"Yes.... What I called you for is that Father's on his way down, and I wanted to be sure you were open."

"Oh, is that right? Well, bless his heart, I'll surely look out for him.... Oh, here he is now," she said, dropping her voice, although the telephone was at the back of the store. "I can see him coming up the step right now—my, he certainly gets around well for a blind man his age. But don't you think somebody'd better see him home, Mrs. Nicholas? Should I keep him here awhile, till you can send for him?"

Dorothea had been reminding herself for ten years that Mrs. Rudd's effusive barbs were not intentional, just tactless. At this last moment, she allowed herself a different judgment.

"I'm afraid he might not like that, Mrs. Rudd. I'm sure he'll be all right. But thank you just the same."

She also allowed herself a little grimace, hanging up. Her husband, coming downstairs, caught her at it.

"Who was that?"

He was a big man, like his father, but like him in no other way. Just as well; the house would never have held two of them. She looked at him with automatic anxiety.

"Where did you get that tie? That's not the one I left out."

"Yes, it is," he said, surprised.

Was it? Momentary uncertainty invaded Dorothea. First the bananas, now the tie ... she really *didn't* remember, about either one!

Her husband came up and put his hand on her shoulder.

"Now, take it easy, hon—you're almost through. Easy does it."

It didn't, of course. She replied, in oblique dissent, "I was talking to Mrs. Rudd—Father's gone down there alone, I wanted to be sure she was open."

"What did he do that for?"

"There were no bananas. He didn't want to wait, or have anything else."

"Oh, Lord," he said, to her tone more than to her words.

He followed her out to the kitchen. The cat was licking itself on the table; he managed to push it off before she saw.

"I better go get him," he said.

"No, let him alone."

He went on watching her uncertainly, as she started his breakfast.

"Look, Dot—why don't I take him with me today? I don't know why we never thought of this, you shouldn't have him all day when you're moving. When you don't even want me around," he said, half joking.

"I have thought of it. They can put his rocker in last and take it out first, that's all. He can stay out on the porch here, and in the patio at the new house. It's a nice day."

"In the rocker, all day?"

"Well, he'll just have to," she said doggedly. "He couldn't stand a whole day downtown with you, he'd be worn out. And so would you," she added, in a rare escape of opinion.

He didn't say anything; but before long he got up and went out, muttering something about going to meet the old boy. By then, she was glad to have him go. Mrs. Rudd would think Johnny had overruled her, but that didn't matter compared to the chance that Father might hurt himself on the way home. She had visions of an ambulance and the movers arriving simultaneously, made herself stop, and went upstairs to wake the children.

That, and breakfast, occupied her mind entirely for some time. Nearly an hour passed before she noticed that neither Johnny nor his father had come back. Then, in a panic, she fled out to the porch.

The old man was sitting there in his rocker, holding two banana skins neatly folded. Breathing hard, she took them from his hand.

"Where's John, Father?"

"Still next door, I suppose. Dorothea, about my trunks—"

"They're all ready, everything's all ready," she murmured, and escaped back into the house. "Next door" must mean Mrs. Thompson; they didn't know the other side. But what was he doing over there so long?

She had to wait nearly a half hour longer to find out; and then she could hardly believe her ears. And Johnny looked so pleased with himself! Standing there explaining to her how Mrs. Thompson—a widow not much younger than Father himself—would be delighted to have her old neighbor spend his last day in the neighborhood with her, only wished she had dared suggest it herself!

"You mean you *asked* her to keep Father today? Oh, Johnny—no!"

"Well, why not? She was glad to be asked, Dottie—I just wish we'd asked her some other favor, all these years. You should have seen how pleased she was."

For Johnny, this was sharp, since Dorothea admittedly couldn't ask favors—though she would go to any trouble to grant them. The original do-it-yourself kid, Johnny said, joking. But he wasn't joking now.

Bewildered, even hurt, Dorothea began to put his breakfast on the table. He stopped her serving hand with his.

"Now, come on—aren't you really a little bit glad? And you don't even have to tell him, I will."

But that was too much. She found her tongue again.

"No, I will—you'll do it wrong. You'll hurt his feelings," she said unsteadily; and as if he had already done so, she left him without another word and went out to the porch.

Chapter 2

Mr. Nicholas was considerably startled.

That the Martyr should under any circumstances lay down any part of her load—or even let it be wrested from her—was enough to shake a man's faith in the laws of nature. Was she going to become a New Woman, in her New House? Was he going to get a New Opponent, flexible and wily, in place of his poor old Martyr?

"Hope springs eternal," he murmured.

But of course she was still there.

"Now, Father, what do you mean by that? No one is hoping anything, we just want you to be comfortable ..."

Suddenly inspired, he lied calmly.

"No, Dorothea—what amuses me is that I hesitated to suggest this very idea myself, because I know how much you dislike asking favors. And now you've gone and done it for yourself."

He knew quite well it was Johnny who had asked. She must know he did. Was she going to admit it?

Was she even there?

He put out his hand, touched her dress, and withdrew at once. Discovered, she said: "Be a good boy now, won't you, dear?"

"Exemplary. But about my trunks, now, Dorothea—"

She was already inside the door.

The morning life of his house went audibly on, for the last time. The Girl came crashing downstairs again, and then the Boy. Presently they would come out on the porch, approximately together, and he would get dutiful light bumps on the head as they went by; these were kisses. On clear mornings he could hear them as far as Haydens', at the corner. If they were speaking. The Girl walked like Dorothea—a lighter echo. The Boy still didn't walk, he loped, or dragged. Usually Johnny's car had come out of the driveway a good half hour before, but this morning he left late, and came out the front way—even sitting on the porch railings near his father for a little while. He didn't want to go at all; Mr. Nicholas had an ironic impulse to invite him next door, too.

After that, there was no one of his family left to listen to but the Martyr; and it often surprised him that he continued to hear and define, day after day, movements that had long since lost all capacity to surprise. In the new house, of course, he would have an immense amount of relearning to do, and he firmly considered that this would be stimulating. He knew that he still kept reserves of energy far beyond what were needed here, in this familiar routine. There was, God knew, plenty of troublesome life in him yet. At the same time, he did not want to leave. Something approaching panic overcame him at times, to his bewilderment and shame. It was entirely irrational, and he was well able to control it, fortunately. Just as he was able to control the depression, equally irrational, which was settling on him now. Because they were farming him out next door.

Not that he minded spending a day with Lettie Thompson, who had always found him sufficiently intimidating to make her behave. She had been a good cook, too, and kept a comfortable house. No, it was a good enough idea—if only he had thought of it for himself! If only it had been he who had gone to Dorothea and said: "Now my dear, I want no part of all this hoo-ha today, and I am going over to Lettie Thompson's until you have finished with it." How upset she would have been, how full of protest! It would never have occurred to her that he might plan to leave her for a whole day, of his own volition. And of course he had not. It was she who was leaving him.

Mr. Nicholas felt for his stick, and pushed himself up. He had had enough of this maudlin trap his thoughts were in. It was time to move around. And once on his feet, he knew where he would go: to Lettie's. Belated initiative, but better than none. Dorothea would see, at least, that he liked the idea very much—that ought to dismay her.

The Thompsons' front walk gave him a little trouble; she evidently didn't keep it up in her widowhood. But he was perfectly composed by the time she opened her door.

"Well, Lettie my dear," he began—but she was too excited to hear any more, seizing his arm and almost pulling him inside, bursting all over him with speech. Poor lonely soul.

"Oh, John, I could hardly believe it when Johnny told me, I was sure he'd done it without Dorothea knowing, and she'd never let you—I told him, I said Johnny, now, don't get me into trouble, darling, you know I've been so careful all these years, girls are so touchy, and Dorothea's always so careful of him, she won't—"

"Nonsense, Lettie, nonsense." But in increasing good humor (and considerable discomfort) he let himself be hauled and bumped along through the house—where on earth were they going? He couldn't match his memory yet to this rough journey. "She's afraid I'll come courting you, that's all," he said, trying to get free—and was astonished at the sudden release and silence that followed. Why, she was taking him seriously! "She's a very sharp girl, Dorothea," he added, delighted.

But Lettie had got hold of herself and said, "Nonsense," in her turn. "Old people like us, John—shame on you!"

He wouldn't hear of being ashamed. Nothing more natural, a pretty widow next door (Was it the kitchen? It *smelled* like the kitchen)—bound to occur to any man, even an old crock like himself. (It was the kitchen; she had him down at the table of course. Lettie always fed people instantly.)

But he had gone too far, and spoiled the fun—she turned sad on him. He oughtn't to talk about himself like that, she said, it really hurt her. If he meant his sight, why, a person would hardly notice, the way he had learned to manage. And it was really very wrong of poor Dorothea, if she had made him feel....

"Oh, bother my eyes," he said, tired of it. "It's my legs I want back. Legs are the thing, Lettie—hang on to your legs, and you hang on to your independence. How are yours, by the way?"

She had varicose veins, of long standing, and after a little struggle couldn't resist talking about them. He got her back to earth nicely in this way, and by eating bits of whatever she gave him; and then the movers came, and they both limped out on her porch. He settled to see the whole thing through Lettie's eyes and memories, perhaps the best way.

Also, he could find out about his trunks.

"Now they'll either be first or last," he instructed her, as she settled beside him. "The attic, you know. They haven't got an attic in this confounded new place, and I know for a fact she's putting some things in the storage warehouse. For a time, she says. I've told her I need those trunks—there isn't a week goes by I don't have one or the other of them open; but she's never given me a straight answer about it yet. You just watch, and tell me what things go with them."

Lettie promised she would. But as the moving progressed, he began to suspect that her eyes weren't much to boast about either. Besides, she got wrapped up in some piece that she either hadn't seen before or else hadn't seen in "years and years," and by the time she finished exclaiming and chattering about it they could have moved a couple of rooms past without her noticing. It didn't help to be sharp with her. If he interrupted, insisting on knowing what had just gone into the van, she always said it was a chair. He began to lose his temper.

"Don't tell me such stuff, Lettie Thompson! Why, that thing weighed a ton, it took three men—"

"It—it was a *big* chair, John ..."

"There isn't a chair like that in the house," he said coldly. For a time, then, she really tried to pay attention.

But to give Lettie credit, it was she who finally enlightened him. After everything was over, and Dorothea had gone off with his poor cat in its basket ("Butter its paws," he reminded her. "The minute you get there, now!")—when they were left alone to talk it over, and Lettie was still insisting that his trunks had gone in, she added thoughtfully: "But I'll tell you what I didn't see, John, and I was particularly looking out for it, and that was Mary's dining-room suite. Now I always admired that fumed oak, and there must have been at least fifteen pieces to it—"

"Twelve chairs," he said.

"That's right, and the table, and the sideboard, and the china cabinet. Why, I couldn't have missed all that! And I didn't see it. Are you sure she's taking it with her?"

"Taking it with her! What else would she do?"

"She might be putting it in storage," Lettie suggested. "She might not think it would go with a modern house. Or maybe she's leaving some of the heavy old things there—to sell, you know, or for the Salvation Army, even. You don't realize what the children think about our furniture, John. Why, when I tried to give Carol my curly-maple bedroom—"

"Dorothea's not Carol," he said shortly. "She's not a fool, either—give it to the Salvation Army! Why, that's good, solid, valuable furniture! You couldn't buy anything like it today!"

"Well, I know that," said Lettie stubbornly. "But the point is, nobody wants to. They think our furniture is *funny.* If Dorothea were your own daughter, you'd know."

"Dorothea is my own daughter. And she asked me when she wanted to change the living room," he added, triumphant. "When she got that couch and put the settee in the attic."

"I didn't see the settee either," said Lettie.

He reached for his stick, and began to struggle up from his chair.

"Well, we'll soon settle it," he said. "Come on—I've still got my key."

"Why, John—I don't think we ought to go in there," she protested. She was struggling up, too, but only to hang on to him. "Now please, dear—I might have been mistaken, I think I was—"

"That is still my house," he said, "and I told you, I have my key."

"But Dorothea wouldn't want you wandering round like this, John—please don't, you don't need to—when you get to the new house tonight, you—"

"When I get to the new house," he said, "I want to know what I'm talking about. Oh, stay there, Lettie—I'll be right back. You don't need to watch me every minute, do you?"

Apparently she felt that she did. Why, if anything should happen to him over there, if those men had left boards and nails and things lying around, and he hurt himself … The end of it was that he had to take her. And she had to come. It was an arrangement that pleased neither of them; but once started, they both made the best of it.

She was incredibly slow. Actually, once he was up, he could cover the ground much faster than she. Probably that was why she hadn't wanted to go—didn't want him to know how bad her legs really were. In order not to embarrass her, he had to pretend to be slow, too, and then she insisted on pointing out every pebble on her wretched path, and altogether it was a most exasperating journey.

But he had been right to insist. The dining-room furniture was still there.

He didn't need Lettie's eyes to assure him of it. His own hands, trembling with shock, with disbelief, traced out for him every familiar piece. Displaced, yes—shoved back. But all there. At last, too shaken to speak, he sank down in his old armchair. Lettie, seated long ago, sounded on the verge of tears.

"Don't take it so hard, dear—I know Dorothea will be able to, will tell you—"

"She's getting rid of everything today, isn't she?" he said, with a laugh that came out like a croak.

"Oh, John—oh, my dear old friend—"

This was intolerable. He pushed himself up again, and went over to her.

"Now stop that, Lettie. Pull yourself together, and let's go see what else she's left. Why, I could probably move right back in here," he said with iron gaiety, "and hardly miss a thing! Come on."

They toured the downstairs, Lettie frankly leaning on him. To her obvious relief, there was nothing else left behind except an old kitchen cabinet which she declared to be a wreck, just a wreck. He paid no attention to her, and investigated every bit of space himself. She was telling him the truth. But there was no reassurance for him in that.

"Come on," he said finally. "The real story will be up in the attic. I don't care too much about the settee, I suppose, but if she's left my trunks up there ..."

"John, she wouldn't do that! All your things!"

"My things have no value for her," he said, tasting his bitterness. Chewing it. "She's made that clear. Come on."

"I can't," Lettie confessed then. "I'm sorry, but—I can't."

"What do you mean, you can't? Just take hold of my arm, and hold the rail on the other side—we'll do it slowly!"

"No," she said. "I don't do stairs anymore, John. Not even at home. I could, but the doctor doesn't want me to. He's very firm about it."

"Oh," he said. Her embarrassment, and the pity of understanding, gave him pause. "No more stairs, eh?"

"No. I don't mind—the children have put in a nice bathroom downstairs, and I've made the dining room into a lovely sleeping room, but—I just can't go up, John."

"Well," he said, depressed for her (and it probably meant heart, too, poor old soul), "well, never mind. You go sit in one of my twelve chairs, Lettie, and have a rest. I'm up there all the time alone, you just sit down and wait, and I'll be right back."

But she wouldn't agree. She wouldn't let him go. Physically—and it came to that—she wouldn't let him go up.

"Why, it's my own house!" he said, growing angry. "What's the matter with you? I go over it every day of my life, I know every inch of it as well as I know my own foot! Don't be so silly, I'm ashamed of you!"

"I can't help it," she said, close to tears. "I won't let you go up there alone! Don't you understand, I couldn't reach you if something happened? I wouldn't even know! I couldn't get up all those stairs if my life depended on it," she burst out. "There! Now, that's the truth, and I don't care—and *you can't go!*"

He accepted defeat. After a moment (remembering that probable heart) he put his arm round her.

"All right. All right, Lettie—my goodness. Calm down, it's all right."

But she was really crying by then, and he led her back to the dining room and made her sit down before he would let her take him back home.

By then she was calmer, but worn out. He had no trouble persuading her to lie down for a while. She didn't even have the energy to make him stretch out on the day bed, when he claimed that he took his own naps sitting up. With no more than an afghan dropped over his knees, she dragged away, to her converted dining room–bedroom.

He heard her shut the door. He meant to allow her five or ten minutes to drop off, more than enough. Then, unencumbered, he would go back to his house and find out the truth about his trunks.

Chapter 3

It was after six o'clock when Johnny came back to DeKuyper Street. After one look at his father's face, he apologized for being so late. The movers were still unloading, he said, and Dorothea hadn't been able to get away—she just had to wait till he came home. Johnny hoped they weren't too tired, waiting.

"We're not tired at all, darling," said Mrs. Thompson brightly. "We had a wonderful morning, watching everything, and then we had some lunch, and just slept for hours. Didn't we, John?"

His father said nothing. Mrs. Thompson didn't seem to notice.

"In fact, I haven't had such a long nap in years," she went on gaily. "You can imagine how I felt, when I woke up and saw how late it was, and thought of your poor father sitting out here wondering where his hostess was! And then I came rushing out, and here he was, fast asleep, too! Imagine."

She was teasing him, he was hating it, and Johnny had no idea what this was all about.

"Well, uh, we certainly appreciate—" he began, when his father interrupted, with one cold sound.

"John."

"Yes, Dad?"

"Mrs. Thompson has very kindly offered to put me up here for the night, and I have accepted. Will you please tell Dorothea she needn't bother about me until tomorrow?"

With no clue, Johnny looked back to Mrs. Thompson. She just nodded and continued to beam.

"Well, uh, don't you think you'd better come home, though, Dad?" he suggested. "I know Dorothea will have your room ready by the time we get there, and she really is expecting you. You don't want to wear yourself out—or Mrs. Thompson," he added, flushing.

"It's the greatest pleasure for me, Johnny," she murmured; and his father said with bitter precision: "We are both extremely well rested. Tell Dorothea she has no cause for concern on that score."

Mrs. Thompson then showed him the lovely day bed, right there in the living room, where she often put up one of her children or grandchildren, since she no longer bothered to heat the upstairs. "And I have some things for your father to use," she said delicately. "And Mr. Rudd has brought us a lovely chicken, I'm roasting it right now, and we're going to have a lovely last evening together. Now Dorothea won't begrudge us that, will she?"

Johnny said, No, he was sure she wouldn't. Actually, with the chaos he had left behind him, he was relieved not to be adding his father to it. Only why was he looking so grim?

"Well, it sounds fine to me," he said, "if you're sure you both feel up to it?"

"Why shouldn't we?" said his father. "We've done nothing but sleep all day."

When Johnny left—still perplexed, but accepting luck where he found it—Mrs. Thompson made exaggerated noises of relief.

"I thought you were going to pitch into him any minute," she declared. "Poor boy! He probably doesn't even know about it."

"Know about what?"

Johnny's departure hadn't changed Mr. Nicholas in the least. He seemed barely aware that his son had gone.

"Why, the furniture—what else?"

He scarcely heard her. To have known nothing, to have wasted in doddering sleep those precious hours when Lettie slept, was a personal betrayal that he simply could not accept. The grudge he had against Dorothea was nothing to the one he now had against himself.

"Or is it the trunks that's worrying you, John?"

Lettie's persistence, very annoying, reminded him that he had nothing against her. On the contrary. Besides, there were hours to pass before he could expect her to sleep again—common courtesy required something from him until then.

"I suppose it is, Lettie."

"But I'm sure they're safe, that's something quite different from old furniture. Besides, didn't you—surely you didn't leave anything ... valuable in them, did you? I mean, for the moving?"

"They're locked," he replied absently.

"Oh, but John—*trunk* keys! Oh, dear, you mean you *did* leave money in them? You really did?"

He lifted his head in surprise.

"Money? What are you talking about, Lettie? I don't keep money in trunks, for pity's sake." She continued to sound very agitated, but made no reply, which was strange. "Why would I do that? Whatever put such an idea in your head?"

"Why—why, I don't see why you shouldn't," she said then, stammering a little. "When it's not possible to go to the bank any longer—and of course you wouldn't want to leave it just lying round in your room, with—with children in your house. I don't see anything very wrong about that ..."

"Well, I do," he said, sobered. "I hope you're not doing anything so foolish. You're not, are you?"

"Oh, no," she said quickly. "Everyone knows I don't keep any money here at all—everything's charged, you know, and then the bills go to George, and he handles everything. Even the paperboy, and the man who does the yard and shovels the snow. Oh, I'm very careful, John. But of course it's different for you," she added. "You're a man, and you don't live alone, and—and I think it's quite all right. Even Mrs.—"

She stopped.

"Well, Mrs. Ryan, who cleans for me—the only thing she thought was that, if there was a fire ... Of course, even to her, I said I didn't believe a word of it. Naturally."

"Well!" he said. "Well, I'm much obliged to you, Lettie. To think I've been a famous miser all the while and didn't even know it."

"Why, that's not being a miser, nobody thinks you—"

"Certainly it's being a miser," he said. "There's no other word for a habitual money-hider that I know of." She was uneasily silent. He began to be curious. "But how did this ever start?" he wondered. "Why? I'm not a rich man, I never have been. Do I just *seem* like an old miser, nowadays? Is that it? Have I grown so unpleasant as that?"

"Oh, John—"

"No, no—that's fishing, isn't it? I'm sorry, I take it back. But how amazing ..."

They sat in silence, until she murmured: "I think it's just that you're so independent, John. I think that's it."

He gave a short laugh.

"Well, if I am, it's not because I hide money in trunks. What a deduction! No, no—I don't mean you, Lettie, I know you've only listened to this nonsense. But it's a sad light on what our poor old street has come to. Or our poor old world, maybe." She sighed; and he changed his tone. "No, Lettie, let me assure you that I have no financial secrets from my son. And I'd be very much surprised if he has any from Dorothea. As for independence," he said steadily, "I'm entirely dependent on my son and daughter in many important ways—the fact that I have a small amount of property doesn't obscure that fact to me. Or to them, naturally."

He was not aware of having formed such a thought before, in all the years of his growing dependence, and he found it curiously satisfying. In some way, it seemed to balance the business of Dorothea and the dining-room furniture—or perhaps to diminish it. Not, however, that he didn't intend to have that out.

But he could tell from Lettie's breathing that it was time to change the subject, and so he began to tell her about his real trunks: not the money-laden ones, but the old steamer that had been Mary's and still held many of her things, and his own sturdy wooden trunk which no moth had ever invaded. Dorothea did not trust it, and always managed to seal away his overcoat and heavy suit in some contraption of her own; but he had kept his woolly blue tam-o'-shanter, for example, quite safely in that trunk ever since he bought it in Scotland, and expected it to outlast him. Without stinking of chemicals, either.

"I always know it's really winter, when I see you wearing your tam the first time," Lettie said. "Oh, dear—I will miss you, John."

"Do you remember Mary's lace collection?" he went on. "I believe you had some of it, before I put it away, didn't you? Now Dorothea really values that," he said, struck by the recollection. "I remember she was upset by the idea that you were going to put it on things and use it— as you ought to, of course. She wanted me to let her rewrap it in some kind of stuff I couldn't get open. But of course I keep it as Mary had it— she knew perfectly well how to care for her lace. Dorothea did value that," he said again. "Even though she wouldn't have any. She wouldn't have forgotten it was there."

"I'm sure your trunks are all right," Lettie replied.

It was like going through the trunks themselves, and not alone, to sit here dredging up one by one their recollected contents. He began to be sorry that Lettie had not been able to come up to the attic with him in fact; they could have spent a very pleasant afternoon, and perhaps she would have liked some other of Mary's things, or even of his. The bits of scrimshaw, for instance. He told her about these, too, and how he had come to have them—the great-aunt in Stonington, Connecticut, who had made him a present of a piece every birthday instead of leaving them to him as a collection. She had hoped he would feel, in this way, that he was making his own collection—and so he had.

It was in Mystic, nearby, that he had met Mary for the first time. Lettie did not know this story, and he told it to her; and then he listened patiently to hear of her own first meeting with poor Thompson—a reedy, nervous fellow who had given up before he was sixty. She cried a little, and he helped her past it.

Altogether, the evening turned into quite a pleasant one, and he lost all sense of wishing it away. Even when Lettie gave up of her own accord, around eleven, and limped off to the dining room, he sat on peacefully enough by himself. He was not afraid of dozing off this time—and, in fact, did so. But his night naps were light, and he always enjoyed waking into the deep quiet of nighttime; perhaps this was why he woke so often then. That, and the bathroom, of course.

Reminded, he used Lettie's bathroom once more before he left. He also pulled the umbrella stand over in the way of the door, so that anyone pushing it open incautiously from the porch would meet an obstruction. It was the best he could do to replace her door chain while he was gone. But he would not leave her long.

He judged the hour to be somewhere soon after midnight. DeKuyper Street lay quiet around him. It was a street of people who worked hard and began early, and only an occasional fast car or some passing gaggle of immature males ever broke its night silence.

The silence within his house had a different quality. He was struck by this, as he mounted its stairs with quiet assurance, until he was able to define the difference. Emptiness, of course (except for the dining room), but an *enclosed* emptiness. Every window and door was shut up tight; trust Dorothea for that.

She had even locked the attic. Against what? Sighing for his poor Martyr, he turned the key and opened the door, and started up the steep enclosed stairwell that led to the attic floor.

Chapter 4

Before Mr. Nicholas had crossed ten feet of floor, he was aware of the other person there with him.

He kept going.

The other person did not move. Still on the narrow ledge of floor behind the stairs—above the door, immobile and almost imperceptibly breathing, someone watched him go.

Presumably watched, if any light was coming in through the windows. Mr. Nicholas, reaching the destination he had set himself, stopped and made random exploration with his stick. No trunks were there. The subject dropped at once from his mind, leaving him without purpose: in this way, he found that he felt some fear.

Realizing this, he at once forced himself round till he faced the stairs, and demanded: "What are you doing there?"

There was no reply. He added: "I see you there—what do you want?"

A small, quick movement, instantly checked, told him his trap had worked. The person knew him, and knew that he could not see—had almost said so.

"Very well," Mr. Nicholas said then. He folded his hands over his stick and leaned on it. "I will wait. The silence will tell me enough. I know how to listen."

It was a calculated bluff, based on the curious ambivalence of the uninformed to blindness. He was considered either entirely helpless or—when he could prove that he was not—possessed of some mysterious new power, kin to extrasensory perception. The truth lay well to the north of both ideas, of course, but few cared to find that out. So Mr. Nicholas tried his bluff. Besides, he did not know what else to do.

The other's breathing had changed. Unfortunately, so had his own; and when the first whisper began, he could not understand it.

"What?" he said. "What is it?"

The whisper sharpened, until it almost had voice.

"Shut the door! *Shut the door!*"

"Certainly not," Mr. Nicholas said at once. "Why should I? Who are you?"

He suspected it was a boy—not a reassuring suspicion to anyone who listened to the boys along DeKuyper Street nowadays. Except that this one seemed timid.

Mr. Nicholas pressed his advantage—or what he hoped was one.

"I mean you no harm," he said gravely, "but you can't stay here. Now jump down, and get out. Hurry up!"

He heard, after a moment, a light scuffle of sound and then a soft jump—as of sneakered feet. A pause, and then the door was quietly closed. But the person was still there with him! His heart gave a slight irregular movement, and he said indignantly: "Why, what are you—"

"*Shut up!*"

The command was so savage that he obeyed.

Another light scramble followed—a return to that perch, over the door. Perplexed, Mr. Nicholas began: "I want to know—"

"You keep quiet, mister," said the small, savage voice. "Just keep quiet!"

Mr. Nicholas took two steps forward, and stopped. "Why, you're a girl," he said. "You're a girl! What girl are you?"

"Shut *up!*"

Whatever girl she was, whatever her purpose here, she was close to hysteria. Mr. Nicholas, trying to adjust, did keep quiet a moment.

In that moment, he heard another tread below them in his house. Someone else was there, and coming up from the first floor.

It was the nature of the ascent, more than the fact of it, which kept Mr. Nicholas immobile. It was so curiously undecided. Not only in pauses, although there were several of these, but in the alternate openness and furtiveness of approach. Someone couldn't decide—

idiotically, since the time for choice was past—whether he wanted to be heard coming up or not. There was no doubt it was a man. The tread was heavy, even when—after one of those pauses—it tried not to be. Then, at the head of the stairs, the man abandoned concealment. Slowly, openly, he came to the attic door and stopped.

"Hey, kid ..."

It was a thick voice, slurred and slow. The girl did not reply. Mr. Nicholas could not even hear her breathing.

"Kid—you all right?"

Time went by. He was a slow thinker, this man. Mr. Nicholas did not interfere, but he took a different grasp of his stick.

There was a metallic rasp of sound. The key, turning in the lock.

"Kid—hear that? It's open."

"Come on," he said presently. "It's open. You better go home now."

After a long wait, he became restless, began to mutter.

"Come on, go on home, it's open ... I'm going," he said, and began to walk with a terrible false loudness—as if he were standing still and trampling in one place.

But he really did move away, and really went clumping down the stairs again.

For the first time since he had taken his stance, Mr. Nicholas allowed his attention to relax. To the girl on the ledge—the presumed girl on the ledge—he said in astonishment: "Who was that?"

"*Shut up!*"

She hadn't relaxed. If anything, she sounded even more feral.

Mr. Nicholas allowed a few seconds to pass, and then said in a low, firm voice: "He can't possibly hear us, he is on the first floor. Now who is that man? Did he lock you in here?"

She replied only by one long, shuddering breath. And a return to ragged breathing. Mr. Nicholas began to understand the depth of her fear, as well as its intensity. She was still scarcely understanding him.

He began to feel very tired.

"Child, what's happened to you? Are you hurt?"

He moved toward her as he spoke—and was checked by another frantic burst of whispering.

"*Don't*—don't make so much *noise!*"

He stopped moving, but said doggedly, "He can't possibly hear us now, I give you my word. Don't be afraid.

"Do you want me to take you home? Come out, child—I'll take you home."

As he spoke, it occurred to him that whatever the man's intention, by turning that key he had probably locked them in again. But he shelved the thought. The main thing at the moment was to get her calmed down, responding.

She did respond, then. But almost inaudibly.

"He's not gone. He's out there."

Mr. Nicholas, remembering that stagy retreat, was inclined to agree.

"Perhaps," he said, "but it doesn't matter. I'm with you now—when he realizes that, he'll take to his heels fast enough."

"He knows. He doesn't care."

"Nonsense, he has no idea—he'll have the shock of his life. Come along, now—come out of there."

"No, he knows, he doesn't care. He saw you come in."

She was obsessed, unmoving. Unreachable. Except by the thread of this dismal argument, which Mr. Nicholas patiently pursued.

"There was no one in the house or in the grounds when I came in. Believe me—I would know. Just as I knew you were here. Wherever he was, he wasn't around here."

She said unexpectedly, "I know where he went—he went back to get another flashlight. I busted his."

Surely she was a very young girl? Mr. Nicholas felt sure of it, with this first sound of a recognizable voice from her. His tone changed, with the opinion, and became at once gentler and more authoritative.

"Would you rather I went down first and chased him away? Then you won't be afraid to come out, will you?"

"*No*—don't go! Don't—"

"All right," he said. "All right, I won't do anything you don't agree to. But don't be afraid."

She was suddenly explosive with rage.

"*I'm not afraid*—quit saying that! I'm not afraid! But I've got some sense and you haven't—you stupid old man, you old dumb, stupid old blind man, you—don't know anything—"

"I know you're making a lot of noise," he said.

She wasn't, even then. But the charge made her suck in silence, sharply, and hold it. She was also, he thought, struggling not to cry.

Presently Mr. Nicholas went on: "Don't you understand that this man believes you are here alone? As soon as he realizes that you are not, you will have nothing more to fear from him. And I hope you are not—I hope you know that you can trust me. Do you know who I am?"

She said, after a long silence, "I wasn't after your money."

"Well," he said, "you would be welcome to any you found. Do you know my name?"

She took time to reply to this, too. And said finally: "I didn't mean what I said, before."

"It's of no consequence. But you must not—you must allow me to help you, child."

"You don't have to help me. I know what I'm going to do."

"What?" he said, patient.

There was a long pause. Then she said: "See this?"

"No. What is it?"

To his surprise, she was confused by her mistake.

"Oh. Well, it's—it's a brick. From the chimley. The minute he comes in that door, I can get him from up here. That's why you've got to be quiet, mister! Because he'll know if he hears anything—and he'll see you, too, if you stand right there! He's got a flashlight now, and he'll see you the minute he opens the door! Please mister—please come back here!"

All at once, for whatever reason, she had accepted him as an ally. It was certainly not the alliance he wanted, to be asked to help with her childish, murderous plan, but it was a beginning. If he was ever to get her unfrozen, off that ledge, it could only be by talking.

He went on talking.

"I don't believe he will come back, you know. He didn't like having to come back and unlock the door, did he?"

"No, he's scared." There was a ghost of satisfaction in her voice. It faded, as she went on: "He'll come back, though—he's got to. See, he's got to find out if I'm all right, or what. That's why we got to be quiet, so he'll think I'm *not*. Then I can get him."

An abyss opened somewhere inside Mr. Nicholas. Not in the head; lower.

"*Are* you all right?" he managed to say.

"Yes, only please come back here—please! You don't have to come all the way, just so he won't see you—please!"

His mind still groped under shock. What did she mean, the man had to come back and find out if she was "all right, or what"? Why should she not be all right? What had happened to her—*how had she been left?*

He was suddenly convinced that she did not come out to him because she could not. Then he remembered the way she had scrambled down to close the door, and up again, and in a confusion of relief he started toward her.

"*Look out for the steps!*"

"All right," he said, shaken by her panic. "All right, child, I know ..."

He found the stairwell and began skirting it with his stick, like a small offer of reassurance to her. She was entirely attentive; and when he came to where the roof sloped, near her perch, she began to make small movements. They were naturally made, not convulsive any more: she was coming to meet him, or crawling into some better position. Her breathing was better, too. And all her attention was on him—she did not hear the small thud of sound in the house below.

Mr. Nicholas heard it. It was far below, perhaps in the front hall. He could not decide what had caused it.

She whispered suddenly, "What is it?" and all her movements ceased. He replied calmly, stretching out his hand:

"Can you reach me, child?"

Her only answer was a convulsive scramble—backward again, away from him.

He said, "Now don't be foolish, give me your—"

"Wait. *Wait.*"

He had lost her to her terrors once more.

Helpless, he listened with her, and the next sound was audible to them both. It was, in fact, the crack of the third step from the bottom, and it was followed by so long a pause that Mr. Nicholas felt both repulsion and surprise.

What was he standing there so long for?

Mr. Nicholas began seriously to consider the attic door. If it was really locked—and it probably was—then there was no use frightening the fellow off before he unlocked it. And the girl seemed to be right: this was a badly frightened man. The question was whether or not he would come even as far as the attic door again. Every sound he made seemed to throw him into a paralysis of caution.

Then there came a strike against the wall below, as if from some loss of balance. That was nearer. He was coming on.

But coming on in a way that Mr. Nicholas did not understand, or like at all. It really seemed more animal than human to be drawn—and redrawn—to an object in such a manner! With so much fear and indecision, and yet with such helpless purpose. Surely his fear was not of the child, and if he knew or suspected that she was no longer alone, why was he coming back at all?

With growing sobriety, Mr. Nicholas changed the position of his body and of his stick. He knew there were men—conditions of man—beyond concern with discovery or shame. Obsessed creatures, who could be checked only by force. He began to think it possible that such a creature was coming up to them now.

And that the man's fear was not of them, but of what he had done. Or what he meant to do.

This time the pause seemed interminable. Mr. Nicholas was careful not to break it. In that long listening, he was coming into agreement with the girl's insistence on surprise. Because they had not much else between them, God knew, to substitute for force.

He still meant to call out, but not until the man tried to enter. At the same time, he now planned to strike down hard with his stick. It was a blackthorn, and heavy—if it should chance to connect it would give a solid blow. But he was not—like the poor child with her brick—counting on any knockout. No; surprise must be their weapon, as total and violent as possible; and their success, he hoped, another retreat on the man's part. At least a long enough one so that Mr. Nicholas might go quickly down and get the key on their side of the door, and lock them in.

For he was convinced by now that no time-weakened old man would get this child safe-conduct through an empty house, an empty yard, with such an animal stalking her. Force alone would do it—and even combined, their only real force lay in a chance of first surprise. Beyond that, Mr. Nicholas really feared that he would not be able to defend her.

Without relaxing, he waited out the long seconds between sounds. Beside him, the girl was shaking hard. He could almost feel the tremor of sound her flesh made against the attic boards. Could almost imagine that other listener hearing it, too, who wanted so badly to hear something!

But they gave him nothing. They were able to do that.

And in the end he went away. With new decision—in what supposed privacy of intention Mr. Nicholas could not imagine—the man turned and tiptoed to the downstairs hall, and out of hearing.

He had not touched the door, or even come near it.

Chapter 5

Mr. Nicholas was amazed at the girl's resilience.

Although she gave no sign until he spoke to her—and none for several moments after that—her first whispering turned into such a torrent that he gave up trying to reply. Not a torrent of terror, either—she was rocketed up, almost to euphoria! And rather inclined to boast.

She had been all ready, with her brick—they would really have given it to him—see, she said he was scared, didn't she? Wasn't she right? He knew she'd be laying for him—but he didn't know where! He didn't even know there was a place over the door! And boy, if he ever came back, if he ever came in—

"Oh, hush, child," Mr. Nicholas murmured.

His own imperative was to sit down, and he was having difficulties. There was no place to sit but the floor, and rather severe leg tremors—due to fatigue—made it hard to let himself down so far without falling.

What he needed was to find the wall and let himself down between that and his stick, but the wall here sloped sharply, and in an unaccustomed confusion, he forgot.

"*Oh!*" she said, crying out for his bump. Then came scrambles, and clutching, that nearly took his remaining balance away. He wasted no breath in protest until he was down, in spite of her help, with his back against the wall and his temporarily useless legs laid out in front of him.

Then he said sharply: "Now control yourself, girl—control yourself! Be still!"

To soften this, he grumbled on: "What a hair-trigger girl you are—I'm surprised you didn't start whacking the door with that brick of yours. I'm surprised you didn't whack me!"

"Oh, no," she said at once. "I knew it was you. I mean, first I just knew it wasn't him, but then I could hear your stick, and I knew it was you."

She meant when he first arrived, of course. When he had sorted this out, he did feel some surprise. It had not occurred to him that he might have been her target.

"Well," he said, "thank you for using your head, then. Instead of mine."

Now she had begun to hiccup, a disarming sound. Her hands he remembered as small and thin, but with strength. He was sorry he had pushed them off so fussily and lost his chance to discover what she was. She sat carefully separate from him now. But this close, she smelled more child than girl.

There was also an odor of blood, which he found himself hesitant to ask about—and then, considering it, to speak of at all.

She was still very keyed up. After a brief struggle with her hiccups she lost patience, and began whispering to him again between clucks.

"Gee, I didn't know what to do about you, mister, I didn't want to get you into trouble, too, but I didn't know what to do! And then I thought maybe if you just got your money and went away you'd be all right, because he didn't have anything against you—and then I thought that would be even better, because then he'd think you left the door unlocked and I already got out, and he wouldn't know where to look for me, so he wouldn't bother. I wish we had done like that," she said wistfully.

"But it never occurred to you to ask me for help?"

He had not meant this as a reproach, but perhaps it came out that way. She answered it quickly, as if it were.

"Oh, sure, I would have, only—well, I didn't know if you might report me, that was all."

"Dear God, child—report you?"

"Well, I didn't know about you then, just how you were supposed to be kind of ..." She couldn't think of a word for what he was supposed to be. Or not a polite one.

"Mean? Crabby?"

"No," she said, and found it: "Strick." Then old anxiety woke in her. "I wasn't after your money, mister—I swear to God I wasn't! If it was laying right in the middle of the floor, I wouldn't have touched it. I wouldn't!"

He said wearily, "I believe you. But why did you come—did that man bring you here?"

"Bring me! No! I just wanted to see inside, that's all—just see what it was like, if it was so fancy, and everything. And they said she left a lot of stuff—but I wasn't going to take anything!"

"Was he here when you came, then?"

"No, I don't think so. Maybe he was," she said, considering. "I guess he could have been, all right. See, it was him told me about the window— like a joke, you know? He said somebody told him it was broke, in case he wanted to get in and have a look for the old—for your money, mister. Like a joke? He said it probably wasn't true though. But it was, I looked on the way home, and it was broke all right. Not the glass, so you could see—just the thing in the middle that would lock it, if it wasn't broke. You wouldn't notice unless you looked."

"There were no broken locks on my windows," said Mr. Nicholas. "Who is this man?"

His question made her silent—or perhaps her own story did, evoking again that trap she had fallen into.

When she whispered to him again, it was a dispirited sound.

"We ought to be listening. He might come back ..."

"I am listening. All the time."

It was true. He had not for one moment tried to foretell what such a man might or might not do. All he had known, in their first moments of respite, was that he needed time to get his legs back; and this he had allowed himself to hope for. Apparently he was to have it. Sitting, he flexed these now, and found them fairly responsive. "Do you think he will, mister?"

Her bravado was gone. She wanted him to say, No. He considered what it was he did have to say to her, and decided to begin with the locked door.

"Child," he said, and then, impatient: "What is your name?"

"My name?"

"Yes, to call you by. What are you called?"

"Oh," she said. "Well, it's—Mary Rose."

She was selecting this name for him. He sighed, and accepted it.

"Well, Mary Rose, I've been thinking about this business of taking you down through the house—"

"No," she said. "No, mister!"

"Just a minute. We can't do that, you see. I'm afraid that when your friend turned the key—"

"He's not my friend!"

"I beg your pardon," he said, vexed with himself. "I'm sorry, Mary Rose. That's just a way of speaking."

"It's all right. I guess I did used to speak to him," she admitted. "Gee—how would you know an old man could be so crazy? I just thought he was kind of stupid. All the kids did."

He said, "An old man?"

"No, I didn't mean that, mister. Just like—grown up." Between her anxiety not to offend him and her curious sense of secrecy, he was finding it very hard to talk to her. But it was necessary to keep trying.

"Yes. Well, about the door—you see, I had left it unlocked, and so when—the key was turned again, that would naturally have locked it."

"I know. But it's all right, he'll think he did it. He's *stupid*."

"Yes. Well, the point is, Mary Rose, that since we are locked in, and since we would much rather be out, the only thing to do is to break the window and—and call."

"*Break the window!*"

"Certainly. It's my window."

"But he'll hear us! You couldn't do that without him hearing us! He's the only one that *will* hear us," she said wildly, "and then he'll know we're laying for him, and we won't have a chance, mister! Don't do it— please don't do it—"

"Mary Rose, be quiet."

Instantly, she was.

"There is no one coming," he said, taken aback. "You don't have to be that quiet. Just let me discuss this with you, will you?"

She still made no sound. And then he heard a small, ragged sigh.

"My hiccups are gone ..."

"Well, I'm glad. But will you let me finish what I'm trying to say? Then I'll listen to you. There is no other way to have a sensible discussion."

"Yes. Sure. Only—I don't think that's such a good idea, mister."

"Well, let's examine it. Your main objection is that you think no one will hear us. That's extremely improbable. If we act together, and promptly—if we both begin to shout as loudly as we can the moment I have knocked the glass from the window—and I can do that very quickly—it is simply not possible that no one will hear us. Don't you realize how many people occupy the houses across the street? And the boardinghouse next door?"

He waited, to make her answer.

"Yes ... I guess so. But they might not ..."

"Might not *what?*"

"They might not come.... They might not know who we are."

"But what possible difference can that make? When you hear someone shouting, 'Help, police!' in the middle of the night, you don't care who it is! You report it, as fast as you can, of course. I assure you, Mary Rose, this is our only sensible course, and we really must not waste any more time. Now help me up, like a good girl, and—"

"Mister! Wait!"

Although he had scarcely moved, she was clutching him with all her wiry strength. But how small she was! Surely not even twelve—?

In this new dismay, he missed what she was saying.

"What? What is it?"

"The *cops*, mister! What would we say? What would they do to us? If we yell like you said, somebody's going to call the cops!"

He said helplessly, "Mary Rose, I don't understand you. At a time like this, you're afraid of the police?"

But before he got the question out, he understood that it was useless. For whatever reason, she was. He would have to start all over on this premise.

"All right," he said. "Now listen to me. This is my house. No one—*no one*—can object to your being here if I do not. Do you understand that? And I do not object. You have my full and complete permission to be here."

"They won't believe you," she said sadly.

"They will. They have no choice. I'm the only one who can make a complaint, and I won't make it. Now if you are afraid of what your parents—"

"But why would we say we were here? They'll think we were doing something bad," she said earnestly. "They'll think we were up here doing something bad!"

It was like crossing a swamp. Trying to run.

He drew a long breath, and abandoned the sticky ground of reason. For whatever fantastic treetop this child lived in.

"All right, supposing that's true—which it most certainly is not. Then I would be taking an equal chance with you. And I agree to take it— rather than wait here all night at the mercy of a criminal lunatic!"

The minute the words were out, he regretted them: the ugly adult words bursting out like a new horror for her, that she would not have found for herself.

But she seemed scarcely to have heard. Lost in her own maze, she murmured on: "And how would we explain about the door being locked? If you—"

"Mary Rose, we haven't time for all this. You will have to take my word for it that you will *not* get into trouble—by allowing yourself to be rescued—from the very real danger you are in *now*."

He made this as clear as he could, speaking slowly. When she said nothing, he added: "And I promise I will do all I can to help you. Now, and later. Do you believe me?"

"Yes ..."

"Then get up, and give me your hand."

"But you don't have to help me.... I know what I'm going to do, I got this brick ..."

In exhaustion, she had gone back to her first premise—and with a limpness that alarmed him. His attempts to reason had only ended by putting her into a stupor: of indecision, of fatigue. They had come to the end of the usefulness of words.

Turning his stick, he deliberately struck the hard end hard against the floor. Only once; but the report was explosive. And to the cry this wrung from her he added harshly: "Be quiet!

"Now get up," he said. "And give me your hand."

Softly, hopelessly, she began to cry.

"Hurry!"

Still crying, in clumsy small movements she started to obey. He did not let himself move or speak lest this distract her. Weeping, she crawled over him, stumbled up onto her sneakered feet. He put up his hand, groping till he found hers. She let it be taken.

"Move back, Mary Rose," he said. "Pull."

Between the lever of her grasp (or his grasp of her) and the wall behind him, he got back on his legs. Then, gently pushing her before him, he came forward from under the roof and stood erect.

His legs held.

She leaned against him, and he put his free arm awkwardly about her. Her head came only to his chest—the hair was rough, and short like a boy's. Her little shoulder felt like a wrist.

"Don't cry anymore," he said gently. "Remember what we are going to do. You will have to shout very loudly—can you do that? Do you want to take my stick and break the window?"

She shook her head—rolling it back and forth upon his chest.

"Well, come along then. Watch me break it."

She did not move. She was guarding her crying, aware of it—perhaps enjoying her refuge, and unwilling to give it up. But he knew that it was no real refuge. And there was not time to pretend.

"Come along, child."

He began to move, moving her with him. She came leaning, in a childish dawdle, which he bore.

Then she stiffened and stood still.

There had been a faint sharpish sound the moment before, but not in the house. Something, somewhere out on the street, had broken or fallen—he did not yet place the sound, and was bewildered by its effect on her.

"What is it?" he said. "What's the matter?"

"The streetlight—he's knocked out the streetlight—"

"What? What do you mean?"

"With a rock—he busted the streetlight!"

He could scarcely hear her. Her body was rigid with terror. The strangeness of this new attack, if it was one, left him at a loss.

"But what difference does that make? It doesn't matter if people can't see us up here," he said, groping, "they can certainly still hear us! Come on—"

"But I can't see! Oh, he's coming back—he's coming back—and *I can't see!*"

It was dark in the attic now. That was it.

Reassured, he said at once: "But I can! The dark makes no difference to me, you know that! Now let go of me, child—here, take my hand. Give me your hand!"

But he could not rearrange her—she was gripping his coat, his body, in such frozen fear that they were both immobilized. Worse, a frenzy of whispers was pouring from her—cutting her off from his voice like a loss of hearing.

"... my brick, I got to get back there and get my brick, I got to get back there before he comes—oh, it's so dark—I can't see, I can't see—"

"Stop it, stop it—*be quiet!*" he commanded. But the words had lost their magic for her, were not even heard. And when in desperation he began to shake her, she only twisted herself free and darted off— became lost to him entirely.

He could hear her blundering about, sobbing and whispering to herself, and fear seized him, too: that she would hurt herself, that she would fall into the stairwell in one of those blind rushes. Pushing his stick before him, still urgently saying her name, he started after her— a hopeless chase, but impossible to abandon. Then she, perhaps blindly answering his voice, ran back toward him, and they met violently.

"I can't find the place, I can't find the place! Oh, mister, take me back, I got to get my brick—"

He muttered, breathless from their hard meeting, "Take hold of my coat. Here! Give me your hand, take hold of my coat!"

This time she obeyed—or at least let her grip be altered so that he could, however awkwardly, move again and draw her behind him. He lost no time in doing so.

Unfortunately, at the moment he did not know exactly where they were. They had done so much gyrating during their separation he had lost his bearings. If she had been a little calmer, he would have made her look to find the windows before they started: as he remembered, these were always to some degree visible. But as things were, he judged it simpler just to set off, pushing his stick before him and holding his other hand half raised to meet any descent of the sloping roof. As soon as he reached any part of the wall or roof, he had only to determine which part it was and then the entire map of the attic would fall into place within his mind. And very soon he felt his hand touch and then follow a descending rafter.

He changed direction, rapidly passing along the slope to determine its length. For a brief, passionate moment he regretted that Dorothea had not in fact betrayed him, and left some familiar object to tell him where it, and he, stood. But nothing was left.

He was continuing intently to finger his way when the girl behind him burst out whispering again.

"Oh, *no*—oh, that's the *window!*"

"Where?" he said sharply. "Ahead? *Which window?*"

Like some echo of his words, he heard quite clearly the report of the sprung board by the bathroom door. Someone had stepped on it.

He said nothing—it was not necessary; the girl had heard, too.

They fell into double silence, intense and brief. In that silence, she let go of his coat.

He still did not speak—not even her name. He only reached across his braced stick to recapture her—but she was gone. That sound had told her where to go, where the stair would be, and she was gone to reach it in total new obedience. She would not obey him now, and he could not match the rapid stealth with which she was leaving him: almost running across the floor on her sneaker-clad feet. He listened dully to hear her fall into the stairwell, but she did not. In some desperate, almost noiseless scramble, she was regaining her lost perch.

And he had, automatically still trying, found his bearings: he was standing near the window, the back window. Overlooking a double row of deserted back yards.

Into their silence, the man turned the knob of the attic door.

Chapter 6

The holding door gave him no trouble. This time, he meant to come in. The key was turned again, and the door opened, and in that moment Mr. Nicholas regained the power to move.

At the same time, the girl fell. Fell, or was pulled down—he could not tell. But there was no mistaking the cascade of thumps that marked her fall into the stairwell, or the rage of growling with which the man received her.

Pushing his stick before him, Mr. Nicholas began to run across the floor.

When the girl screamed, he stopped dead. She screamed twice, sounds of animal pain, which Mr. Nicholas answered with all the force of his voice.

"Let her alone!" he shouted. "For God's sake, let the child alone!"

He might have been an echo, a ghost of that attic, for all the difference he made. Some scuffle, hard and violent, continued until his stick reached the edge of the floor. Then it stopped.

There was not a sound of the girl. Only of the panting, lurching man down below. Then only the panting.

Mr. Nicholas struck the floor as hard as he could, and then raised his stick high.

"You murderer!" he called. "I know you! Get out of here—get out of this house!"

The faintest grayness bloomed upon his vision. Some radiance was turned full on him: the flashlight. Mr. Nicholas stared sternly, desperately downward, beneath his raised stick.

"Get out of here!" he said loudly. "Get out!"

Like a slow reply, the man whispered: "Why, you dirty old bastard, you. You dirty old bastard ..."

It was not even a voice. To Mr. Nicholas, listening as a stifling man might breathe—with his whole concentration in the effort—no clue of humanity came with the words. Barely the words themselves, on harsh, heavy breath.

Mr. Nicholas said nothing, and stepped back. To this invitation, the man slowly began to ascend, still whispering.

"... you doing up here with the kid, eh? Dirty old bastard ... dirty old ..."

With a sudden, sideways slash, Mr. Nicholas brought his stick down. It was caught, and held. After one tug, Mr. Nicholas let it remain briefly in this double hold. Then, with all his force, he thrust forward.

The man's backward stagger nearly pulled him down into the well, too. There was a moment when the stick was nearly free ... and then he knew his legs would not do it, would not give him the support he needed, and at once Mr. Nicholas let go. Doubly freed, the stick clattered down the steps and stopped.

The man laughed.

At first, Mr. Nicholas did not recognize the flat, open-mouthed sound for what it was. Then he identified and dismissed it, continuing slowly to back away—a magnet, if nothing more. And a magnet that could grip and hold, when the time came.

Going slowly backward across his attic, Mr. Nicholas began to feel that the time would never come. He had, in his last resource, invented a game too satisfactory to this dead-minded beast he drew after him—at once a respite and a long chance to threaten, which the man was in no haste to alter. With his flashlight steadily trained—but not too near, there was no warmth in the grayness—he came shuffling after, spewing slow obscenities for his pleasure as he came.

There was no doubt that they pleased him, that his slow mind took pleasure in groping out words for the girl's debauching, and grotesquely attaching them to the old man in his view. Mr. Nicholas, far past squeamishness or any sense of shock, listened with great care to the voice. But it never became one. It was not that the man took any counter-care to deceive. He had no need to. He was producing sounds at the level of one in delirium, or in sleep, and no more recognizably. Because no thought was there, no individual voice ever appeared.

Mr. Nicholas was also trying to gauge to what degree the man was drunk. There was no doubt that he had been drinking; the still air stank of him by now. He muttered and moved like someone far gone. Yet he had caught Mr. Nicholas's stick soon enough. No doubt he had caught the girl's arm on its descent, too, in order to pull her down so quickly. And he had succeeded in breaking the streetlight with a stone, no matter after how many tries. Mr. Nicholas decided there was no use trying to guess how much of the man's behavior was due to drink and how much due to sheer animalism released by the drinking. The main thing was that he was still physically competent.

Resigning himself to this, Mr. Nicholas took the initiative and stood still. The man was not prepared for this. As at the thrust stick, he lost balance. The light's grayness went away, came back. The drone of loose words stopped.

A younger man might have leaped forward then, with some chance of success. Mr. Nicholas did not even try. He simply stood, keeping his hands open and ready—thank God, they were still strong.

The other did not like this stopping. For himself, he chose to keep in motion, in a slow, peripheral circling of the motionless man. He made no more sound except for his shuffling and breathing; perhaps he was engaged in some attempt at thought. Mr. Nicholas waited, turning as necessary to keep their encounter face to face.

Mercifully soon, the man struck. It must have been with the flashlight, to cause such a painful blow. Fortunately he caught Mr. Nicholas's shoulder instead of the portion of the head he had no doubt aimed for—and in addition, he dropped the flashlight. But these mishaps only ended his attempt at planned attack, and he reverted much more successfully to a simple seizure of Mr. Nicholas, which immediately brought them both to the floor.

Then Mr. Nicholas took hold. He took the best and most secure hold he could manage, with each hand, and locked on—in one case to the underarm part of a jacket, and in the other to a fistful of hair, of which there seemed to be plenty. Still conscious, still not too much distracted by pain, Mr. Nicholas felt that these gripping hands of his were well placed, and would not now fail no matter what happened. Even in unconsciousness, even—if that was to be—in death, his hands would not unlock, this beast would not get free of him to go back to the girl at the foot of the stairs. And if he tried, he would have to drag Mr. Nicholas's body along with him. The hands would not unlock.

At first the man was distracted by the grip on his hair, and tried to prize it off. While he was fumbling, Mr. Nicholas heard the child trying to come silently up the stairs. If anything could have loosened his grip, the weakening despair that flooded him then would have done it. For she was after—oh, God, she was after that brick again....

The fumbling stopped, and two savage hands seized his throat. No cry from Mr. Nicholas could have passed them. But with all his heart, his mind—his bursting mind—he thought to her: *Run, run, run away....*

He heard her suddenly clatter down the stairs.

The hands heard her. They did not slacken, but were still. Then they were gone.

Mr. Nicholas's hands did not unlock.

His heavy old body hung from them—twisted, jerked, flung, struck, kicked, his body still depended from those hands that were his mind now, his life, all that remained of him. And the hands held. As long as he knew of them at all, he knew they held.

When it was always dark, sound was the light you woke to. The mind's real darkness then became no sound; and this was surprisingly rare. There was always some sort of sound, somewhere, to a total listener; and so when Mr. Nicholas began to be aware of himself—as a consciousness, and yet as a consciousness within a void—he seriously considered whether he had not entered some form of afterlife.

As much as by the void, in which he knew he lay, he was influenced by the altered quality of his own consciousness. He was himself, and yet not his known self; and this more than anything convinced him.

To his faint surprise, he found that he did not know what to do. His first impulse, one of respect, was to offer prayer. And yet, what prayer? His altered consciousness, feebly revolving all the known words, could find none which seemed appropriate to say *now*. And then he came, as an afterthought, to the Gloria Patri—so brief that it was almost gone before he recognized it: ... As it was in the beginning, is now, and ever shall be, world without end ...

Was it even a prayer? Yet his anxiety was subsiding, surely this was the one. Firmly, he thought his prayer again and then—closing his mind—submitted himself once more to the new void.

After a while there were hands, a child's hands.

He murmured without stirring (and somehow without sound): "Get in, get in, don't catch cold"; but the child was crying.

He made himself wake further. Some very pleasant sense of dreaming still clung to him, and he could not at once tell which child this was. But he put his hand up to it. There was pain somewhere, too.

The crying child had begun to whisper, "Get up, get up—oh, mister, don't be dead, don't die—get up—"

Mary Rose.

He said her name, but she paid no attention and only went on whispering, "... get up, please get up, I'll help you—I got your stick, here's your stick—please get up, mister, I'll help you ..."

"No," he said, breaking into this firmly but kindly. "No, I can't do that."

There was silence for a time. He could go back to sleep.

Then she spoke to him. In a real voice, neither a whisper nor a mutter. It was the first he had heard of her voice, and the surprise of it woke him entirely.

"Are you sure? Did you try?"

It was his own normal voice that had evoked hers, of course, and so he used it again.

"No, I haven't tried, Mary Rose."

"Aren't you going to?"

How desolate she sounded! He turned his head, and became aware of the floor boards beneath it, and the capacity for pain within it. And of much else.

"Child, what are you doing back here?" he said, appalled. "Where is that man?"

"It's all right," she assured him quickly. "Don't worry, it's all right! I locked everything, with the chains up—even the door down to the cellar! And I put those shutters over the busted window, with that fasten they got, and I pushed that big chest over in front—he couldn't get back in here in a million years!"

Something had gone very wrong. He could not yet grasp what it was.

"But why did you do that?" he asked; and said, believing it, "I told you to run home!"

"I know, I did—I did, mister! First I was going to try and get him off you, and then I didn't know if I could—he twisted my arm pretty bad, and I couldn't work it. It's not broke," she said quickly, "it's just twisted. But anyway I thought if I made a noise like running away he'd get off you and come after me. I can run about sixty times faster than him any day. And I was going to tell Bud about you, honest I was—I would have told him, and he would have come back here and got you. But he wasn't home. His car wasn't in the yard, I guess he stayed at Lou's. Sometimes he does that."

Out of his total confusion, Mr. Nicholas asked: "Who is Bud?"

"My brother."

She was crouched close against him, speaking very fast, with long pauses. Recurrent small spasms of shuddering went through her, and echoed in Mr. Nicholas, but she paid no attention to them. Except for these, her breathing was fairly regular, and her voice—her small, high voice—seemed normal too.

"You're bleeding," he said.

"It's just my nose, it bleeds all the time. If I fight, or if anybody hits me on the head. Everybody around here knows not to hit me on the head. Except him." She burst out: "He's in our yard—in that old Chevy that don't run. I don't know if he passed out or what. Or if he's just *waiting* there!"

Mr. Nicholas sighed in defeat.

"I don't understand this, Mary Rose. You were home? You went home, and then came back here?"

"Well," she said, "sure—I had to go *somewheres* fast!"

But he had infected her with doubt. She began to argue.

"See, our back door don't lock. And I could see him out there in the Chevy, I could see him. And he could see Bud's car wasn't there, he'd know he wasn't home just the same as I would. And everybody knows it's pretty hard to wake up my dad, and he isn't—he's pretty old anyway.

So I thought, what if he comes in here and does the same thing to my dad? Like he did to you, mister. So I sneaked out the front way and came back here—this place locks up good. If he came in our place and I wasn't there, he wouldn't stay.

"I put up all those chains," she went on presently. "Boy, she has them everywhere, doesn't she? But it's a good thing for us, though."

She meant his daughter-in-law. Confusion began to overtake Mr. Nicholas.

"She's a fearful woman," he murmured. "Always was. Yet nothing has ever happened to Dorothea, that I know of ..."

"Even if he comes back here and gets into the cellar, he couldn't get up here. I don't think he will, though. He might have passed out, I couldn't tell. And anyway the light's on in Millers' kitchen and that means it's after four o'clock. He won't hang around anymore so close to daylight, he won't do that."

The light in Millers' kitchen. What kitchen this was—what kitchen had become Millers' kitchen, he had no idea. And yet he saw that light, that beacon, that promise of release which she had ignored. A little groan escaped him, at the thought of the wakened household, able to defend her, to call in help. Why had she run away from it, back to this ghost house—and to him?

"Oh, Mary Rose—why didn't you go there?" he murmured.

"Go where?"

He had forgotten the name.

She said, "You mean to *Millers'*?"

Apparently he did. It was her turn to be bewildered.

"Gee, I wouldn't go there, mister! I guess you don't know what they think about us—they hate us worse than rats! They're the ones that keep reporting us all the time, they want to get me put in Children's! Only Bud won't let them," she said quickly. "He makes good money, and he might get married, too. Only I hope it's not Lou ..."

She fell quiet, pursuing some uneasy speculation. He could not follow her any more. Nor, somehow, could he get back—back out of the maze she had led him into. At its far end shone a light, a kitchen light, that they might not approach. He could not remember what light this was, or even if it was real.

At his chest, his vest button, her fingers worried lightly. His main awareness came to center in this touching, which was like his cat's when it wanted to wake him. This was not his cat, he did not know where his cat was—and yet he recognized a similar persistent message. He ought to get up.

She suggested as much, presently.

"Couldn't you get up, mister? Couldn't you try?

"I got your stick," she said.

He heard her hunting it, beside them. Then the knob end came to his hand. He closed his fingers round it.

"If you could get up, we could just go home when it gets light. Nobody would have to know. I could help you."

He had, at that moment, no quarrel with any of this. But he did not move.

"Bud might not even come back," she went on, explaining their position to him. "He might go right to work. I could call him and he'd come and get you, except how would I say I knew you were here? He wouldn't think it was anything bad," she said firmly. "He knows I wouldn't ever do anything like that, because that's the one thing he couldn't stop them taking me, if I got into that kind of trouble. Besides, I wouldn't anyway. He knows that. But he'd know I busted in."

She considered this. Mr. Nicholas, relieved to be still following, waited. He gathered that they were not afraid of Bud, but that he presented some sort of problem.

"I don't mind a licking," she said.

"No," said Mr. Nicholas, to his own surprise.

"But the worse thing is if he doesn't give me a licking, if he just gets fed up. See, like he says, by now I ought to be able to look after myself, and help with Dad, too—and I *do*," she said. "We don't need anybody, he doesn't have to marry Lou! He'd be crazy to marry Lou," she said with sudden passion. "If he doesn't want to already, he'd *hate* it if he did! And believe me, mister, she doesn't act so nice when she doesn't have to. She doesn't want us. I don't care what she says, she doesn't want us. She wants Bud, but she don't want us, and she'd get rid of us pretty quick, too, if they got married!"

Mr. Nicholas's fingers tightened on his stick. He believed her.

"But when—if something like this happens, then sometimes he really gets fed up. Mostly he just gets mad, and yells at Dad, or gives me a licking—that's all right. But I hate it when he gets fed up. I *hate* it....

"Someday he'll get so fed up he'll marry Lou," she said. Her voice was hushed with that fear.

In his own bed, Mr. Nicholas always rose first on one elbow and then put his legs over the edge of the bed. Once he got into that position, he was as good as up. Or if he were sitting up with a wall behind him—they had managed that, he and Mary Rose. But the problem here, he began to realize, was not the lack of support, or a place to put his legs over, but a curious lassitude that kept him from making any beginning. He lay and *thought* movement, but somehow he made none.

Could he move? Convulsively, he pushed an arm out from his body—and it went. Now if he could roll sideways and brace upon it ... But at these first efforts, she eagerly seized upon him and began to help. To *try* to help—by tugging him upright.

The result of this was such a vertigo of pain that Mr. Nicholas could not even speak, to protest. He could not get loose from her, he could not make her stop—and he began seriously to fear that the child was going to kill him.

The horror of this idea—that he might suddenly sag lifeless in her poor little arms, in this deserted house—was probably what got him upright at last. Certainly none of the equipment by which he had to raise himself could have done it. Even when he finally stood—or hung—between his stick and Mary Rose's small body, he could hardly believe in their accomplishment.

Or be glad of it. He felt, to tell the truth, like a homemade Lazarus—a clear mistake.

But there was no doubt of the child's joy. She was incoherent with it, and with praise for him.

"See, you could do it, mister—you could do it! I didn't do it, I *couldn't*—I was so scared! But you did it, mister! Oh, you got up so *good*," she cried, embracing him.

Her embrace hurt him. Her voice hurt him. He could not reflect one particle of her joy. But here he was, raised, sober, with a clearing mind.

He said glumly, "Hush, child. Let go ..." and began to try if his legs would hold.

Chapter 7

Somehow they got down the attic stairs.

Although he had no spare energy to remonstrate, the child quickly learned to restrain her rough help. By the time they reached the stairs she was behaving as intelligently as a guide dog after months of training, staying close for support but never tugging or pulling at him. He felt some pride for her, and intended to speak of it when he could.

Thank God, his mind had cleared. And he had become more familiar with the sources of his pain and able to define them. Nothing vital seemed to be broken.

On the other hand, his general condition was extremely poor; and leaning between the wall and his stick—with Mary Rose breathing anxiously beside him—he had to admit that this was as far as he could go, just now.

It was going to be a blow to the child. Her goal was the dining-room chairs, where she seemed to envision them sitting in a civilized manner and waiting for daylight. It had also occurred to her (she was a very bright child) that if he waited on a chair, they would avoid the problem of getting him off the floor again. She was right; but he simply was not able to go on.

He was going to have to speak of this soon. Already, with controlled but rising anxiety, she had twice asked him if he was all right.

He drew a careful breath and answered:

"Yes. Thank you. But I am going to rest in my room now. Come with me."

Most of this journey could be made against the wall; and in addition, he was remembering the radiator cover. This was built in; Dorothea would hardly have gone to the trouble of removing it. And it could be sat on. He wished he had the energy to explain these things to Mary Rose, who was behaving in a disconsolate—almost a frantic—way, at this change in plan. But he had to keep on, wordless, leaning his way down the wall, until at last he opened the familiar door and crept in.

She followed, still trying to urge him back.

"... like a piggyback, see? I can do it, honest I can, I'm strong and I'd be careful! And you could keep one hand on the rail if you wanted, but you wouldn't have to. I'd be like your stick, see, only better, and you could lean right over on me, so you wouldn't hardly be walking down on your own legs at all! Please try it, mister—please!"

Around the wall, halfway along the next. And there it was. He found his radiator cover and began to lower himself on it. And was seated at last. He put both hands over his stick and found a balance. Now there was no part of him without support. The relief was enormous.

Silenced at last, the girl had come to stand in front of him. Suddenly she gave a small cry. It jarred him, but he didn't move.

"Mister! I can see light around you! It's getting light, look!" She added hastily, "I mean, the window's all gray, like—you can see it. I can see the whole shape of you!"

"Good," he murmured, not stirring.

Then she laughed. A real laugh, of pure delight.

"Hey, it's tomorrow! Get it? Like all that stuff was yesterday, and it's not yesterday anymore—it's tomorrow!"

She was absolutely enchanted by her discovery. He wouldn't have interfered with her logic for the world. Now everything began to interest and please her.

"Hey, that's a pretty good seat," she said, exploring it. "What is it? What's in it? She sure left a lot of good things, didn't she?"

He muttered, "Don't knock my stick ..." and she replied, content, "No, it's okay, I can see that, too. I can see *every*thing, sort of! Honest I can. Even out the window ... Well, no," she admitted. "Not down. I can see up, a little, but down still isn't anything yet. Up it's tomorrow, down it's yesterday. Right?"

"Yes," said Mr. Nicholas.

He had a new trouble. A new embarrassment. For he needed very much, very suddenly, to get to the bathroom. Was, in fact, going to have to get there—without delay.

He *must* move. He must move, get up, and go back down that hall to the bathroom. Now.

Instead he kept on sitting there. Remembering the time he had heard Dorothea tell his boy how he was—"anyway"—such a clean old man. As if, given the rest of him, she might well have expected him to be dribbling his food, wetting his bed. He had been too amused to be angry. Poor Dorothea, poor Martyr! It must have been a low point for her, that day.

Then, in great haste, he got up.

It startled the child.

"What's the matter?" she said, back to panic. To whispers. "Mister, what—"

"Nothing." The worst of it was, he had to keep moving as he tried to reassure her. "Stay here. I'm just going to the bathroom."

"But I'll help you! Here—lean—"

"*Stay. Here.*"

He said it between his teeth, and it stopped her. In the interval he got clear out of the room.

Then down the hall. Into the bathroom. Door shut.

His subsequent relief was so great that he was in no way prepared for what happened. In no way capable of defending himself against it, or even of controlling himself. Perhaps he had used up his stock of control.

What he did was to flush the toilet.

The gesture was habitual, he gave it no thought—until suddenly, washing all thought away in terror, the roaring echoes of that loosed water seemed to dissolve him in despair.

He had given them away. The man would come back. There would be another beating.

For the first time in his life, Mr. Nicholas was lost in absolute physical terror. This had nothing to do with the child, left unprotected behind him. For that moment, for him, there was no child. There was only the lurking man, who would hear—whom he had *summoned*—and his own aching, beaten body.

He would be beaten again.

He could not survive another beating.

How long this madness of terror lasted—for it certainly was nothing else—Mr. Nicholas did not know. When it left him, he found himself half collapsed against the sink, clutching the taps with all his mindless strength.

It was a fortunate position, because he vomited.

Sometime later—again, time unknown—his hands managed to turn the taps. The time that it took to rinse himself, and the sink, and then to capture and feebly suck in some of the water, he was very conscious of. It seemed endless. His clumsiness was past belief. But his mind was his own again.

He was even numbly aware of his fortune in having water. Why had Dorothea not turned this off, too?

At last he was finished, and could allow himself to close the toilet seat and let himself down upon it. With pain and patience, he retrieved his stick from the floor, and crossed his hands on it, and rested.

He felt no shame. His experience did not leave that residue; apparently it was not that kind of experience.

But as feeling did return to him, he found that it was taking the form of anger. Deep, rooted anger, such as he had rarely known—anger quietly and steadily growing in him as he rested there, and giving him something of its own strength, like a miraculous form of nourishment or rest. Anger that he meant to act upon.

When he heard the girl whispering at the door—"Mister! Mister, are you all right?"—he got himself up and answered her calmly.

"Yes, I'm coming."

"Oh, mister, open the door—please! Please come out, please let me help—"

He opened the door. Instantly her little hands were on him, touching, exploring, claiming—but carefully. She remembered to be careful with her hands, though her worrying flowed all over him in words. In whispers.

"Oh, mister, I was so scared—you were so long! I was so scared you passed out or something.... Oh, mister, I swear to God, I—"

"Don't say that," said Mr. Nicholas, in his own voice. He added, "It's very rude to call people 'mister.' You must say my name—Mr. Nicholas."

"Yes," she said. "Yes, sure, I know—Mr. Nicholas."

"That's right. Mary Rose."

"Come on," she urged him. "Come back!"

As soon as they were back in his room he heard her turning the key in the lock. (She had trouble with it; no one had turned that lock in years.) So she must have known fear, too, beyond her fear for him. His anger took note of this, as he went back to his radiator cover and let himself down upon it.

The minute he was back in his place, her spirits went up again. This time he wasn't deceived. The fear was still in her, waiting to leap up at any moment—at many moments, perhaps all her life long.

"Oh, now I can see you so *good*," she exclaimed. "All around you—and like where the fences are, out there, and *everything!* What do you think, mister—Mr. Nicholas? Do you think about fifteen more minutes we should go? Do you feel all right? Or half an hour? Where do you have to go?" she said suddenly. "Do you live far, now?"

"Just next door. I'm staying with Mrs. Thompson. Do you know her?"

"Oh, sure, everybody knows her." Her need to be polite made her add: "She's all right, she never reported me."

"Then she knows you, Mary Rose?"

He was only puzzled, that indoor Lettie should know a child he himself could not place; but his question somehow warned her into silence.

He said, "Why are you afraid to tell me your real name, child? You don't think *I'm* going to report you, do you?"

"It's my real name," she said quickly.

He let this pass.

"Do you honestly think I would do anything to make trouble for you, Mary Rose?"

She wanted to answer him, and answer well—the desire brought her closer to him, and she put her hand on his shoulder. Lightly; remembering not to hurt.

But she couldn't find what to say.

"You wouldn't mean to," she said at last.

"I don't do things unless I mean to. I won't make that kind of mistake."

She said shrewdly, "You still want to tell the police, though."

"I'm going to tell the police. I'm going to do everything in my power to see that they find this man who attacked you."

"No, he never did attack me," she said in instant withdrawal. "Mister, don't you ever tell anybody a thing like that because it's a *lie*, he *didn't!* And if you ever even said a thing like that they'd put me in Children's, there wouldn't be anything Bud could do about it, because that's the one thing he—"

"Mary Rose, stop it," he commanded. "This man attacked *both* of us, if you like that better. He beat us up," he said distinctly.

"But you fought him! You fought him *good*, mister—Mr. Nicholas! Boy, I never would have got away if you didn't fight him the way you did—

and I would have helped you, if it wasn't for my arm. We could have got him, between the both of us. I never even *thought* you would fight so good!"

He did not say, "I only hung on. I wasn't even trying to fight." The moment when he meant to say it passed—and he let it go. But that small vanity distracted him.

She rushed on, relieved that their difference was over, or that the subject was changed.

"I was the dopey one! Gee, I don't know how he got hold of my arm so fast, though—except it was like I couldn't get it up again, you know? Without I let go my brick, I mean, and I didn't want to do that. But he knocked me loose of it anyway," she admitted. "The thing is, you have to practice on something like that, like hitting down with a brick, because the *brick* makes a difference. You know? It's not like just hitting—it makes your aim different, because of the brick is heavy, like. I should have practiced on it, but I didn't know. I will now, though."

He was not deceived. Under this confident tomboy the frightened child still lay. And he could see no way to learn what he must know without reawakening that child.

He said gravely, "You realize that this man is extremely dangerous, Mary Rose. Especially to you—because you know what he is really like."

"I sure do," she said. "Don't worry—he'll never catch me again!"

"No. We'll make sure of it—that he never again can harm you, or any other child."

Uneasy, she murmured: "He isn't after anybody else. I'm the one he likes. And he won't—"

"*Likes!*" Mr. Nicholas exclaimed.

"No—okay, I didn't mean—I'm the one he's *after*," she said, despairing. "And I *know* he's a creep, I know it! He's crazy—I wouldn't go anywheres near him again for a million bucks, I'm not even going to make him sorry, or anything. I'll just keep away from him, I promise!"

Mr. Nicholas said to her, with care: "Tell me this. Do you have any possible reason for shielding this man, aside from not wanting anyone to know what has happened?"

"What?"

"This man, Mary Rose. Is he some—friend of your brother? Or of your father?"

"No!" Shocked, she said, "Gee, that's a lousy thing to say, Mr. Nicholas!"

"I'm sorry. But you don't care what happens to him?"

"No! Why should I care what ... What do you mean?"

"This is what I mean. If I can have him arrested, and put into jail, without bringing you into it *in any way*, would you be glad?"

"Sure," she said, a minimal agreement. "I guess so. But how could you do that? What could they arrest him for?"

"For what he has done to me," he said quietly. "That will be better than nothing."

In a voice hushed with discovery, she said: "Hey. *Hey!*" she cried. "You could *do* that—sure you could! Why, it could be like he broke into your house—he was going to steal your money! And you caught him, and you had a fight, and he beat you up! You could say like he robbed you, too—boy, then they could really get him. Couldn't they?"

"Yes," he said.

"But you ought to get the money out of here first! You could take it away and hide it, before you call the cops—you better do that," she said earnestly. "Do you want me to go up and get it for you? I could, right now—it's getting lighter, I could see up there. And then we could go!"

"But there isn't any money, Mary Rose."

"Oh," she said. And then: "Oh, sure. Okay. It's okay." She didn't believe him. And she was bitterly hurt.

He sighed. His small return of energy was not lasting ... and there was still so far to go.

Too tired for guile, he murmured, "I'm sorry you believe that story about me. I have many faults, but I'm not a miser."

"I didn't think that! It was just—everybody said—"

"Yes. All right. It doesn't matter. What does matter," he said doggedly, "is that this man should be kept from doing more harm. You want that, don't you?"

"Yes. Sure. Only ..."

"Only what?"

"Well, how would you know who he was, Mr. Nicholas? I mean, how would you say you knew? If you didn't want to say who told you?"

He recognized the need for care, here, and took time to answer.

"Well, it's this way, child. When you lack one of your senses, then you learn to use your other senses more. They get sharper because they have to. There are many ways in which I recognize people—the way they walk, the way they talk. Even the way they breathe, or the odors they carry about them. Little habits. My son jingles the change in his pockets, in a certain way. Mrs. Nicholas rubs her fingers together when she is thinking. You snap your socks, don't you?"

She was delighted.

"Hey—that's pretty sharp! I guess I do! Hey, I could practice on that—I could keep my eyes shut like two hours every day, and—"

"But you do understand that I can tell who people are, even though I can't see them?"

"Yes," she said. "Except—you didn't."

He didn't what? Then he understood. The man was someone he ought to have recognized.

"That's true," he said steadily. "But that's because this man was, quite literally, not himself. All the ways in which I would ordinarily have recognized him were changed. His voice, his step. Even his smell. His whole personality. But I *might* have recognized him—no one can prove that I didn't."

"Well ..."

"Of course they can't. It's a known fact that I can recognize people, Mary Rose. In any ordinary circumstances. And you remember, I am not going to tell how unusual these circumstances were. I shall simply say," he went on, wearily finding words, "that I came upon him here—"

"In the dark! And that was why he didn't see you coming—because you wouldn't *need* any light!"

"Exactly."

"But he didn't know you could tell right away it was him, in the dark, and so he tried to get away—and he beat you up, and got away!"

"Yes."

Her energy was remorseless. Even the force of her speaking, so close, with her hand upon his shoulder, shook him like a too-powerful motor attached to some ancient chassis.

Then the hand left him.

"He'll tell them it's not true, though. If you tell on him, then he'll tell them I was here."

"He'll be the last one to do that," he said dryly.

"No. He will. He'll say I was here—he'll say it was us that was here, and him that found us. Like when he came upstairs, remember? Remember what he said? That's what he'll tell them."

The panic was back in her voice—so unexpectedly, this time, that he could not adjust to answer it.

He said uncertainly, "No, child, that's not true," and put out his hand. But she eluded it.

"Sure he will—that's what he'll say, if you tell the cops on him. Because if you try to get him in trouble, then he'll try to get us in trouble. Oh, mister—don't!" she burst out. "Please, mister, please—don't tell them!"

He said helplessly, "Mary Rose, you are very wrong about this—now come back here, and don't be so unreasonable."

"But it's not! It's what he'll do, I know he will! You don't know him!"

She said again, but differently, "You don't know him ..." and he knew she was realizing that this was, literally, true. He did not yet know.

Nor was she going to tell him. The intensity of her silence, the continuing small movements of retreat, told him how narrow she felt her escape had been, from making such a confidence.

He said with a last effort at command: "You are making up things to frighten yourself. This man will be so—"

"No, mister."

Very soft, very final, her breath of answer crossed the room to him. He heard the soft fumbling of the key in the lock.

"What are you doing?" he said sharply. "Mary Rose!"

But he knew what she was doing. She was going away from him—now, quickly, before she could betray herself anymore. Or perhaps his mysterious power of recognition, in which he had wanted her to believe, had grown to enormous proportions in her mind: as if he might also have some entry to her thoughts.

She got the key round, and opened the door.

"I'm sorry, mister—I'm sorry—"

He said nothing. She would not have heard him in any case. Her sneakers, that carried so small a weight, rapidly crossed the hall boards and went rushing down the steps. He heard the front door chain come down, and the door open.

On daylight, he prayed. On clear daylight. The urgency of his hope brought him to his feet once more; and he was crossing the room, doggedly, hopelessly following her, before he realized that he did not even know where she would go.

Chapter 8

By nine-thirty the next morning, Lettie Thompson had decided to call Dorothea. She got the new number simply by trying the old one, and was rather proud of her efficiency. But at Dorothea's instant response, she got flustered.

"I'm awfully sorry to bother you, dear—but it did seem so odd, that note, I mean. It really frightened me until I looked in and saw him sleeping. But I thought I'd better just tell you, on account of the responsibility. What do you suppose it means?"

"I'll be there in half an hour, Mrs. Thompson," was Dorothea's sole response. So grimly made that Mrs. Thompson began to feel frightened all over again.

The telephone was in the hall, so she had not needed to disturb John to use it. She did risk another peep at him, lying there deeply sleeping on top of the day bed in the daylit room—of course the light would not bother him. But surely he did not usually sleep in his clothing? On top of the covers?

Fear nudged her again, and she tried to slip into the room for a closer look—she wanted to see him *breathe*. But her days for stealthy movement were past, and he heard her—his hand began to grope on the bed beside him. Relieved, she stood still.

He said, "Mary Rose ..."; but it was a sleeper's voice. She did not reply. When he was still again she got herself out of the room and limped back to the kitchen to wait for Dorothea. She had the note propped up on the table there, so she would not mislay it; but returning, she found it had lost most of its power to unsettle her. It was so clearly untrue, and so clearly—now that she looked at it calmly—the work of a child.

On a child's lined paper, in pencil, someone had painfully written: "Mr. Nicklis is in his house Upstairs. He is hurt very bad."

It was such a queer little message, unlike any child mischief in her experience. Lettie gave a shiver, and put it down again. She felt unexpected concern for the child itself—what confusion had possessed it, to come putting such a note under her door? And so early, too! She hadn't even considered rising to answer the bell at such an hour. The note had lain there a long time, until she did come out to unlock the door and take in her paper. How awful, if its message had been true!

She began to be vaguely sorry she had called Dorothea. Some mystery was here, that she ought to have talked over with John, first. Now perhaps they would both be angry with her—John, and Dorothea too. Well, she couldn't help it.

Yet when Dorothea came—in less than half an hour—Mrs. Thompson's defensiveness died at sight of her. Without makeup, her head wrapped in a plain scarf, Dorothea looked so tired and resigned that Mrs. Thompson's heart went out to her.

"Oh, I shouldn't have bothered you, dear—it's really nothing, and I know how busy you are—"

"No, you were right, Mrs. Thompson," Dorothea said. "I'm the one that's at fault. I knew it all day yesterday, I couldn't sleep last night for thinking about it. Where is Father, please?"

"Why, he's asleep, he's perfectly all right—now at least sit down, dear, and have a little coffee. I've made it fresh for you. And here's this silly note, I don't know why I even paid any attention to it! It's just some child's idea of—something, I don't know."

Dorothea picked up the note and read it standing—read it carefully. Then she put it down, and shook her head. Mrs. Thompson was startled to see tears in her eyes.

"No, it's true—I know it's true. He went over there. And he hurt

himself. However he got back here, he's hurt himself. Have you called
the doctor?" When Mrs. Thompson stammered that she had not, that
such a thing hadn't occurred to her, Dorothea said decisively: "Then I
will. May I use your phone?"

At the thought of her rather frightening old friend waking to find
himself under medical examination (and through her fault, too) Mrs.
Thompson gathered strength to resist.

"Why, I think that would be a mistake, Dorothea—before you've even
looked at him. I've looked at him, and he's—he's just sleeping. He even
called me 'Mary' in his sleep—'Mary Rose,' I should say. Though I
didn't know he called her that."

"He didn't," said Dorothea flatly. "That wasn't Mother's name. Is he
upstairs, Mrs. Thompson?"

"No, no, right in the front room, dear. I don't heat the whole house
anymore.... Right in here, you see. I don't know why he chose not to, not
to get ready for bed. I had a pair of George's pajamas laid out for him,
but—"

Mrs. Thompson was considerably startled then to have her own
sitting-room door closed in her face—with Dorothea on the other side
of it. Helpless, she stood there a moment longer and then wandered back
to the kitchen and sat down. With relief. Of course Dorothea had not
meant to be rude—she was incapable of such a thing. Just overwrought.
And to tell the truth, Mrs. Thompson was not anxious to be present
when John first woke and found Dorothea poking at him. Let them
settle it first, and then she would bring in some nice hot coffee. And the
coffeecake that Mr. Rudd had brought down with their chicken
yesterday.

Dorothea, alone in the strange parlor, made no attempt to touch her
father-in-law. She went and stood over him for some time, noting with
exact despair every evidence of disorder and accident that she could find.
Nothing surprised her, not his streaked and filthy shirt, nor his torn coat
pocket, nor even his visible hand with dried blood on it from some
wound. When she came to his head—the poor white hair in such a state
as she had never seen it, the whole side of his face discolored with ... with
dirt? Or bruise?—she paused for a long time.

Then, quietly moving a chair to the day bed, she sat down and put her
face in her hands and began—silently, passionately—to cry. This was
the one relief that Dorothea allowed herself, and she had learned to do
it very quietly. In such a world, and from such a faulty creature as
herself, she knew that real grief was not wrong, if it did not call
attention to itself or frighten others. That she had never done. And over
the years, her occasional crying spells had come to seem a privacy in

themselves, where she disturbed no one and no one disturbed her.

Yet all at once he spoke to her.

"What is it? What is it? Where are you, child?"

Immediately, assembling her self-control, Dorothea pulled herself together. She needed a moment before she could speak, and put her hand on his, that seemed to search for her. He took it—seized it—and then grew still.

"What? Dorothea?"

"Yes, Father. I'm here."

He let go of her hand, and began another kind of searching, which she recognized—wanting to know where he was. She told him.

"You're at Mrs. Thompson's, dear. I've come to take you home. How do you feel?"

He didn't reply at once. Then his hand, a little furtively, began exploring himself, his clothing. He wanted to know what she saw. Sadly, she watched him.

"Torn my pocket a bit, haven't I?" he muttered finally.

"It doesn't matter." Unable to bear any more, she said: "You've had a fall, haven't you, dear? I just want the doctor to have a look at you, you won't mind that. To make me feel better."

"Good Lord, what's Lettie told you?" he said—but absently. "Where is she, anyway? What time is it?" Then, canceling these questions in irritation: "Where's my stick?"

She had moved it away, and left it where it was. "Please don't get up until the doctor's seen you, Father. I don't want to alarm you, but your head—"

"I want to go to the bathroom," he interrupted coldly, and pushed himself up.

She retrieved the stick without further comment. Once—only once—she had tried to bring him a bedpan. He got himself up, struggling against a distress which he could not conceal. Dorothea rose, too, but did not touch him or speak. She saw with a heavy and patient heart that he was going to fall.

He did not. Erratic, staggering a little, he got under way. It was the wrong way; and still in silence, Dorothea walked toward the door. This was the only form of guiding that he permitted, and he turned and followed her. At the door, he put out his hand and found her arm.

"Now stay here, child—don't fuss. Don't worry, I'm all right. I'll be right back."

"I'm going to call the doctor, Father."

"Do as you like."

She turned to the telephone as he reeled into some near-by door. And shut it firmly.

Her own doctor was not available at this hour of the morning, except through messages relayed to the hospital. With no obvious breakage to offer him, she felt shy of making so much trouble—and besides, it would mean delay. After some hesitation, she looked up the number of a semiretired doctor not far away, whom her father-in-law preferred. He was out on neighborhood calls, but his wife promised to find him and send him over. She wanted to know what was wrong with Mr. Nicholas. Dorothea said without expression that he had had a bad fall. Possible concussion. The doctor's wife said, "Oh, dear ..." and Dorothea cut her off with a polite "Thank you," and hung up.

She did not want to go out into the kitchen, where Mrs. Thompson was hovering in wait, and so pretending to be absorbed in thought she returned to the sitting room and began tidying away all traces of the old man. When this was done she sat down and waited, her dry fingers working upon themselves. He was being very long. She was not going to interfere.

Presently she heard a door open, and her father-in-law's voice saying: "Lettie? Lettie, where are you?"

Had he forgotten she was here, or did he mean to hurt her? Dorothea stayed where she was. She could hear Mrs. Thompson replying, coming to him—trying to urge him into the kitchen. But he did not want that.

"Where's that nice chair I was sitting in last night?" he wanted to know. "I'm a bit turned round, since you changed everything, you know."

They came into the sitting room together, with Mrs. Thompson clumsily attached to him, and he allowing it. Mrs. Thompson gave her an apologetic look, as Dorothea rose in place.

He had done his best to straighten himself up. His face and hands were washed, and his hair was combed, and he had buttoned his jacket over much of the shirt. A button was loose, the torn pocket gaped, and it *was* a bruise on the side of his face. A big one. He looked heartbreaking, and he didn't even know it—Mrs. Thompson was too nervous to mention it. She kept murmuring about coffee.

"Just fresh, and hot. And that coffeecake I showed you last night—"

"I usually take a banana first thing," he replied, "but it doesn't matter. I don't believe I want anything just now, thank you, Lettie. Except to ask you—"

"But Dorothea, you'll have some coffee, won't you?"

He had forgotten her. Unmistakably. Her heart swelled with a kind of bitter pride, to see how startled and guilty he looked. In a low voice, she thanked Mrs. Thompson and refused.

"But I would like to speak to Father a moment, if you don't mind."

Mrs. Thompson, once she grasped what was meant, made a second retreat to her kitchen—urging Dorothea to come and tell her when she wanted coffee. When she had gone, Dorothea came across the room. He still looked disconcerted, but said to her approach: "Well, Dorrie?"

She got down on the floor in front of him, and put her hands on his knees. Warily, he waited for her to speak.

She said earnestly, "Father, I know what's in your mind. I know you're angry with me, and I deserve it. I was angry with you when I left those pieces—when I planned to leave them! That's why I let Johnny take you away from me. But don't punish me by punishing yourself, dear. Don't do that."

"How do you mean?" he said. And then, "Why didn't you say you didn't like that stuff, Dorrie?"

"I didn't dislike it. It went with the house. But I was worried about fitting it in the new house, and I knew you were upset about moving anyway—and when Mrs. Bohr said how much she wished she had dining-room furniture like that, I—"

"Oh, she's taking it, is she? Well, that's something. I thought you'd left it for the Salvation Army."

"No, dear. I wouldn't have given it to anyone who didn't value it. But you know she's going to have a boarding-house there, and—"

"You gave it to her?"

"Well, sold it. But you know furniture like that doesn't bring a great deal nowadays, Father, and I was afraid you—"

"How much?"

"Well, twenty-five dollars," she said, resigned.

He thought about it.

"I suppose that's a fair price, considering," he said at last. "I can't see why you didn't tell me, though. That's what I minded."

"Because I was a coward," she said at once. "And because I was a coward, I blamed you in my mind for it—I imagined you blaming me, and so I wanted to blame you first. And then it seemed to me I had every right to avoid unpleasantness and just do what was sensible—except that I had to make myself angry at you first, in my mind. So I should have known I was wrong. I was wrong, Father."

"Well, I'm sorry you had such a time of it," he replied.

He sounded a little vague, and she raised her head, noticing how large the bruise looked in this light. It seemed to extend down the whole side of his face. He must have run into something very hard, or else fallen with great force—all alone, miles from her, helpless and deserted. He might well have died at that moment, leaving her to live the rest of her life knowing that he had done so. And why. She put her head down on his knees without a tear. But great pools of tears welled up within her, waiting for solitude.

He put an absent hand on her hair.

"But what did you do with my trunks? I couldn't—"

Chimes interrupted them; and Mrs. Thompson called out from the kitchen: "Oh, Dorothea, would you go?"

"It's Dr. Linen," she said, and got up. "Now, Father—if you forgive me, you must let him see you. If you aren't nice to him, I'll know you mean it for me."

"Good heavens, child, let the man in," he replied.

He listened to hear if she came back, but she was being very scrupulous: only the doctor came into the room, and the door shut behind him. Dorothea's slow steps went on down the hall. Poor Lettie.

"Well, John, you're up, are you?" said Dr. Linen's loud voice. "From what Dorothea said I didn't expect that. Been in a scrap, have you?"

Mr. Nicholas flinched, and said crossly: "Stop that, Roger. Behave like a civilized being. I'm perfectly all right—but as a matter of fact, I'm glad you're here. I think you're the very person ... What are you doing?"

"You just let me have my innings, here, and then you can have yours," said Dr. Linen. "How did this happen?"

"A little accident," said Mr. Nicholas.

"Is that it? Well, your little accident had shoes, didn't he? Big ones. Let's get you over on this couch, where I can tell what I'm doing. Want help?"

Mr. Nicholas found that he did. Without comment on either side, he was returned to the day bed, and a businesslike silence ensued—broken only by Dr. Linen's "Does this hurt?" and his own "Certainly" or "Certainly not." There were several sharp Certainlies.

Finally Dr. Linen sat back.

"Well, if there's concussion at all, it's very slight," he said. "But I want those ribs X-rayed. An ambulance would be the simplest way to get you there. And it would save trouble all round, of course, if you'd spend a few days at the hospital while we're at it."

"No," said Mr. Nicholas.

Dr. Linen hadn't waited for an answer.

"And you've got a lot of nasty contusions there, as you know. I don't understand you, John—why don't you want to report this?" he asked. "I'm used to family close-ups, God knows, but that's not your case. Young John could no more do this to you than he could fly, and Dorothea hasn't got the weight. How big is that grandson of yours now?" he asked suddenly.

Mr. Nicholas showed his long teeth.

"Enormous. But we keep him strait-jacketed. Now if you're finished," he said, "I'd like to ask you about a family in this neighborhood. There is a father, ill or otherwise burdensome. A working son named Bud, unmarried. A daughter, probably not named Mary Rose. About eleven or twelve—possibly a small thirteen. Not more."

"Well," said Dr. Linen, and thought. "No idea where, around here?"

"No. Except that the house is probably in considerable disrepair, and there is an automobile that doesn't run standing in the yard."

"Put three or four more in with it, and I'd say Haydens'," said Dr. Linen. "Lord, that place is an eyesore. As a matter of fact, it could be the Haydens," he added. "I don't remember the boy's name, but I suppose he's out of school and working by now. And there was a little girl—Mrs. Reilly on Cross Street used to take her by the day before she went to school. I patched her up a couple of times, haven't seen her since. The father worked for the railroad—engineer, or something. Nothing wrong with him that I know of, except he lost his wife before he got his kids raised."

"Perhaps you are right," Mr. Nicholas said, after a pause. "There aren't many people left around here who occupy a house to themselves. And I have a strong impression that no one else was there."

"When do you mean—when this happened? You were in some strange house when this happened?"

"No, no." Mr. Nicholas's tone became, for him, hesitant. He said, "I would like very much to be sure that the Hayden girl is all right, Roger. Would there be any way of finding that out, without asking directly?"

"You mean of me finding out?" the doctor said bluntly.

"Yes. If they're not your patients, perhaps you might have a patient who's a neighbor? Whom you might drop by to see?"

"Well, what's the point of all this, John—why shouldn't she be all right? I don't like to blunder around completely in the dark, you know."

"No, of course not." Mr. Nicholas hesitated, again, and then apologized for it. "I'm a little tired this morning, I'm afraid. This person who was involved in my accident," he said. "I want to make sure he's done the girl no harm."

"One of her family?"

"No. As a matter of fact, I don't yet know who he is."

"But you mean to find out?"

"If I can. But not at any cost to the girl. Mainly, I want to be sure that she is at home, and all right."

Dr. Linen said as he rose: "This sounds to me like a small part of an ugly story, John."

"Yes. I'm sorry I can't be more help. If the brother's name were Bud," he said, "you could be sure it's the right girl. Perhaps you could find out her name for me."

"Well, the Millers next door to them are patients of mine," the doctor began, when the old man interrupted with a sharp cry.

"Then it's Mary Rose! How stupid of me, I knew that there were neighbors named Miller. I think my mind must be going," he said, exasperated.

"I shouldn't be surprised, the way you treat it. All right; then I'm definitely interested in the Hayden girl, am I? To see if she's home, and all right."

"If you can—indirectly, Roger, please. I gather that the two families aren't on very good terms."

"All the better. People can't wait to talk about their enemies. Well, all right," he said. "I'll have the ambulance round for you within the hour I can call from here. And I'll come tell you what I can, as soon as I can. At the hospital, that is."

An awful silence followed him. He turned at the door, to enjoy it.

Mr. Nicholas said with restraint, "I think it would be wrong to worry Dorothea that way, Roger. If I were kept at the hospital, she would assume that my injuries were serious."

"They are, at your age," said the doctor. "And if you want to bring Dorothea into it, how's she going to manage you and a new house at the same time?"

"I don't need to be managed. I'm perfectly capable—"

"You're perfectly capable of going out and getting into more trouble. Now fair's fair, John," he said firmly. "If I've got to run mysterious errands for you, I want you off my mind while I'm doing it. And don't worry about Dorothea, I'll talk to her."

"You talk to the Millers," said Mr. Nicholas bitterly. "And just overnight, mind you—that's the absolute limit."

Dr. Linen didn't even bother to reply.

Chapter 9

It was night before Mr. Nicholas had any profit from his bargain, but the profit was considerable when it came.

Meanwhile he underwent exactly the dehumanizing process he had foreseen: was delivered, handled, dulled, manhandled, and stashed away in smelly, echoing solitude. He did not get the particular strong-minded type of nurse who found his independence an offense and set out to quash it—no, his was sweet, with cloying hands, and thought he was cute. He also had a maddening harness round his middle, and bedpans.

Dr. Linen showed up after dinner, the easy author of all this humiliation. Mr. Nicholas forced himself to civil replies, and waited.

"Well, I saw your girl," the doctor said, after minimum preliminaries—he was a fair man. "You're a fine pair, you are. That fellow must be marked up, too, you know—ever thought of that?"

"You saw Mary Rose? She's hurt?"

"There is no Mary Rose, forget that. Your cherub is Mickey Hayden, the terror of the block—according to Mrs. Miller. She's eleven, she looks like an undersized jockey, and I doubt if there's much about this world she doesn't know. That's not worth knowing," he amended. "I wish you'd tell me what this is all about!"

"Is she hurt?" said Mr. Nicholas patiently.

"Well, she's been in a scrap, and looks it. In fact, she's confined to quarters for fighting—her old man yelled out the window at her while she was talking to me, and she skedaddled back inside. So you won't have to worry about her getting into any more trouble for a while—the block's safe from both of you," he said.

"How did you come to talk to her? What did she say?"

"Well, she was waiting for me when I came out of the Millers'—hanging around behind the bushes between the yards. I didn't even see her, just heard somebody whispering 'Mister, mister' in the bushes, and there she was—glaring up at me like some little one-eyed wild creature. She's got a lovely shiner. Pain?" he asked, to Mr. Nicholas's checked sigh.

"No."

"I held up your dope, so you can hear all this good news. There isn't much more. She wanted to know what happened to the old man that the ambulance took away. I asked her why she wanted to know, and that threw her. I said, 'Do you know him?' and she looked as if she couldn't remember the Fifth Amendment. Then all of a sudden she got brave and said, 'Yes! He's Mr. Nicholas!' So I told her you were all right, and just needed a few days' rest—and that if she was a friend of yours she could come and see you here, after tomorrow. How's that?"

"What did she say?"

"Said she couldn't. Got in a fight, and was being punished. But would I tell you hello? I said, 'Who from?' but she couldn't think of the answer to that one, either. Then the old man yelled at her, and she said very fast, 'Tell him love from Mary Rose—that's another girl, he knows her.' And that was that. She holds her arm wrong when she runs," he added. "Something happened to that, too."

"I wish you could have looked at it," said Mr. Nicholas. "Although I can't believe they seriously neglect the child.... What did the Millers say?"

"Mrs. Miller," the doctor corrected. "I don't think I'll bother to repeat it, she doesn't seem sane on the subject. All I had to do was glance out the window and remark on the cars in the yard next door, and her beloved hemorrhoids went right down the drain. The boy is a gangster, with gangster pals, the child is a vicious delinquent, the father is a whisky soaked bum, and they all ought to be forcibly removed from Mrs. Miller's vicinity. Would be, if she could manage it."

"I see," said Mr. Nicholas. "No, I don't think Mrs. Miller is much use to us. We'll have to try someone else."

"You mean I will," said Dr. Linen. "By the way, I ordered that bedpan—I consider it necessary for a time. I wouldn't like to think you were refusing it."

"I haven't much choice, have I?" said Mr. Nicholas mildly. "What about the Rudds, at the corner store? They deal with everyone round there."

"I'm ahead of you. I went there. I don't care much for them," he said frankly. "They're too damned obsequious—makes me feel like a brute, or a health inspector. I bet she could be a devil, too, without much trying. However. At least she could tell me the facts—which I had forgotten, or didn't know. It seems that shortly after Hayden's wife died he did begin to hit the bottle, and one day while under the influence he ran his train past some stop signal and hit another train. Nobody killed, but several people injured, and lots of damage. And that was the end of him with the railroad. Pretty much the end of him as a man, too—he didn't know any other trade, and was too old to learn one. The boy went right to work out of high school, seems to be a hard worker and a good car mechanic, or whatever they call them. I have a feeling he's good-looking, too—Mrs. Rudd talks about him very indulgently. And she's sorry for the father. Got no use for the girl, though—she's a bad one."

Mr. Nicholas said, "And did she strike you as a bad one, Roger?"

"Well, she's a wild one—no doubt about that. In fact, the whole family sounds like something out of the backwoods—clannish, touchy, hot-tempered. Hard up. One fellow swears the old man keeps a shotgun handy, but I wouldn't take that too seriously."

"What do you mean, one fellow? You've asked other people about them?"

"Oh, here and there. You've got me intrigued, you know. But don't worry, I've got the perfect opener—all I have to do is mention that yard full of cars, and I hear all about the terrible Haydens. Wouldn't think a place like DeKuyper Street would be so sensitive to a few junk cars in somebody's yard, would you? Considering all the ones along the curb. Well, have you got enough to sleep on tonight?" he asked. "You've got to face Dorothea tomorrow, you know. I hadn't the heart to keep her out another day."

"Yes, all right," said Mr. Nicholas absently.

But Dr. Linen, perhaps against his own judgment, still lingered. An active and vigorous man in his sixties, warned into semiretirement by a heart attack, he found himself these days with not enough life to satisfy a lively temperament. And reticence teased him.

"What do you think of your Mary Rose now?" he said curiously. "Still think you should have got mixed up in her battles?"

"I think so. This one."

"Well, I'll say one thing—whatever she did, that was a damned vicious brute that attacked you both. It wasn't Miller was it?" he said suddenly.

"I've told you, Roger—I don't know."

"Yes. I remember. Well, let me know when you get ready to find out," he said, half joking. "I seem to have unsuspected talents in the detective line. Only don't wait till his bruises fade!"

When he had gone, Mr. Nicholas felt an ungrateful relief. The information his friend had brought him was useful, he was glad to have it—but the grotesque, almost caricatured view Dr. Linen had presented of Mary Rose and her family had begun to tire him. He understood that the Haydens now offered this view of themselves to the world—indeed, forced it, with their stubborn junkyard, their feuds, and probably their careless appearances. They were responding with defiance to their difficulties and ill-luck, no doubt, and increasing both with every gesture. But this was the outside view of them. Necessary to be aware of, perhaps, but bearing about as much relation to Mary Rose and her brother and father as did the crabby old attic miser to Mr. Nicholas himself. No; he had needed to know about Mary Rose, in order not to lose her. But to know her, that was a matter between Mary Rose and himself.

The loneliness of the child appalled him. To be in such danger as she had been in, and to fear every authority to whom she might turn for help! The police, her brother, the neighbors—even, in the end, himself. And yet in this forest of fears she was living almost jauntily—"practicing on" her brick-swinging, and on other fierce accomplishments, he supposed. Observing her world with inventiveness, and even delight. Prepared to cope singlehanded with her enemies, so long as she could, whether they were an irate neighbor-woman or a lethal madman. For Mr. Nicholas had no doubt that Mary Rose would have died in that attic, if things had gone otherwise.

"What did you say?" said the nurse.

He hadn't even heard her come in.

"I don't want that," he said, fussed. Meaning, go away.

"Don't want what?" she said, taking his arm. He withdrew it at once.

"That injection. It's not necessary."

"Yes it is. You don't want to be in pain all night, do you?"

"I want the use of my mind. If the price of that is some pain, I'm quite willing to pay it."

"The use of your mind!"

This wasn't the one who thought he was cute. This one thought he was mad.

"You've got plenty of nights to use your mind," she said finally. "This one you need to sleep."

"I haven't got plenty of nights left for anything," he retorted, "and it's my business how I spend them. Now go away!"

She said she would have to report him, but she went.

Of course he then began to mind the harness a great deal—he had been much better off without it, in the first place. Besides, she had broken his train of thought, leaving in him some mounting sense of urgency for which he could not account. About Mary Rose ... but what? She was home, she was being closely watched (for whatever reason). She was not hurt, in any grave sense. And she knew her enemy now, he could not surprise her again.

But did she know him to be a *mortal* enemy? Did she fear him *enough*? Did she realize what extreme cause she had to fear this man— *and he to fear her?*

For how could he ever be assured that she would not tell? If not at once—and he knew by now that she had not told at once—then eventually. He would not dare to trust her with so terrible a secret as his other identity.

The back door didn't lock.

Mr. Nicholas began to doubt his own sanity.

Why was he lying here, keeping this man's secret for him? What possible choice could there be between some mild discomfort for Mary Rose and her very life? He could not understand why it had even mattered to him that he did not know the man's name—he knew and could testify absolutely to his existence, to his mad behavior, to his victim; and once this much was known, and Mary Rose questioned, why should she keep back his name?

Except that she would deny everything. He could hear her doing it. Would deny everything, including him, and turn to fight him as relentlessly as she fought Mrs. Miller, or any other who wanted to get her "put into Children's."

Well, he could accept that. But what *was* "Children's"? Children's Court? Children's Home? Children's Protective something-or-other? He had a shrewd idea that Mary Rose's picture of some ravening institution, lying in wait to snatch her, must be pure fiction. Surely so long as any family group could manage without becoming a public charge, or a public nuisance, no one wanted to interfere with them.

Was Mary Rose a public nuisance?

Or could Bud abandon them, if he became sufficiently "fed up"?

Mr. Nicholas saw that he could no longer answer his own questions. He knew little of legal matters. In a long and rather autocratic career as a frame maker, without peer in his craft, and accustomed to making his own terms with museums and collectors alike, Mr. Nicholas had done almost no litigating. His private affairs he had simply turned over to an old friend who happened to be a lawyer. About municipal facilities, for those who needed them, he knew next to nothing; and about family responsibilities as laid down by law, nothing at all.

But at least his puzzling had quieted down that echo of last night's panic (for that was what it had been). Mary Rose was not safe, in any way. But he had no real doubt that she was safe for the night.

Mr. Nicholas rang his bell.

When it was answered—not very soon—he said: "I think I should like that injection now, nurse. I'm sorry I was sharp with you."

"I thought you'd change your mind," she said briefly. "Through using it, are you?"

"Yes. Or rather, I'd like to be."

"Wouldn't we all?" she said mysteriously, and pushed up his sleeve.

Chapter 10

John was a good son, if a little too easygoing (he had his mother's nature), and he showed no annoyance with his father next morning. Probably he felt none. Even his father's obstinate dismissal of what had happened to him as a "slight accident" failed to exasperate him, although clearly Dorothea had charged him to get the details. His father wasn't going to give them; and after a short struggle he gave up, and accepted this.

Mr. Nicholas then thought it fair to point out to John some other reasons why he, John, might be expected to feel annoyed.

"I'm sorry to cause all this inconvenience just when we're moving, John. And to take you away from your work, too."

"It should happen oftener," John said. "Skipping the office, I mean."

He had been employed for many years in the drafting department of a large engineering corporation. He seemed safely niched there, and fairly content. It was not Mr. Nicholas's idea of a career, but he knew that times had changed.

"I hope Dorothea didn't mind your coming alone."

"No, afternoon's better for her anyway. How long are they going to keep you here, Dad? It's not like anything was broken, is it? I should think you'd be just as well off at home."

"Why? The expense is going to be negligible, with my insurance. And it gives Dorothea a chance to settle."

"Yes, but she doesn't. She won't, till she gets you back under her eye. And don't tell me you like this! I think you'd both be a lot better off if you came home. You'll like the house—your bathroom's like Florida."

Mr. Nicholas was touched, but wary.

"Well, we'll see," he said. "I'll talk to Dorrie. But there are a couple of things I want to talk over with you, first. I wish you would ask Mr. Marks to come and see me, Johnny. We should get the date for the closing put up. Mrs. Bohr doesn't need all this time, we can make some other arrangement. The main thing is that we should get the money, or whatever it is, transferred over. Do you realize how awkward it would have been for you if this—business had finished me? That house, and the sale price we'll realize from it, are still in my name—and the new title is in yours. We don't want a lot of probate delays in between. You tell Mr. Marks what our problem is, and ask him to come talk to me. Will you?"

"Yes," said John. He added: "You feeling mortal this morning, Dad?"

"I'm feeling sensible, and about time, too. We should have done something about this years ago."

"Well, we tried, didn't we? It's not the world's easiest job to sell a house on DeKuyper Street. For a decent price."

"Then I should have put it in your name," said his father. "Well. Enough hindsight. But get hold of Mr. Marks."

John said he would. He sounded depressed; he had never liked coping with money problems. Neither did Mr. Nicholas. But he could think of no other excuse for summoning his lawyer. Besides, the problem was quite real.

"Well," he said, dismissing it, "now I have a favor to ask you. You know the Haydens, up on the corner?"

"I know who you mean. That beat-up place with all the junk cars in the yard. I think they lost us a couple of chances to sell."

"Yes. Now the boy is a mechanic, I think, in some garage or filling station. Probably in the neighborhood. You wouldn't know which one it might be?"

"Gosh, no, Dad. I wouldn't know him if I saw him. Why?"

"I'd like to talk to him, and I don't want to approach him at home. I wonder how we could find out where he works?"

"Well, I don't know—I could ask around, I guess. But why? What do you want to talk to him about?"

"About his sister," said Mr. Nicholas, who had thought this out. "One of the little girls on the block. I have reason to believe she may be in some trouble, and I think he ought to be warned, to help her. They're not a very popular family locally—there's no mother, and the father drinks. I suppose the children run rather wild. And yet they're not bad people, you know. It seemed to me that I might be able to talk to the boy, as another old resident. Like his own people."

This had seemed to Mr. Nicholas, when he arranged it, a very good explanation. He couldn't imagine why Johnny just sat there in silence.

"Well?" he said—and heard his son move.

"Why—yes, Dad, I see. But—you want this fellow to come over and talk to you? About his sister?"

"Certainly. If he will."

More silence. What was wrong?

"What's wrong?" he said impatiently.

"Nothing—nothing. I just don't understand it. You've never gotten mixed up in neighborhood stuff before."

Too late, Mr. Nicholas recognized the justice of this. The fault was not in his story; it was in himself.

"Well, not for many years," he said weakly. It was all he could think of to say.

"Is this something Mrs. Thompson's put you up to?"

Mr. Nicholas's temptation was brief, and he won. "Of course not."

John, however, marked the hesitation, and so discounted the reply.

"Well, all right. I don't suppose it can do any harm, if you really want to do it. After all, you won't be around there anymore. In case the guy resents it, or something."

"I'm not going to cause any resentment," his father said. "And by the way, John, I wish you could find time to stop by and apologize to Mrs. Thompson. For me. I didn't intend to let her in for so much bother. Perhaps you could take her some flowers."

John said he would. He said, "I'll go by the old neighborhood, and see what I can find out for you, and then I'll go on down and see Joe Marks. I suppose I could ask the Rudds about this fellow. They seem to know everything about everyone."

"You call Mr. Marks 'Joe'?" said his father.

"Sure. Everybody does."

"But he's many years your senior, John."

This made his son laugh—that bright burst of pure enjoyment which occasionally escaped him, and which neither Dorothea nor his father could resist. If he had been a calculating man, he could have got away with almost anything at home. Except, his father felt sure, no calculating man could laugh that way.

"It's true," said Mr. Nicholas, sticking to the point.

"Sure, I know. So does Joe. But you better not remind him."

"And about the Rudds—isn't there someone else you could ask? Dr. Linen has already picked up a point or two from them, and I think it would be better to spread things out more."

"A point or two? About the Haydens? Look," said John, "just what are you up to, Dad?"

Luckily, Mr. Nicholas had an idea just then.

"Actually, we may be able to find out what we need to know by telephoning," he said, and groped on his table. "Here—let me see if I can get a number for them. The Haydens. Then you can simply ask where to get in touch with the boy—his name is Bud. As if you had a car to be fixed, or something of that sort. You needn't give your name," he added.

"I gathered that," said John dryly.

Mr. Nicholas, after some polite negotiation with the hospital switchboard, was able presently to hand John a receiver already registering ringing. John took it hastily, clearing his throat, but several more rings went by before a sharp male voice answered.

"Yes? Who's this?"

"Is Bud there?"

"Bud? No, he don't get home till round six-thirty. Who's this?"

"Where could I reach him? It's about a car," said John.

"Well, you can get him at the station, I guess. You know the number?" John said he didn't, and wrote down the number he was given. Then he asked, "Where is the station?"

This was a mistake. The voice sharpened again. "What? Say, who is this?"

"Never mind," John said hastily, "I guess I can find it. Thanks."

Anxiously following this, his father demanded: "What's the matter? Wouldn't he tell you?"

"Wanted to know who I was. If you know Bud, apparently you know the station. Never mind, it's simpler just to call the station and ask where they are."

"Well, as a matter of fact, John," his father said, "there's no reason I can't call this boy up myself. I don't know why I didn't think of this before," he added, vexed with himself. "It seems to be possible to do everything over the telephone nowadays. I rarely used it, myself."

"I remember," said John; and his father heard him smiling. "When they did call you up, they used to say: 'Do you think Mr. Nicholas would come to the telephone?' Boy, you really had it made, Dad."

There was pride in his voice, not a trace of envy—a selflessness that Mr. Nicholas did not find entirely comforting.

"Well, those were different times," he said glumly. "I suppose I could call Mr. Marks up, too, couldn't I? So it seems I've bothered you for nothing, Johnny."

"So you have. You can even call up the florist, for Mrs. Thompson's flowers, can't you?"

But he was teasing, he knew better. His father replied only: "Perhaps you'd better get her something in a pot, in case she feels the way Dorrie does about buying cut flowers. And please express my thanks to her, for a most enjoyable stay."

"I'll also suggest she do her own dirty work from now on," said John.

Since his father was clearly not going to do any telephoning until he left, John left. He would have given a good deal to hear Mr. Nicholas's end of the conversation with Bud Hayden—and a good deal more to hear both sides.

Mr. Nicholas, intent simply on the mechanics of reaching Mary Rose's brother, had no time to worry about other aspects. John had told him the number, and had also rewritten it heavily, in case he forgot. Just the same he was relieved to be answered by someone who said: "Al's Service Station."

"Good," said Mr. Nicholas. "Now—is there a Mr. Bud Hayden employed there?"

"This is Bud."

"Excellent. Now, Bud, this is Mr. Nicholas, of 143 DeKuyper Street. Do you know who I am?"

"Yes," said Bud. "Sure. You just moved, didn't you?"

"That's right. I'm now calling you from United Hospital, where I am spending a few days. I'm sorry to disturb you at your work, but I wonder if you could come by and talk to me for a short while, sometime today. Do you think you could manage that? It's important, of course, or I shouldn't ask you. Important to you as well as to me."

Bud said, "Was it you that called my old man just now?"

What a beleaguered family, Mr. Nicholas thought. The father at once needing to report so small a strangeness!

"Yes, it was I. Or rather, someone calling for me. I didn't know where to reach you during the daytime, you see. Now, if you could come—"

"Well, just what would this be about, Mr. Nicholas?" Bud's voice broke in with impatience, or nervous irritation—controlled, though, for so young a voice. Nor was there any intentional rudeness in it. "Is it a car, or what?"

"No, no—I'm afraid we were trying not to alarm your family—not very successfully. No, I want to talk to you about your sister. Rather urgently, in fact."

"About Mickey? What about Mickey?" The question was flatly asked; those controls had tightened, Mr. Nicholas was sorry to hear. "You got some complaint about her, mister?"

"No, I have not. On the contrary," said Mr. Nicholas, with an emphatic wish to reassure. "Entirely to the contrary. I have her welfare very much in mind, and that is why—"

"Well, I tell you how it is, Mr. Nicholas. We're pretty busy here right now, and I wouldn't be able to get away. You say you got no complaint about the kid—right? So maybe I could give you a ring about this sometime later. All right?"

It wasn't in the least all right. The instant evaporation of interest from Bud's voice was startling. If it wasn't a complaint, he didn't care what it was. Only a thread of minimal politeness held him there at all, with his real interest already returned to the clamor in his background.

Mr. Nicholas swallowed his indignation—or most of it.

"No, Bud, that is not all right. What I have to say to you about Mary Rose is both urgent and important, and—"

"*Mary Rose?*" The boy's attention was back, sharply. Then: "How come you call her Mary Rose?" he asked, clearly entertained.

"Because I was told that was her name. Isn't it?"

"Well, sure—but you better not call her by it! I didn't think there was anybody around that remembered, even."

He sounded almost friendly. Encouraged, Mr. Nicholas said: "Oh, yes. Mary Rose remembers."

"You mean she *told* you that was her name?"

"Of course." In the small succeeding pause, Mr. Nicholas added: "I can't tell you how important it is that you find some time to come and talk to me, Bud. I would come to you if I could, but that isn't possible. It isn't more than a fifteen-minute drive, is it?"

"No, I guess not." With sudden decisiveness, he said: "Maybe I could drop by on my lunch hour, but it would have to be fast. You care if I bring my lunch?"

"Bring it by all means. And come directly to my room—it's 214. In the left wing."

"Okay, 214 in the left wing. I'll see you around quarter past twelve then, okay?"

"Yes. Thank you," said Mr. Nicholas.

He was invaded by a sadness that he did not understand, after he had hung up. Quite suddenly, like some emotion remembered from another time of life, sadness came down upon him. He lay quietly, not attempting to reason it away, and it turned into sleep.

He was wakened by his lunch, which meant that Bud would be coming soon. The sadness was gone. He remembered, and sensed for it, like a presence in the room; but it was gone.

The lunch, however, was there—and his "cute" nurse, who still hoped to feed it to him. To save time, he allowed this, and they finished up rapidly. He then boldly proposed that coffee and cake should be brought to his room for a friend. She gave in so easily he was sorry he had not asked for another lunch.

Bud was a little late. He was also, Mr. Nicholas became aware, sorry he had come. And intending to leave as soon as possible.

But he had felt obliged to keep his word and come. That was something.

Mr. Nicholas struck for his attention firmly, and at once.

"First, Bud, I want to tell you something I haven't been able to tell Mary Rose—how much I admire the courage, and generosity, and strength of character she showed me at a time when there was no obligation whatsoever. And nothing possible to be gained by it. It was simply an expression of her true character—and I hope that you know it's a fine one. A very fine one."

Bud, having declined to sit down, heard this standing by the bed. He was entirely silent.

"You don't underestimate your sister, I hope, because she's a child?"

"Mick's a good kid. Nobody has to tell me that."

"She's much more than a good kid," said Mr. Nicholas severely. "She is a most unusual person, both in character and intelligence. And more than that, Mary Rose has a loving heart. The rest would be meaningless without that."

A sudden sound escaped the young man standing beside him. It took the form of a laugh, an uncertain and explosive laugh—but it was an involuntary escape of voice, Mr. Nicholas felt, and might have taken any form. Bud covered it by an immediate noisy adjustment of his chair, and by sitting down.

He said then, "It really hits me, the way you keep on calling her 'Mary Rose'! You don't know how weird that sounds."

"They gave me some coffee for you," Mr. Nicholas replied. "Can you see it? Would you like some?"

"Yes, sure," said Bud. "Thanks." He didn't move, though, nor did Mr. Nicholas interrupt his tense silence. It broke again, with the same abruptness.

"God, you don't know what it's like, to hear somebody say something decent about the kid! Just once, just something!" Now he was leaning forward, his restlessness jarring Mr. Nicholas's bed. "Sure I know she's bright—I knew it a long time before they did, with their crappy tests and all. And you know something? When they found it out, that was just something else to hit her with! 'Potential,' " he said bitterly. "Boy, that's a word I'd like to take, I'd like to ram it.... It's like they want to punish her, for being smart. You know? If she was some rich kid, okay, it would all be roses. They could believe it, then! But some poor little snot-nose mick, what right has she got to be a genius? It's like, if she is one, then they got to prove she's a bad one—you know? Otherwise the whole system don't work!"

He had let out too much hostility, there was no place to use it in this quiet room. The tail of it swung round on Mr. Nicholas.

"So how come you know so much about her?" he demanded. "And what's this 'Mary Rose' bit, anyway? Just when did she tell you about that?"

Mr. Nicholas answered carefully.

"Night before last, Bud. When we were both hurt. Her 'fight' was actually an attempt to help me, in great part. I'm not supposed to tell you this, of course."

"Yeah," he said, intent. "I can believe it. That's another thing—all of a sudden I'm not supposed to know anything anymore. So what happened?" But before Mr. Nicholas could begin to reply, Bud swept past his own question. "You see how it is? Now I got to go ask around, I want to know what's happening in my own family! Or else stand there while some creep gives me a long story, I don't know what they're talking about. Not you, mister—I don't mean that. Believe me, they're not all like you! Even the ones that start out nice, like what a bright little girl she is—boy, they are the worst. I *know* she's bright," he said with passion. "I *know* she's a little girl—I know she ought to have a nice home, and a nice mama and papa, and pretty stuff to wear—she's the one that don't know it! You know that? You know what's in that kid's closet right now, she won't even look at it? Not any junky stuff—I got a friend that knows exactly what girls ought to wear, she's got very good taste. Well, I gave her fifty dollars to get Easter stuff for that kid—fifty bucks, that's not raisins, right? And she got it. Everything. The best. So where is it? Did she ever wear it—did she ever even put it on? You just guess, mister. Just take one guess."

Mr. Nicholas sighed.

"Well, there's no doubt it's a considerable burden for a man, to bring up a little girl."

"Listen, she's no burden to me, she's my sister—I'm not complaining! All I'm saying is—"

"Oh, a boy would have been far easier, Bud. A younger brother. There's no harm in admitting that. And surely you see that Mary Rose figured it out long ago."

"How do you mean?"

"Well, how does she come to call herself 'Mickey'?" he asked.

Bud said quickly, "She didn't call herself 'Mickey,' it's her nickname. We always called her that."

"When your mother was alive?"

Bud now discovered the coffee Thermos. Mr. Nicholas heard him fiddling with it, before he asked: "Sure it's okay if I drink some of this?"

"Yes, it's for you. Please have your lunch. I've had mine."

"Oh, I left that in the car. It's okay."

At least he wasn't troubling to disguise his former intentions. Mr. Nicholas drew faint hope from this, and waited. Bud also found the cake.

"As a matter of fact, I can tell you exactly how that got started," he said presently, munching. "She didn't have a thing to do with it. There was this old biddy used to take care of her in the daytime, when Dad was working—I still went to school. Well, she meant well—I guess she was kind of a nice old biddy, but she used to make this big thing of it every time Mick fell down, or something—call the doctor, and she was always plastering stuff all over her. A real fusser. Well, we didn't want to hurt her feelings, but finally my dad did say she shouldn't worry so much. You know, she might make the kid nervous, or something. So he just told her, like a joke, he said, 'Hell, she's a little mick, they're tough, you can't hurt a mick.' So Mi—so my sister naturally says, 'What's a mick?' and Dad says, 'You're a mick, that's what, and don't forget it!'"

It was a pleasant recollection. Mr. Nicholas could hear him smiling as he recalled it. Or perhaps a pleasant time to recollect, when he had still been a boy, and his father had still done a man's work, and they had lived a fairly normal life.

Before he had got so fed up.

Chapter 11

The empathy between Mary Rose and himself, so briefly and deeply established in his empty house, persisted in curious ways still, Mr. Nicholas found. One was in the flurry of panic that could rise in him all at once—like hers, absolutely resistant to reason—in which her violent destruction seemed both certain and imminent. As, indeed, it had nearly been. He felt sure these echoes of their common terror still rose in her, and even wondered if they happened at the same time as his— Mr. Nicholas was not averse to wonders.

Another persistence lay, he now realized, in his attitude to Bud. He knew perfectly well that Bud was not really the arbiter of anyone's fate. But to Mary Rose, he was—and this emotional aura hung round him and hampered Mr. Nicholas in speaking out.

Both these remnants of empathy hampered him. He needed a clear mind to realize just what Mary Rose's situation was, and to take steps to correct it. The main trouble was that her immediate danger was so bound up with her precarious family life that Mr. Nicholas did not know how to protect her from the one without destroying the other. He preferred to begin with Bud, but he did not know if Bud was capable of hearing what had really happened without losing his head and rushing into disastrous action.

Certainly the boy was too tightly wound up, too nervously guarded, for his years. His feeling for his sister seemed genuine, but confused. Where the father came in was another blank—except that his misfortunes seemed to have turned him almost paranoid. On the whole, Mr. Nicholas felt the need for great care.

Bud, having gulped down his cake and coffee, now wanted a cigarette—and remembered to ask.

"Okay to smoke in here, Mr. Nicholas?"

"Perfectly, Bud. Is there an ash tray?"

"I can use the cup. I guess you don't smoke, right? Is that on account of, uh, you don't see?"

"Yes, it is. You've heard of that, have you?"

"Oh, sure. At first it sounds nuts, but all you got to do is try it in the dark sometime—I mean real dark. It's no good. Funny, isn't it?"

This was such a poignant echo of Mary Rose that Mr. Nicholas's caution melted.

He said, "I'm extremely glad you came, Bud. I appreciate it. Your sister's been much on my mind."

"Well, she's on mine, too, believe me. Only most people that want to talk to me about her, well, they don't really like her. You know? That's no good."

"No."

"I mean, I can tell you like the kid."

It was a kind of question, and Mr. Nicholas answered emphatically. "Very much indeed."

"Yeah. I could tell."

He was savoring this. Mr. Nicholas decided to risk the moment.

"What particularly worries me is that I'm afraid she may have made an enemy, in our—our difficulties the other night," he said. "Even a dangerous enemy."

"Who?" Bud said sharply.

"Well, that's it. I don't know who this man is."

"What man? What do you mean," he said suddenly, "some *man* beat her up like that? It wasn't kids?"

"Oh, no, it wasn't kids. This was a man of, I should say, forty to fifty, perhaps older. A heavy-set man, with a good head of hair. A beer drinker."

"Miller," said Bud. His chair scraped back violently. "By God, that's Miller. I'll kill him. I'll kill him ..."

"Now, just a minute. Bud! Listen to me. I don't think it was Miller."

Bud came back, but altered.

"What do you mean, you don't think it was Miller? You said you didn't know who it was. So how do you know it's not Miller all of a sudden?"

"I don't, of course. But from something Mary Rose said, I doubt it very much. Besides, however unpleasant your neighbor may be, he isn't a criminal lunatic, is he? This man is, I can assure you."

Bud said, almost in a whisper, "Oh, Christ—what are you talking about? You lie there—you lie there talking—"

"I'm lying here because I also got in his way," said Mr. Nicholas. "Fortunately I'm out of it now. Mary Rose isn't. Will you let me tell you about it?"

For a moment Bud didn't speak. Then, in his original tight voice, he replied: "I guess I'll let my sister tell me, thanks. That'll be a straight story, at least."

"It'll be a story, I can promise you that," said Mr. Nicholas. "You don't get truth from anybody when you behave as you're doing, at the first hint of it. Go home and make a fine scene—she expects you to. That's why she doesn't tell you things anymore."

"I guess I'm pretty sick of you telling me about my own sister, too—

how come you're in the middle, all at once? You get her into bad trouble—you get her into some mess she don't even dare tell me about, and then you lie here and talk like you're the only person in the world can handle Mick. Mary Rose!" he said, with savage contempt. "Giving me all that crap about the kid—what was that for? To soften me up, so I wouldn't get sore you nearly got her beat to death? What kind of an old guy are you, anyway—hiding behind a kid?"

Mr. Nicholas said steadily, "I was not able to protect Mary Rose, that's true. I'm not able to now. I had hoped you might be able to—she needs protection, and she needs it badly. Go do what you like, and think what you like, but remember that—your sister needs all your protection."

The boy above him was a hard breathing—nothing more. Then, with a muttered word, he turned and slammed out of the room—became a pounding of hard soles down the hospital corridor. And then nothing.

Mr. Nicholas had failed. Worse, he had brought Mary Rose's affairs to the crisis she most dreaded—and at a time when she had already borne more than a child should bear. It was worse than failure, it was disaster.

And he was too angry to care.

He was so angry, in fact, that his anger affected him like a tonic. A freedom. For what had failed was his last attempt to follow Mary Rose's way—a child's way, in a world of total enmity and one shaky refuge. Which was no refuge at all. He had known better all along. Now he would act as he should have acted from the beginning, like a sane adult, a citizen of a sane adult world. Instead of a cautious intermediary between two madmen! Because the father was as mad in his way as that devil in the attic, and he had already infected the son. What if she did lose a home like that? She was better off without it!

His "cute" nurse had come in, indignant—was checking his pulse, his skin, clucking all over him. He barely noticed. The first thing was Marks. To call Joe Marks. Then ...

His nurse gave a cry, and rose.

"You get out of here, young man! Don't you dare come in this room!"

"That's for him to say. Let him say it," said Bud's tight voice, from the door.

"If you don't leave this—"

"Just a minute, nurse. What is it you want?" Mr. Nicholas demanded, turning his face toward the door.

"You know what I want. I want to know what trouble the kid's in—and that's all, old man. That's all!"

"Mr. Nicholas, I can't allow you to be excited like this," his nurse protested. "Doctor gave very strict orders—"

"I'm not in the least excited," said Mr. Nicholas. "Stay and make sure, if you like. And you may come in, Hayden, if you can behave like an adult."

"This is private," said Bud, still from the door.

"No. No longer. I tried to keep it so, but that was a mistake—you are no more capable of protecting your sister than I am. This is man's work," said Mr. Nicholas, in the warmth of his anger, "and neither you nor I qualify for it."

Unexpectedly, Bud gave a short laugh. He came in and shut the door—quietly. The nurse's hand moved on Mr. Nicholas's, but she did not speak.

"He's quite a talker, isn't he?" said Bud. He was speaking to her, and his voice was different—the voice of a man at ease with women because he was attractive to them.

"You should be ashamed of yourself," she said.

"Yeah. That's what they tell me."

"No, I mean it. Mr. Nicholas, if you must see this man, I really think you had better wait until—"

"No. This will be very brief. I would rather be finished with it," he said. He turned his face to where Bud now stood, at the foot of his bed. "There is no reason why I shouldn't tell you what I intend to tell the police. Your sister was attacked—nearly violated and murdered, in my empty house. The night before last. I interrupted the attack by accident, and the man got away. She knows who he is. And she is more afraid of telling you what happened than of anything else he may do to her."

There was total silence in the room.

The nurse whispered, "Oh, dear ..." under her breath, and moved toward the door. "Please don't stay long," she murmured, passing Bud. He didn't reply.

When they were alone he came round the bed and stood over Mr. Nicholas.

"Tell me what happened. Tell me what happened to her."

"I've told you what matters. This man lured her into my house by breaking a window lock and telling her that it was broken. Like any normally adventurous child, she went in to explore. He either entered after her or was lying there in wait. She managed to escape from him, and he locked her in my attic—I suppose she had run there to get away from him. That was where I found her. She was simply crouching there by the door, waiting to fight another hopeless battle with him whenever he should come back. She even hid from me."

"Oh, God," said Bud. "Why didn't she ..."

He was as tense for her as if it were still happening. But he couldn't think what it was she should have done.

"Why didn't she break a window and call for help? I suggested that—after he came back and locked us in again. But he knew her better than I did. He knew she belonged to a family that makes a profession of being at odds with the world—to whom the police are enemies. The neighbors are enemies. And enemies that she has to fight alone, so that her brother won't get fed up and leave."

"You said he came back."

"He came back twice. In between, he went down and broke the streetlight outside. He had a healthy respect for her, you see—he didn't want her to be able to see at all when he came into that attic."

"Wait a minute," said Bud.

But he did nothing in the pause, neither moved nor spoke. He seemed hardly to breathe.

"You had better sit down," said Mr. Nicholas.

"God damn it, I know what I better do!" he broke out savagely. Then: "No. No. I don't mean that. Go on. Tell me."

"He came in, of course. And we were no match for him. But while he was dealing with me—he hadn't known I was there—Mary Rose was able to escape. She made a lot of noise," said Mr. Nicholas, "so that the man would leave me and follow her. As he did. She came back later and told me he was hiding in an abandoned car in your yard."

"She came *back?*"

"Yes. You weren't home, and she says the back door doesn't lock. Apparently she didn't feel her father was any protection—she was afraid this man would beat him up, too, if he came into your house looking for her. So she came back to my house. There was nowhere else she dared to go. She came back and barricaded us in to wait for daylight, even though she thought at first that I was dead. That frightened her."

"All right," said Bud. Stopping it. He turned and walked away, to some distant part of the room.

"I've got to get her away. Now. Right now."

"Have you someplace to take her?"

"I'll keep her with me. Every minute. She'll never go near that place again without I'm right there with her. Never."

Mr. Nicholas accepted this for what it was—an outburst of horror, and grief. He didn't comment.

"By God, she'll never go back," Bud said then. "I'll sell that pile of junk—I'll make the old man sell it, even if he has to give it away! Or else he can sit there alone in it and rot in his drink.... I'll get a trailer," he said rapidly. "We'll get the hell out of here, I can make good money any place. She'll live in a decent, clean trailer, in a nice place. A new place. She'll go to a new school, and she won't have anything to be ashamed of! And she'll dress like the other girls. Better. She wants to be Mary Rose," he said, "that's what she'll be. From now on."

He came back beside the bed. Mr. Nicholas felt his inspection.

"You put up a fight for her, didn't you?" he said.

"I'm far past the days of being able to do that. She does her own fighting. She has to."

"No, she wouldn't have got away, if you hadn't of been there. I owe you that."

It was an aggressive statement, and Mr. Nicholas was irritated by it.

"You owe me nothing. If your sister had any debt to me, she paid it herself."

The consideration of him went on, above him there. Finally Bud said: "Those things you said about her, before. You meant that, didn't you?"

"I meant it. I also meant what I said about reporting this man to the police." In spite of himself, an urgency came into his voice. "He's broken out of control, Bud. He isn't safe to be at large. He'll do it again. If not to Mary Rose, then to some other child."

"Not when I get through with him."

"Oh, yes. Unless you mean to kill him, of course. That would certainly solve all your problems."

"I got no quarrel with you, Mr. Nicholas," Bud said suddenly. "Just don't needle me... Look, I'm going home and get the kid now. I got a friend she can stay with for a while. A woman. She'll be okay there, till I can get things straightened out—and I will. But don't you—"

"Is this Lou?" Mr. Nicholas inquired.

Bud drew a long breath.

"You two really had quite a session, didn't you?" he said.

"We had a lot of time. And Mary Rose has a great deal on her mind."

"Yeah," said Bud. "I can see that. All right—I get your message, Mr. Nicholas. It's time Mi—my sister and I talked things over, and we will. But—"

"Privately, I hope. And before you rush into anything."

"Look, I said I got your message. I got it. Now try and get mine," he said earnestly. "You call the cops on this, and the kid's going to get it just as hard as this guy. If it's Miller, or some bastard like that, his word's as good as hers. Maybe better. Sure you were there," he said, as Mr. Nicholas opened his mouth. "So who was it? Whoever she says? Don't kid yourself, Mr. Nicholas—we don't have that kind of reputation. And what was she doing there, anyway—maybe she went in with him, herself, and then he got a little too rough for her. How about that?"

"Bud—"

"You want to hear this from me, or from them?" he said savagely.

"Wake up, Mr. Nicholas—you're a nice old guy, but you got a different orbit, that's all."

"The man will be marked, too," said Mr. Nicholas rapidly.

"You're damn right he'll be marked.... So suppose it all goes like the book says," Bud said, quieting. "They believe her. They take in the guy. What happens to him? You think they're going to lock him up for life? Brand him? I'll tell you what happens—he gets about six months for assault, and he goes on the books to watch. Along with about a million other queers. You think they can watch 'em all? So he does his six, he comes out, he moves. And he's back in business. And meanwhile my sister's on the books, too, for being in an empty house at night with a dirty man. That she says she didn't know was there."

"You know she didn't."

"Sure I know. So do you. And if you're the kid's friend, like you say, you'll keep it that way—between the two of us that do believe her. Once you start talking, you're going to find out I'm right. Only that'll be too late."

Mr. Nicholas said thoughtfully, "Bud, I know you believe everything that you're saying. But what if it simply isn't so? If there's another side to this, won't you at least listen to it?"

"Sure. Like what?"

"I don't know. But I intend to find out. Exactly what the procedures and penalties are, for what this man has done. And what protection is available to your sister."

"You want to talk to your lawyer, right?"

"Yes. Without mentioning names."

"Well, you do that," said Bud. "And if he tells you any different than I tell you, you let me know."

"Also, there's a strong possibility that this man may be mentally unbalanced. And able to conceal it only if he's not challenged. If that's the case, he must be found at all costs."

Above him, Bud gave a checked sigh.

"Mister, how can you live so long and be so innocent?" he said, almost kindly. "Sure he's a nut, there's no maybe about it. If you want the God's truth, my old man's another. The street's full of 'em. The world's full of 'em! Once they start rounding up the nuts, where do you think they're going to put 'em all?"

Mr. Nicholas lost patience.

"Don't be absurd—there's a great deal of difference between what you call a 'nut' and a dangerous criminal lunatic! You're the one who's being naïve! A man who would trap a little girl in a deserted house, with the intention of violating her—undoubtedly of murdering her—"

"Now stop right there," said Bud. "How much of that can you prove? No—hold it. Think it over. This guy didn't kill anybody. He didn't rape anybody. He—"

"Do you mean to wait until he does?"

Bud's urgent voice became more remote. He had straightened up.

"Not me," he said. "I'm not patient, like the legal beagles, Mr. Nicholas. I know what was in his dirty black heart as well as you do. As well as he does. And I know what to do about it. There's no red tape round my hands. And no headshrinker telling me what to do. I can get through to him just fine—the way he'll remember every time he looks at another kid, his whole dirty life. And strictly private, Mr. Nicholas. He'll take what he takes and keep shut about it, don't worry about that."

"Why?" Mr. Nicholas demanded. "If he has as little to fear as you say?"

Bud gave his short laugh.

"You should be a lawyer yourself," he said, without rancor. "All right, call your guy—take your time, talk it over. That's the bargain, right? You don't blow any whistles, I don't make any move. And then we'll see who's right."

He was moving toward the door. Mr. Nicholas said urgently, "But when will I see you again? Are you coming back?"

"Sure, I'll drop by—or I'll give you a ring. I'll be in touch with you, don't worry, Mr. Nicholas. And don't worry about my sister anymore. I mean it. Maybe it's a rotten thing to say, but I guess we needed something to happen to us—thank God it wasn't worse. So don't worry about her—she's going to be all right from now on, believe me."

"She won't be all right unless you are, Bud," said Mr. Nicholas. He called it out, despairingly, to the closing door; but either Bud did not hear or he did not want to talk any more. The door shut quietly, finally, and his rapid steps went off down the hall. They were the steps of a man impatient to be on his way, with a lot to do. And no intentions of coming back again.

Chapter 12

Whatever Bud's intentions had been, something changed them. He came back the next morning.

To Mr. Nicholas, he seemed almost a different person—much quieter, much less hostile. Almost diffident in his need to talk things over with someone he could trust. He was, in fact, the young man Mr. Nicholas had tried to find the day before—and now here he was, a day too late.

For something had happened to Mr. Nicholas, too. It was not exactly discouragement. Perhaps it was partly cumulative fatigue—and no doubt all those bedpans were beginning to tell on his spirit. Mostly, though, he was just homesick.

Dorothea and his grandchildren had come to visit him the afternoon before; and while the visit had gone very well, even cheerfully, he had not felt homesick then. Not even when they told him about his cat, who missed him and cried in the night, shut into his room alone (apparently Dorothea had known about this all along). Nor about his trunks, which she had finally decided to keep right in his new room, no matter how it looked. And all the details of the new house, and the new neighborhood—he had enjoyed these, but felt no particular haste to confirm them. But that night, he had dreamed that he was home. Home was not the old house—it was not, in fact, any particular place. So far as he could puzzle it out after he woke, it was just a long awareness of being where he belonged: of hearing Dorothea's coming and going, her occasional voice, her footsteps and perfectly definable activities. That was the whole dream; it seemed to go on a long time, and it absorbed him completely. When he woke and knew that it had been a dream, he felt quite lost, and rather humiliated. Why, that was no better than a big baby, content simply to lie all day listening to its mother! Had he really sunk to such a state? He knew, of course, that he had not—and yet the memory of the dream clung, nostalgic and shameful, long after he had repudiated it.

The dream had also cut him off from Mary Rose. She lay somewhere on the other side of it, as if in a far past—a puzzling and pitiful little girl whom he had not been able to help. Someone else's little girl, though, and not really his concern at all.

He thought, I'm being old this morning, that's what it is. This is what old age is like. I suppose it's time…. But it depressed him; he did not like to be so good.

Nor did he want to cope with Bud again. Even a good Bud. Why was he here? What did he want? He sat politely on the chair beside the bed, smelling of shaving lotion and car grease, and asked if Mr. Nicholas had talked to his lawyer.

Mr. Nicholas had. He was able to say, without satisfaction, that Bud had been quite wrong about the light sentence. From the way the man had behaved, Mr. Marks thought it more than probable that he would be given extensive tests, and probably sent to a mental institution: the criminal assault would serve as a legal control to get the man where he really belonged, before he qualified for a life sentence—or the electric chair.

Besides, Mr. Marks doubted that the man had got to this stage without some preliminary troubles, or warnings, which should be on record.

"Already on the books, hey?" said Bud thoughtfully. "Well, maybe. Could be."

What Mr. Nicholas did not go into was Joe's insistence on their being able to identify the man absolutely. Mr. Nicholas admitted that from this particular encounter he couldn't do it. But if he was to be confronted with him again, even sober, he felt sure that he could.

"Could, or would?" said Joe shrewdly. "Come on, Nick, you're completely dependent on this girl's word for it, aren't you? And how's she going to stand up for a witness? She ever been in any sex trouble before?"

"Certainly not! And what do you mean, *before?*" added Mr. Nicholas, angrily.

Still, faintly, his anger came back when he thought of it. In the end, Joe's advice had been to report the attack at once, and let the police take over from there. Without any more delay, either. A day or two was allowable, at his age, and being in the hospital. But no more; or else it would begin to look fishy. As if he didn't trust the girl himself, maybe.

"I trust her absolutely," said Mr. Nicholas.

He still did. But he was beginning to have a faint, exhausted resentment at the Haydens in general. They were the hardest people to reach he had ever come across. It would serve them right if he did as Joe suggested, and reported his own attack and the presence of the man and the girl without identifying either. After all, Mary Rose had carefully not told him who she was.

Yet he couldn't bring himself to this deception. Nor could he report her. How could he expect anyone else to understand that she would conceal such an experience? They would think the worst of her. They might even think, as Bud said, that she had gone with the man voluntarily, and then taken fright.

No; he couldn't do it.

He didn't even want to talk about it anymore.

Yet here was Bud, troubled and persistent, camped beside his bed. Mr. Nicholas had a good idea what had happened: Mary Rose wouldn't tell him who the man was, either. He lay and waited for Bud to confess this, so he could tell him it served him right.

But Bud was taking the long way round.

"I admit I can't see Pop in the trailer," he was saying. "And I can understand how she don't want to go anywheres without him. But it's crazy to think we can fix that place up and live there different, with him like he is. No woman's going to put up with him, even if I could afford to hire somebody. Or even if I got married ..."

Mr. Nicholas made no comment.

"Well, it's not your worry," said Bud, accepting this. "It's just that yesterday you—I guess you made pretty good sense, and it's the first time I ever talked about it with anybody. I mean, that didn't have some crazy ax to grind."

"I had an ax to grind," Mr. Nicholas said grimly.

Bud laughed.

"Yeah. You sure are for that kid, aren't you?"

But Mr. Nicholas wasn't falling into this trap again. He said nothing.

"Well, so am I," said Bud. "But what the hell am I going to do with her? She can't handle Pop, and he can't handle her—and I can't handle the both of them! Brother, if he knew what happened this time, she'd really get it."

Against his better judgment, Mr. Nicholas said: "You haven't told your father about this?"

"Jeez, no—he'd blow the roof off!"

"Do you mean he would beat her? For being attacked and beaten?"

Startled, Bud said: "No—he wouldn't do that—"

There was a long silence, and then Bud got up.

"Maybe you got something there, Mr. Nicholas," he said. "Okay. Thanks. I'll see you."

Mr. Nicholas had never heard of a family so completely out of touch with itself and the world around it. He was thoroughly out of patience with them. All of them.

He was out of patience with everybody.

Dr. Linen came by and approved of his gloom. He said, "You're letting down nicely. Now you can see just how much that business took out of you."

"Is that what you intended?"

"Well, there's no way round it. Unless you keep on going till you drop. Like me," he said cheerfully.

Mr. Nicholas lay silently hating him till he went away.

His family came that evening and found him totally unresponsive. If he had spoken at all, he would have been particularly disagreeable to Dorothea, and he wasn't going to give her that much satisfaction. As it was, she kept a hurt silence, and Johnny did the talking.

He said he had gone by Mrs. Thompson's and taken her a Spring Assortment. She was feeling lonely and rather dull, after all the excitement, and John had taken it on himself to offer to bring her over for the day as soon as they got settled. Was that all right? Mr. Nicholas supposed it was. Then John produced the queer little note someone had left at Mrs. Thompson's house, the morning his father had been there, and read it out.

"What do you think of that, Dad?" he said. "There must have been some kid peeking in at you—and you must have lost consciousness for quite a while, you know. Did you realize it?"

"Let me have the note," said his father.

It was crumpled and much folded by now, and he could feel nothing except periods, and perhaps a crossbar. But his fingers went over and over it, in some idiot hope of their own. From which they got nothing, of course. It didn't even have any smell, except Johnny's tobacco.

That night he got only a pill to sleep on, and it didn't carry him through. In some still pre-morning hour he had another attack of panic for Mary Rose—not quite so severe, but entirely sobering. In the morning, as soon as he could hope for an answer, he called Al's Service Station.

Bud wasn't there, somebody told him, but they would tell him to call Mr. Nicholas when he came in. Time passed; he didn't call. Mr. Nicholas decided that he would come by instead, in his lunch hour. By two o'clock he conceded to himself that the lunch hour was past, and called the service station again. At that point, he began to wonder what he had to say.

In fact, he had only to say his name, and Bud's voice warmed into loquacity.

"Gee, I wanted to get over and see you, Mr. Nicholas," he began. "But I already took so much time off yesterday, I got kind of behind here. But you really started something with us! I told my old man about the kid, like you said, and you know what he did?"

"What?"

"He sent for the priest! How do you like that? All these years he won't let him in the door, and last night I had to go over after him. Boy, I was scared to go."

"The priest?" It would never have occurred to Mr. Nicholas, an active Episcopalian, to send for his own priest at such a time. He said with interest: "Why, Bud?"

"Who knows? Anyway, he's really in for it now. The kid isn't even confirmed, the old man hasn't been to confession in ten years—me, too—it's a mess! And I was bringing the kid over here with me after school, you know? She could sit in the office here, and do her homework, and talk to the guys—she wanted to. But no more. Now I got to take her over, she stays with the Father's housekeeper till I can pick her up, she works on her catechism—brother, I'm telling you, it's one mess!"

But he sounded cheerful about it.

Mr. Nicholas said urgently, "But that man, Bud—hasn't she said yet who he is?"

Bud's voice altered. He said, "Well, you know, I think you might have been wrong about that, Mr. Nicholas. That was another thing I wanted to ask you about. What made you so sure she knew him, and all? It's more like she really didn't, you know? Like she says, it was pretty dark in there, and everything happened so fast, when he showed ... What made you feel like she knew him?" he asked again.

Mr. Nicholas opened his mouth, and closed it. His first exasperation went down almost unrecognized. Caution settled on him, like a calmness.

"Well, I did have that impression, Bud," he said.

"Yeah, I know—but why? From the way it sounds, it was more like some bum that was holed up there for the night. I guess she was pretty scared when you were talking to her—but if you could have heard her last night, I think you—"

"As a matter of fact, I would like to see her again," Mr. Nicholas said, adding cunning to caution. "It would give me a great deal of pleasure to talk to her in ordinary circumstances, you know. It's difficult to efface the impression of her as a child in trouble."

This piece of diplomatic pleading went down very well. Bud said thoughtfully, "Yeah, I see what you mean. I guess I should have thought of bringing her over, but everything's been happening so fast—"

"Why don't you bring her to me after school today?" Mr. Nicholas suggested. "And leave her here till you want to pick her up? I'm sure we can find plenty to do, and she could have something to eat here with me."

"Well, thanks—maybe I could check with you later?" Bud sounded embarrassed. "See, I don't want to upset the old man's applecart, you know it really hit him, how she didn't dare stay in the house because I wasn't there. He's thrown out the bottles, he's cleaning the joint up, I got to clean up the yard, and so on. How long it's going to last I wouldn't know, but right now it's like he's got all these plans, him and the Father, and I wouldn't want to mess them up. Maybe I could call you?"

"If you will. I hope very much you can bring her, Bud," said Mr. Nicholas.

It was an understatement.

Around four o'clock Bud called again, still embarrassed. He had just dropped his sister at the priest's, but he was going to bring her by the hospital that evening for a visit, if that was okay? They wouldn't stay very long, but she wanted to see him—only she thought she had better stick to the new plan about afternoons. Was that okay?

Mr. Nicholas "got the message." She wanted to have her brother with her when they talked. She didn't want to upset any applecarts either. The past was past; no one but dogged old "Mr. Nicklis" threatened her new life, and she didn't want any interference from him. He said grimly that this was quite all right, and settled to wait—without pleasure—for an encounter that would be false, and brief, and useless.

Yet for the second time, she took him by surprise. Her pleasure at seeing him again was real—he couldn't doubt it. In the quiet bustle of the evening visiting hour she came into his room almost running (in some light, hard-soled slippers) and then stopped dead at the bed's edge, without sending one tremor through it. He was sitting up; and to the hand he automatically raised—half in defense, half to see with—she eagerly touched her own. He enclosed it at once; it was Mary Rose's hand.

She said delightedly: "You know it's me, don't you? Even if you didn't know I was coming, you could tell—couldn't you, Mr. Nicholas?"

She was turned away, wanting her brother to hear, and to acknowledge her friend's accomplishments.

Her brother said, "Kid, the whole world knows it's you. Now simmer down, you're not supposed to run in hospitals."

"It's all right," said Mr. Nicholas hastily. "How are you, child? How are you?"

He was astonished by his own happiness—as instant as it was unexpected. As if he had told Bud the truth without realizing it: that all he wanted was to encounter the real Mary Rose, really freed from her fears and dangers. For that moment, he was as willing to forget as she.

Evidently, she was nicely dressed, and wanted him to notice—or wanted to show Bud that he *could* notice—for she guided his hand to her chest.

"It's my new dress," she explained. "It's purple—my father bought it! He went with Mrs. Reilly, she used to take care of me when I was little, and she might come and housekeep for us if he gets a job ..." Her voice grew absent; she said suddenly: "It's the first time I saw you so good, Mr. Nicholas. Do you want to see me?"

"Yes," he said, not understanding or caring much what she meant, absorbed in her lively nearness. "Yes, I should like that."

She sat carefully on the edge of his bed and put his hand against her cheek, and left it there. After a moment he understood, and not to disappoint her, made a careful exploration of the small face. He was not expert at this, and did not learn much, except that her rough hair had been carefully smoothed.

"Why," he said gravely, "you have blue eyes!"

She drew in her breath so sharply that he added at once: "I'm only teasing, child."

"But it's true!"

"Guessing, then. Bud, look on my dresser—are there cookies?" There were, and bottles of Coke—he had asked for them out of a sense of duty, but he was glad now that they were there.

And he did not disturb their brief party by any warnings, or references, that would make Mary Rose withdraw. But as it became clear that the Haydens were not going to leave their neighborhood but were, on the contrary, going to pull themselves together and face it down—Millers and all—a grave intention began to grow in him.

Mary Rose could not build her new life on this pact of secrecy with a vicious, dangerous man. Nor could Mr. Nicholas—yet—persuade her of this. Especially not with Joe Marks's skepticism still in his own mind, about the child's reliability as a witness. *But if Mr. Nicholas himself could identify the man*—independently—then there could be no more reason for keeping quiet. He would have no more hesitation in openly urging Mary Rose and her family—and her priest, if necessary—to start their new life as they meant to go on. Openly, and lawfully.

Only how could he manage it?

Mr. Nicholas grew so thoughtful that Bud took his sister away, afraid she had exhausted the old man. She went obediently, but left him a present—a small box filled with things which, she said, were nice to feel. Some of them he could—absently exploring—identify without trouble: stones and marbles, stripped and smoothed twigs of odd design. Others, such as a piece of new chamois, took him longer. But there was a plastic or celluloid shape he could make nothing of; and during the long night he returned gratefully to this puzzle, when he needed rest from the graver problem weighing on his mind.

Chapter 13

By morning he had his plan, and felt that he was ready to put it into action.

Dr. Linen, perhaps in remorse, had taken him off the bedpan the day before, and by now he was navigating pretty freely. His legs were fine. His head was fine. He didn't even mind the harness round his middle. He could, in fact, have gone home—the doctor himself agreed with this.

But Mr. Nicholas didn't want to go home. What he desired—and proposed—was that he should be a kind of latchkey patient for another day or so, with the privilege of spending his evenings in Rudds' Grocery Store, staying until they closed. Then he would taxi back to the hospital and go to bed. Since this was Friday, he had every hope that one or two evenings of listening would suffice. Rudds' was the only local source of beer in the evenings, and their weekend trade must comprise the whole neighborhood, surely.

Dr. Linen wanted to know what he meant to do if he did identify his attacker—trip him up with his stick and then step on him? Mr. Nicholas replied seriously that he meant to ask the Rudds, now and then, who some customer had been, and in this way obscure the real information he wanted. When he had it, he would simply leave—after an interval.

"And what's the fellow going to think, if he comes in and sees you sitting there?" Dr. Linen demanded. "Don't you think he'll guess what you're up to?"

"I hope so," said Mr. Nicholas. "There isn't much he can do about it. He certainly won't risk attacking me in a public place. Of course he might see me and not come in, but I'll try not to be visible from the outside. And I'll know him this time, Roger—no matter how he tries to walk or speak, I'll know him."

Dr. Linen then pointed out that the hospital was not a hotel, and that he certainly could not go out for the evening and come rolling in at midnight. Of course, if he thought Dorothea wouldn't mind his having a little night life, Dr. Linen had no objection to his going home.

Mr. Nicholas now perceived that his earnest plan was making no impression—that his friend was worse than skeptical, he was amused.

He said, "I think I had better tell you why the identification of this man is so important, Roger"; and then, much as he had told it to Bud, he repeated the story of their encounter in the empty house. He added to this what he had learned of Mary Rose and her circumstances. And finally, he explained the necessity for a positive identification, as Joe Marks had explained it to him. Dr. Linen listened without interrupting, as he did to interesting symptoms.

At the end, he said only: "Well, I agree with your friend Marks, that you ought to turn the whole mess over to the police and bow out. But if you're going to adopt little wild girls at your age, I suppose I can't expect rational behavior."

His manner was different, though. He was serious now. Mr. Nicholas said, "Perhaps Lettie Thompson would put me up again for a night or two."

"You keep away from that poor woman, she's had enough of you. No," said his friend decisively, "if you're set on this business, you'd better come to us. Then I can keep an eye on you. And my wife's used to characters, she'll see that you behave."

Mr. Nicholas said that was very kind, and would be considerably easier to explain to Dorothea than another visit to Lettie.

"And I want to take you there and pick you up," Dr. Linen added. "You're not to set foot out of the place without me, do you hear? Actually, someone ought to wait with you—Johnny, perhaps. I don't like you sitting there alone so long."

"It won't be long, I'm only interested in the evening hours, and they close at eleven." Mr. Nicholas, relieved to find his friend being drawn in, went on: "Besides, the Rudds are always there, one or both of them, I'm sure. And an able-bodied person sitting there with me would be much too obvious. No one minds an old blind man sitting around, he's quite anonymous," he said impersonally.

Dr. Linen was taken aback by this self-description—which he wouldn't have used, himself, of his friend, and didn't much like to hear Mr. Nicholas using.

He said, "Well, get some rest, and I'll pick you up later today. Since you're bound to do this." And went away in a state of indecision not usual to him.

Explaining their proposed visitor to his wife, he said: "I don't suppose it'll hurt the old fellow to sit there playing detective for an evening or two. It'll relieve his mind, anyway—he'll have done what he could, about a very nasty business. Though I wouldn't want to spend that long with the Rudds myself," he added. "But that's his problem." And having in this way made up his mind, he began to be amused again at the idea of this unlikely company, and curious to see how Mr. Nicholas would handle it.

Both Rudds were on duty when they arrived, at a little after seven that evening. Mild weather, and the beginning of the weekend, had brought DeKuyper Street largely out of doors; and its corner store was still doing a brisk "supper" business. Mrs. Rudd, behind the counter, noticed them first. Her expression altered, to a different intentness, and she came out to them.

"Well, good evening, doctor—and here's Mr. Nicholas, looking just as spry as ever, isn't he? My, you certainly gave us all a shock, that day you went off in the ambulance—first the moving vans and then the ambulance, I thought my goodness, I bet Mrs. Nicholas doesn't know which way she's going. A fall, was it?"

"A slight accident. Thank you. Very nice of you to be concerned," said Mr. Nicholas. "And now I wonder if I might trespass on your kindness, Mrs. Rudd."

"You want some bananas," she said, with a quick glance at the doctor.

"I'll get them for you right now. About how many?"

"No, as a matter of fact, I don't require anything. But I should like very much to wait in some corner here, if I may, for a while."

"Wait here?" Mrs. Rudd glanced at the doctor again, who was looking idly round, nodding to an occasional patient. "You're waiting for someone?"

"Yes," he said. "I should appreciate being able to wait here."

"Oh." Her glance went to the back of the store, to where her husband had been when they arrived—a broad back at the big refrigerator. But he was no longer in sight. She made up her mind alone, and quickly. "Why, surely," she said, with her anguished smile. "No matter how busy we are, I guess we can still do a favor for an old neighbor, isn't that right, doctor? After all, we're not one of those supermarkets that don't even know who their neighbors are, not that Mrs. Nicholas doesn't have the right to shop anywhere she wants, that's what a democracy's for. But I wouldn't want anything else to happen to you, it gets so crowded in here sometimes—we wouldn't want that, would we, doctor?"

"Nothing will happen to me, Mrs. Rudd," Mr. Nicholas said patiently. "Thank you. I wonder if I might use the chair you used to keep here? Perhaps you would ask Mr. Rudd."

"The chair?" she repeated. There was a small pause; then she said tightly, "Just a minute," and left them.

Dr. Linen watched her go into the back premises, past the three or four remaining customers—a small bustling woman in search of something she wasn't going to find. Rudd, a pale-eyed, heavy blond man, given to striped shirts under his soiled butcher's apron, was popularly supposed to be henpecked; but Dr. Linen did not agree. He preferred to consider him a potential wife-beater, whom Mrs. Rudd could not rouse to his duties.

She reappeared alone, her pale face pinched with annoyance, and began to wait on the nearest customer without another glance at the two men by the door. Dr. Linen murmured, "I don't think your plan is going to get off the ground, my friend." To which Mr. Nicholas replied quietly: "Why don't you go, Roger? I'm all right."

"I want to see what happens when she finds out how long you mean to wait."

But less patient than his friend, he presently walked over to the counter.

"If your husband's busy, perhaps I can get the chair, Mrs. Rudd," he said briskly. "Mr. Nicholas ought not to stand long."

She looked up at him then—with such open longing to quarrel that he felt some sympathy for her. But her control was remarkable. She managed another of those aching smiles.

"He's gone to deliver. We're very busy."

"I see you are. You'd better let me help."

Without a word, she turned and went into the back premises—returned past the curtain, awkwardly bearing the chair herself. It was an old wooden straight chair which had stood in one corner for years, certainly no invitation to loll, and usually covered with boxes. But she said in a rush of sweetness, handing it over: "People hang around so if they can sit down—I had to put it in back. But you're welcome to use it, doctor."

Remarkable control. He thanked her gravely, and then looked round for a place to put Mr. Nicholas, who was still standing patiently by the door. He found a niche behind the bread stand, from which his friend could not be seen from the street, and placed the chair there. Then he guided Mr. Nicholas to it.

Seated, Mr. Nicholas said in a low voice, "Thank you, Roger. I hadn't expected so much difficulty—Mrs. Rudd always seemed excessively pleasant, the few mornings I came down. Do you think something is wrong?"

"No more than usual," Dr. Linen said, grinning. "Sure you want to stay?"

Mr. Nicholas hesitated and then said: "I think I must. But you go along. And thank you."

"Call me if you change your mind. And remember—stay put."

Mr. Nicholas said he would, and the doctor left—wondering how long his friend would stick it out.

Mr. Nicholas himself had no such wonder—he meant to stay until closing, unless he were actually put out, which seemed unlikely. But he hadn't foreseen the obstacle of being unwelcome, added to the general unpleasantness of his task.

For he did not want to do this. Dr. Linen's idea of him as "playing detective" was far from true. He dreaded these lonely, public hours of listening for the entrance of a man whom he abhorred more than he had realized. His dread was not physical—certainly no second beating was going to take place in this open, lighted store. Only an encounter lay ahead, if he was lucky. A second encounter, when the man would see him sitting there and in that moment of surprise—he hoped—would betray himself in his breathing, his movements, his whole manner. That was all that could happen; Mr. Nicholas did not know why he dreaded it so. And afterward, he had only to inquire who that man had been.

But he would have to inquire of Mrs. Rudd. A hostile Mrs. Rudd, who perhaps would not even bother to answer? He considered this, anxiously, and tried to gauge her temper from her voice. There was no doubt that it changed, whenever it came in his direction. She did resent his being there.

Why? Did she have some grudge against his family that he did not know about? Did she dislike him personally? Or did she simply feel that her property was being encroached upon, without profit to her? Mr. Nicholas began to realize that his supposed familiarity with the Rudds was one of hearsay, rather than experience. They were emergency suppliers for Dorothea, who would send one of the children down to the corner for something she had run out of; and his knowledge of them was based almost entirely on this long, reluctant patronage of hers. He wasn't pleased to find a part of his mind stocked with Dorothea's opinions disguised as his own; but since he had no others, he attempted to sort these out. His impression was that Dorothea preferred to deal with Mr. Rudd, who was less tense than his wife, and that Rudd usually took the evening hours in the store. Certainly Mr. Nicholas had never encountered him there on one of his morning visits. So probably the wife opened the store, and the husband closed it, and if this was true Mr. Nicholas might hope that Rudd would soon relieve Mrs. Rudd, and prove less hostile. He could hardly be more so.

A pause came, in which there were no customers in the store, and Mr. Nicholas was not surprised when Mrs. Rudd came over to question him.

"Well, you're having a long wait, aren't you?" she said (although he had not been there half an hour). "Don't you think I'd better call up and find out what's the matter? I'm sure Mrs. Nicholas wouldn't want you to be sitting around this way, with every nosy person on the block asking about her business—now would she?"

It was true that several persons had stopped briefly to speak to him, rather to his surprise. On the porch, probably, he had been too far for casual conversations. But he did not like this interpretation of their neighborliness.

"I'm competent to deal with nosiness, Mrs. Rudd," he replied. "If there should be any. You have very pleasant customers," he added. "You're fortunate in them."

"Well," she said, distracted, "of course we've been here a long while. People know us. And we don't encourage the riffraff—that cheap candy business, I had to get rid of that. It just wasn't worth it, for what it brought in."

"I suppose not."

"Well," she said, returning to business, "I don't like to hurry an old—an old neighbor, but I don't want to go upstairs and leave you here, Mr. Nicholas. I just don't feel your daughter-in-law would want me to do that, especially after all the trouble she's had already. Why don't you let me call up and see what's the matter? Is it your son you're waiting for?"

"No, my son isn't coming for me tonight," he replied. "Dr. Linen will pick me up again when you close, if the person I'm waiting for shouldn't appear. You needn't worry about my being left on your hands."

"When we close!" she repeated. "Well, that's quite a time, I mean that's quite a responsibility, Mr. Nicholas! We always like to be as obliging as we can, but after all, we're busy people! This is a business, and that's a long time to have to be responsible for someone's—for someone. I just think you'd better go wait somewhere else, Mr. Nicholas!"

That controlled waspishness was escaping at last, with no Dr. Linen to appreciate it.

Mr. Nicholas said, without expression, "I'm afraid there is nowhere else to wait for this person. I have no other way of reaching him. Privately, that is."

"Well, I don't know what you mean by *that*," she exclaimed, in a luxury of release. "*'Privately'* isn't exactly what I'd call a busy store, where hard-working people are trying to earn a *living*—!"

"Myra ..."

This one low sound, from the back of the store, startled them both. It silenced Mrs. Rudd, but only momentarily. In the next moment, she had turned and started rapidly toward the speaker.

"Where have you been?" she demanded, in a new, more fretful voice. "Do you realize I've been alone here nearly an hour? And you didn't even take the beer down to ... and leaving me with ... sit there all *night* ..."

She was behind the curtain that partitioned the back premises from the store, and had lowered her voice, but not much. Her husband's lower voice obscured whatever words he was offering in reply. They were not many.

Whatever they were, his wife received them indignantly. Mr. Nicholas, a helpless audience, heard her say: "... think I'm made of! You didn't even ..." He interrupted, his words still obscure, and she broke in upon him—and then a customer came into the store.

It was a man, absently whistling. Tapping with his nails on the counter, while he waited. His brief inspection of silent Mr. Nicholas didn't reconcile him to waiting.

"Hey!" he called out. "Anybody home?"

Mrs. Rudd's rapid footsteps went up some stairs; and presently, a slower bass accompaniment, her husband's steps came into the front of the store.

He said nothing, not even to the impatient man's "Six Piels—you got it cold?" For answer, the heavy refrigerator door opened and shut, and then the cash register. The impatient man went out, still whistling, and the door shut behind him.

Mr. Nicholas, raising his head, said: "Good evening, Mr. Rudd."

Rudd shifted his feet, there behind the counter. He muttered finally, "Don't mind about her. It's her nerves. She's a very nervous woman. Afterwards, she's sorry."

"She has no need to be sorry, so far as I'm concerned," Mr. Nicholas replied.

The feet moved again.

"You can sit here if you want," said Rudd's voice.

"Thank you."

"It don't bother me."

Mr. Nicholas said nothing to this; and after a moment the refrigerator door opened again.

"You want a beer?"

Mr. Nicholas declined. He heard the rush of escaping gas as a beer can was punctured, and then two women came into the store, talking together. This time Mr. Rudd greeted them: "Good evening, ladies," and the three of them talked while the women's purchases were collected and paid for. When they had gone, the silence returned. Rudd broke it.

"It even makes her nervous if I take a beer in the store," he said, a man continuing conversation. "So—what can you do? I wait till she goes up."

He laughed, and drank. Mr. Nicholas's continuing quiet seemed to encourage him.

"A nervous woman you can't argue with. You know? You can't even talk to a nervous woman, it just makes her nervous."

Another customer entered while he was speaking, and two more while the first was still there. When all three finally were gone, another beer can was punctured.

"So you just want to sit here and wait awhile, that's right?" said Rudd, when he had drunk. "Till the doctor comes back for you?"

"That's right."

"Well, why not? It don't bother anybody. You can sit here, I don't care." His first constraint was gone; he sounded at ease now, even slightly contemptuous. Mr. Nicholas faced across the room toward him.

"Will you come and help me up, Mr. Rudd?" he said then.

"You want to get up?"

"Please."

With interest—and without moving—Rudd said: "You can't get up by yourself since you got hurt?"

"I'll be glad of your help."

"Sure, all right."

But he still did not move.

"What happened to you, anyway? I heard you went in the ambulance."

"Nothing of any consequence."

Neither of them spoke, until Rudd spoke again. "Maybe you better stay there like the doc put you," he said. "Maybe that's better."

"Nonsense," said Mr. Nicholas. "There's no reason why I shouldn't get up. Is there any reason why you shouldn't help me to?"

"Sure, I'll help you," said Rudd again. But his feet, coming into sluggish motion, went toward the refrigerator. "You don't want a beer?"

Mr. Nicholas didn't answer. The heavy door opened and shut again, the can was punctured. Rudd drank. No one came in.

Then the can was set down, the slow steps came round the counter and down the middle of the floor. Within several feet of Mr. Nicholas they stopped again.

"What did you want to get up for?" he asked.

"I want to use your telephone, if I may."

"Sure, I'll call for you," said Rudd. "Who do you want to call up?"

"Thank you, but I had better make this call myself," said Mr. Nicholas. As he spoke he reached out his hand, saying firmly: "Just take my hand, please."

He had his stick braced and ready, in his other hand, and kept his posture of readiness until, after a pause, Rudd shuffled forward. An experimental hand touched his. He took it at once, checking its movement of withdrawal, and at the same time forced himself quickly up.

"There, you see?" he said. "Quite simple."

As he said this, dropping the supporting hand, he seemed in some overconfidence to lose balance, and his hand flew up again—far up, touching and then grasping the other's hair. Only for a moment; before Rudd could strike out, cursing, at the grasping hand, Mr. Nicholas had withdrawn it.

"Clumsy of me ..."

Leaning on his stick, a little out of breath, he heard Rudd blunder away, out of reach, and stand with his own harder breathing filling the little store's silence.

"You startle easily, Mr. Rudd," said Mr. Nicholas. "You have caught some of your wife's nervousness."

Like an evoked nightmare, the familiar thick whispering broke out: "You devil! You old devil ..."

It stopped, abruptly. There were several fast, heavy steps, and then the sound of the front door being slammed and locked. And then the blind was pulled down.

Chapter 14

Mr. Nicholas said quietly, "What is the point of that? I am known to be here. You had better not make your position any worse."

Rudd, breathing, went on drawing down blinds—one for each large window on either side of the door. When he had done this, some feeling of refuge let him stop. He did nothing but stand waiting—breathing. As if the next move were Mr. Nicholas's.

Who went on: "I suppose you realize that you were lucky, in my house. You did not commit any serious crime, at least not according to the law. Don't spoil your luck now, Mr. Rudd."

He didn't expect an answer at once—not from this slow mind with its wild underlay of alarms. But with hardly any delay, Rudd blurted out: "You come here to make trouble for me—don't do it! I'll make trouble, too—"

"You already have. Be glad it's no worse. Now open that door again, before someone notices it."

Rudd went past him. Widely round him, to the back of the store. The refrigerator door opened and shut again.

Mr. Nicholas briefly debated whether or not to go and open the door himself. Rudd was twice the distance from it now that he was. Rudd was also twice as agile; and above all, Mr. Nicholas knew he must avoid throwing the man into a panic, in which he would use his physical strength without thinking of consequences.

Oddly, Mr. Nicholas felt no fear. That seizure of physical terror in his own bathroom had left no echo in him. In fact, he felt no emotion, now that he was beyond the emotions of wonder and surprise, and had come to certainty. A certainty without anger, without satisfaction or any excitement. Only a grim determination filled him—to finish this, and be done with it forever.

He said deliberately, "I intend to identify you as the man who entered my empty house and attacked me there when I surprised you. Deny it if you like. If you attack me again, here, you will simply prove what I say. And this time, Dr. Linen is my witness."

"I never touched you," Rudd muttered, from his refuge. "I never would have touched you before, but you hit me first! You were up there with that kid—that dirty kid—everybody knows she's a liar—"

"I'm not interested in your story," Mr. Nicholas said coldly. "You had better keep it. Now are you going to open this door, or shall I?"

Rudd didn't move. But he went on talking, with gathering grievance.

"What do you want to believe that dirty kid for? Everybody on the block knows about her—she got into your house herself, I seen her! I only went in to make her come out, that's all! And I only knocked you down because you jumped me like that, you hit me first! How did I know?"

"I see you have your story prepared," said Mr. Nicholas, with contempt.

"I only went in to make her come out," Rudd repeated doggedly. "On account of her old man—he already had enough bad luck, everybody's sorry for him. Everybody knows what kind of a kid he's got! And then you jumped me like that—how did I know who you were? You better not say I was up there with that kid, because I wasn't—that was you up there, you was the one up there with her! I only went in to make her come out, that's all."

Someone came up and rattled the door, knocked on it.

Mr. Nicholas moved, but Rudd was faster. The beer can dropped clattering to the floor, and he passed Mr. Nicholas like a running bear.

"Closed! Closed!" he bawled against his blinded door. "We got sickness—we're closed!"

Someone spoke inaudibly from the other side—and went away. Immediately, Rudd ran back again to his refuge, and there came the click of a light switch—then another. The smell of his sweating fear hung in the air where he had passed.

"You are making your own story absurd by behaving this way," said Mr. Nicholas. "When Dr. Linen comes back and finds the store closed, he won't go away—I promise you that."

Rudd burst out, almost in a sob: "What do you want to do this for? Why do you want to make all this trouble? I told you—I told you I wouldn't have touched you, only you come at me like that—you and that kid! You was the ones that was up there! I only come in to get her out, and then you both jumped me—"

A door opened, somewhere within the building, and a woman's voice called faintly: "Will! What is it? What's that noise?"

"Nothing—nothing! Go to bed, Myra!"

"But what was that noise?"

She was coming down the stairs. His helpless silence waited to be found.

Her voice became clearer, and sharpened with discovery.

"What have you got the lights out for? Will! *Will!* What are you doing—where are you?"

"Here," he said, hopeless.

He was evidently near her; her voice sank at once.

"What are you doing?"

He mumbled, "That old man—he's trying to make trouble, I had to shut the store—"

She took this in. Then her voice came again, tense and quiet.

"Will, where is he? What did you do?"

"I'm here, Mrs. Rudd," Mr. Nicholas said clearly. "Waiting for your husband to control himself."

Instantly she spat at him: "You get out of here! Get out!"

"Gladly. But your husband has locked me in, for some reason."

She was silent again, perhaps turning to her husband.

His sobbing voice broke out then: "Myra—oh, God, he's got some crazy story, he's going to tell the police—"

"What story? What are you talking about?"

"Oh, God, I don't know—some dirty kid got in his house that night, I only went in to get her out—I didn't know he was there, I wouldn't have touched him, only he—"

"*What kid?*"

Her fierce demand froze him. He couldn't produce any more coherence, only sobbing breath. There was a sudden scuffle of sound, as if she had seized on him.

"It was that dirty Hayden kid, wasn't it? Wasn't it?"

"Myra—the old man out there, be quiet—"

She was quiet.

There was a muted click—perhaps some other light switch in the back, which would shed a smaller light throughout the store. Mr. Nicholas, halfway to the front door, stopped and turned as her rapid steps came toward him.

She came directly to him and slapped him hard across the face. There was a hoarse cry: "*Myra!*" from the back of the store. She paid no attention to it.

"So you came here to make trouble, did you?" she began in a rapid, low voice. "We're not good enough for you and your stuck-up family—the whole neighborhood's not good enough for you! Well, all right, get out! Nobody wants you around here anyway! But don't you try to make trouble for hard-working people, don't you dare try it! You hear me, old man?"

Mr. Nicholas had recovered his balance, with the aid of the bread stand, which was rather shaky.

He said breathlessly, "The trouble has already been made, by your husband. I advise you not to—"

"You advise me!" Her voice went up to a low shriek. "Don't you dare stand there and tell me what to do! Who do you think is going to listen to you—a useless old man that can't even take care of himself—that can't even see! And you come in here and tell me filthy lies about my husband—and that filthy girl, that dirty kid—!"

She burst into dry sobs—to Mr. Nicholas's relief. He had been trying to brace himself for an attack that would land him on the floor.

He said uncertainly, "You had better talk this over with your husband, Mrs. Rudd. He is in trouble—and he would have been in much worse trouble if I had not happened to interfere. Your husband is a dangerously ill man. He came very near to destroying a little girl the other night."

"Myra, Myra—don't listen to him! It's not true!"

Rudd, eager with despair, came half running toward them. His wife had fallen quiet, checking her sobs, listening.

"Myra, listen—nothing happened, he's lying—listen, wouldn't the kid have said something? Wasn't her father in here today—yesterday—wasn't he just like always? He's lying, Myra—he's lying!"

She said in a new voice, dulled and savage: "Tell me what happened, Will. You took that girl in his house? At night?"

"No! I never did! She went in by herself, Myra—by herself—I only tried to get her out so—"

"You followed her in? And the old man followed you?"

"No! I didn't! I mean, I don't know what he—"

"Wait," she said: a command. Then her dulled voice turned to Mr. Nicholas. "You tell me what you've got to say about my husband. Right now. Quick!"

"Myra—"

"Shut up!"

Mr. Nicholas hesitated. He saw no use in saying more to her than he had said. On the other hand, she was in no state to be refused. In his slight pausing, she seized his arm and shook it. Hysteria lay beneath a very thin control.

"Tell me!"

"I intend to," Mr. Nicholas said hastily. He did not try to alter or soften the facts he had already related—to Bud, to Dr. Linen—but simply began to relate them once more.

He had just begun, when someone came and rapped sharply on the door. To his wearied, sickened mind, hope came that this was the doctor; and with a sigh, he fell silent. Neither Rudd spoke. When the rapping came again, harder, Mrs. Rudd turned to her husband.

"Take him in back," she ordered, low.

"That is probably Dr. Linen," Mr. Nicholas said.

She went directly to the door, an act of courage he had not expected, and said sharply: "Who is it?"

The answer was indistinguishable to Mr. Nicholas, but it was not his friend's voice; he could tell that before she answered.

"No, we're closed early tonight. We're closed!"

Her husband hissed at her: *"Because of sickness!"* But she disdained this cue, and returned in hard silence. Passed them by.

"Bring him back here," she said, passing.

As he obeyed orders, Rudd's confusion vanished. He seized Mr. Nicholas's arm and began, as if he were a sack of potatoes, to haul him away.

If Mr. Nicholas could have got his stick free, he would have struck at him—but his wretched legs made this impossible. Made it all he could do, in fact, to keep upright on his journey. Grimly silent, he allowed himself to be hustled along. A heavy curtain brushed his face, and then he was past it and allowed to stand still. Rudd's dutiful hand still grasped his arm.

"Myra, don't let him—"

"Don't talk, let me hear. Go on," she ordered Mr. Nicholas. "You said the door was locked."

Mr. Nicholas went on. It seemed impossible to him that she should hear what her husband had done—what he was capable of doing—without collapsing in horror. He waited every moment for her to stop him, to say: "No more!" or simply to cry.

She did none of these things. From her silence, one could not guess that she was learning anything—or hearing anything. It was Rudd who found the recital unbearable to hear—who dropped Mr. Nicholas's arm and went into restless wandering, a peripheral protest that was all he dared make. Even when Mr. Nicholas had finished, he did not speak.

It was his wife who spoke to him.

"All right," she said, flat-voiced. "I told you. I told you you'd get into trouble with those rotten kids—you and your candy! I know what went on behind that counter! But that Hayden slut wasn't so easy, was she? What did you have to give her to get her into that house? What? Money?"

"I think your mind must be as diseased as your husband's!" said Mr. Nicholas.

She paid no attention. Neither to him nor to her husband's unhappy protests.

Her voice sharpened. She said, "And why didn't she say anything? Are you sure she didn't?"

The telephone rang, startling Rudd so badly that he knocked over some heavy pile of goods. A hand instantly took Mr. Nicholas's arm—a smaller, harder hand than Rudd's.

"Let it ring," said Mrs. Rudd.

They let it ring.

In the following silence she said thoughtfully, "No. She wouldn't dare say a word, that one. She knows better. And you should have known better, too, old man! Do you know how long we've worked to keep this store? How hard we've worked? Do you think I'm going to let you come in here and ruin us, at our age, on account of some rotten brat that ought to be in a detention home anyway?"

Mr. Nicholas said earnestly, "If it's not this child, it will be another. Your husband is out of control, Mrs. Rudd."

"Oh, no, he's not. I can control my husband." And as if in proof—triumphant proof—she said crisply into the room: "All right, Rudd. You got us into this, now do what I say and I'll get you out. He'll have to go down the cellar steps."

Rudd said humbly, "I don't know what you mean, Myra."

"Yes, you do. He had to go to the toilet. He asked to use the toilet. Then he fell down the steps."

She allowed them a brief silence.

Mr. Nicholas cried out: "Are you mad? God help you—do you mean to become *murderers?*"

Rudd blurted, "You keep still." He didn't move.

His wife said rapidly, "The doctor doesn't know, or he wouldn't have left him here. The girl's too scared to talk. It's only him, Rudd. Just him."

Rudd didn't answer. But in his farther part of the room he stirred, began to come forward. A door near Mr. Nicholas was flung open, a light switch snapped.

He exclaimed, "But what are you thinking? Don't you realize you are—"

"You shut up, old man," Rudd said softly. "You ought to been dead a long time anyway."

He was coming up behind Mr. Nicholas, who suddenly swung round, raking air with his rising stick as he turned.

It was an instinctive movement, the movement of a much younger man—and it cost him his balance. But that loss of balance, the glancing stagger against Rudd, somehow entangled them with the partition curtain—and caught Rudd's reaching hands in the curtain as well.

Mr. Nicholas staggered past. He did not fall. He did not know where he was at all, and could not think for sheer horror. He knew he had no hope of reaching the front of the store, and that his voice would not carry from here to the street.

Nevertheless, with all his might, he shouted for help—and shouting, grasped at whatever he could reach, with both hands—letting his stick fall—and threw these objects as hard as he could toward the front. One of them—a can of something—crashed dully against the blinded glass.

Then he was seized, and his mouth covered by Rudd's large hand.

Rudd was almost weeping with rage and fear.

"Shut up, shut up, shut up ..." he gibbered, over and over.

Mr. Nicholas flung himself violently left and right, Rudd swaying behind him, struggling to enforce his grip. He was hampered by the need to cover that shouting mouth, still making muffled calls into his hand.

"Myra, *Myra—!*"

She was there, too, a vicious and silent attacker, not what he needed at all.

"Hold him...."

One of Mr. Nicholas's arms flailed free, and instantaneously the hand grasped and flung another can. This one hit some pile of goods, or fragile display, and the entire structure toppled and crashed in echoing reverberations.

Above these echoes, a louder thundering came upon the front door, and a shouting that was perfectly clear to the wordless, struggling three within.

"Open this door! Open this door!"

It was Linen.

With something—perhaps his foot—he broke glass. Instantly Rudd dropped his prisoner and turned and ran.

Mr. Nicholas, catching at shelving to keep from falling, half falling against a counter and gripping that, was still aware that Rudd did not run far. His wife, crying out shrilly, had caught up with him and would not let him go. At the front of the store, a shouting Linen was knocking out more glass, and Mr. Nicholas continued breathlessly to call to him.

But Mrs. Rudd screamed louder than all these sounds, as if oblivious to them all.

"No, Will—no! Don't leave me—don't—"

"Let *go!*"

From Rudd, there was only the one hard snarl. Then abruptly, scuffle and scream broke off together. There was a moment of some violent suspension; and then began a gagging, retching sound that choked off Mr. Nicholas's own voice. Rudd had the woman by the throat—trying to choke her loose from him as he had done to Mr. Nicholas. And there was no way to stop him—if he left the counter, Mr. Nicholas knew that he would fall. He could only cling, and hear, and his faint, exhausted attempts to cry out were lost in the doctor's shouts and smashing of glass.

The front door slammed open. The ghastly noises stopped. Rudd was running. Some back door was torn violently open and his running footsteps pounded beyond it—away, out of hearing. It was the doctor's running steps he heard now, coming toward him—and knowing this, Mr. Nicholas sagged forward, with his whirling head on the cash register.

Chapter 15

"I don't think it was a thing the man could ever have done, consciously," Dr. Linen said. "Killing that damned woman, I mean. He certainly must have hated her like the devil, and yet he's absolutely lost without her."

With the moral superiority of a man wearing his clothes, and free to walk in and out, he gave this opinion down to his friend lying in bed.

Mr. Nicholas murmured, "It may be as he says, that he didn't mean to do it."

"Well, his hands meant to do it, whatever he says—or thinks. You don't get that much damage from halfhearted squeezing. And he certainly wasn't hesitating much about pushing you down those steps! No, I had that man pegged all along, John. All along. A very violent type, potentially."

Mr. Nicholas forbore pointing out that a little advance pegging would have been welcome, in this case; and as if scenting forbearance, the doctor added: "What threw me off—or never put me on—was the little-girl business. I certainly never heard anything like that about him, and apparently he had no previous record at all. But I told you that."

"Perhaps that poor miserable wife of his protected him."

"Maybe. But it's a tricky business, this child molestation. The children themselves are often hesitant to say anything, out of a vague feeling they've done something wrong, too. And too many parents, if they do find out, regard it as some kind of disgrace, and keep quiet about it. If no violence has occurred to the child—which was apparently the case here. Often the father will go over and settle it himself, especially in a neighborhood like ours, where people are leery of the police in general. But I never even saw him in bad shape—certainly never patched him up. He had some dandy scratches on his arms, by the way," he added. "Your little friend must never cut her nails."

"You did go talk to Bud, didn't you?" said Mr. Nicholas.

He turned his head anxiously on the pillow, toward his friend's face.

"I did, I told you I did. And it was a waste of time—everybody on DeKuyper Street knew last night that I broke in and caught Rudd strangling his wife. The latest version is that I also pursued and caught him—I don't know what all the police cars were supposed to be for. Background music, maybe. You don't figure in the legend at all, you know," he said cheerfully. "It's all brave me."

"Well, actually it *was*, Roger. If you hadn't come ..."

"What did you expect me to do, when they wouldn't answer their damned telephone? I was worried about you! And then to find the place shut up and dark ... Do you know what I thought at first?"

"What?" said Mr. Nicholas, obligingly.

"I thought you'd spotted the fellow, and got Rudd to come after him with you! I could just see you hobbling down some dark street, dragging Rudd along, and some devil waiting with a blackjack for you both! No, really," he said, drowning his patient's faint laugh with his own much heartier one. "What else could I think? It's exactly the kind of thing you'd do, and I knew it—and I was standing there cussing you out—and myself—when all of a sudden the ceiling fell down inside. And then I noticed the cracked door, of course. And began improving on it a bit."

He was enjoying himself enormously, no one could doubt it. Mr. Nicholas, who was not, didn't begrudge him his pleasure. He was glad not to be a total Jonah to everyone who offered him hospitality—first Lettie, now Roger. And Mrs. Linen had been noble about receiving him back into her house, in spite of the forbidden excitements he got her husband involved in. She was also coping with Dorothea, he understood; he didn't dare to inquire how.

He really felt quite subdued this morning, and not inclined to inquire about anything. It rather surprised him that the doctor—the great subduer—should not notice this, and should go on sitting there and roaring at him in this way. Mr. Nicholas, both guest and patient, could only respond politely, and endure.

Perhaps his endurance began to show, for Dr. Linen got up.

He said reluctantly, "Well, I'll get out of here now and let you rest. You may be indestructible—I think you are —but damn it, you're still mortal. And eighty-five!"

"Eighty-three," Mr. Nicholas corrected.

"Oh, is that all? Well, I told your people they could see you this evening, but your little girl friend and her handsome brother are going to have to wait another day or so. Lord, the men certainly have the looks in that family! Even the father's not bad-looking, you know, now that Mrs. Reilly's got him cleaned up. I think she's rather got her eye on him, too."

A faint, familiar twinge of anxiety touched at Mr. Nicholas. In spite of himself, he murmured: "Isn't Mary Rose pretty at all?"

The moment he said this, he was so cross with himself that he turned his head away, deliberately shut out the doctor's tactful reply. What earthly difference did it make? And what could he do about it, if she wasn't?

Nothing. His brief responsibility for Mary Rose was over, and he was glad it was over. It had been too much for him in the first place.

Besides, all girls were pretty, once they got old enough to do something about it.

Alone in his room once more, he relaxed, turning his head back toward the open window. Calm air floated in to him the familiar sounds of his old neighborhood. It was not DeKuyper Street, but it might have been; the same busy echoes were washing round his old house not far away, although it stood closed against them, and empty (except for the dining-room furniture).

The house was empty in his mind, too. All that he cared for was out of it, and his long life of responsibility there was ended. It had really ended long ago, he knew; that little girl—that unexpected little girl—had been his first real responsibility in many years. No doubt she would be his last. Perhaps that was why his tired mind still clung to the idea of her. She was, for him, the essence of all that would not come again: the anxieties, the necessities, the painful care. The love.

He really did not want any more of it. What he wanted now was his room and his cat and his trunks. The ordinary sounds of Dorrie, going about the house. His in-and-out Boy and Girl. Johnny, laughing.

But he would have one unexpected last treasure for his trunk, now. That box, with its smooth stones and peeled twigs, its poker chip and marbles and bit of chamois, and that plastic or celluloid object he still couldn't make out....

What *was* the confounded thing, anyway?

Well, it didn't matter. He was too tired to care.

On the other hand, the box was right beside his bed. To make sure of this, he reached out and found it. Then he took off the lid and found the plastic thing, baffling as ever.

He sighed, and took it out for another try.

THE END